CITY OF SNAKES

MARIET KAY

AUTHOR'S NOTE

This book includes content that may be difficult for some readers. The intended reading age is 18+ years old. Within this book there are depictions of violence, references to domestic violence, and themes of oppression and war. This book also contains on page sexual content.

To my mom, Dawn. Thank you for leaving your paranormal romance novels in easy-to-steal places. I learned how to use all my best curse words from you.

Realm of Henosis

Sahlmkar
THE SAHLMS
Sahlmsara
The Plateau
Brennac Ruins
Helos
Kullworth
Lamoreaux
NORTH CORRIDOR
NORTH TOWER
Kruthin
Belray
CENTRAL TOWER
EAST TOWER
WEST CORRIDOR
EAST CORRIDOR
Luz
CENTRAL CORRIDOR
Phynnic Ruins
WEST TOWER

N
S

SOUTH TOWER
Eros
Ikanten
SOUTH CORRIDOR

PROLOGUE

LARK

The glass marble rolled down the palace hall and veered left, slipping beneath the door Mama always told me *never* to open.

"Shucks!" The only frustrated expression Mama allowed me to say burst out of me. I slid my fingers under the door for my precious marble—it was my favorite from the set that my cousin had gifted me. Inside the glass, the thread of silver and royal blue reminded me of a waterfall.

I had no luck retrieving it. My prized possession seemed to have rolled too far.

The man behind that door—the one the adults tried so hard never to let me see—was quiet today. Some days, when I passed, I could feel the stir of his restless anger. I wasn't afraid of him, though. His rage didn't reach for me like it did for others, at least not always.

I glanced both ways down the hall. The usual guards who flanked the doors were not there.

It wouldn't hurt to break the rules just this once, would it?

I was going to be ten soon, after all. Double-digits. I could retrieve one tiny marble without getting caught.

Before I could overthink, I turned the silver doorknob and pushed. I gasped quietly as the door hinges creaked, and it opened to unveil quarters fit for a King. Fresh shimmering roses stuck out from a vase on the vanity, and thick blue curtains were drawn back to let in the sun. The far wall's fireplace was lit, and the bed was so abundant with pillows that it was hard to see whoever slept there.

I frantically searched the floor, my heart quickening.

"Lark! What are you doing here?"

Caught.

Aunty Lora sprang up from a chair by the other side of the bed, looking sad and startled. She held a black mirror. Instead of her reflection, the glass showed only a shining black swirl that seemed to sputter out as soon as I eyed it.

"I'm sorry...My marble." I pointed to the shining orb next to her boot, and her posture softened. "Were you crying, Aunty?"

She wiped beneath her eyes. "Of course not. Run along. You should not come in here. Do you understand me?" She kicked the marble toward me.

I picked up my precious trinket as Aunty Lora approached, ushering me back to the door. My boots stuck in the floor's wooden grooves. If only I could peek at the mysterious man over all those pillows.

"Is he sick?" I asked, rising to my tiptoes to catch a glimpse. Aunty stepped between me and the footboard.

"Lark. I mean it."

She never used that tone with me.

"You are not to come in here." She guided me away from the bed.

"Wait!" I whined. "Can I read to him? Can I please? I need my practice—you said so! He seems lonely, Aunty."

She glanced back at the stoic figure, who was wrapped in sheets. Aunty wore an expression I did not understand.

Her hands landed on her hips, and she gave me a hard look.

"I think he would like to be read to," I matter-of-factly stated. Who wouldn't love to hear stories if they slept so much?

Aunty hesitated but finally said, "Fine. But this is our little secret, okay? Go get the blue leather-bound book from the library—the one your Papa reads you."

Ugh. That dusty old thing always confused me.

I would not complain.

From that day on, whenever Aunty Lora visited, I sat beside her, behind the door that I was never meant to open, and read to the man who seemed never to wake.

PART ONE

Thousands of years before you will read this, the seven natural Origins arrived in the lands that you call your realms. It happened in a single day.

At dawn, Origin Asterie fell from the night sky as a star that struck the ground. Her brother, Astros, followed, ascending as a ray of morning sunshine.

Next, in an open field, Siro entered the world in a destructive swirl of wind that uprooted neighboring trees. From the torn roots of those trees, Origin Atla bloomed like a flower in the wild meadow.

Lightning struck that same meadow, and Lira rose from the ashes of the wildfire.

As the moon set that night, Origin Elara dropped from the crescent into the glistening sea, and the ocean's tides carried her and Origin Aquas ashore.

The Origins were born into a world of mortals who welcomed them, worshiped them. They gave thanks for the new gifts the Sources bestowed upon them: immortality, magic, prosperity.

On that same night, I was born, too, of flesh and blood.

The mortals in my village knew I was different from a young age.

All things were clear to me: the thoughts and emotions of those around me, the past and future. But what struck fear in the mortals,

Origins and immortals alike was my power to completely control the whims and actions of others—the power of compulsion.

They called me the First Reverist.

Something new, something coveted.

Men bowed at my feet. The Origins put a crown of thorns on my head and made me share their fates and prophecies. And when my children were born, they, too, held some of my gifts and lived peacefully among the mortals, Origins, and immortals.

Until two sinister powers joined us...

Chapter 1
SYBILLA

My city lay in ruins. Through the dining hall window, nothing more than a ramshackle mess of fire-torn buildings and ash-coated streets greeted me. I wanted to scream, cry or throw something across the dining hall.

What good would my sulking do for the people of my city?

Unlike the other four Corridors of Henosis, which had many provinces and cities, mine had only a single sprawling metropolis—Luz. Without it, the Central Corridor was nothing but vast countryside and wetlands. While I was grateful that the farming industry had not been impacted by the attack, it still pained me that our landmarks, our history, now lay in rubble.

When fucking Firose Van Gran marched into my city with Death-wielding defectors from the Sahlms in tow, the heart of my kingdom had been torn out and shredded in a single night.

The Phynnic people had once built a city like this one. It had fallen centuries ago in much the same way. The relics and remnants of Phynx, which had never been rebuilt, were a day's travel from Luz and a reminder of what could have been.

How much pain could one woman cause?

Instead of lingering on that thought, I sipped my bluebell vine tea and then took three deep breaths while rattling off the things I was lucky for...

No civilians had been harmed. We'd evacuated the city quickly.

Cities could be rebuilt. My Source-wielding new advisors, Fen and Asterie, would see to it.

My people were resilient. I would be resilient with them—even with the constant aches in my body and my general exhaustion.

I'd won powerful allies before—King Sheffield, the Nadiars. More could be won.

Silence rang heavily in the room. I took in the final moments of uninterrupted quiet, looking around the blue-curtained space with its ornate silver sconces and chandeliers. It was hard to imagine this palace had been under attack not even seventy-two hours ago.

Now where was King Darvanda?

I'd come up here to meet with the man that I was oath bound to ally with. Last night the other three *willing* rulers of the Corridors had met with me, insisting on speaking to me alone before they would allow King Darvanda's participation.

An alliance with Darvanda was an alliance with Source magic.

I had to remind myself of that; otherwise, the thought of aligning myself with such an insufferable warlock would have completely revolted me.

Who would partner with a man who'd burned down — decimated—the city of Phynx all those centuries ago? I understood the other rulers' concerns. But Darvanda had something I wanted—a depth of magic ready to be tapped into. And the King of the Sahlms might be a dick, but if he'd wanted me dead, there was no doubt I would've been.

His soldiers had saved my city. I owed him a debt.

An arrogant, putrid feeling hit me as a familiar loathsome energy approached the dining hall door.

My fucking cousin Haward. Did I need to deal with him today on top of all else?

I turned toward the door, awaiting him. The hinges on the white birch creaked, and my horrid kin, from my father's side, stepped into the room. His disparaging thoughts about me were thick in the air.

I smiled nonetheless.

"Dear cousin, come to wish me safe travels?" I asked, unwilling to rise to his petty ire.

Sources. Not today.

Haward's younger brother trailed behind him. Barden had always been a gentle boy, but under Haward's mentorship, his grip on moral decency was loosening, too. As soon as the boyish chub had left Barden's cheeks, he'd been swept up into Haward's hatred for me, albeit in a more half-assed manner. His thoughts were never quite as cutting as his elder brother's.

Keeping my placating smile, I crossed the room to where Haward stood.

He fought a grimace as he thought, *"A whore's daughter deserves no crown."*

Grinding my teeth, I tried to focus on the way his dress robe collar was flipped up, out of place.

Haward scoffed. "I just received word about your appointment of advisors. I am a Wymark—and yet you trust Luz to two Source-wielders? Clearly, you are unfit to rule this Corridor, *dear* cousin."

His spittle hit my cheek, and I fought the urge to step away. It took every ounce of control not to bite back with venom.

"Useless woman," he thought. My nails bit into my palms.

Haward's unearned sense of self-worth swelled within him. I wanted to tell him exactly where to shove his condescending thoughts; instead, I shut down my senses and forced him out of my head. It was difficult to do when my anxieties were heightened, and it took much of my waning strength.

Barden loitered behind Haward with his hands in his pockets, ruddy, pale skin collecting sweat at his temples. They were a mirror of each other, with rounded noses and light features that were not unlike my own.

"Do you feel the same, Barden?" I asked.

Barden flushed and fiddled with his pocket watch. "Yes, Queen Sybilla. It seems unwise to leave the Corridor in the hands of acquaintances. Unwiser still to go willingly into the Wastelands with the Brennac King. He cannot be trusted."

His thoughts were peculiarly quiet today. Brainwashed into thinking whatever Haward thought, I was sure. Already too fatigued to try to push in and uncover his emotions, I sighed.

"Hm," I mused, nodding. "You're right. It does seem unwise. And yet..." I reached out and straightened Haward's dress robe collar. "I still trust this Corridor more in the hands of two capable acquaintances than with two entitled lords who do not know their asses from that of a hog."

As I smiled up at Haward, his freckled face grew red. He ran one hand through his dull-blond, too-thin hair with a scowl. "You will regret this."

"I can assure you—I will not."

I'd made the right choice. Asterie, my starlit friend, and Fenris, her Fire-wielding Source Match, would keep my Corridor safe. They would rebuild it to its former glory. I trusted them to handle all that, and these two blubbering idiots.

As I turned toward the door, I was yanked to an abrupt stop. Haward had reached out and grabbed both of my wrists, causing me to stumble forward with a gasp. I should have seen it coming. The pressure of his hands around my already-aching wrists made tears swell. I would not let them fall in front of these two.

"Haward," Barden mumbled in warning and glanced toward the open dining hall door.

Right. Wymark men liked doors closed when they bullied others.

I glared into the eyes of a pitiful man who longed for nothing more than the silver crown of thorns and acorns adorning my head. He craved the adoration of my people. If he wore my crown, he would have no adoration. Under his rule, when the crops refused to grow and prices rose, he would sit up on my throne and demand to be fed from a silver fucking spoon.

Men like Haward Wymark were the reason our realm had fallen so far from the peaceful, prosperous place it once had been centuries ago.

My temper flared hotter as his hold grew tighter. My odds were slim of escaping his grip, and he towered over me by a foot, but I growled in protest anyway.

"Is it customary in Henosis to put hands on your Queen when she doesn't want them there?" A rough, deep voice carried from the doorway where a tall, shadowy figure leaned.

Just what I needed—another man to insert his opinion.

King Krait Darvanda of Sahlmsara spoke every word as though it were an order—an impressively intimidating feat. The intrusion did not loosen Haward's grip.

For the second time since Darvanda had ridden in with his flaming Warhorses, I was somewhat grateful to see the Sahlmsaran King. If he could help me avoid further interaction with my dreadful cousins, then I'd happily face the greater evil of him.

Darvanda may have saved my city, but it would be foolish to think he didn't have his own agenda. I had my own agenda, too—keep my Corridor out of the hands of men like Haward and bring magic back into my lands to reintroduce balance.

For too long, the people of Henosis had been taught to fear Source-wielders under the Order. Those laws were crumbling faster than the rulers of the realm could amend them.

My thoughts would've sounded like treason to my Phynnic ancestors, who'd cast out magic from these lands over four centuries ago. As Henosis entered a new era, I saw no other way forward.

I was no stranger to compromise. Conditions.

"She is my cousin," Haward snapped back as the brooding King entered, his gait stiff and domineering. Darvanda's iron-gray eyes scanned Haward, sizing him up.

The King shrugged before he said, "Does that make her any less your Queen?" His face was all hard lines; his sculpted biceps were flexed and sported rough scars where his tunic had slid up. He was a man who had been spat out from the Great Wars ready for retribution.

The whites of Haward's eyes showed and he more carefully said, "With all respect, this is a family matter."

My wrists stung from the bite of Haward's fingers.

Darvanda let a low, dark hum leave his throat. He grated out, "With no respect at all, she is under the ward of the Sahlms now. And I don't let others break what is promised to me." His voice seeped out like a smoky threat, in a timbre that hung heavy in my ears.

Never mind being grateful to see him. I wanted to kick King Darvan-dick in the groin.

As a Queen in my own right, I *was promised* to no one—blood oath to be his ally or not. I imagined my fist smashing against the King's commanding countenance.

He may be the King of the Sahlms now, but he'd also been the King of Brennax—the kingdom that had orchestrated the destruction of Phynx. It would serve me well to remember that this alliance would be a tenuous one; the history of my ancestors was an ominous reminder of the ruin he could bring upon us.

Barden seemed jumpy, but Haward dared to meet the King's glare and answered, "So we've heard."

As Darvanda neared, putting Haward in his shadow, the darkness flickered around my cousin, looking like tendrils of nothingness that sought something to devour.

Haward dropped my wrists. His mind warred between his fear of the Shadow-wielding King and his anger with me, but his cowardice won out, and he said nothing more.

Good choice. Although, it would've been fun to watch those Shadows descend on him.

I'd encountered the Sahlmsaran King's Source power only once, and being gripped by his Shadows had left me terrified of ever feeling them again. To be encased in a depthless pit, devoid of all light and being—Haward would crumble under that weight.

What terrified me more was my inability to slip into Darvanda's mind like I could with others. Fighting the urge to shake my hands out, I shot Darvanda a scowl that said, "I could have handled them." He met my gaze with a quirk of his dark brow.

The King looked well rested for our journey—that made one of us. He was neatly dressed in a well-cut red tunic that suited his light-brown complexion. Dark stubble accentuated a strong chin, and his dark hair glistened as though tamed with pomade.

At least he was appealing to look at, so long as I didn't have to interact with the prick.

"Tall, dark, handsome and *my savior*," I crooned with enough sarcasm that I caught Barden's lips quirk up at the sides.

King Darvanda only grunted a response before stepping away from us and finding a seat at the round birch table. He sat with his back to where we stood, as though *we* had interrupted *his* quiet morning.

Haward snarled at me, "Just remember, Sybilla, you have two years until that throne is mine. And you're not exactly in your prime seasons."

I rolled my eyes. "I'm well aware of the laws pertaining to my future reign. Thank you."

Darvanda didn't stir from the table or show any interest in our conversation.

"Then where are your heirs, Sybilla?" Haward's snide smile made my temper bubble.

"The law requires no heirs of me."

Haward carried on, "It states that by age thirty, you need—"

"She's right," Barden cut in. "The law only requires her to marry."

I shot a look at my younger cousin, my shoulders deflating at the slightest notion of camaraderie.

"We'll see what the Central lords think five years from now when there's still no heir to your line. That assumes any poor sap will even want a ruined woman," Haward said as he pointed a finger at me.

I wanted to cut it off and feed it to him.

"Maybe you should have tried harder to make one of those failed betrothals stick. What was it, two?"

I glared at him. "Three, actually. And I'll have a husband and a dozen tiny Sybillas running around before you know it if only to keep you off my throne. Mark my words."

I'd just need to find a King consort that wanted little to do with the crown on my head and had little ambition toward ruling my Corridor. That shouldn't be so hard.

Haward leaned in and gruffly whispered, "The lords once voted to take your mother's head. It'll be no different when it's your turn. Come, Barden." He stormed out of the room.

Barden paused momentarily, looking at his pocket watch again. Before he walked away, he caught my eye and winced, as though maybe some remorse still lived within him.

Standing tall, and fighting the impulse to sigh or slacken in relief, I watched Barden follow after his brother.

"Do you always let that nonentity speak to you that way?" A low grumble from the table reached me.

I jumped, having forgotten that the King of the Sahlms was in the room. Darvanda's back was to me still, and he sat completely stiff.

"It's easier to have him believe he's won. It keeps him out of my hair for a while," I answered, unable to mask the annoyance in my tone.

I rounded the table and sat across from him, keeping a skeptical eye on his hands as he drummed his fingers against the table. Glancing up, I found him tracking me with those eerie dark-gray irises.

He grumbled, "What laws did he speak of?"

"Nothing that pertains to you," I snapped. "When do we leave?"

"Soon. And don't change the subject. I am owed an explanation if my ally is soon to be legally unable to offer any aid. Is your crown secured?"

"Our laws require any female ruler of mortal birth to marry before her thirtieth birthday. I assure you, I have it handled."

His eyes narrowed, and he said with subtle sarcasm, "Sounds like it."

"Why are you even here?" I huffed. "What is in this for you?"

He scowled. "It seemed like a good political move to have at least one connection in this realm. The Sahlms have grown crowded, and some wish to return to the lands they once were free to live in."

I couldn't tell if that was a dig at my ancestors' decision to cast out magic but chose not to rise to the bait if so.

With my hands on the armrests of the dining chair, I said, "I will ensure they shall be free to return—that is why I wanted to speak to you before we leave."

"What is your little plan then?" He sounded as though he doubted me capable of any plan.

I straightened in my seat, fighting the desire to slump against it. *Deep breaths.*

"The rulers of Henosis have agreed to hold monthly trials. It would allow Source-wielders reentry to Henosis on a case-by-case basis. Those who wish to return will need to appear before the council with proof of their identity. Mortals and immortals without Source power will follow the same process for record keeping."

"*All* of your rulers agreed to such a plan?" he asked.

"Not exactly." While Emmerick hadn't attended the meeting last night, I knew he would support this plan.

"The North King," he guessed.

I trained my face to not react but nodded. "King Mattock has not *yet* agreed. But only because he needs time to rest after the attack on Luz. He will accept his crown and my support."

"If open borders are not what is proposed, then to make this alliance worth my while, Queen Wymark, I'll need more from you than '*Mattock will come around.*' The North Corridor borders my lands, and we need the cooperation of our neighbor's ruler."

"What exactly do you suggest I do?"

It was now evident that this insufferable man saw right through the professional ties between me and my former Constable. He'd made snide remarks in the bailey during the battle. *"A Queen warming her bed with those on her payroll. Leash your dog. If I wanted to kill you, I would have done so already."*

"Get your affairs in order," he said coldly. "Keep him close. Marry him if you must. Two birds with one stone, as they say." Then he stood and walked out of the room without so much as a farewell.

Fucking prick.

CHAPTER 2
EMMERICK

S he'd lied to me.

She was leaving with a King of a land we knew so little about. My Queen, my lover, was now oath bound to an unknown evil.

I should be kneeling, thanking Krait Darvanda—it would've been the noble thing to do. He'd saved my city, after all.

But he intended to take Sybilla away, and regardless of whether his men fought alongside mine, regardless of the debt we owed him, I despised him. I'd never felt so raw and bitter down to my core. It was so unlike me.

Her betrayal seemed to have broken the good-natured man within me. I wanted to shake her—to force her to stay. But her fate was set in blood. She would leave, while I'd be left to love her and hate her for breaking the trust I'd put in us.

"Emmerick," a warm, feminine voice soothed from the door. I hadn't realized Amara, my birth mother, had been let into my chambers.

The guards had been keeping watch over me since my outburst toward their Queen. I hadn't left my chambers since she'd agreed to go.

No part of me had wanted to be in the dining hall last night. I hadn't cared to wear a crown or talk politics with a bunch of silver-spoon-fed royals around a table like I belonged there.

You do belong there. You're a King. That is what Sybilla would have said to me, had I not been avoiding her like the plague since realizing how long she'd withheld the truth of my identity from me. She'd known for a decade; she'd known what fate lay before me and said *nothing.*

I sat on the foot of my bed, elbows on my knees, hands cradling my head.

"If you're feeling overwhelmed, take deep breaths and count backward from ten, my love."

A mother's love knew no bounds—it was something that the mother I'd grown up knowing, Angeline, had taught me. Amara might be my mother by blood, but I barely knew her, and I'd never met my birth father, King Corric Mattock, before he died. The revelation of my lineage was still so fresh.

"I don't want to fucking count," I snapped back. I winced at how unfamiliar my surly tone sounded.

Amara sighed and said, "Sybilla is not in danger with Darvanda, Emmerick."

"How do you know?"

When I looked up at her, her posture slackened. The shape of her nose and her almond-shaped eyes were so familiar to me. I'd taken the warm tones of her dark skin, and our curls were the very same pattern. Nature had molded me as her duplicate but in a heaping male form. It surprised me that it had taken Asterie, my friend and Amara's former ward, so long to notice our similarities. It surprised me more that I hadn't immediately seen them myself.

"Because I know Krait. We were friends—once, maybe more than that—before Corric. Krait is not the monster he puts forth to the world, and he will keep his word not to harm her. I don't know what he came here for, but I am confident in that much."

Something between a strangled gurgle and a growl left my throat upon hearing her speak kindly about Darvanda.

Sybilla's agreement had replayed in my head a million times. *I agree to your demands. I will go willingly to the Sahlms so long as no harm shall befall me or my Corridor until the trials end.*

"How could she do this?" I pulled at the hair at my temples.

Was I the only one who could hear the risk in the blood oath she'd made? The trials could take centuries—Henosis was built on the foundation of fearing magic's rise. She was trying to fast-track a flimsy plan in a land that wouldn't welcome Source-wielders without a long legal negotiation.

A warm hand landed on my shoulder, and I felt the weight of Amara sitting beside me. "She sees an opportunity, I presume."

I rubbed my eyes with the pads of my fingers. My head had been throbbing since that night Firose had poisoned me and Asterie. The details were still so blurry around the edges.

I shivered, thinking about my time in the Central Tower. The events that had unfolded there were becoming less foggy—events I wanted to bury deep in the depths of my subconscious because they no longer mattered.

Firose was dead.

You could not remain bound to a dead woman.

"What do you mean?" I asked.

"Sybilla is a capable ruler. This realm is depleted of magic and sitting helpless. Like it or not, Krait holds the allegiance of Source-wielders far more powerful than the ones who attacked this city yesterday. He's lived away from this realm in peace for four centuries."

I sighed. "So you trust him?"

"I do," she said without hesitation. "Rough around the edges, that one, and not one to be crossed. But if he'd wanted to turn on Henosis, he would have already. We would not stand a chance."

Letting that sink in, I nodded. Amara rubbed my shoulder, and I relaxed at the sensation of her calming touch. I imagined what it would have been like to be raised by her. My friend Asterie knew her as more of a mother than I did. The Sisterhood, Amara chiefly, had raised Asterie in the High Enchantresses' towers. I trusted Asterie, but could I trust my mother?

Amara cut through my thoughts. "Why didn't you attend the meeting last night?"

I groaned and craned my neck back to look at the birch-planked ceiling. "I don't want it," I answered.

"Don't want what, dear?"

"A crown, a Corridor, my life to change...any of it," I answered.

Amara squeezed my shoulder again. "I know. But sometimes, we rise to fill a need. I see a great King in you. A King like your father used to be—before Firose sank her claws into him, before his downfall. I want you to know he was a very good man. Consider attending the next meeting, please? He would want you there."

My jaw tightened at her words, but I nodded.

Like it or not, I was going to take my birth father's crown. I would try to be worthy of wearing it, however incapable I felt for that duty.

CHAPTER 3
SYBILLA

Without knocking, I pushed Emmerick's bedroom door open.

He had practically worn a track into the carpet from his pacing. A ring of shining golden light formed in his irises when they found me, as though anger ignited the power in his veins.

The new Sun King. A Source-wielder. Immortal.

And I'd known and never told him for over a decade.

Em stilled, throat bobbing, arms tensed at his sides. The rise and fall of his chest was the only movement in the room.

"Leave us," I told my personal guards who had trailed me up the stairs.

"My Queen, Sir Emmerick—"

"King Mattock," I corrected.

The guard wavered. "Well…Yes. King Mattock is angry. It may be better if someone stayed to—"

"That was not a suggestion," I snapped. Fucking insubordination.

My guards gave a shallow, reluctant bow before leaving us. The door closed, and all that filled the silence between us was the bubbling sensation of Em's boiling resentment. It took all my restraint not to let his emotions overtake mine—they were so strong. So volatile.

Emmerick had lived here since he had become my guard as a teenager. Every ounce of this space was filled with him—from the burgundy quilts to the collection of wooden figurines that his father had carved for him, to the table in the corner where he cleaned his weapons. He had branded himself on the space. I'd never be able to enter this room again without thinking of him.

I wanted to run into his arms as I had so many times before. I imagined wrapping my arms around his neck and leaning in to smell the rosemary of the soap he liked to use. His embrace would be all the peace I needed, yet he offered me no comfort today.

I'd let him down in such a stupidly selfish way.

His lips drew into a taut line, and his jaw locked into a pained grimace. I knew that look.

He was angry, yes, but what I felt roiling off him was fear, too.

"Em...please," I said, my voice cracking. I didn't know what I was pleading for.

His breath deepened. *In, out, in, out.* I shut down my senses fully, not wanting to feel the claw of his disappointment. Unveiling whatever awful thoughts lurked behind that scowl would have been simple. But now wasn't the time to wound myself.

He hated when I slipped into his mind and invaded his privacy, and I hated the thought that he might loathe me. I couldn't bring myself to face that.

So, I stood and awaited his words—they would likely be sharp and cutting, but this man would never lay an unkind hand on me.

Emmerick had been my best friend since we were children. Even as we'd warmed each other's beds in recent years, I'd clung to his friendship most. If he was never my lover again—I could handle that. The thought of not being his friend? That raised the hairs on the back of my neck.

"I am supposed to be by your side, protecting you. Let me go with you." The vulnerability in his words lashed through any last shred of my defenses. He placed his hands on his head, fingers digging into the hair at his temples that he frequently pulled when his nerves ran high.

Fuck.

"Emmerick," I whispered. "I don't have a choice. I am not allowed Luz guards, and you are no longer my Constable."

Normally, I would rib him, say that I didn't need his protection even though I very much did. He'd prevented countless attempts on my life...and now I would leave him to enter my ancestors' enemy's territory.

"I go where you go, Syb. That's always been the case."

I shook my head. "This place—me and Luz—was always a detour on your path to greatness. You have been here for too long already."

That had been my fault.

He took one step toward me. His jaw slackened, and a tear ran down his cheek, looking like a crystal on wet sand. It shone in that same eerie gold as his irises.

Closing the distance to him, I placed a hand over his heart.

"You *lied* to me." The word "lied" hit me with deliberate weight.

I tried to raise my hands to his cheeks, but he gently caught my wrists and pushed them back down to my sides.

The glass castle I'd fortified around myself was shattering one pane at a time. There had been so many chances to tell him who his father was. But to tell that truth would have been to lose him. To acknowledge that he was immortal and would long outlive me would have been to admit he deserved a love that could outlast my time.

So, I'd held onto the facade of his mortality. I'd never allowed him to grow into a King because I wanted him near me. Why would a King who could live forever anchor himself to a Queen who would grow old beside him?

"Em...I'm so sorry."

Now that I was closer, his fear tasted coppery and metallic—it felt like suffocating on one's own breath.

"Those words are empty. If you are truly so sorry, then don't go—be his ally from here. Stay with me. Why do you insist on going with him?"

I sighed. "That prick has things I need. *We* need. You know it's only a matter of time before every town in the Central Corridor looks like Kullworth—a slum. The magic in his land gives us leverage, hope."

"*Us?*" Sounding skeptical, he searched for my gaze.

I avoided eye contact as Darvanda's words echoed in my mind. *Marry him if you must.*

I knew in the depths of my heart that I couldn't let Em marry me—not when he was bound to lose me, not when he could potentially find an immortal woman to accompany him through eternity.

"Yes. *Us.* This alliance can help strengthen *both* of our rules." I needed to frame this politically.

"Our rules..." He'd never been able to stay angry with me for long—and I hoped now would be no different.

"Yes. I will soon come back to Luz. We can still—"

Before I could finish, his arms wrapped around me. I let my former Constable, my late father's secret ward, and my dearest friend, hold me, not knowing when the next time might be. "I'm still so angry with you," he whispered.

"I know." Letting my nose nestle into the space between his head and neck, I clung to him, having missed the warm steady feeling of being in his arms.

My lips instinctually found his pulse. He groaned as I trailed a kiss down to his collarbone, and I said, "You need to focus on the North. You are their *King*. You cannot keep avoiding council meetings."

He abruptly pulled away from me. "You always have an angle, don't you? Did you come up here to apologize or to seduce me onto a throne I don't even want?"

I stiffened.

Had that been what I'd done?

"Will you ever consider anyone else's desires but your own?" he continued—his words like rocks pressing on my chest.

My temper flared. He could not think that of me.

Immediately missing his warmth, I watched him turn and brace his palms down on his weapons table. His broadsword lay flat there—rubies encrusted its pommel.

"Be mad at me, but don't let your fear turn you into a coward. Those people deserve a King who can rule them fairly, not a scared boy running with his tail between his fucking legs." As soon as the words left my lips, they felt wrong.

Emmerick sucked in a breath. "You're really something, Sybilla."

I wanted to scream, *"Look at me!"*

He added, "You had no issue keeping my identity from me when it was convenient for you. Now you care about the people of the North? What do you want me to do? Step into my father's shoes like I have any right leading a Corridor?"

"I can help you—"

"No, Sybilla." He cut me off with a raised hand. "You can't. I need to figure this out on my own. You need to give me the space to do so."

Through tears that threatened to spill, I huffed a short laugh. "You don't mean that. You're just angry."

He scoffed. "Of course I am angry. You leaving? It's a terrible idea, Sybilla."

"We were almost decimated out there, Emmerick! Wake up. I am going to secure us a powerful ally."

"No, Sybilla. You are going to secure *you* a powerful ally. There is no *we* or *us*," he said with a shake of his head.

"This has nothing to do with me," I shot back. "We don't all get the luxury of doing things for ourselves. You will learn that when your people need something from you that requires compromise to obtain."

He needed to understand me.

He turned toward me and braced as though he wanted to throw me across the room. He wouldn't, of course. Yet there was an intent in his posture that I'd never seen before, and the shimmer of gold in his eyes winked out.

"Leave," he said with a tightened jawline.

A lump grew in my throat as I pressed, "I will see you at the next council meeting, King Mattock."

He only glared at me.

I left the room with shaky knees.

Just as I'd always feared, I was losing him to his crown.

CHAPTER 4
KRAIT

"Why are we here, Krait?"

The singsong cadence of Elsedora's voice reached me, but I pretended it hadn't. If we hurried and left before sundown, we'd make it to the Plateau in a little more than a week and to the heart of Sahlmsara a week after that.

"Boy, why aren't these packs loaded?" I barked at a young groom who was tying his bootlaces. He startled and fell over before lifting himself and scurrying to toss packs into one of the horse-drawn carts. We stood at the south gates of the Palace of Luz. Its spires and turrets were still blackened from battle. The gardens were upturned, only a few rose bushes remaining in place. The south wall, where I'd first met Queen Wymark, rose above us.

Death had nearly conquered this city.

I had felt *him* in the air as soon as I'd arrived, and the sensation had not ceased. I itched to get out of here. This battle reeked of Death's influence—which meant the prophecies were all coming true. We didn't have the luxury of time. We were due for a black moon in just a few years.

"Kraiiit," my officer prodded. How the woman could turn my name into a three-syllable word was mind-bending.

"What?" I snapped.

"Oh no," El warned. "We do not bite the hand that steals for us."

I rubbed my face. "I'm busy, Elsedora." I only used her full name when she got under my skin, which was growing more and more frequent.

"I see that. But something is bothering you." It wasn't a question.

She was right. My mood had went sour the minute that entitled brat of a Queen had offered herself in her friend's place to join us in the Sahlms. *That* had not been the goal. Yet my plan had gone awry long before that.

I'd already had enough time to assess whether the starling, the one they called Asterie, was who I thought she might be. My interest had been piqued when Elsedora had brought word of an Oracle in Luz.

Powerful? Yes. But the Star-wielder was not the right one; by her age, she would have been capable of so much more if she'd been the one.

I'd been wrong to come, and I hated being wrong.

"It's nothing," I said.

"Oh, Krait, I told you it wasn't her." El sighed, figuring me out far too quickly.

"Not the time."

"When *is* it the time? Are you going to have me tear the world apart whenever you catch wind of someone with a sliver of Reverist magic?"

"Yes."

"All because of some prophecy in a dusty old book?" she lamented.

"Yes." My patience wore thin, as we'd had this conversation too many times to count.

She questioned, "What about the Central Queen? She can read minds. That means she has a bit of Reverist power. No?"

I shook my head. "Too weak—if she were the full Reverist, she'd be out of control by now with no training. But she can be useful in other ways."

Elsedora sighed again and looked up at the clouds. "You're impossible," she muttered as she practically bounced away from me, through the south gates of the Palace of Luz. It was hard to dissuade her of her enthusiasm for life. Even my shit demeanor didn't knock her down.

At least I'd gotten one thing out of this. I *did* need an ally in this realm. Only that ally came in a petite, foulmouthed and willful package. She embodied everything I hated about the old Phynnic ways—belligerent righteousness and rigid traditionalism.

She couldn't even command the respect of her own family, so at least she wasn't a threat. I could get what I needed and then send her on her way to Luz and out of my hair.

I didn't *need* her to come to the Sahlms to ally with me, but her presence would assure my people that we were making progress toward a solution to our resource constraints.

Whether the realm of Henosis stood or fell concerned me less than what resources I could gather from its state of being.

Currently, it would serve me better standing. Unfortunately.

CHAPTER 5
SYBILLA

A small wooden cab, pulled by Darvanda's Warhorses, stopped just outside the gates. The horses were clad in charmed armor that glowed and emitted flames that matched the darkening sunset. It might have been a beautiful sight if it hadn't meant it was time to leave.

Maids wheeled a large wooden trunk of my belongings out and a groom loaded it in the back of an open-air cart sitting behind the cab. I looked up at the war-blackened walls of the Palace of Luz.

This courtyard was once where I'd liked to sit and think, where I'd stolen kisses behind wisteria from a young Constable who'd thought the world of me, where I'd studied arithmetic and history in the grasses beneath the trees. Now, the ramshackle space only served as evidence of my failure.

Asterie approached from the eastern lawns, holding a small latched wooden box. I lingered just outside the palace doors, the steps down to the courtyard a thin barrier between everything I knew and whatever future awaited me.

Vangard, the horned wolf-beast that sometimes rested in an inked form on Asterie's arm, was left free to roam. The dark-coated canine got distracted by a scent along the palace wall and whined.

So much death. I wondered if Van could smell it or if the souls of the soldiers we'd lost still lingered.

"Sybilla." Asterie reached out to take my hand with her free one. When my fingers wrapped around hers, she squeezed. "Are you sure?"

Are you sure you must go in my place?

Are you sure leaving your court to two inexperienced rulers was wise?

Are you sure you'll be back?

Asterie didn't give voice to any of those things—instead, her emotions were steady, calm and soothing. Her belief in me and complete lack of doubt helped to push away some of my own hesitation.

I nodded. "I'm sure—the Sahlms will make a good ally if we can maintain peaceful negotiations."

"And a dangerous one if we cannot," Asterie warned.

I offered her a weak smile and reassured her, "This is the right move. Are those the tonics I requested?"

"Yes." Asterie lifted the small wooden case. "This is a remedy for most common ailments. It's likely what Healer Mortag was offering you."

I opened the snap closure of the wooden box, unveiling a couple dozen vials of green liquid. "It's usually blue," I commented.

Healer Mortag had evacuated to the countryside with other civilians, and he had not yet returned. I'd been desperate enough to confide in Asterie—well, partly. I'd made the excuse that I might need relief from illness if it struck me. She'd seen through my fibs with her hawk-like stare.

"Yes, well...Wyeth and I are unsure how to replicate his remedy. Maybe if you told me what you take these for—"

I held up my hand. "They will do. Thank you, Asterie. You and Fenris are going to do well here in Luz. I can feel it, and I'll be back in no time at all."

Asterie's face brightened when we heard Fenris' voice float over the palace walls as he said his temporary goodbyes to his sister, Elsedora. He soon joined us on the steps.

"Did you smell a compliment and come running? I was just telling Asterie that you both will do well here."

Fen grinned and drew me in for a hug. "Oh, we know we will."

"Don't burn anything down while I'm gone," I warned as Fen released me. "And don't let Van piss on any of the remaining rose bushes."

"I can't speak for Van any longer, but I wouldn't dream of letting him—I've seen you with a bow. I try not to piss off women that can kill me from a distance," Fen joked.

"Not entirely true." Asterie smirked and nudged him with her elbow. But I will watch both of them."

"Good then," I said, not wanting to linger in case my feet grew too cold to leave the only place I'd ever known as home. "I will write as soon as we arrive. And an Egress will be built between the realms."

Long ago, Egresses—magical portals between cities—had been closed in Henosis, but since the Order had fallen, I was determined to pass amendments to re-open them. Fen's arm wrapped around Asterie's waist as I turned toward the gates where the carriage awaited.

Elsedora leaned against the cab. Her posture straightened upon seeing me, and her lips quirked up. "You wore...wool? For a trip into the Sahlms?"

"It's a sturdy fabric," I defended, and Elsedora laughed and nodded.

I'd tied my curls atop my head with a long Luz-blue silk ribbon—something blue, a royal tradition when traveling. Our crest's color remained with us, holding a piece of home wherever we ventured.

I didn't know what Elsedora was so tickled by. My garb was travel ready—a plain wool skirt, thick socks and leather boots. My black long-sleeved velvet bodice was tucked into a leather belt bag. It was all perfectly appropriate.

She chuckled and said, "Very sturdy."

Amusement roiled from her—it tasted like sugared fruit and felt like bubbles across my skin. She held no resentment toward me despite our first meeting having been less than ideal.

Prior to the attack on Luz, my court had been infiltrated by northern guards in a pathetically ill-planned attempt to assassinate me. Elsedora had found herself in the wrong place. She'd been falsely accused of opening the Egress into Luz's underground tunnels, which I'd known she had not done—a perk of my abilities. If only I knew who *had*.

I tried to glimpse what Elsedora wore beneath the thin rust-colored robe that adorned her, but it was buttoned up to her neck. "Well, what was I supposed to wear?"

"Nothing, if you prefer it." Elsedora's smirk deepened. Her playful nature, chestnut waves, and hazel eyes matched her brother's perfectly. She and Fenris were undoubtedly cut from the same cloth.

"It's warm in the Sahlms, is all. You may want to borrow something—"

"I'll be fine."

Elsedora shrugged, but my sharpness didn't deter her smile. "It's been a long time since I've had a female friend."

"We aren't friends. Your King is detaining me," I reminded her.

"Detaining, yes, but he has agreed not to *kill* you. Deep down, that must mean he likes you. At least enough to allow you to keep breathing."

I huffed out a laugh. There was no way that this agreement would end well for me. "Yes, *that's* surely it," I mused sarcastically. The idea of Krait Darvanda liking anyone, or anything, was unfathomable.

"What? You mean to tell me that two royals can't bury old resentments and get along for the greater good?"

She put the massacre of thousands in Phynx so lightly. Krait Darvanda was a monstrous pig. He had condemned Phynx to death. Four centuries had not been enough to heal that festering wound.

It was meant to be a coup, not a massacre, he'd said.

He'd claimed that when white flags flew, his army had been instructed to retreat—that his Commander had betrayed him. But how much of his story could I trust? It seemed convenient that he should pass the blame onto a Commander who hadn't survived the attack and could neither confirm nor deny the allegation.

Speak of the insufferable, enigmatic ass.

King Darvanda approached atop a gray horse with a dished nose that flared. Beneath furrowed brows, his steely gaze assessed me.

"You're wearing that?"

I huffed. "What is wrong with what I'm wearing?"

Elsedora motioned for me to step up into the carriage and offered me a hand. "You'll see," she mused with a light laugh.

Once I was seated, Darvanda scowled at me through the cab door. "You'll stay in there. The doors will be locked for your safety—in case we run into any trouble. Elsedora will carry the key."

Well, that brought me *great* comfort.

I didn't want to think about the implications of his words. I wasn't safe while traveling with them.

Or he enjoyed seeing me caged—that made my nostrils flare like his horse's. Before I could retort, he lifted a foot out of his stirrup and kicked the door closed. I wiggled the handle.

Fucking locked.

Darvan-dick had not been kidding. Aside from getting out to relieve myself behind trees in the northern woodlands, I stayed in the carriage for over a week. Rain delayed us for a couple of days when the woods grew too muddy for the carts. I ate the rations of bread, dried fruits and meats that were offered at each stop. Elsedora was never far, and her humming was becoming a constant irritant.

The carriage rattled on as light seeped through the too-small window at the top of the door. We had begun descending beyond the Plateau today. I peeked out the window and saw glimpses of beige mountains in the distance. We passed a heavy presence of Sahlmsaran guards, who wore chest plates with the rattling-serpent symbol. He guarded the border.

Sweat crept between my breasts, down my back and forehead and well...everywhere. If it *could* sweat, it was sweating. But out of principle, I would not tell Elsedora she had been right. Every garment I'd packed was unsuitable for this heat, and it wasn't even summer yet.

The carriage jostled down the switchbacks of the Plateau for hours before we found flat ground. At the bottom, the path was laden with rocks, and every movement was jarring to my stomach.

I was going to be sick.

Thinking it might help settle my stomach, I dared to look out the window again. It didn't work. An unforgiving wave of nausea overtook me. I banged on the door.

Oh Sources, no. I didn't want to be sick—not in front of them.

The carriage creaked to a halt, but I kept banging on the door until Elsedora came around the side and unlocked it. After throwing myself from the cab, I ran behind a boulder across the trail and emptied the contents of my stomach.

"Woah," Elsedora said over my shoulder.

"What is this place?" I heaved out, trying to distract her from having time to tell me that she'd told me so about the wool.

Glancing around at the passing guards, I sighed. There was no sign of an ill-tempered warlock on a gray horse. Good. He hadn't witnessed me weak and hurling.

"Sit, sit. This is Skull Valley," Elsedora answered as she guided me toward another boulder, away from where I'd vomited. Elsedora wore a silk pair of pants, with suede chaps that protected her while riding, and a silk tunic that was entirely indecent—a portion of her *stomach* showed.

However, the ensemble did look far more forgiving in the heat than my heavy skirts and tunic.

Warhorses and soldiers passed us on the trail, unfazed. Trained soldiers set on their destination. None of them regarded me, as though their orders were to pay me no mind at all. They were all dressed in light linen, which prepared them for the sweltering sun of this valley of death.

"Pleasant name," I mused and then heaved up a bit of bile.

I heard approaching hoofbeats crushing the rocky ground. "It isn't a pleasant place," Darvanda answered from atop his horse. This man loved to look down at me. "What are you doing out of the cab?"

"Oh, enjoying the sunshine," I snapped. "Why is it called that?" I chugged the flask that Elsedora offered me.

"You can often find skulls of fallen Brennac exiles here."

"Why would there be skulls here?" I stood, bracing at the thought of having to climb back into that suffocating cab.

"The switchbacks didn't always exist. They're man-made. When the Phynnic began their crusade against all magic, this land bordered their territory. They would push exiled Source-wielders, and the mortals who helped hide them, off that cliff." He pointed up. The cliff towered hundreds of feet above us. "Also, when Source-wielders began to flee after the Great Wars, many died of dehydration. We weren't prepared during the early days."

After the Great Wars—after he'd destroyed the city of Phynx. I tried to remind myself that he was not merely a victim of the suffering. He'd contributed.

Yet that had been more words than I'd ever heard him speak—each one more horrible than the last.

"How could *anyone* survive it? The fall, the travel without water?"

"Many didn't, hence the skulls. Immortals who fell shattered so many bones it took them weeks to heal enough to be able to walk. Mortals who caught onto rocks and branches sometimes got lucky and could scale down. Broken, thirsty, hopeless, cast out of the only home they'd ever known. The journey killed many. Not even immortals can live without water."

Heart racing, I started pacing to settle my stomach. During the Great Wars, thousands of mortals and immortals were exiled here. I stepped back onto the worn dirt path, avoiding looking up at Darvanda or the cliff beyond him again.

"Why should I believe—" My voice cut off as I passed something ivory on the ground. My knees hit the sand, and my hands trembled as they dusted away rock and soil.

It was a human skull...a small one.

Darvanda dismounted and stepped behind me.

"Like I said...you still find skulls here." His tone was gruff.

"This was a child."

"Yes."

What do you do when faced with the horrific actions of your ancestors? I'd spent so long thinking the Brennac King was a monster for the fall of Phynx...but two treacherous wrongs never truly made a right.

I stared into the empty sockets.

No. This couldn't have been the way of the realm for so long. My ancestors couldn't...wouldn't have done this.

"Why were they not buried?" I asked, throat tightening.

CHAPTER 6

KRAIT

Why hadn't we buried our dead? That, at its core, was a painful question.

"We still find so many...It's hard to delay every time." Elsedora offered the simple answer.

Queen Sybilla brought her hands to her wool-covered hips, wiping her palms. Wool. For a journey through the desert.

We'd been traveling for over a week, but it was only our first day in the Sahlms. If she didn't stop being so stubborn and put something more suitable on, she'd die of heat stroke before we arrived in Sahlmsara.

So be it.

"That's a horrid excuse," Sybilla said plainly. "Bring me a shovel. I know you've got one for digging holes to shit in."

My mouth hung open, and I thought about disagreeing. "Fine."

"Fine," Sybilla grunted back at me, mocking my curtness in an artificially low voice. I didn't sound like *that*.

Elsedora chuckled. I shot her a glare, and she responded, "What? That was pretty good."

As El went off to find a shovel, Sybilla wandered toward the side of the trail.

"Over there," Sybilla said as she stared at a desert meadow. Late spring in these highland areas meant the usually sparse, sharp brown grasses were somewhat green and Larkspur shot up in bright blue patches across the otherwise rocky terrain. "It looks...peaceful. And those wildflowers are beautiful. I like those."

After being brought the shovel, Sybilla spent the next fifteen minutes attempting to dig a hole large enough for the skull. The unforgiving rocky ground fought every strike against it.

Pathetic...yet slightly endearing.

She let the shovel rest against her shoulder and rubbed at her wrists. The sight of her attempting to bury the fallen of my land stirred something in me. It was a gesture of respect to bury another ruler's dead.

Respect went further with me than kindness or likability. I pushed off from where I'd been leaning against the carriage and approached her.

"Move." My command only resulted in her raising one choice manicured finger.

No shredding her to pieces with Shadows.

No violence toward our new ally.

Instead of biting back, I let my Shadows reach out and grab the shovel, pulling it away from her. She gasped as the dark tendrils brushed her fingers, unraveling them from around the wooden handle.

"That is creepy," she mumbled. Yet, when I lifted the Shadows to create shade for her, she didn't hesitate to step beneath it. "And nice to know you could have done *that* sooner."

I hummed a dull response, taking the shovel in my hand, and finished digging the hole.

"I loosened that dirt for you," she justified with a smirk as I wiped my brow and glanced down at her red face. Sweat beaded down her neck and then disappeared between her breasts. My eyes had only been drawn to the spot because a sun rash had formed across her chest.

"You're going to overheat if you don't change," I grumbled. After pushing the shovel's head down into the rocky terrain, I crossed my arms.

"Only if Elsedora has something that will cover me more than. ..that." Sybilla waved her hand up and down at El, who was out of earshot offering water to the carriage horses. She typically pushed fashion boundaries even by the Sahlms' standards, but I wasn't going to tell Sybilla that.

My lips fought the urge to creep up at the sides. "Not a fan of staying cool?"

"Don't play coy. In my land, royals just started to be allowed to show their *shoulders*."

"How virginal," I droned.

I found myself a bit disappointed when she didn't shoot back an insult. She looked flushed and dead on her feet.

Bending, I set the skull into the grave we'd dug and offered her the shovel to cover it.

As she pushed dirt in, she said, "That's a much more suitable resting place."

I let a wordless response rumble in the back of my throat. Elsedora often mocked me for not being great with words—which wasn't entirely true. It was just that not much compelled me to use them.

"Oh, why, you're great company, too."

My brow furrowed before I realized she'd pretended to fill in the response I hadn't offered.

I grunted in agreement.

She answered again, "You think I am the Sources' gift to this world? I'm flattered."

At that, I couldn't help but crack a vicious smile—would she tire of talking to herself, or was this the way it was to be? She glanced at me before she tossed the last bit of dirt back into place and patted the ground.

"Woah...his teeth are showing," she called across the trail. "Elsedora, does he bite? I think he might be rabid."

Elsie rounded the cart with an airy laugh. "He is all bark."

The thought of them teaming up to rib me sounded like torture. I lowered my voice and said, "I don't need to bite."

"Is that so?" Sybilla whispered back.

Feeling like I'd fallen for bait, I grumbled, "Mhm."

"Well, you should smile more—it suits your face. The whole brooding ass thing is dull and overdone," she said as she rested her forearms against the shovel.

I knew she was trying to provoke a reaction. It worked. "Do you frequently advise people on what to do with their face when you have no right to?"

"Yes. And seeing as I'm 'under the ward of the Sahlms now,' I thought maybe you might like to get to know me."

"I have better things to do."

"Right," Sybilla huffed, and her nose pinched up. "Why exactly do you hate me? I understand why I hate you—but I wasn't even *alive* during the Great Wars."

She pointed the shovel's blade at me.

Great, I'd armed her.

Drawing a deep breath to steady my temper, I reeled my Shadows back and let the sun descend on her again.

"What do I hate?" I ground out. "For starters—your entire upbringing was rooted in hating people for no other reason than the Source in their veins. I'd say my hate is justified. Your Phynnic ancestors paved the way for your realm to fall apart, and yet you blame my actions centuries ago for your own downfall. You look at my land now, and you see only what you can gain from that power. Don't you?"

It felt odd to use so many words and yet it still had not been enough to cover even half of my qualms with the Central Queen and her shit realm.

Queen Sybilla dropped the shovel, and her hands fell to her hips. "If your people are so strong, why did you leave?" she retorted. "You could have stayed—overtaken it all. You were more than positioned to."

I growled under my breath. "We didn't *need* to leave. I could have let my troops take every city in the Kingdom of Phynx, spill more blood, destroy more homes. But after centuries of persecution, my people wanted *peace,* not more war. So I led them away from those who would sooner see them dead than cohabitate with Source-wielders."

She straightened. "That isn't what the history texts say, and—"

I cut her off with a dark laugh and said, "And you believe everything you've ever read? Everything that has been fed to you about your *hero* ancestors? Source-wielders were bound with magic cuffs in their sleep and thrown from that cliff. The Phynnic invented weapons against us—gasses and tonics that could suppress magic. Mortals always find a way to see magic as a threat. They seek to destroy it out of fear.

"You can hate me for the fall of Phynx and for fighting for my people. I'll happily play the villain in your storybooks if it means you don't yammer on for the rest of this trip."

"You're one to talk. I haven't been able to get a word in." Her hands fell to her sides. "You act like *I* am my ancestors—as though I am not here, willing to negotiate. My father and those before him might not have been capable of change, but I am ready for it."

I said nothing.

That response had been unexpected—I'd anticipated more fire, more denial.

Emerald-green irises of pure determination met my gaze.

She continued, "It is no mystery that I want things from you. Henosis has long suffered from the suppression of magic. But that doesn't mean I have no care for the needs of your people in the Sahlms. If I'm to be your ally, then I should know their needs too. So, instead of being Darvan-dick the Terrible, work *with* me and not against me."

It was unnerving how quickly she'd disarmed my temper. No cutting response came to mind, so a low growl built again in my throat.

She mimicked the sound, her brows knitting together, attempting to imitate my expression.

"Stop that," I commanded.

She stopped mimicking me but did not stop trying to persuade me. "Come now. What harm would it bring if I better understood what you're trying to accomplish?"

"I don't need to tell you anything."

"Why?" she insisted.

"Are you always this persistent?"

"Only when I want something," she said.

Why did that statement make my cock twitch?

Probably because she'd leaned in with that ruthlessly anticipatory smile and unnerving eye contact when she'd said it.

"Fine."

"Fine," she repeated back to me. I'd expected her to be petulant and spoiled. I hadn't anticipated that she might be willing to work for anything.

I added, "There's a difference between hating a person and hating a system."

"A system...like the Order?" she asked. "That is being dismantled as we speak."

"Your history under the Order won't be forgotten or forgiven. Those laws were erected to—" She snorted a laugh. "Are you giggling over the word '*erect*'?"

Impossible woman.

I should have known there would be nothing redeeming in her character, but for a second, I'd felt a spark of hope.

"I'm sorry. The sun has worn me down. Plus, it's a funny word. Especially coming out of your mouth. Go on, I'm listening."

I glared. "I have no trouble with that word."

Sybilla's cheeks flushed an even deeper crimson. I almost smirked, proud of myself for catching her off guard.

"And you will learn what the people of my realm need when we get there."

She rubbed a bead of sweat from her forehead, looking like she might fall over. "Alright then," she said finally. "Sources, it's hot out here."

"The heat slows you down, but you get used to it," I said.

She nodded and called out, "Elsedora—I'll take that change of clothes."

At least she had enough sense not to die of stubbornness in that wool and velvet.

A rattling sound came from the brush nearby, and I stepped between her and a thicket of half-dead grass. "Might want to stay back."

"What is that?" Sybilla asked as she instead stepped forward to peer around my arm.

A horn-nosed snake slithered out from the brush. Its rattling died away as it peacefully made its way into another patch of thicket.

Sybilla stepped up beside me and glanced down at the symbol of the rattling serpent on my silk tunic. "Why are they on your crest?"

Fighting the urge to shrug away her question, I answered, "Because they are precise and lethal, but they always provide a warning before striking. They are docile until provoked."

"Is that what you think you are? 'Docile until provoked'?" she asked.

I looked over at her and shook my head. "Not anymore."
***

The red rocks surrounding us seemed to ebb and flow with the midday heat. Elsedora had slipped a change of clothes into the carriage for the Central Queen, and we waited for her to change as my soldiers watered their horses.

"You two were looking chummy. I haven't heard you talk that much in a century. What's your angle there?" Elsedora questioned in a hushed tone.

"No angle."

"I know you better than that. What do you think of her?" Elsedora prodded.

"I think nothing of her," I said.

El crossed her arms, blowing a stray red lock from her eyes. "She doesn't seem as bad as we'd thought, does she?"

Not quite as bad, but infuriatingly talkative.

"No comment."

"Whatever you say, my King." The click of the carriage door interrupted us. Elsedora smirked, pushed off from where she'd been leaning against the cab and went around it to go address the thirty or so soldiers that had stayed back. "We move again in five!" I heard her call out.

Immediately skeptical as to why she'd fled so quickly, I turned toward the carriage door.

Sybilla stepped down with a hand shielding her eyes. "I'm not in a skirt anymore—I can ride. *Please* don't put me back in that oven.

I don't give a shit if we encounter bears or criminals. Either would be a quicker death than being cooked alive."

Elsedora had provided the Queen with a pair of emerald silk pants, which flowed too long on her. Slits ran up the sides of her legs, revealing a dagger strapped to one hip. That's what drew my eye—not the supple skin there. It was smart, after all, to keep track of the weapons on someone who might want to kill me.

"No," I said.

"Do you think you get to make all decisions now?" Sybilla asked.

"Yes."

"*That* is not what I agreed to. *Allies* don't lock each other in small boiling carriages for a week. Technically, that blood oath you took was to keep me safe—is letting me die of heat in that cab 'keeping me safe'?"

She was rambling, but I was preoccupied with how the matching silk top snaked around her waist and cinched at the back, leaving no curve a mystery. The thin fabric cascaded down at the neckline and drew my eye downward with it. Fucking Elsedora.

"My eyes are up here, if that's what you were looking for."

I bit my inner cheek but made no move to correct my gaze; instead, I let it trail back down to the dagger at her hip. "You're wise to stay armed."

"Was that a compliment?" she asked.

"No, it was an observation."

"You seem to have made *many* observations just now," she teased.

When my eyes met hers, she was smirking. Let her think she was ribbing me. I'd never been embarrassed to appreciate a woman's appearance.

"So, a horse, Darvanda? Are you capable of producing that, or would you like to continue trying to make me uncomfortable in this silk napkin that I was given to wear?"

"Are you uncomfortable with being looked at?" I asked.

"No," she said. "But I can't tell if you're trying to determine the best way to fuck me or filet me. And *that* makes me uncomfortable."

"Both. You pick the order," I grumbled.

"You are vile," she said with a scrunched nose, but a bubble of laughter escaped her lips.

My crude joke had landed.

She rolled her eyes. "I'm not getting back in that cart, so either I walk, and slow us down, or you find me a horse."

I let my hand run down my face before I stepped away from her. She was altogether too amused; it would be easier if she were more intimidated.

If the small victory of not riding in the cart would keep her from bothering me the rest of the trip, then so be it. "Unload a mule's pack into the carriage," I instructed the nearest soldiers.

With a hand on her hip, she said, "A mule, really?"

"You are more than welcome to ride with one of my men or go back in the carriage."

She took one look around at the bloodstained tunics of my men, unbathed and well traveled, and another glance at the carriage. "Mules are built for tough terrain, even better than a horse."

For the next week, the sun was unrelenting. Not a cloud had marked the blue sky. A few times, Queen Wymark had looked so unsteady on her mule I'd nearly opted to Shadow her to Sahlmsara. But this journey, the harsh reality of it, was important for her to appreciate. I always traveled with my soldiers, and she should have to as well.

The rocky terrain did nothing to cool the ground, so the heat of late spring enveloped us. These red rocks and this unforgiving land were home to me now. In the low desert, the greener brush was already becoming yellow and dry, and the towering spiky plants did nothing to shade us. Nearly a century of making this trek to secure exiles' safety, and then four centuries more living here myself, had hardened me to the conditions.

"Is everything in this land designed to be deadly?" the Queen said from the mule to my left. She motioned to the spiked foliage. In juxtaposition to the dying grasses, the cacti were blooming with various colored flora.

"Mhm," I answered. I'd tried to pawn her off on Elsedora, but my flighty officer kept wandering off, so I was forced to stay by the ever-talkative Queen.

"They're pretty. In a very prickly stay-away-or-else sort of way. Like you."

I squinted and hummed a response, not letting myself react to her statement, which had most definitely been aimed at baiting me into conversation.

We were approaching the switchbacks of the canyon that led down into the city, and the spires of buildings were beginning to peek above the horizon.

She spoke again. "Are you just going to keep grunting at me?"

I shrugged. The horses and carts at the front of the procession began to crest the canyon and travel downhill. I watched as the riders leaned back on their horses, freeing the animals' shoulders to navigate the mountainous terrain unobstructed. The Vallic Mountains, which separated us from the volcanic shores, created a backdrop against the deep valley, painting the view in reds and browns. Colors I'd grown to love.

At Sybilla's gasp, I finally looked over at her. Her eyes were as big as saucers. She steered the mule to the side of the trail and stopped at the canyon's edge.

"Sources," she breathed out. Her heart-shaped lips were chapped from the sun and hung open.

I followed her line of sight, realizing that, from our vantage point, Sahlmsara was now in full view. I'd helped build the city stone by stone, one canal and crop yard at a time. The population had boomed, and the city stretched the full width of the canyon, with the densest sector around Umber House—my home.

I imagined what it might be like to see it for the first time. Judging by her reaction, it was not what the Queen had expected. I didn't ask but watched her take it in.

"It's marvelous." She didn't spare a glance at me. "You built all this?"

"Yes."

She swallowed hard. "I couldn't even keep a city that was handed to me out of shambles and yet this..."

Did she blame herself for the destruction of her city? Judging by the Death-wielding I'd witnessed, there would have been little she could have done to prevent the ruin that had occurred. No mortal, even one with a hint of Reverist magic, could take on an army of Death-wielders. I voiced none of that.

I knew the feeling of being responsible for a city's demise...

"That is Sahlmsara."

"It's truly marvelous," she repeated.

Chapter 7
SYBILLA

S till reeling from seeing the city for the first time, I gave the mule enough slack in the reins to navigate down the rocky trail.

We weaved through smaller towns built into the canyon side. People stood on stone porches and waved rust-colored fabric to greet us. They kissed two fingers and held them out to the soldiers and their King as we passed.

"Return the gesture," Krait instructed before he placed the pads of his pointer and middle fingers to his lips and extended them out to each family. I held the reins in one hand and mimicked his movement.

"Is it a sign of respect?" I asked.

"Yes."

I found myself thankful that the mule seemed to know the route well because my head snapped from one side to the other as I looked at the surroundings, too entranced to steer effectively.

It was far more vivid than I'd imagined. We rode through rural areas with quaint rounded clay structures. As we neared the heart of Sahlmsara, colorful tiles of turquoise, burgundy and orange adorned doorways and windows. Intricate lines of tiles stretched across the full face of some of the larger buildings.

And the *size* of the city. If it weren't hidden in this canyon, you might have been able to see it from the Plateau at the north border of Henosis.

As we traveled toward the city's center, the buildings grew denser. The skyline of towering buildings was only interrupted by canals that ran parallel to each other, with bridges to allow crossing. Stucco balconies lined most of the multistory buildings. In the street gutters, a surprising mix of spiked vegetation grew, adding green and blue hues to the bustling streets. People stared as we passed, but I was too consumed with the breathtaking beauty of the city to fully pay attention.

Until their thoughts began to seep in.

"Our King has returned..."

"This must mean news is coming about the Henosis border..."

"Who rides with him?"

I shut down my senses—a habit of self-preservation. It wasn't always pleasant to hear first impressions of yourself.

"Stay with her," Darvanda said to Elsedora before he trotted up to lead the soldiers. She clucked to her horse and glanced over at me.

"It's something, isn't it?" she asked as she extended her fingers to a little girl who waved with a smile.

I nodded, unsure how to articulate exactly how splendid it was. The red rocks of the canyon walls complemented the city—making every color pop that much more. "It looks very prosperous here," I managed to say.

"What did you think it would be? A pile of rocks?"

"I honestly didn't know," I answered. "I expected more...doom and gloom?"

Elsedora snorted. "Oh, because of him?" She held her reins in one hand and waved toward the front of the procession. "Most people here have made a comfortable life for themselves."

"If that's so, why did so many leave to attack Henosis?" There was still resentment against Henosis in this realm—my city lay in ruins as proof.

"There is another city, just beyond the Vallic Mountains." Elsedora pointed straight ahead. "It is called Sahlmkar. It's where those who continued the attack on Phynx civilians were relegated when we traveled here. Most are still imprisoned. It's less fertile ground and has harder living conditions—a punishment for disobeying their King's orders. We suspect that is where Firose was able to rally recent support. The people there still worship the Death Origin, Caym."

My throat constricted. Darvanda had punished those who'd invaded my ancestors' city. He'd said the first day we'd met that the attack had only been meant to be a siege of power, that once white flags had flown, it hadn't been his command to continue the attack. This supported his claim, yet I still held doubts.

I didn't get time to ponder that more before a towering building with arched dormers, a large bell tower and many arcaded windows came into view. Colored tile encrusted every arch and numerous balconies that looked out over the main canal.

"That's Umber House. You'll be staying with us there."

I gripped the reins tight. It was by no means as large as the Palace of Luz, but Umber House seemed too enchanting of a place for such a surly, brooding King to reside.

"Do many live there?"

"Krait only has two officers, me included. The few lords here in the city hold their own residences and a few from rural regions visit every so often. The political structure is much flatter than in Henosis. Fewer laws and regulations—really the only laws surround stealing, violence and Death-wielding."

"So Death-wielding is outlawed?"

Remembering that awful smell of the amber smoke that the attackers had used against my city knotted my throat and made the hairs of my arms rise.

"Mhm, it is the worst offense someone can commit. Death only aids Death—it's thought when enough is harvested, it can bring forth the Death Origin for a reckoning. At least, that is the belief in Sahlmkar."

I sucked in my cheeks as I let that sink in. In Henosis, the Source Origins were thought to be non-sentient ideals rooted in superstition. Yet I knew what I'd seen that night in the bailey challenged that belief. Amara had summoned an Origin, right there within my palace walls.

The sun was beginning to set behind the mountains, casting a bronze glow over the city that mingled beautifully with the hues of the tiles and painted stucco. Around Umber House there were no parapets, no protection walls, no guards at the gates—no gates at all. The large front entrance featured an enormous arched wooden door that opened right into a large courtyard, where a market was setting up for the evening. High above the courtyard was a bell tower, which sat as a focal point at the center of the house.

The soldiers continued around the estate, and Krait peeled off and dismounted by the front door. He handed his reins to a groom, who then followed the soldiers—I assumed to a stable somewhere beyond the estate.

We approached the door, and Elsedora did the same; she handed off her reins with a polite thank you to a second groom. I dismounted, and a boy, no more than nine, approached with an outstretched hand to take the mule. "Thank you...your name?"

The boy turned a shade of crimson. "My...I'm sorry, miss?"

"Your name?"

"Oh, um...Hurley," he lisped through a missing front tooth.

I could feel the heat of the boy's embarrassment creep up my neck. His thoughts were scattered and nervous. *"She must be the Queen from Henosis."*

I supposed, like in any kingdom, news traveled fast here.

"Thank you, Hurley."

Krait stepped beside us. "Carry on, boy," he barked. "Get some help to get her things up to her bedchamber."

"Please," I added too brightly before I shot Krait a glare. The boy took the reins, nodded and walked away with my mule. "Iron fist over pleasantries, I see. He was, what, barely ten years old?"

"How far did pleasantries get you in Luz? And all children go to school here. Can you say the same? How their parents choose to let them spend their excess time is not mine to dictate."

I rolled my eyes. "You don't know any of their names though, do you?" I retorted.

He shrugged. "I pay well. That boy will have a small fund for his future after he's done with school."

Prick.

"Plus, you should be careful not to get too close to anyone here. I can't be around at all hours to keep you from harm's way."

"Am I at risk of being harmed?" I asked.

He shrugged again. "Probably."

I felt the tickle of Elsedora's amusement.

"Let me show my new friend the city." Elsedora rested an elbow on my shoulder. "Please, please, please—"

I couldn't fight the pang of excitement in my gut at the idea of venturing out into this newfound oasis.

"Elsedora..." Krait sighed her name while pinching the bridge of his nose. It seemed this wasn't the first time he'd disagreed with her whims. I wasn't about to get in the middle of it, having not yet figured out their dynamic.

"What? Don't 'Elsedora' me. Not many know her face yet or that she's even here...There will be little chance for her to see it once they do. And she will be with *me*."

"That's entirely what worries me," he argued.

"Just this once. Please, please, please—"

"No gaming houses," he warned.

The redhead's face lit up like he'd just made her day.

"Or pleasure halls or pubs."

Elsedora smirked. "What do you think of me?"

"I know you better than most," he said.

His skepticism didn't dull Elsedora's enthusiasm, which grew contagious.

"Go get cleaned up." She bounced around me and twisted a finger into one of my curls. "I'm going to have fun doing something with these."

I smirked. No matter how much my body ached, or how much I longed for a bath and a bed, I didn't think I could refuse her if I tried. Then she skipped toward the entry of Umber House.

"There are underground baths—I'll assign someone to show you around," Krait said. "Unless you'd rather explore my city smelling like a mule."

"It's a rather fine deterrent," I answered, though a bath after our long trip sounded divine. Not even my desire to be contrary to him would prevent me from taking him up on that offer.

I felt slighted that he wouldn't even be showing me his house or city himself though.

The sight of the main hall of Umber House took my breath away as we stepped inside. The way the dark wood domed above us made the space look larger than it had from the outside. Above us, tapestries depicting the Vallic Mountains hung between the beams and stretched up to the ceilings. The mountains were woven in silk of deep hues of red, brown and gold. The air was noticeably cooler, like an ever-present breeze fended off some of the stifling heat.

My mouth hung open, and I tripped over something while admiring the tapestries.

A broom?

The stick righted itself and continued sweeping into a dustpan. "Oh, sorry…" I glanced around, and a maid giggled from the corner.

"It is charmed, my lady."

I stepped out of the broom's way. "Marvelous!" The maid was tall and lanky with straight brown hair, looking to be in her early twenties. "What's your name?"

"Maddi," she said and bowed.

"I am Sybilla," I answered while spinning on my heel to get a better look at the way the candles and sconces seemed to hang and float on nothing but air.

"Oh! You are the Central Queen—"

I waved my hand to dispel her alarm. "If the estate is charmed to clean, what are your duties?"

"Well, I charmed the broom." Her eyes went wide as saucers. "If the magic offends you, I can stop it."

So Source magic was as common here as I'd imagined. The possibilities of such efficiency swirled through my mind. Farming, trade work, all of it aided by magic.

I shook my head and smiled. "I was merely curious. You like working here?"

The girl's shoulders relaxed, and she nodded. "Very much. King Darvanda keeps a full staff during the day, and it is much less dull than working in textiles like my mother did."

I noticed movement on the steps. A man with long silver hair greeted Krait, who had, unsurprisingly, walked away from me as soon as we'd arrived.

"Nice to meet you, Maddi—I'll watch out for the brooms next time." Offering her a smile, I approached the steps where Darvanda and the mystery man were discussing something in hushed tones.

CHAPTER 8

KRAIT

Any respect I had for Queen Sybilla had faded after she'd questioned my approach to dealing with my *own* staff. She acted as though she were trying to remember every face, every acquaintance. I now understood why her people accepted her even though her nobles did not.

In the old courts, nothing would've slighted a noble more than being treated the same as a commoner—she must have offended her nobles' sensibilities and made them feel too small.

A lump formed in my throat. Not my problem.

El could tote her around the city. I knew better than to think my officer would stay away from the pubs, but at least my warning would make her think twice about the more unsavory options.

When I strode into Umber House, Sybilla followed me but quickly got distracted by a broom and the tapestries of the Vallic Mountains hanging from the ceilings. She wandered off and began chattering with a maid.

I let out a frustrated sigh—she was bent on talking to *every* damned person in this estate.

"Look what the canals dragged in…" An airy male voice carried from the staircase.

My other officer, Ryn, peeked down over the balcony before descending. While Elsedora liked to be considered my second-in-command, no such role existed. I trusted either of them with the leadership of my city in my absence.

They were the only officers I'd ever appointed for the Sahlms—the only two allowed to speak for me.

"Ryn," I greeted him. His silver hair was pulled back, but a few stray strands framed his face. He looked as though our arrival had interrupted something—his tunic askew and unbuttoned at the collar.

"Who is *that*…?" The interest in his voice was not subtle.

I shook my head. "She is your new assignment. If you bed her, then you lose your cock. We don't need to complicate things any more with Henosis."

"Oh, but complications are so very fun," he teased me. "And I'm *assigned* to her no less."

"Ryn, not now."

"Fine. I'll keep my hands *mostly* to myself." He wiggled an eyebrow. "In more serious matters, you have a trial this coming week."

I stilled. "What happened?" I was only brought in to make calls on cases when Ryn and Elsedora couldn't decide on something between themselves.

"A man in the east quarter of Sahlmkar killed his wife—he says it was an accident. But he Death-wielded nonetheless. Something feels off about it though…"

"The decision is simple: he's sent to the Sahlmkar prison, questioned, and then sent to the guillotine." I swallowed a lump in my throat.

Sybilla interrupted and stepped up beside me. "Your staff is delightful—not that you would know," she jabbed.

I sighed.

She straightened and opened her mouth, ready to say more.

"Queen Sybilla, meet Rynall Toth. Ryn, meet the Queen of the Central Corridor—she will be staying in Umber House. Your job is to keep her out of trouble and out of my hair."

Queen Sybilla's whole body stiffened, and her hand froze in midair. She appeared hesitant to touch Ryn. Her green eyes widened as though my officer had hung the moon. A dumbfounded expression crossed her features. She outright swooned. I ground my teeth.

"Call me Sybilla," she breathed out.

"Oh, Sybilla, it's been a *long* time since someone's looked at me like that." Ryn winked and leaned against the railing, toward her. As he took Sybilla's hand and kissed it, I wanted to grab him by the collar and drag him back up the stairs.

A pit grew in my stomach. Seeing my ruthlessly flirtatious friend take interest in an objectively beautiful woman had never bothered me before.

CHAPTER 9
SYBILLA

R ynall Toth.

Before the Corridors existed, there had been two kingdoms split down the center of the realm, each with its own King.

Brennax, which had been ruled by the Darvanda dynasty. And Phynx, which had been ruled by the Toths. Without the fall of Phynx, the realm of Henosis would never have been—the Enchantresses would never have selected new rulers to replace the failing political system, and the realm would never have been divided into five Corridors.

None of the Toths had survived. Or so I'd thought.

"Does she always stand there with her mouth agape?" Rynall glanced at Darvanda before raising his silver brows in my direction. The room somehow got hotter.

"No," Darvanda said.

I shook my head. "Rynall *Toth*? The Prince of Phynx? And you are here? With *him*?" I hadn't meant to let the contempt slip into my tone.

It didn't make sense.

"Oh, *that* Rynall Toth. People get us confused all the time." Ryn's sarcasm was paired with a charismatic smile.

There was more to the history of my land than I could have ever imagined.

"Have we broken her? She looks ill."

"Not yet," Darvanda ground out, which caused my head to snap in his direction. "*That* was a joke."

"It's hard to tell with you," I breathed out before turning back to Rynall.

I scanned the Prince's face; it was much the same as I'd seen in history-book portraits and statues. Portraits and statues that I'd kept for...commemorative reasons. Taking a deep breath, I allowed my mind to slink into his momentarily, looking for anything threatening.

Was he a prisoner here?

A cool wave of amusement skated up my neck and caused me to gasp. His thoughts were mostly of my appearance, and a lick of his surprise slid down my body that made me physically shiver. *"If you're going to slip into my mind, I can make this far more amusing for us. I have a* very *vivid imagination."*

My back straightened at the realization that Rynall knew what I'd been doing. "How...?"

Darvanda cut in, "You're not as subtle as you think. Most Source-wielders, if taught, can feel the attempt of unrefined Reverist magic—those of us strong enough can block it entirely."

That was why Krait's thoughts were off-limits to me. That prick was blocking me out.

Heat rose in my cheeks, and I placed a hand across my neck, attempting to hide the flush that had grown there.

"Reverist magic?"

Krait sighed. "It's where your mind-intruding power comes from."

Fenris had told me that Elsedora, while immortal, had never inherited any Source magic, so her thoughts and feelings came to me more easily. I made a mental note to try to suppress my power in this land. If I could help it. No one else needed to know about my abilities.

"I'm sorry for the intrusion. I won't dream of it again."

Rynall chuckled. "Oh, I will."

My cheeks grew even hotter. I didn't think I'd ever met a man this forward. Maybe Fen, but he had eyes only for Asterie.

"Enough," Krait said, giving him a warning look. "Ryn will show you around and to where you can bathe—*alone.*" Darvanda pointed a finger at Rynall.

The silver-haired Prince lifted an eyebrow at that, and I couldn't help but laugh in a girlish pitch, which I wanted to swallow immediately. "Are you assigning the last Prince of my ancestors' homeland, a legend to my people...to be my caretaker?"

Rynall was biting his lower lip, but Darvanda was unamused as he said, "Yes." He glanced at Ryn again. "No complications."

"I heard you the first time," Rynall called after Krait as the King ascended the steps. "Don't worry, you get used to his moods. And quit looking at me all starry-eyed. Truly, it's an honor to meet you, Queen Sybilla—we'll be friends in no time. After all, we have worlds in common."

Ryn offered me his arm to lead me through the halls of Umber House. The same tilework as outside was prominent inside, and the brown-speckled terrazzo stone floor kept the space cool despite the heat outside. Even the halls of the estate were cozy. Warm-toned, thick curtains hung around every window and large wooden beams ran the length of the ceilings.

"So, if you are a Toth, what is your Source power?" That seemed the simplest question, though I bubbled over with eagerness to ask him more. The Order had long stripped magic out of our history, and meeting him in the flesh was an opportunity to uncover tendrils of my land's roots.

Ryn smiled and answered, "Moonlight—my twin sister, Freya, and I both."

Not much was known about what had happened to the Princess of Phynx all those centuries ago.

"You have a sister?"

"Had," he corrected, and a subtle pained expression crossed his features.

"I'm so sorry," I offered, and he squeezed my arm.

"It was a long time ago."

Ryn looked no older than thirty with a strong jawline, crystal-blue eyes and sleeves pushed up over thick biceps. I'd always had a weakness for strong arms.

"My friend Asterie is also of the night sky," I noted lamely, unable to come up with anything more intelligent to say after his disclosed tragedy.

The corner of his mouth turned up slightly in thought as we approached another curved hall. He explained, "The house has four quadrants on each level, and the halls form one giant loop."

I was surprised to find each space he led me through as enchanting as the last. Wooden bookshelves adorned the walls, along with portraits of men and women I didn't recognize. Above each doorway, there was a wooden carving of the rattling-serpent crest of the Sahlms.

We were on the fifth level, having just passed several windows with views of the main canal, when we passed a plain closed wooden door on our left.

If I was judging the space appropriately, it was about where the bell tower I'd seen from the exterior would be, yet the door looked as though it led to nothing more than a broom closet.

"Is that the bell tower entry?" I asked

"It is—but it's Krait's private study. None of us are allowed in there. I'd advise, if you'd like to keep your fingers intact, that you don't even touch the knob. He's likely laid traps with Shadows."

"Noted." What the King might keep in his personal study intrigued me. "I have to ask. You're here with the enemy of your fallen kingdom..."

"Is that a question, Princess?"

I blushed, too enamored with him to be offended by the demotion. After all, if he'd stayed, I would not be sitting on a throne. A lump grew in my throat. "It doesn't make any sense."

Ryn shook his head and patted my arm as we stepped past Krait's study. "You know, some stories are mine to tell, and some are only partly mine. Come back and ask me after you piece together some parts that aren't mine."

He gave me a wink and held out his hand to let me walk first down the main staircase. "I'll show you where your bedchamber and the baths are so you can get cleaned up before you leave with El. If you drink with her, keep your wits about you and don't try to keep pace with her. She's a wild one."

My chamber was a decent size, a double bed with an abundance of pillows on one side and a vanity on the other. It was decorated simply with a few paintings of the red rock mountains. I was thankful not to be held in a cell. So far, Darvanda had kept his word that he wouldn't harm me, however, there was no guarantee I'd be treated as royalty.

Ryn explained on our way down that the bathwater in Umber House, and bathhouses around the city, was filtered through sand,

and the gray water was used to water the greenhouse crops. No waste in the desert.

He left me at the door, and I entered, *alone*, to a divine space. Three exquisitely tiled pools of crystal-blue water sat side by side, large enough for ten people each.

After stripping out of my travel-worn clothes, I soaked in the pool for so long that my hands had become pruned. The dust and grime washed away with lukewarm water and lilac-scented soap. After drying and wrapping myself in the robe that'd been left for me, I padded up the cool tile steps to my bedchamber.

After a few minutes, Elsedora came into the room like a hurricane.

"There you are. Sit!" she commanded.

She spent an hour ironing out every one of my curls with a pronged contraption that she heated over a candle. I was uncomfortable with it so close to my face, but the more I moved, the more likely she was to catch me with the edge of it.

"Put this on." She handed me an emerald silk dress that felt far too light. "It will suit your eyes."

"*This* is not a dress."

Elsedora chuckled. "Trust me. As we get into the heat of summer, you'll be thankful for the lack of modesty here."

Offering her a mock glare, I took the dress behind a changing partition. Slipping off the robe, I pulled the slick green fabric over my head. I was thankful for the extra fabric that wrapped around the bodice but not for the back being left open.

Long ribbons hung from the sides, and the sleeves would need to be tied. I stepped out from behind the partition, trying to hold the dress together. "What exactly do I do with all of these?"

"Let me," Elsedora said and stepped up behind me. With surer fingers, she crossed the extra fabric over my shoulders and then around my waist before tying it there. "This is the fashion right now, so many ties...It's rather fun to be unwrapped like a present, though."

A laugh burst out of me. I couldn't imagine King Darvan-dick taking his time with a woman enough to 'unwrap her like a present.'

It also seemed as though nothing, not even the Shadow-wielding King, could tame the wild gust of Elsedora's winds. She was like a beautiful tornado that could sweep through and dismantle even one's thickest defensive walls.

While she was Fenris' sister, she had grown up here, apart from him. I admired her independent streak.

"Does your King like the gifts you offer?"

"Who?" Elsedora asked as though the question was outlandish. "Krait?"

"I assumed..."

Elsie threw her head back with a snorted laugh. "Oh, how I wished as a girl. Practically threw myself at him on my eighteenth birthday, and he was mortified."

"It was wrong of me to assume."

"I will deny I ever told you this, but I once had a portrait of him hanging on my wall as a girl."

"No!" I gasped out.

"Yes. Such a girlish dream—the Brennac Prince whisking me away. The infatuation took years to squash. And many, many sexual encounters with other people—it's funny now."

I couldn't judge her. The man *was* lethally attractive. I'd give him that.

"You've spent many years together—it never changed for him?"

"No. After Freya, his heart is too wounded to have eyes for anyone else. But Krait is a loyal friend. Once he chooses you, little will deter him from being there when you need him. He and Ryn have been a constant in my life since I left the North Corridor."

It was odd to think of the growling, grunting King as anything more than a sadistic prick. That he might be loved by anyone was intriguing, and it was clear from the adoration in her emotions that she did love her King.

"Princess Freya?"

"Yes. Rynall's sister. I urge you never to say her name in front of Krait unless you want a catastrophic Shadow tantrum. She was beheaded centuries ago—it was a tragedy. The people of Brennax loved her. Krait loved her."

I filed that all away—the last Prince of Phynx was here. Krait had loved his sister. She'd been *beheaded.*

The very word sent shivers down my spine. What could the Princess have done to deserve such a fate? Or had she deserved it at all? My heart sank for Ryn.

In my mother's case, it hadn't taken more than hearsay. For female royals, their position on a throne was always a precarious one.

But Krait had destroyed her city and killed her family...aside from Ryn.

Something wasn't adding up.

"Was it hard for you—leaving your land?"

Elsedora contemplated that for a moment before she shook her head. "No, at the time I thought there was nothing left for me there. But I do miss the Hussa Mountains, the crisp air, the frost melting away after a long winter."

I extended a hand to squeeze her shoulder and said, "Soon you can travel back there whenever you please. The wards are down, and an Egress will be built."

Elsedora smirked. "Like the wards ever stopped me. There are some things that are nostalgic not because of the places themselves but because of the people that once filled them."

From discussions with Asterie, I knew Elsedora's parents had been killed during the Great Wars—that they'd harbored Source-wielders and had been punished for that crime.

She interrupted my thoughts by asking, "Ready to break some rules?"

"As I'll ever be." I had a feeling that Elsedora wouldn't allow Darvanda's skepticism to change any plans she'd made for her evening.

My hair was too slick and soft to tie back with the Luz-blue ribbon, so instead, I wrapped it around my wrist as a bracelet and followed her out of the bedchamber.

CHAPTER 10
SYBILLA

The roads of Sahlmsara were enchanting by day, but they were downright mesmerizing at night. Golden lanterns hung in the air, held up by nothing but whatever charm allowed them to float and sway in the night wind. Rowboats lined the canals, charmed to carry passengers unmanned.

In the courtyard of Umber House, a quartet of brass instrumentalists played atop the low wall separating the space from the canals. People sat picnicking on woven blankets around the musicians, watching them play and throwing them coins. Elsedora went over to speak to a woman selling something on skewers and came back with one stick outstretched toward me.

"What do I do with that?"

She laughed before taking a bite of the meat off the stick.

Oh no—I couldn't.

"C'mon. I know you've got to be hungry."

I took the skewer stiffly and took a bite without letting anything drip onto the dress Elsedora had loaned me. It was chicken—in a savory, spiced marinade that hit my tongue with such a mouthwatering depth of flavor.

Some storefronts were closed for the night, but others had stayed open. The city bustled and came alive when the sun no longer accosted it. Elsedora grabbed my hand and pulled me along through the crowds. Despite my limbs feeling like stone and my longing for sleep, I couldn't compel myself to take a break from exploring this wondrous city.

"Is it always this busy?"

"Most nights. In peak summer it's quieter. The night heat is not as moderate then."

We weaved through the market. Floating tealight candles lit the balconies above, revealing people sitting out and enjoying their wine and spirits. I would kill for a glass of wine.

"Do you have a favorite pub?" I asked, biting off more meat—from a stick! It was freeing to be so present with the people—to be on the ground with them, to experience the city as they did.

Elsedora looked downright devious. "Of course. Where did you think we were heading?" She released my hand once we'd made our way through the night market and the traffic was easier to navigate.

"Thank the Sources," I breathed out. A drink would settle my nerves from having arrived in this strange, marvelous place.

She'd left me here.
Alone.
In a pub.

It had only taken Elsedora thirty minutes before getting distract-ed and chatting up a dark-haired man at the next table. She'd left on his arm, saying, "This won't take long. Promise. Stay put—drink, relax."

It shouldn't bother me, but my shoulders tensed from unwanted gazes and my hands gripped my wineglass. The leather bench seat was slippery against the silk of my borrowed dress, and I felt far more exposed than I preferred even though the booth was in the corner.

The pub itself was a rather nice establishment for something named "The Royale Cock."

I'd half expected Elsedora to take me somewhere with a rowdy crowd, sticky floors and ale-stenched air. Instead, colorful tapestries lined the walls—they illustrated some fairytales I recalled having heard as a girl, but all the characters looked red-eyed and drunk. The brown-speckled terrazzo tile floor was similar to Umber House.

The ceiling was tented with crimson curtains, and the flickering light of sconces dimly lit the space. Hanging in one corner, on a giant golden perch sat a taxidermy peacock.

Ah. That's what the name was about.

I ran my fingers through my hair, not used to the silken texture or the lack of snagging. Maybe going and sitting at the bar, where a couple was drinking together, would feel less awkward. I'd never been out to a pub unaccompanied before...or to one ever. It would be an unsavory thing in Luz—a Queen in a pub.

It felt unnatural not to be trailed by a dozen guards.

I shouldn't have suggested this.

Downing the last gulp of my wine, I decided that finding my way to Umber House wouldn't be too difficult.

Before I could leave the booth, a man slid into the seat to my left, where I'd intended to move. I reared back into the cushioned bench.

"Excuse me. I was just leaving."

"Why so soon? I haven't seen you here before."

He reeked of ale and sweat. He was somewhat handsome, but his predatory expression killed any interest and made my heart thump. "I'm meeting a friend," I lied.

That was the wise thing to say, right? Someone waiting for me would deter him.

"I saw your friend leave a few minutes ago. Come on now. A pretty face like that shouldn't be drinking alone. Let me get you another."

Unsure of if he was a Source-wielder or if he would be able to tell if I slipped into his mind, I avoided doing so. If he felt me as Ryn had, it would only draw more attention to who I might be and could provoke him.

"I should really be going." I began to scoot out of the booth in the other direction, only to meet a hard body on my right. It was as if he'd materialized out of shadows.

"She'll be staying. You'll be going. Unless you'd like those eyeballs that are undressing my guest removed." Darvan-dick sat to my right with an arm slung behind me over the back of the booth. He looked unbothered despite the command in his tone.

"Yes, my King—my apologies."

"Don't apologize to me. Apologize to *her* for your unwanted attention."

Humiliation brought redness to the man's face. His gaze landed between my nose and forehead.

"I'm sorry for my advances," he grumbled.

Darvanda waved his hand as if to shoo him away, and the man quickly scooted out of the booth and rushed toward the front doors. The barkeep barked after him, "Oi, your tab!"

"What are you doing here?" I asked Darvanda, and despite his alluring spiced and smoky scent beckoning me closer, I slid left to put an arm's length between us.

"I made a blood oath to let no harm come to you," he said. "I may not like you, but an oath is an oath. I figured El would leave you for dead at the first whiff of debauchery."

"Ah, so you're here to moderate our fun," I said.

"Would that have been fun for you?" He waved toward the door with his free hand, the other still lazily draped behind me but not touching me.

Refusing to look at him, I stared into my empty wine glass. "No," I answered. Agreeing with him was painful. Truthfully, I was happy he'd intervened.

"I'm not going to tell you where to go or what to do in my city. But next time you want to go out drinking—bring Ryn. He lives for that doe-eyed adoration you give him, and he's more reliable than El."

"I am not 'doe-eyed' toward him," I retorted.

Darvanda caught the attention of the barkeep. The man grinned at him, seeming proud to see his King in his establishment. Darvanda held up two fingers and pointed to my wineglass.

I glanced at Darvanda. "Wait, we're staying?"

He shrugged.

Cleaned up and under the warm lamplight, his skin glistened with a thin glow of sweat. He'd shaved and the collared red satin tunic he wore dipped to reveal the hair on his chest. Even frowning and brooding, he looked attractive. In a frightening sort of way. Or maybe it was in an exciting way.

Now that was the wine talking.

"I'm surprised. You were eager to hand me off earlier," I added.

Something akin to a grimace crossed his face. "I was tired, and you're exhausting."

Two glasses of wine were set before us. "Not the worst I've been called," I mused.

He took a long drag of his wine, and his throat bobbed. He dipped his head, and when I followed his gaze, he was staring at the sleek hair draped over my shoulder.

"The curls suit you better." He professed the unsolicited observation as though I gave a shit.

"Well then, I will have Elsedora iron my hair with that terrifying contraption every day."

His gaze ran down me. For some reason, it didn't bother me that he seemed to be assessing me. The wine hitting my stomach left me light-headed and relaxed.

"But that dress brings out your eyes." His tone was flat, and he cleared his throat afterward.

"Thank you. They're one of my better features."

I let my head fall against the seat and loll to look at him, too tired to feel bashful about staring. I took another sip of wine, and he mirrored my movement.

My lips turned up at the sides.

"What?" he grunted.

"I think that may have been a genuine compliment."

He shrugged. "I've never had any trouble recognizing beauty."

"Are you calling me beautiful, Darvanda?"

"Yes. But you are already well aware of that."

I covered my mouth so as not to spit out my wine. "You've got me pegged, huh? Self-centered, difficult, exhausting. It's alright—we can hope for the sake of my people that beauty alone can win over a husband before Haward can step in and display my head on the gates."

No...*that* was the wine talking.

I set down my glass.

"You are exhausting. But I am exhausted by most people. I said none of the other things."

I sighed and shrugged. Our wine glasses were nearly drained.

"Finish that," he said. "I have something to show you."

"Why do I feel like this is your way of luring me into an alley to be rid of me?"

"Take your chances here then."

I rolled my eyes. "Fine."

We downed the final sips of our wine before Krait walked up to the bar and paid the tab—their coins looked similar to ours but were bronze instead of silver. I scooted across the slippery leather and stood. I was thankful for the flat velvet shoes Elsedora had given me. After weeks of not drinking any wine, two glasses was enough to make my head spin.

Fighting the fatigue of alcohol was simply an added obstacle. It was familiar territory—I was always tired. My body often rebelled against being awake. The buzz of liquor would dull the pain in my joints until the lousy morning hours.

I followed Darvanda outside, where the air surrounded me like a warm embrace. Light from the floating lanterns above blurred together in a glow as the wind knocked them from side to side. The night market vendors were beginning to pack up their carts and booths, using spells and charms to quickly stow goods into trunks and crates.

"This way," Darvanda said as we walked further away from Umber House. It took nearly a half hour to reach what appeared to be the city's edge. As we navigated down a trail, the lantern glow began to fade behind us.

"This trail is hard to navigate at night. Do you want a hand?" he asked. I found it oddly comforting that he'd asked instead of assuming.

I grasped his offered fingers, and he led us down into a dry wash. His hand was rough in mine with calluses from where one might hold a sword.

I joked, "Here lies Sybilla Wymark: She took the hand of her enemy."

"I am not your enemy," he ground out as we veered left around some low branches. Thorny trees grew denser in the riverbed, the water allowing life to thrive here even in the middle of the desert.

The rocky bank was steep, slick and smoothed, and his grip tightened. My ankles felt stiff and unreliable, and I was glad for the darkness that veiled my grimacing.

"Fuck!" My foot slipped on a smooth rock.

I squeaked as Krait pulled me upright and steadied me.

"You use such charming language."

"Oh, please," I huffed. I could hear a trickle of water now.

He let out a "hmph" in response.

If I squinted through the darkness, I could make out the glimmer of the riverbed below. "What do you need to show me in this death trap?"

He brought me closer to the wall of the canyon, and then guided my hand to press my fingers against the rock face. We were so deep in the wash that the walls surrounding the riverbed formed a cliff above us, blocking out the city lights above. I felt a rough line where the smoothness of the rock ended. "This is one of the reasons you're here."

"I'm here...to fondle some rocks in the dark with you?"

He let out a ragged laugh. "No...This is where the waterline used to be just a few years ago. This is my realm's only water source, and it runs off the Hussa Mountains. We divert it to the canals."

The warmth of his hand left mine, but I continued to feel the rough edge. My throat grew tight as I tried to determine how far we were from the trickling water below. Too far.

"You're running out of resources."

"Water is a pretty damn important one. Without it, immortals can sustain themselves longer than mortals, but not forever. Our population has thrived, but as our droughts grow longer with each passing year, that river runs lower. Soon the canals will be impacted. It will grow harder and harder to live here."

He stood facing me, watching me. I could only see the outline of his features in the darkness. Standing here in a wash, shadows of sad bare trees above us, and nothing between us but our own breath and the trickling sound of a too-low river below, I began to understand the King of the Sahlms.

"How long do you have?" I asked.

"A few years, give or take. Then many will need to leave."

I blew out a breath.

Darvanda shifted to lean against the canyon wall on one forearm. "And where do I play a part in that?"

He wasn't only aligning himself with me because of some silly power move. His people needed *water*.

A basic necessity. A right of all in Henosis.

He took a deep breath between his teeth as if it pained him. "You have connections in the North. Mattock senior long ago stopped corresponding with me, but his son, the boy you've been wrapped up with, might be willing to break down some of the dams. They prevent the full flow of water into our realm."

I scoffed. "I can try. But that relationship is still...strained."

"Then unstrain it. I thought you'd prove more useful." His breath rustled the hair at my temple as he loomed over me, and his tone baited me.

I stood up a bit taller, not wanting to admit my alliances were weakened beyond repair. "Nothing I can't fix."

If this was what he'd brought me here for, it was best he didn't think I was incapable of helping him.

"That's what I like to hear," Darvanda mumbled.

"You said one of the reasons. What are the others?" I rested against the rock face, my energy depleted.

He tipped his chin down—the moon's light outlined the harsh lines of his face.

"Let's see if you can accomplish this for me first."

I ground my teeth. "I'm doing this for the people up there. You? You have nothing to do with it."

"We'll see."

I huffed in frustration, feeling my brow pinch. "What makes you so sure I give two shits about what happens to you personally?"

He stared down at me, unmoved by my sharpness. "Your hastened breath. The way you look at me. It's only a matter of time before you try to—how did you put it? 'Fuck me or filet me'? It will be interesting to see which you attempt first."

Stifling a growl, I turned on my heel and began climbing the rocky wash.

He was wrong.

Admitting your ancestors' enemy was attractive was one thing. Warming your bed with them was another. That was a line that wouldn't be crossed.

I knew he'd been trying to rattle me. It had worked.

CHAPTER 11

EMMERICK

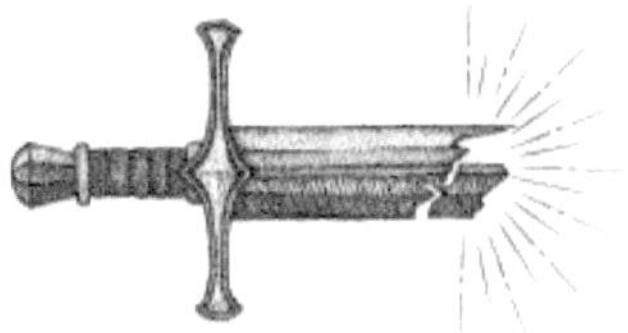

Crowds gathered outside the Sun Temple in Helos. As soon as the heavy golden crown was lowered onto my head, they cheered. The Lynx formed a protective row at the bottom of the steps. The horrid rat-faced, feline-like creatures roared.

The bell tower rang in celebration of a new King.

I looked to Barden and Haward, Sybilla's cousins. They'd come to petition that *they* should be my advisors.

"I'm ready to return to the castle," I told them.

Hundreds of North Corridor guards escorted us back to the mechanical lift, which pulled us up the mountain in a sickening, jolting manner. Perched atop the highest peak of the Hussa Mountains, Helos Castle was a marvel. Towers stretched up into the clouds, and the granite stone shined with dew.

I didn't remember making my way to the dining hall; my mind was too dazed with the feeling of metal at my temples and the weight of dozens of eyes gaping at me as we passed. I'd always been partial to Luz's silver and royal blue. Everything here was black and gold.

Too much gold.

A feast had been prepared and laid out before me on a long gilded table lined with faces that I barely knew.

Most royal heirs grew up knowing they would one day rule—they were prepared and excited for this moment. Conversation hummed around me. It felt wrong to sit in the chair of a man I'd never even met.

"Emmerick," Amara greeted.

My birth mother sat to my left. Next to her sat Angeline, my mother by all other standards. She was the woman who'd raised me as a baker's son turned Knight—she would always hold the title of Mama. My father had stayed in Luz to help with the grounds after the attack. He'd been the groundskeeper there for thirty-five years and stayed devoted even as his body protested.

Mama leaned over Amara and squeezed my arm, reassuring me. "You've done well."

This had just begun. I'd done nothing yet. Aside from accepting the throne of the Mad King, who had let Firose lead him to war.

The ashes of King Mattock, my birth father, were somewhere in the tombs below this gaudy castle. Forks scraped against plates; bottles were drained.

I didn't know how much time had passed, but the lords were drunk on mead, and Sybilla's cousins seemed to have them wrapped around their grubby fingers.

"Not hungry?" Amara asked, staring down at my full plate.

Mama glanced over Amara's shoulder, frowning. "Eat, my boy."

Great, now there were two of them.

When Amara had lifted the charm on our memories, she and Mama had both cried tears of joy at their reunion. I'd only felt emptier. Less of me felt *right* even though my mama had reassured me that I was no less hers, that shared blood alone did not make a family.

There were now fragmented memories of Amara visiting us, posing as my father's sister. I'd been too young to understand the weight of her presence.

I hadn't liked seeing the confusion cross my mother's face when the veil had been pulled back. She had lived so long under the guise of magic. What other evils could such magic could do?

I shook that thought away.

Magic was still forbidden in the North Corridor.

Sybilla would tell me that should change.

I was not so sure.

"It's just been a long day, Mama," I reassured her. "I'm fine, just feeling a bit green."

With doubt in her eyes, she said, "If you say so, my love. Why are the two lords from the Central Corridor here?" My mama wasn't unwise—she knew Haward and Barden had long spoken out against Sybilla's rule.

"As lords in the Central Corridor, they hope that their support 'adds legitimacy to my claim on the crown,' as they put it," I told her. "They could be useful." Haward and Barden were weasels. But they were great at shaking hands.

My mama pursed her lips, seeming skeptical. I was, too, but I needed to be accepted by the stakeholders in this Corridor. Sybilla's cousins had invited numerous lords and ladies of the North Corridor—I couldn't remember a single name.

My eye caught on one woman who stood out amongst them. She wore a burgundy veil, which she had not removed for dinner. The fabric looked charmed to obscure her face—how appealing. I'd give anything to be able to hide. I hadn't been introduced to her, so she must have been escorted in late.

A prickle of cold hit the back of my neck. It was sudden and chilling, as though someone had let in a draft—though no window was open.

How odd…

The northern nobles filtered out as soon as dinner plates had been cleared, and I didn't offer drinks or cigars in the sitting room. Amara agreed to see my mama up to her bedchamber. They chatted all the way up the stairs. Haward and Barden lingered.

Apparently, no one had told them it was rude to loiter about a royal's home—then again, that had always been their way. Barden stood behind Haward, looking nervous as usual.

"Can I help you, Haward?" I asked.

"Yes. I was waiting for a good time to introduce you to someone. She is the Lady of High Tower. That is a township a few miles east of here."

"I do own a map, Haward," I said and gritted my teeth. *Play nice.*

He nodded. "Then you know that she owns one of the largest estates in the North. She has requested to speak with you. So be *polite.*" Haward held his arm out toward the door.

When I stepped inside the drawing room, a petite figure, clad in a dark-burgundy cloak with the hood up, ran a gloved finger along a golden bust of a horse's head.

The veiled woman rounded the room and took in the books on the shelves—her movement eerily smooth. None of her skin was visible, and where her features should be, there were only shadows.

Hayward continued, "This is Lady Ryssa of High Tower. She tells us she has extensive experience in Source law. Should you need an advisor to help manage the changing landscape of the realm, she could be of great help."

"It is a pleasure to meet you, King Mattock." Her voice was distorted, and it rippled at the edges through the veil. I grimaced at my new title and new surname.

My late "father" had let Firose infiltrate his throne…his mind. Now I had to share his name as if he meant something to me.

"It's customary to lower your hood when speaking to a royal, is it not?" I asked. Distrust itched at my stomach.

Lady Ryssa drew in a deep breath and stilled. Her body language showed discomfort but no threat.

Barden explained, "Lady Ryssa told us she suffered scarring and burns as a child."

The thought of the hand-shaped burns on my chest, of the pain Firose had inflicted that night in the tower struck me. No one should be forced to bear their scars openly. I relived those moments whenever I saw my own.

Lady Ryssa nodded. "If you will allow it, King Mattock, I prefer to wear the veil. Forgive my broken customs, but—"

I waved away her explanation. It wasn't my way to make a woman do anything she wasn't comfortable with—customary or not. I felt bad for having required a reason, but I didn't know if I could trust any advisor Haward and Barden recommended.

"It's okay. I do not mind the veil, Lady Ryssa."

"Thank you, my King." The rippled sound of her voice was sweet at the edges.

"And I appreciate your willingness to help a green King. How did you gain experience as an advisor?"

"A green King is a blessing to these lands. Your presence brings excitement, the hope of change for the people. I once advised the late King Mattock a long time ago, but his allegiances changed. I could no longer support him, but it would be my honor to serve you."

Haward and Barden looked at me expectantly. I was too tired, and too eager to retire for the evening, to question it further.

"Very well. When can you start?" I asked.

Lady Ryssa curtsied her thanks. The delicate placement of her limbs hinted at a training in classical dance. "Whenever you wish, my King. Just send word to High Tower by hawk."

How very like me. I'd found myself intrigued by another woman who hid parts of herself from the world.

Chapter 12
SYBILLA

After slipping into the only light-fabric nightdress I'd brought, I sat at the edge of the bed and combed my silken hair. My fingers grew full of blonde strands, and I shook the hair from my hands. They floated to the floor like feathers in the wind, and I cursed under my breath, wondering if eventually I'd have no hair at all.

Darvanda's accusation ran through my mind.

It will be interesting to see which you try first

Filet. Absolutely filet.

The curls suit you better.

I'd choke him with my curls in his sleep, then.

"Who the fuck does he think he is?" I grumbled to myself as my brushing motion grew more aggressive; the bristles scratched against my sensitive scalp.

I blew a raspberry and rolled my eyes. The brushing didn't relieve my pent-up aggression. Instead, my wrist began to ache in a telltale manner, so I stopped.

It dawned on me that I was hundreds of miles from home, in the company of complete strangers. No guards trailed me, no maids whose names I knew well lingered and no familiar views waited outside the windows.

There was no Healer Mortag to send up the right tonics to relieve the way I ached all the damned time. I would not admit to any other healer how my glow of health was merely a facade.

Worse yet—no Emmerick.

I sighed. He'd come around.

Dropping the brush, I shook out my wrists. That recognizable fog of fatigue had been plaguing me all evening.

Not now. Not here.

It was almost a relief. I could rely on old weaknesses to be present at the least convenient times, could rely on my body to flip a coin to determine whether I'd find comfort or pain.

I dropped to my knees in front of my oak trunk from Luz. After unlocking it, I felt between the too-heavy dresses and skirts for the slick feeling of the small wooden box. Once I plucked it from the depths of the trunk, I opened it, revealing dozens of green vials inside.

Only one healer in Luz knew that I struggled to remain well. I wondered if these tonics would suit me the way Mortag's had. They would need to be enough for now—so long as the flares didn't get progressively worse. I'd be fine. I'd conserve them.

My health had fared well without any slowdowns for months, but the stress of the attack on my Corridor had taken a toll. Holding one of the glass bottles in my hand, I slouched over the trunk.

I contemplated whether it was worth it to use a dose so soon.

A creak in the floorboards caught my attention. A figure moved in the corner of my vision.

I started to scream as I stood, but my wail was cut short.

A rope came around my neck from behind, and I was yanked backward against a hard chest. The wooden box of remedies fell from my hands and the vials shattered at my feet.

I gasped. "Get off m—"

The rope tightened, cutting off my voice. I gagged and heaved. Pulled to my tiptoes, I couldn't find any leverage.

I hadn't heard them coming. Hadn't felt them coming.

Panic set in as another entered the room—a sandy-haired man with too few teeth, flipping a dagger in his hand. Every awful thing they imagined doing slammed into me as I lost control over my thoughts.

"Cut her."

"Bleed her out."

"Kill her."

The frenzy of their wrath painted my mind with rotting, wretched hatred. I choked on the mental onslaught as much as I choked for air.

"Be quick about it," the one holding me growled. I tried to shake my head, tried to scream, tried to do anything.

I'd never felt so fucking hopeless. I dug my nails into the man's arm, trying to claw him away. Time slowed; icy-cold terror spread through my veins.

No one was coming.

Darvanda had probably planned this after realizing I couldn't help him.

A small boy stood frozen in the doorway, watching in horror. Hurley—the damned groom.

The sandy-haired man approached with a predatory expression. He grinned before pointing the dagger at my forehead.

I closed my pooling eyes, praying to any Source who would listen. Please, please, please...

Make it stop.

"Open your eyes, Henosis whore. I want you to watch while I carve you up..."

When I refused, I felt a cool swipe across my cheek and then the burn of the cut he'd left there. My vision blurred.

This was how I would die?

Pathetic.

Weak.

I channeled all of my anger and let it fill the room; it clung to the curtains and dripped from the wooden chandelier. When I opened my eyes, my gaze sharpened and my face contorted. If I was going to die, then it wasn't going to be while whimpering like a fucking fool.

The ruddy-faced dagger-wielder drew back the blade, lining it up to pierce my heart.

Then, I reached out.

But not with my hands...

It was as though all the fury, all the fears I'd let out were being pulled to me and then pushed out, like a tide.

Every painful memory.

Every night my mother had slept at my bedside, waiting for a fever to break.

Every bruise my father had left behind.

Every ache and pain my body imposed on me.

I unleashed it *all.*

The dagger dropped from the man's hand. He fell, hitting the ground with a thud, and began to convulse.

The rope around my throat loosened. My skin itched where the coarse hairs had dug in.

As I gasped for air, the man behind me stumbled backward. When I glanced back, he landed on the ground, writhing and screaming. Both of their shrieks filled the room with agonized pleas.

"Stop! Stop!"

"Sources. Oh, Sources!"

I wanted them to hurt.

The boy groom—Hurley—watched, his mouth gaping. I had no voice, but I mouthed the word, "Run."

The boy scrambled away from the door, tripping before he tore down the hall.

I didn't know what I was doing to these men.

But a child shouldn't witness it, even if that child likely had something to do with this attack.

A feral part of me felt fed—a part that craved violence. A side of me I'd never met nodded and encouraged me. "You can kill them…" the feminine fury whispered. "It would be so easy."

Their fate lay in my hands.

I didn't know how long I watched the two gasping, flailing men. "Sybilla!"

Krait's voice woke me from my wrath and pulled me from the web of pain I wielded. Standing over the two red-eyed, bawling men, I held my hands down toward them. I looked at Krait and then at the men. Piss had soaked through their pants. The dagger and rope lay on the ground.

What had I done?

Then, the world snapped back into focus.

It was a light and heady feeling—as though I hadn't just twisted pain into the minds of others.

The men stopped screaming, but they stayed on the ground, twitching and trembling.

Krait looked me up and down before his Shadows snaked across the floor like dark vines and wrapped around the men's necks. He slammed them both up against the far wall, away from me. The paintings that had hung there clattered to the ground, shelves snapping and breaking beneath the men's weight.

He took a step toward me. "What did they do to you?" he shouted.

CHAPTER 13

KRAIT

I'd been in the bell tower quarters, lighting the candles, when a prickling sense of danger had hit the back of my neck. Legend said that Shadow-wielders were more attuned to forthcoming Death since the Death and Shadow Origins were brothers. I could usually see Shadows of the dead in the moments after someone had passed away, and had a keen sense of when Death neared.

Sybilla.

Leaving the candles, I Shadowed to her bedchamber door.

"Ryn?" I shouted. He had been told to watch over her room. I pushed through the door. Sybilla stood with her hands stretched out toward the ground.

Blood dripped from her cheek.

A ring of red circled her neck.

Someone would be dying for that. An annoyance or not, the Queen should not have been touched in my home. My vision blurred with rage.

For a moment, I didn't register what she was doing. Then I looked down and saw the state of the two men on the ground.

Shit. I might not even need to help kill them.

The men were clawing at their own skin, trying to escape the inferno of their minds.

It was her.

I'd doubted it could be possible, but she had been right in front of me this whole time.

I wanted to watch her fry their brains like eggs in a pan, make them husks—punish them. Standing there in nothing but a pale-blue, blood-spattered nightdress, she was a vision of violence that struck me as terrifyingly beautiful.

But I needed to know who'd sent them and why. Logic won out.

"Sybilla!" I didn't tell her to stop. Killing was a personal choice.

Her shoulders slumped, and she glanced down and then up at me. For a split second, it seemed as though she might extend her magic to me; she looked drunk off it.

I tilted my head. "Come on now. Don't do *that.*" She didn't seem to hear me.

She stared down at her hands.

Then she gasped and took in the product of her vengeance. As soon as the men's bodies slackened, I let my Shadows do as they wished—which was to dig into the intruders and slam them to the far wall. I'd deal with them later.

I took one step toward Sybilla. "What did they do to you?"

She fucking flinched.

I softened my tone. "Sybilla, which one of them did that?" I pointed to her neck.

Her breath heaved, and she gestured to the dark-haired man. I smirked as my Shadows wrapped around his fingers and mangled every single one. He shrieked as they snapped, though it paled in comparison to his shrieks from just moments ago.

"What about that?" I pointed to her cheek.

Her eyes darted like a caged animal, as if she didn't know whether to strike out at me or back away. But then she motioned to the light-haired man.

"My King, please—" he begged.

The snap of his bones and cries of his pain pleased me. They were both pleading now, squabbling like children. Not wanting to hear them anymore, I let my Shadows consume them completely and cut off their air.

"Did they touch you anywhere else?" I whispered. I didn't want to startle her again.

Sybilla shook her head.

Ryn burst through the empty doorway, glancing around. "Sources...what happened?"

"I don't know, Ryn," I growled. "What happened? You were supposed to be guarding her door."

Ryn's face paled. "Krait—I went to take a piss. I was gone for five minutes."

"A lot can happen in five minutes," Sybilla's rasped and strained voice cut in. "I should have locked the door."

Hearing her take any blame made another snarl gather low in my throat.

Sybilla pointed at the men. Their faces were turning blue.

"Stop that," she ordered.

"Why?" I retorted.

"Because I'd like to interrogate them tomorrow."

Elsedora jogged down the hall in what she'd worn that evening, except with no shoes. Her eyes widened at the scene. "What in the Sources' names..."

"El, take these men to the cell," I reeled in my Shadows only enough to allow my *newly appointed* second to step inside and take the rope from the ground. I could kill Ryn.

"Happily," she said. She crossed the room and tied the men's hands with frightening ease. She turned to Ryn with a narrowed gaze. "Answers later."

"What will you do with them?" Sybilla asked.

"They will die," I said plainly. "After we question them."

"They attempted to kill *me.* Don't I get a say in their fates?" she retorted though her posture told me the wind had been knocked from her sails. It felt like she needed to pick this fight—like it centered her to have her claws out.

My teeth involuntarily ground together. "Fuck no, not in my realm."

When I stepped toward her, she braced again—it made her look smaller. Her hands began to rise as though I would...

I frowned, and her eyes grew wider.

A learned reaction.

She thought I would lash out—hurt her too.

"You can't go around killing anyone who tries to harm me. Your people need to trust this alliance. You kill them for attacking me, and you make them martyrs."

I drew closer to her, and she took another step backward.

Now I was growing pissed. But not at her. At anyone who'd dared to touch such divinity, such power, with an unkind hand.

Ryn was still standing there with his hands loosely at his sides, body tense, when I glanced back at him.

"Help El get them to the cell. And have the maids bring a cot up to my chambers."

"A cot?" he asked.

"Are you really asking questions? Go."

I trusted my friend implicitly—he'd never slacked off or slipped up on anything this important. And the Central Queen had just become *incredibly* important to us.

He nodded with a short "Alright." Looking defeated, Ryn left the room without another word.

Sybilla's breath finally slowed. As I approached, she gripped a bedpost, her knuckles white, but she didn't try to back away from me this time. I leaned down as gently as possible, trying to remind myself that she was still in shock, still shaken.

"I don't know who in your life gave you the impression that someone can hurt you without consequence." I should stop speaking and let her be, but all I could see was red. "In my residence—if anyone so much as intentionally gives you a paper cut, I will let my Shadows tear them limb from limb. Slowly. Do we have an understanding?"

Knowing who she was changed everything. Her safety was no longer just about a political arrangement.

With a skeptical expression, she nodded and her posture softened.

The way her wet lashes stuck together as she looked up through them added fuel to my fury.

"No one lays a finger on you unless you want them to—not me, not your cousins, not that Constable. And I will teach you how to stop any who try. Because what you just did, what you are—with training—is a weapon worth protecting."

"How do I know it wasn't you who sent those men?" she rasped.

I scoffed. "If I wanted you dead, I'd have never made a blood oath that binds me to keeping you safe. Plus, what good would a dead Queen of a realm I need a foothold in be to me?"

Keeping her safe wasn't a matter of a silly blood oath. It was a matter of life and Death for the realms.

To let her fully into my head would've been unwise, but as she stared up at me, I realized she needed to know that my words were true. I focused on my emotions—the swelling sense of protection, the desire to see her unharmed, to see her power outgrow mine.

When I opened those emotions to her, she wrapped a hand around her bruised throat and stared at me with a furrowed brow. I stepped out of her personal space. I hadn't touched her, but the warmth of her breath had heated, and left condensation on, the silk shoulder of my tunic.

I pushed her back out of my thoughts before she could unravel the truth. I wasn't ready to lay that bare to her—not yet.

"Why a cot?" she asked. The roughness in her tone made me want to follow El and Ryn down to the dungeons and get rid of those men. But that wasn't *my* pain to deal.

"Because you're no longer under Ryn's watch. You're under mine. You'll be staying with me for the rest of your time here."

She opened her mouth like she might try to disagree, but the words died on her tongue as her gaze caught on her own blood mixed with the green liquid from the shattered vials. Curious vials. Had she intended to poison me? I wouldn't put it past her.

"Let's get you cleaned up, yeah?"

She nodded.

A breeze blew through the curtains from the open balcony as I held my bedchamber door open for Sybilla. She stepped inside, glancing around, stiffly clutching her dark-blue robe closed. Her bare feet planted on the terrazzo tile at the entry, not moving further into the room.

"The balcony is warded. This is the safest place in the realm you could be," I assured her.

The maids had already brought a cot in. Atop the footboard bench were healing salves and a bucket of warm, clean water. Sybilla sat and wet a rag, not speaking, for once.

There was something odd about seeing someone so exquisitely feminine in this space—all dark leather and crimson. The bedsheets were a deep brick color, and the ceilings were made of dark wood.

She bristled. "Repeat it."

It seemed she'd come to the conclusion of whatever thoughts had been wracking her.

I felt that conclusion would inevitably be bad news for me.

"Repeat what?"

"Repeat what you said in our blood oath. I need to hear it again."

My teeth ground, but I remembered every oath I'd ever made. Every word. To forget one was to leave yourself vulnerable to loopholes. Blood oaths were fickle magic if not ironclad. Outside forces could break them rather easily with no consequence if both oaths were broken at once.

I repeated my oath to her: "'No harm will come to the Central Queen, or her Corridor, so long as she is an ally to Sahlmsara in all negotiations with the rulers of the Corridors.'"

Her distrust was misplaced.

Yet, her eyes narrowed on me.

"'I will go willingly to the Sahlms so long as no harm shall befall me or my Corridor until the trials end,'" she said, repeating the terms she had agreed to. Her shoulders were still stiff as she looked around at the contents of my room—the dark wood vanity, the shelf of my favorite volumes and the standing globe that still reflected the Old World.

My face paled as she touched her cheek with one hand and her throat with the other.

No harm.

The marred skin on her neck and the slice across her cheek taunted me with the truth. She was no longer bound to be here by flimsy magic. No oath tied us together any longer.

"It seems we don't need to hold up this alliance, do we?"

I swallowed hard. "So you'll return to Luz?"

"That depends. Would you try to keep me here if I said yes?"

"No." It was the easy answer. The more complicated one burned in the graveness of my voice. She couldn't go—not now, not after I'd just found her.

"Then I am willing to stay."

The air deflated from my lungs, but her tone told me this wouldn't bode well for me.

She added, "With a few conditions." Blood dripped onto her neck as she gingerly wiped her cheek with the cloth and winced.

I stepped across the room and sat beside her on the bench. Outstretching a hand, I offered to take the rag. "You're just smearing it around. Let me? While you share your conditions," I said, trying to feign indifference as my mind grappled with what she might propose.

She hesitated but reluctantly handed me the cloth. I dunked it in the lukewarm water and began to dab away blood from her cheek. She met my gaze with resolve.

"An Egress, built immediately so that my advisors may come and go as they please and I can aid them in rebuilding Luz."

"Done," I grunted. She pursed her lips, which dragged my gaze down. "You want that in blood?"

She shook her head. "Enough has been spilled—and blood oaths can clearly be broken. But I am not done," she said. I dabbed my finger in the salve and gingerly pressed it to the open wound on her cheek. "I want your assurance that what happened tonight remains between us."

I stilled, glancing at the blood running down the side of her neck over the purple-mottled skin. "May I?"

She pulled her hair to the opposite side and nodded.

"I agree with your condition. But what exactly happened tonight, Sybilla?"

"I don't know," she admitted and sucked in her cheeks. "You said you can teach me how to control it...and that's another condition. If I'm to stay, I want to understand how to wield *that*."

I fought a smile and trained my face into a neutral expression, as I slid the cloth down her neck. That was a condition we both wanted. The stronger she grew, the better she could contend with Caym in the years to come.

"Then we begin tomorrow." I took a dry cloth and wiped the water off her neck where it had dripped. My fingers trailed over her soft skin. Those stunning green orbs of determination held my gaze. "Is that all?"

"No. My last condition"—she hesitated—"is that you marry me, Darvanda *dearest*."

My whole body stiffened. I'd heard her wrong.

The proposition struck me in a way that raised the hairs on the back of my neck and made my palms grow clammy.

"Why would you want to marry *me*? You've made your opinions of my character rather clear."

She looked a bit smug about having taken me off guard. "Because, Darvanda, you don't seem like the kind of King who needs, or wants, a wife or another ruler's crown. I have two years left to marry to keep my position, and I'd rather focus on matters of my Corridor than court prospective consorts. It's a wise political move for both of us. It's no secret that I want to bring Source power back to Henosis, and you need resources for your people."

I didn't need her crown, or a wife. I needed a child. That was a more complicated matter—one that would become less complicated if we were to marry.

She continued, "You are powerful in your own right; you have your own lands and no desire for mine. We would maintain separate rules and stay out of each other's affairs for my mortal lifespan. It's a perfect arrangement."

I shrugged. "Very well then." My heart raced.

"Utterly romantic," she scoffed, and I had to fight a smirk.

"Do you wish to be romanced into marriage?" The question left my lips before I could think better of it.

"No."

Her answer was abrupt enough that it brought me relief and, more confusingly, some disappointment.

She scanned my face. "One more thing."

I raised my brows. "What's that?"

"I get the bed."

I'd already planned to let her have that.

"Fine." I sighed.

She cast me a skeptical look but rose and stepped around the bed to rearrange my pillows. She was ruthlessly flattening them.

I rinsed my hands in the bucket and then dried them. Not saying goodnight, I got into my new bed on the other side of the room.

I had the Last Daughter of Isleen beneath my roof.

Willing to marry me.

I'd sleep wherever it took to keep her here.

And although my feet hung off the edge of the cot, I'd rest better knowing that no one could get to her unless they got through me first.

CHAPTER 14
SYBILLA

When I awoke, the sun seeping through the curtains stung my eyes. Darvanda wasn't in the room, and the cot was neatly made, as though he'd never slept in it.

I'd proposed to a man who did more grunting and growling at me than speaking. Yet, when he'd let down his mental walls the night prior, his intentions were clear. He wouldn't let harm come to me—I didn't understand why, but I didn't need to so long as I dictated the conditions of our marriage contract. There wasn't any rush.

Deep-crimson curtains hung from wooden rods, and the room was paneled and wainscoted in dark stained oak. My trunk of belongings had been hauled up and now sat on the far side of the room. I felt groggy as I rose, and it was tempting to curl back up under the covers and sleep the rest of the day away.

Instead, I padded with bare feet across the room and opened the trunk, searching for a vial before remembering they'd all shattered.

"Shit..." I said, blowing out a deflated sigh. I didn't wish to bring attention to my health to any healer here. It was always tiresome to explain, and my weaknesses were my safely guarded secrets.

I would be fine for now.

"What was in the vials?"

I jumped. "Sources!"

The whole Shadow-roaming thing he could do gave me the fucking creeps.

He could be anywhere...

Darvanda stepped from the balcony. "Was it poison?"

"No," I bit back. "And it's none of your damned business what was in them."

I'm betrothed to this man. My stomach turned at the thought—what was I thinking? Why had he agreed? He must have deemed water for his realm and reentry into Henosis worth shackling himself to me for the length of my mortal life.

He shrugged. "How are you feeling this morning?"

Shuffling through my trunk, I found my stationery box and pulled that out. "Like I was nearly strangled and killed last night. So, by all standards, *wonderful*."

There was a small, practical three-drawer vanity in the corner of the room where I set myself up to write Asterie.

He glanced over my shoulder for a moment before settling on the bench at the foot of the bed. I pretended he wasn't there.

Gathering the parchment and ink, I noticed a crystal decanter of port and a glass on the desk. Might as well ease my nerves and headache. I poured myself a glass; my hands were still shaky, and I spilled some on the page.

"Shit..." I wiped it away with my palm.

I wouldn't worry Asterie with what had happened or what I'd just agreed to. The letter was vague but reassuring.

It isn't as awful as I imagined—charming even.

I ended the short letter with a promise to see them soon.

P.S. I have negotiated with King Prick to allow you and Fen to Egress in for weekly dinners so that I can advise you. More importantly—to speak amongst friends. I will send word when the Egress is built.

That was as much as I was comfortable sharing on paper.

"Your hands are shaky...were the vials some sort of drug you're withdrawing from?" His shadow covered the page as he hovered behind me.

"For Sources' sake, since when did you grow so fucking chatty?"

"Charming language."

I snapped, "Then leave me alone if you don't want to hear it."

When I glanced over my shoulder, his jaw was tight. But the flicker of mischief in his iron eyes told me he had been ribbing me.

"Glad to see you're in such a great mood. Now, seriously"—I shooed him toward the door—"I need to change."

To my surprise, he listened. I looked back down at the page and began to fold it.

"You should go back to sleep, Sybilla. It was a long night," he said, still leaning in the doorway.

Why was that oddly alluring?

His tone quickly changed from light to grave again when he added, "And you have men to question this afternoon."

He didn't wait for my response before closing the door.

Though I hadn't meant to, I did end up back in bed.

I'd fallen asleep over the covers and awoke hugging a pillow. I hated admitting that the pillowcases smelled divine—like warm spice and smoke. It was an erotic scent that I would happily bathe in.

The weight of another on the bed next to me shifted my hip. I gasped, shooting upright.

"Woah, now," Elsedora soothed. "I'm sorry to wake you. It's past noon."

She knelt on the bed beside me, hands clasped in her lap, looking like the saddest puppy I'd ever seen. Big hazel eyes glistened as she took in the ring of bruising on my neck.

I didn't love being inspected for cracks, like a fine vase.

"Stop staring at me like that."

"I *left* you—and then you were attacked."

Lying back on my elbows, I narrowed my gaze at her. "You're right...I'm unhappy you left me in that pub to fend for myself. But what happened last night had nothing to do with that."

She shook her head. "I will work on being a better friend."

"We're friends? I don't recall ever agreeing to that," I teased with a smirk. It was nice having someone seem genuinely worried about me—flighty as she was.

Elsedora had a wild energy that made me feel like she would walk over flaming glass to keep someone she loved out of harm's way. If she was around that day.

She scooted up and let herself flop down onto the pillows beside me.

"We might not be friends yet. But you had a part in bringing my brother back to me. You sent Asterie after him—I owe you more than being unreliable and horny. But we'd been traveling for so long...I had *needs,*" she said as she threw her hands up toward the ceiling.

I tried to laugh but coughed instead. Recovering, I asked, "Was he worthwhile?"

"Not in the least." She raised her eyebrows and tipped her head toward me. "He called out his *own* name when he reached release."

"No…" I hurt everywhere and winced against my laughter.

Elsedora returned her gaze to the ceiling, smile fading. "I wanted to go down to the dungeon and play target practice with my daggers, but Krait wouldn't let me—killjoy he is."

Sobering from the humor of the moment, I realized that I still needed to know who wanted me dead this time. And I also could go for a cup of tea.

"Do you have bluebell vine tea here?" I asked Elsedora.

She scrunched up her nose. "You drink that? It tastes so medicinal."

"Don't judge my choice of tea," I said as I gently smacked her arm.

"Well, no, I can't say that grows here," she contemplated. "I don't know anyone who would put that in tea."

I tilted my head. "My healer, Mortag, used to prepare it, with other herbs for taste; it's good for inflammation."

Elsedora, ever perceptive, narrowed her gaze. "Why would you need that?"

I stilled for a moment, realizing my slip. Elsedora had such a warm energy that it had just spilled out of me. I rolled my eyes, trying to think of a logical excuse. "What? Do immortals not get their cycles? It's a painful business."

At that, Elsedora shook her head. "Not typically after a female immortal's hundredth or so year. It becomes much harder to conceive after that."

"Why does it always have to be the woman's scourge to bear?" I huffed. The thought of children sounded nice but only in the distant future. Yet my body would unjustly dictate the timeline for me.

She smirked. "It's not impossible for us. But my birth was practically a miracle. My parents liked to joke that I was their 'happy accident.' Being a hundred years younger than your sibling has its challenges."

"I can imagine. Especially when that hundred-year-older sibling is a dallying idiot sometimes."

Elsedora nodded. "Most men are."

That much she and I could agree on.

My heart tightened to think of the one man who had never wandered. I missed the feeling of his strong arms around me.

I feared his reaction when he learned that I was to be married to another. Again. He'd seen this play out, and I'd skirted the altar more than once.

Which begged me to consider whether I would be able to go through with it this time.

CHAPTER 15

KRAIT

While relighting some candles in the bell tower quarters, my blood pounded in my ears. With a shaky hand, I used a soft cloth to polish the stand of her statue. Thick gray curtains were drawn, and no sunlight leaked into the space. Only twinkling flames lit the small room and the stairway, which led to the bell.

The weight of having found Sybilla—of what that meant hit me. Even the thought of her name while standing in this space felt wrong.

I set the cloth down and moved to the desk, where *The Book of Isolde*, the First Reverist's prophecies, lay safe in a glass case. No one else was allowed in this room, where I preserved the book from hands, dust and sunlight.

The prophecies of Isolde were full of stupid fucking riddles.

But my ancestors had decoded each line with great precision and lived by them for centuries to keep the Death Origin from rising. Until me.

My disobedience, my choice to marry Freya, to not wait to find the Last Daughter of Isleen—everything I'd done had set chaos in motion four hundred years ago. It had lost me the love of my life. I'd fought my father's insistence on following the prophecies until her death.

Those stained pages had sealed my fate long before I'd been able to speak for myself—long before I'd met a Princess who had been my Source Match yet hadn't been destined to be mine. Long before she had been taken from me.

Now we had a chance to stop the Death Origin once and for all. A new royal wife and I, a child of ours. Maybe none of my mistakes had to be in vain.

If it wasn't already too late. It had taken so long to find her.

The cards had fallen so perfectly—a political marriage for her, one of dreadful fate for me. There would be no replacing Freya, and the Central Queen offered me the type of arrangement that wouldn't sully what we'd shared.

I pulled open a desk drawer abruptly.

Grabbing ink and a piece of parchment, I thought for a moment. I then scribbled down a few faults of the Central Queen. This list would act as a reminder if I ever began to see her as anything more than what she was—a convenient means to an end.

I. Phynnic idealist

II. Stubborn as a bull

III. Has little control over her own power

Staring down at my rushed penmanship, I felt better already. There was no room in my life to enjoy the company of Sybilla Wymark, no matter what she was prophesied to be to me. I slipped the parchment back into the drawer.

I didn't need a wife, didn't need a partner. I just needed her to be willing to consider what the prophecy required of us, and that might be easier to justify through marriage.

Two rulers could have a child without romance. It happened all of the time.

I shouldn't feel guilty.

Unable to look Freya's bronze statue in the face, I stepped toward the door. There was a knock as I reached for the handle, and my brow furrowed.

"What?"

As soon as I turned the knob, Elsedora pushed the door to poke her head in. "Pleasant greeting."

I practically snarled, "What are you doing up here?"

My mood didn't deter her. She slinked inside. "Lower your hackles—there isn't a place in this house where I haven't been. But I haven't taken anything from this room. It seemed wrong..."

Elsedora's gaze caught on the bronze figure, tracing over Freya's gentle, eternal form. My late wife was depicted reaching out to hold up a crescent moon. She wore a billowing gown reminiscent of the one she'd worn on our wedding night.

Her essence could never be fully captured. Nothing set in bronze nor painted ever matched my memory of her. Or maybe I simply misremembered her. That pissed me off the most—forgetting.

"She was beautiful, truly."

My throat tightened at the simplicity of her adoration.

I sucked in a breath and nodded. "Truly."

"And judging by the sour look on your face...I take it that you found the Last Daughter of Isleen, didn't you?" El fidgeted and ran a finger over a candle's flame, letting fire dance toward her and away.

"We aren't discussing this. Not here."

She sighed. "I saw those men that attacked her...they were haunted. *Husks.* I know there is only one type of power that can do that. The same one you've had me searching for."

"It isn't her," I tried.

Her hand stilled, and she snapped, "Don't you dare lie to me. It's an insult to my intelligence."

I headed toward the door, but she stepped into my path. "El, please. Not here."

"Then where? When? What are you going to do, Krait? I deserve to know."

Maybe she did deserve answers. Instead, I growled, "Don't be dramatic."

"I'm not! Are you dense?"

I rarely heard Elsedora angry.

While rage also crept into the corners of my mind, I wasn't mad at El. She'd just forced me to think about the repercussions of every action I'd taken in my five centuries of existence.

"Why aren't you with her?"

My concern must have been answer enough because Elsedora's entire posture softened. "She's with Ryn—they're eating lunch. Now answer me. Is it her?"

"Yes. She's the last full Reverist, and you cannot tell a soul."

"And?" El pressed.

"And..." I struggled with the next part. Elsedora knew *The Book of Isolde* as well as I did. She'd spent centuries searching for hidden artifacts mentioned in it that might've led me to Sybilla.

She just needed me to confirm what she already knew.

"According to the prophecy, the child of the fifth heir of Shadows and the Last Daughter of Isleen will end Death's second reign."

Elsedora snorted. "Well, Fifth Heir of Shadows, I'd suggest you be a tad nicer to her then. I don't know a single woman who would choose to procreate with such a gloomy asshole."

If she only knew the proposition Sybilla had laid before me the night prior.

"Such high praise for your King," I mused. My normally light and airy friend was stone-faced and solemn.

"After you have an heir—how long?"

I shrugged and said, "My father was immortal until my birth. He lost control of his Shadows and passed them to me by my twentieth birthday and then lived a long mortal life. It won't be instant. You aren't getting rid of me so quickly."

"Yes—but you will be *mortal*. Me, Ryn, the Sahlms, we'll all lose you eventually. Are you sure there's no other way? I can go to the East Corridor ruins again..." The idea died on Elsedora's tongue.

"There is no other option. You'll need to guide them. Maybe my heir will be less of a 'gloomy asshole' to you."

Elsedora pursed her lips and narrowed her gaze.

Mortality didn't frighten me. As a younger man, it had. My father built dying up to be some grand, dreary occasion. He was buried somewhere in the catacombs beneath the Brennac ruins. He'd endlessly harped on me not to take my immortality for granted.

My mother had been mortal, a spitfire that everyone in Brennax had loved. She threw loud parties, never took no for an answer and loved fiercely. I'd grown up feeling as though she might be the only person who could truly love my father for all he was.

They got lucky. None of the prophecies in that old fucking book had relied on *them* procreating with a specific person.

I looked away from Elsedora and up at Freya—my Source Match, my everything.

She had been the only reason I hadn't Shadowed the whole world apart by now. Freya had been gentle and loved by all. She'd always known about the prophecy and had reminded me often that even though it could never have been our child, she would've raised any heir of mine as her own. That had been our plan then.

Now, she wasn't here to offer me a kind hand on the cheek or to tell me to go on. She would have wanted me to do the right thing for the realms. It still put a sour taste in my mouth...

Elsedora eyed me with skepticism. "You don't intend to force her to—"

"Of course not." I held up a hand and ground out, "You've known me far too long to ask that question."

"Then *how*? You need to tell her about the book—about how she fits into the prophecy. Soon...Now. Should we go tell her now?"

I shook my head. There would only be one chance to convince a woman who loathed me to agree to have a child with me. I damned well wasn't going to try it in front of Elsedora. "It's my choice when to tell her, and it will be her choice to accept or decline when she knows the full prophecy."

"And if she chooses against the prophecy, what then?"

"You won't have to worry about losing me."

Elsedora sighed. "Well then, the least you could do is bring her flowers or something. After all—your people just tried to kill her under your roof."

I sighed.

Elsedora rolled her eyes and motioned for me to follow her out. "Fine...Maybe just growl at her less."

Happy to have ended the heavier conversation, I joked, "Some women like the growling."

She laughed as we made our way down the stairs. "I have always wondered what the appeal was."

We approached the kitchenette. Laughter carried into the hall. It sounded like cool rain on a hot day—like pure, unfiltered joy.

Despite everything that had happened to her the night prior, Queen Sybilla laughed as she leaned into Ryn's shoulder, looking at something on the table. The two of them were arm to arm, heads drawn close. I could imagine them painted like that.

They were too chummy already.

Sybilla gasped out another chuckle, but it rasped, and she coughed, which drew my eye to the back of her neck. I knew bruising still lay beneath the blue ribbon she'd decorated her throat with. She'd refused to see a healer, and that had pissed me off.

Peeking over their shoulders, I caught sight of lewd sketches splayed out on the table.

"Look at how crooked his—" Her words caught in her throat upon seeing my shadow on the table. From the side, I could tell her face had sobered, and she turned the parchment at once.

"We were just taking a look at some of the *literature* that was on our prisoners when we stripped them," Ryn explained, choking down a laugh as I rounded the table.

Their proximity to one another twisted something inside of me.

Enough of that—remember the list.

Let Ryn be there if she needed comfort, laughter, happiness—he smiled enough for the lot of us. Plus, those comforts weren't things I could ever offer her.

As if sensing my displeasure, Ryn scooted over to put a hand's distance between himself and our new ally. He couldn't help but smooth her emerald silk tunic sleeve before folding his hands on the table and peering at me with a cocked eyebrow.

One out-of-place strand of silver hair, still wavy from his braid, hung loose, and he shook it away. "Good morning to you too, Krait."

I hummed a response. Maybe it was a grunt—El would have called it a grunt.

He didn't need to ask what my problem was. Instead, he glanced over at Sybilla, and a dimpled smirk crept onto his face.

Both Ryn and El knew the implications of finding the Last Daughter of Isleen. They knew what the prophecy entailed...

Sybilla's attention shifted between the two of us. She skeptically said, "It is as if I am *not* the one who can read minds around here. Can you boys use your words, please?"

I huffed out a sigh. "Learn to break in if you'd like to hear our thoughts," I deadpanned.

Her gaze narrowed on my lips while her fingers danced momentarily across the wood table as though playing the same piano chords repeatedly.

"Are you ready to question the prisoners?" I asked.

"As ready as I can be." She straightened.

She rose and rounded the table toward me—all business now. It was irksome that all prior amusement had left her when she'd seen me. From behind her, Ryn stared at me with a look of sheer mischief.

He mouthed, "It's her, isn't it?"

I glared at him and led Queen Sybilla out of the kitchenette.

Silence stretched between us as we walked down the hall leading to the main staircase. Light was cast in through one of the floor-to-ceiling windows we passed by, illuminating her golden hair, which was still slick and mostly straight from the night prior. She wore a loose-fitting green silk skirt that matched the draping silk tunic. While more modest than Elsedora's typical wares, it still hugged her hips in a way that made my fingers itch to dig in.

Sucking in my cheeks, I broke the silence. "Do you want me to be there when you question them?"

She flashed me a wide-eyed look, seeming shocked to have the option.

"I..." She paused as we neared the bottom of the stairs and turned toward the doorway that led down to the cell. We only had a few holding areas in Sahlmsara—most of our prisoners were held in Sahlmkar.

The steep stone stairway to the cell was lit by the flicking fire of too few sconces. "I'd prefer not to be alone," she admitted.

"Good," I answered, secretly reveling in not having to let her walk down those stairs and out of my sight. I might have many reasons to dislike her, but her well-being was now tied to something larger than our feelings toward one another.

CHAPTER 16
SYBILLA

The men were chained to the far wall with magic-binding cuffs and sitting slumped over in their own waste.

They held Source power yet had chosen to attempt killing me by hand.

That ignited an indignant sensation that burned to be let out. I'd felt all the intentions of their cruelty—felt their wretched hatred—and it had been like an ugly brand on my skin. That would last far longer than the extent of my injuries.

I was no stranger to the unkindness of men.

There had been prior assassination attempts.

Poisons.

Convenient carriage malfunctions.

A few attempted break-ins that Emmerick had squashed.

Sources, I missed Emmerick. His steady presence would've been a welcome reassurance right now.

No attempt on my life had ever come so close. He'd always been there.

I clapped my hands to get their attention. "Good afternoon, jack-asses."

The sandy-haired man who had sliced my cheek woke first. He paled when his gaze landed on me. The dark-haired man lolled his head. When he woke, his stare was distant, but he trembled.

I steadied my voice. "The faster you cooperate, the more likely you are to live."

Neither of them moved. Neither of them spoke. When I glanced back at Krait, he was leaning against the bars, and offered a nod of approval.

"Who sent you to kill me?"

Silence. Their fear coated my tongue in a metallic, sticky flavor.

Fear made men stupid.

"I will give you until the count of three. Then I'll inflict the same wrath I did last night and see how long you last."

I aimed one palm at each of them.

"One..."

"We will tell you!" The light-haired one broke first.

"Nice bluff." The caress of Krait's voice in my head made a chill roll down the back of my neck.

"Who?" I demanded.

"The direction to kill you came from the North."

I straightened. "'The North' as in north of here? Sahlmkar?"

"No," the dark-haired man answered. "The North Corridor. Our orders came from Helos."

My tongue grew heavy in my mouth. "You're lying," I growled and stepped closer.

"We're not lying!"

"Who from Helos wants me dead?" I spat and crossed the room. I wanted to strike the man, to unhear what he was telling me. Emmerick was in Helos—he could be in danger.

"The Death Origin, Caym, has influence in the North Corridor. We answer only to him. We pray only to him."

The man glared at Darvanda as he appeared between me and the prisoners. I almost slammed into his broad, muscular back. His Shadows stretched out of him like tendrils of dark vines and lifted the men off their asses and slammed them to the wall. Both prisoners grunted on impact.

"Your necks can be snapped. I can let my Shadows shatter every bone in your bodies. *Or* you will tell the Queen everything you know about whoever from Helos you spoke with."

The light-haired assassin said, "Caym knows that Queen Wymark is the Last Daughter of Isleen, and she is a threat if not contained. His envoy told us she'd be here in Sahlmsara, that she'd be an easy kill, but clearly, he *lied*." His words were hurried and panicked as he stared over Krait's shoulder at me. "We do not know what name the Origin goes by now, or his face, only that he is in Helos. He sent an envoy to Sahlmkar who brought a dagger for us to use to kill you. We caught the boy leaving the estate—he was able to lead us to your quarters."

Krait glanced at me over his shoulder with a creased brow. "*What boy?*"

Shit.

I swallowed hard. "I'll explain later."

So would he...because I didn't know what being the Last Daughter of Isleen meant, but every perfectly sculpted muscle in Krait's shoulders and back had tightened when the title had been stated.

"Let them down," I ordered.

Krait hesitated before dropping his Shadows and letting the men fall into a foul-smelling heap with a thud.

"You live only because I do..." I swallowed. "But I imagine a century in prison would suit you both."

"Three," Krait concluded. "And her mercy doesn't match what I'd like to do to you. So thank her."

The men blubbered their gratitude.

My mind raced, and I began to grow a bit dizzy. Someone from my own realm wanted me dead, the Origin of Death was hunting me. I turned and walked away, up the narrow stone steps. At the top, I took my first deep breath since I'd entered the cell.

I worried for my Em, who lived among people who wished to see his former Queen dead. Thoughts nagged in the back of my mind—what if he knew? What if he had conspired against me?

Those were the sort of intrusive thoughts that had kept me from telling him about his lineage in the first place...

Knowing there might be some part of my identity that had been hidden from me in the same way made my skin crawl with rage. Krait's heavy footfall on the stairs behind me egged on my anger.

Spinning on him with the ferocity of a cornered animal, I questioned, "Did you know?"

"Did I know *what*?" He stopped at the top of the stairs and leaned against the doorframe with crossed arms, having the nerve to look both pissed off and attractive.

"Are you the Origin of Death?"

He let out a few breaths of heavy, grating laughter that sent chills up my arms. "No. That would be my uncle."

My eyebrows rose. The old texts told stories of the Shadow and Death Origins being brothers. Caym and Desidero.

Those were stories.

"Be serious," I warned.

"Oh, I am serious," he answered. "I'm not the Source of Death. But I am the Shadow Origin—the fifth heir of Desidero."

His willingness to disclose this disarmed me. All of my steam and anger came crashing to a halt. He hadn't balked at telling me that he was a fucking *Source Origin*—as though it were common knowledge, as though that shouldn't rock the ground I stood on.

I shook my head, unable to believe it. The Origins were fables and fairytales—not living, breathing, growling, frowning men.

"Let's pretend I believe that for even a moment," I began. "Why do those prisoners think that the Death Origin rises? Why do they think I have anything to do with him?"

"Because he is, and you do." He stared down at me intently, searching my face for a reaction while offering me no glimpse into his stakes in any of this.

I rested my hands on my hips. "What are you trying to say? Use more words."

"Only if you explain why you didn't tell me there was a third person in your room last night."

"He was just a child," I defended. I couldn't blame the boy, who had been pale with shock and fear.

I'd witnessed people I loved being hurt.

I'd stood by and done nothing when my father's hands landed on my mother.

There was a remorse that I'd recognized in that boy's stare. He did not belong strung up in a dungeon with those men.

Krait pushed off from the doorframe and stalked forward. I took a few steps back. The hallway was narrow, and my back soon pressed against the cool mixed-tile wall before he stopped. I didn't love the idea of being backed against a wall in most contexts...but something about the way he moved was both intimidating and alluring.

He wasn't touching me, but his proximity brought an intoxicating smell—the same warm spice and smoke of his pillowcases. It made me want to step closer.

"It pains me to tell you that it doesn't matter if that boy was a toddler. He sold you out. Like it or not. I can't keep you safe if you omit information."

"I'll remember that next time someone in your court tries to kill me. Since my safety seems to be *very* important to you." Tilting my chin up to meet his smoked-gray eyes, I narrowed my gaze.

"There won't be a next time," he said.

"Because I am this 'Daughter of Isleen'?" I retorted—wanting to know what that meant but not wanting him to sniff out my desperation.

He nodded and grunted a muffled, "*Mhm.*"

"What does that mean?"

He swallowed hard before he said, "It means you are descended from Isleen, a daughter of the First Reverist, Isolde. You are the last full Reverist aside from Caym himself—who took Isolde's power. It means you are the only one who can continue Isleen's line."

I searched his face for any hint of a lie. Even if I couldn't hear his thoughts, he would give something away.

He added, "You will be a target of Death because of it."

When he spoke, I could feel his breath on my cheek. He still made no move to touch me, despite leaning down into my space. I could slip out past him on either side. Barely.

My heart clenched. I'd always known that an heir would strengthen my claim over the Central Corridor, but I'd never considered that I would pass the magic that coursed through me to them.

Once upon a time, I'd imagined a life with children—before my mother's death, before the glum reality of what being a royal in Henosis meant had dawned on me.

What he was saying was a weight I wasn't ready to bear and one that I'd never wish on another.

"Which is why no one touches you..." he whispered.

I stepped forward into his space—a challenge. The rise and fall of his chest brushed against mine. He clenched his hands at his sides, knuckles turning white, and stared down at me.

"You haven't ever touched me without asking." The statement flew out of my mouth before I could rethink it.

For all of Krait's brooding, barking, big-bad-wolf ways, I realized that this man, the Shadow Origin, seemed to keep me at arm's length. He'd taken my hand at the river only briefly and with permission. He'd only let his Shadows descend on me once upon meeting me.

Maybe once was all it took for most people to learn to not cross him.

I'd always been a slow learner.

"As I said...you can be taught to prevent *anyone* from laying a hand on you against your will ever again. Me, those men, Caym. I, frankly, don't understand why your powers haven't grown completely out of control by now."

I didn't understand what he had invested in my being the Daughter of Isleen, in my power. That made me weary. "Because I am a full Reverist?"

"Yes," he answered. "You should be lethal by now—unstoppable. Your power is one that even the Origins feared. I don't know what has stifled your magic's growth, but you have the capability of compulsion—to completely control the feelings and actions of others."

His closeness did weird things to my body.

I shouldn't trust him.

Instead, heat gathered low in my abdomen, and I licked my lips. The way he gazed at me wasn't full of fear. It was full of something akin to excitement or adoration.

The iron ring of his irises glistened, making me wonder what he would have done if I climbed him like a tree right there in the hall.

No man had ever infuriated me this much, and somehow that equated to attraction.

"Fine," I agreed. "Then we start figuring out how to make me 'unstoppable.' You teach me about what it means to be a full Reverist, about everything you know."

I let my gaze lower to his lips, then past them to the stubble that ran down his neck and further to where the dark hair on his chest disappeared below his tunic. My hands had begun to sweat, so I wiped them on the silk of my skirt, which drew his attention downward.

He might not have been touching me, but there was something about the way his stare lingered that felt heavy and sensual.

He cleared his throat. "We'll need to announce our intent to marry soon. Write who you need to write beforehand. If the threat comes from within your realm, our marriage will be a show of strength."

Those words nearly jolted me out of whatever lust-filled fog I'd slipped into. I'd need to write to my friends...to Emmerick. This was not news that I wanted to reach any of them secondhand.

"I have a sneaking suspicion that there is more that you're looking for in me than just an ally," I whispered.

"There is," Krait whispered back as he ran a hand through his dark tousles of hair, which I imagined pulling in a different context.

"There you two are." Ryn rounded the corner of the hall, and Krait stepped away from me with lifted brows. The last Prince of Phynx smirked as though he knew exactly what he had interrupted.

What had he interrupted?

Two angry royals undressing each other with their eyes?

My head swam with confusion, fear and need.

I had to share a bedchamber with this man for Sources' sake. I couldn't keep fantasizing about ways to get him in some state of undress in the middle of a hallway.

Ryn reached us. Krait's cheeks flushed mauve, which gave me a sense of satisfaction.

"Happy to report that an Egress has been built into a warded building in the courtyard. We are heavily guarding it—but travel for your friends in Luz is ready," Ryn explained. "We also received notice that the next council meeting will be moved up to next week."

I smiled—the thought of seeing familiar faces, ones I trusted, filled me with a warm sense of ease. "I will send word to Asterie and Fen. They'll join us for dinner after the meeting."

Who I really *needed* to see was Emmerick. I doubted he'd come anywhere near the Sahlms even if I begged.

The reality of what the prisoners had shared set in, and my smile faded. There was a chance that visiting him would put me in danger—something Em wouldn't want.

I wondered if he would join our next council meeting.

I hoped he would.

CHAPTER 17
SYBILLA

A man selling fruit from a cart straightened and glanced around, uneasily. *Caught.*

"Fuck," I groaned.

Ryn and I sat on a bench in the Umber House courtyard. I blew curls from my face, convinced I'd never learn how to access the minds of others unnoticed.

"No one is perfect after just a few days of training, Princess. Keep trying." He rambled on. "There are front entrances of the mind and back entrances—the front, most Source-wielders can *feel* when someone with Reverist magic is accessing them. My guess is you have no idea which way you're getting in."

"This all sounds oddly sexual," I mused, and Ryn cracked a laugh.

I was glad for the large umbrella he had placed in a base beside us. The courtyard was bustling with people, most of whom were visiting the produce markets, which had fewer hot-food vendors than at night. The heat was too stifling.

"It *is* sort of like having your brain caressed," he said, wiggling his brow in a way that made me smirk. "It's how I could tell you were in there when we met. However, it's said that skilled Reverists of the past could access the mind through less obvious entries...poke around a bit."

We spent an hour like that—he would point to an unsuspecting person in the bustling crowd and tell me to focus on the threads of their mind and find all the access points. Once he'd helped me visualize it that way, it became easier to determine when I'd failed.

A woman pulling her toddler by hand behind her quickly scooped up the child, looking shaken. I'd gotten it wrong.

The tune of a mandolin stopped, and the musician's brow furrowed. Wrong again.

I began to pick up on the subtle differences between threads—my mind had never felt clearer, even if I was failing at the exercise. To know how not to just be a passenger in the minds of others was refreshing.

I decided to try one more time on Ryn.

Ryn wiped his brow and muttered, "I can't wait for the first rain."

"Why's that?" I asked. He still hadn't noticed me there, slipping into his head.

"It's a night of debauchery, and I could use a good fuck to get her off my mind." His unspoken words made me smirk. He answered, "It typically brings a short cold front, some reprieve. And a natural reason to drink and celebrate. There's usually a festival."

"Lovely. And who are you trying to get off your mind?"

Ryn's eyes widened. "You did it!"

My smile widened at his excitement.

"Now try that again on someone *else*—stay out of here. I assure you my love life is not all that interesting."

I doubted that but laughed anyway. My next few attempts failed.

As the sun became too hot to bear, I sighed. "Where is Darvanda this morning?"

"Miss him?" Ryn said in jest.

I scoffed. "We're to be married," I blurted out, and Ryn's posture straightened.

"You don't say."

"You don't sound surprised."

He smiled and said, "He is addressing some cases—there was a murder in Sahlmkar while he was gone and some complex land disputes we needed him to weigh in on."

I stood and put my hands on my hips. "Then why are we not present?" He tilted his head, and I added, "I would like to see how things are accomplished around here."

"He's going to hate this," Ryn warned.

I was counting on it.

Part of me was just curious to see how he appeared before his people.

When Ryn led me to the throne room, there were guards present at the doors. They stepped aside to allow us through, bowing their heads.

The throne room was simpler than I'd imagined, with drab brown curtains and white stucco walls. Krait was perched on a large wooden seat at the center of the room. Guards held the chains of a kneeling man. His hands were extended, clasped together in a ball, and his wrists were cuffed together with what I recognized as magic-binding cuffs.

"Please, my King—it was an accident!" The man leaked spittle onto the ground, unabashedly crying.

Krait's gaze landed on me, and he frowned. He didn't interrupt his dealings to greet us, and Ryn gently guided me toward the far-right wall, where we found a seat beside Elsedora. On the other wall, a row of unfamiliar faces, in neatly pressed and expensive-looking garb, sat—lords, I assumed.

"What did he do?" I whispered to Ryn. Elsedora glanced over at me and offered a quick smile that crinkled her eyes.

"He is a Source-wielder, of the Soil. But he Death-wielded. It resulted in the killing of his wife."

My stomach sank.

"Your crime is grave enough to sentence you to death. But I'll instead send you to the prisons of Sahlmkar for a minimum of one century."

"Please, my King!"

I extended my mind to the kneeling man and found the thread that I thought might let me in undetected. The man didn't react—either too distraught to notice or I'd succeeded.

His memories flooded mine—*a woman lying in bed in a dark room. She was so pale, so thin, coughing, shaking. Her gray hair was plastered to the sweat on her forehead.*

"Please, make the pain stop," she asked him.

"I will, love. I will."

"I love you."

"I love you too, my sweet."

A dead pig lay on the ground beside the bed. The man drew back his hands, and when he extended them, an amber smoke flowed from his fingertips. It filled his wife's nostrils, ears and eye sockets. It worked so quickly, blackening skin and bone until there was nothing more than dust. His fingers looked stained with coal. A sign of Death-wielding I recognized from the attack on Luz. It'd happened quickly; she had not suffered.

The chair screeched below me as I shot up, surfacing from the dreadful memory as guards began to drag the man away. "Stop!"

Krait leveled a look at me that raised the hair on the back of my neck. Ryn tugged on my elbow, urging me to sit.

I blurted, "It was not an accident. It was a mercy kill."

The man's eyes widened as they landed on me. I stepped closer to the bound man, drawing sideways glances and side conversations from the lords on the other side of the room. I could feel the sensation of their confusion.

"Wasn't it?" I asked the man.

Tears leaked down the man's cheeks, and he nodded. "It matters little—I knew the cost."

"Your wife was mortal." It wasn't a question.

"This end offered her less suffering than any other option."

The guards carried the man away, and I was left staring at an insufferable, unjust King.

Krait clenched the wooden armrests of his throne with white knuckles.

"She wanted to die," I said to Krait, and the room quieted. "He killed a pig in order to Death-wield, hardly a punishable offense."

Krait's Shadows were whipping around him violently, as though they craved striking out at me. "Death-wielding is always a punishable offense. Be seated, Queen Wymark."

Fuck no, I would not sit down.

"A century? For doing as his wife wanted?" I spat.

"Leave us," Krait commanded the rest of the room, and the lords bowed, seeming eager to exit the room. Krait's growing Shadows vined up the ceiling, and a lump grew in my throat.

Once Krait and I were alone, he rose and crossed the room. He stood so close that I had to tilt my chin up to meet his gaze, so close that there seemed to be no light left in the room. He leaned into my space—still not touching me. I had to fight the urge to back away.

"You cannot walk into my throne room and dictate how I deal with my realm's matters," he snarled. "I would not interfere in your rulings if it were the other way around."

I stiffened and he withdrew a step.

That was what I wanted, wasn't it? A King who would leave me to my own devices.

"It wasn't murder. It was done *out of love*, Krait."

"As I've stated, *Queen Wymark,*" he said, seeming to throw formality back at me like an insult. "It does not matter. Death-wielding is outlawed here. It strengthens Caym. It weakens us whether done out of love or hate, or indifference."

My hands balled at my sides. I wanted to argue.

But this was *his* court, *his* home, *his* law.

"You Death-wielded in Luz. I saw your hands—they were coaled at the fingertips when I met you."

At the accusation, Krait's Shadows snapped around my feet. I finally lost composure and flinched, blinking hard once. He noticed and took another step backward, the angry lines in his brow fading abruptly.

"That night, we used the energy of the dead already on the battlefield. That is different. While it is still dark magic, it is not the same as creating *new* death. That is what Death-wielding is, killing for the sake of harvesting energy, using death."

Darvanda's whole life had been devoted to stopping the Death Origin's rise, and that was exactly what he'd been up to in Luz.

"You didn't come to help us, to save Luz," I realized out loud. "You simply came that night to stop those who were Death-wielding."

"Among other reasons," he snapped back.

The weight of his gaze unnerved me. I nodded. Instead of spitting more fire over this, I spun on my heels and went to find Ryn.

Ryn and Elsedora were waiting in the main hall. The smile and slap on the back I received from the silver-haired warlock snapped me out of my anger.

"You did it again. You got into that man's mind unnoticed."

My shoulders deflated as he squeezed them. I had.

Little good it had done for him.

Elsedora offered me a sad smile and said, "You meant well. But our laws are in place to prevent Caym from gaining strength before his Reverist abilities are returned."

"Does Death-wielding risk giving him the power of compulsion too?" I tried to remember what Krait had told me outside the holding cell, but all I could recall was the way his warm spice scent had surrounded me.

"No, not yet. He will not have that power until the next black moon. He took that power from Isolde—he forced her into a bargain," Elsedora explained. "It's all in the book."

None of this explanation helped calm the churning feeling in my stomach as I thought of the man's desperation to end his wife's suffering.

"How do you know so much about the Reverists?" I asked, wanting to move the subject away from what had happened in the throne room. Away from having uncovered my soon-to-be-husband's motives in Luz.

"We saved many of the Reverist texts that Phynx wanted destroyed," Ryn answered. "Despite being a Source-wielder, my father strongly opposed the spread of magic. He wanted it moderated, controlled and only accessible to the wealthy. My earliest memories are of the rebellions that followed some of those laws going into effect."

To think of a realm even more torn than it was today saddened me. "And you have Reverist texts here?"

"Yes—they're mostly written in old Brennac, which Krait knows well," Ryn answered. "He'll be able to help you."

Of course, I'd need *him*. "Where might I find these texts?"

"In Krait's hole," Elsedora chimed in.

"Excuse me?" I gasped out.

Ryn smiled wide, which told me I'd delivered the exact reaction they'd been hoping for.

"It's what we call his private library—his hole. I can show you his hole," Ryn carried on.

"Stop that." I would have a fit of giggles if he used the word "hole" one more time regarding the King of the Sahlms. "But also, I would like to see the *texts*."

"C'mon, Princess," Ryn said before offering me his hand. He pulled me further into Umber House.

My ankles felt like an inferno of pain as I followed him. I'd think about that later—maybe I could find a cold compress somewhere in this Source-forsaken desert.

"I will swing by your room later," Elsedora called after Ryn as he whisked me away.

Before I could react to Elsedora's comment, Ryn stopped just beside a stairwell—there was a small door there that was my height. He leaned over and whispered into my ear, "Say the words 'In the Shadows we trust.'"

"In the Shadows we trust?" I asked. Before he could answer, the door's lock clicked open.

"I *knew* he liked you," Ryn said as he ducked through the entry.

"What do you mean?"

He answered, "It won't open for anyone Krait doesn't trust."

"You're mistaken. That man hates the ground I walk on. You saw him in the throne room—he wanted my head on a platter."

The Prince shrugged and formed a ball of white moonlight in his palm. The light cast beams down the stairwell into a windowless chamber that was lined with the most beautiful wooden bookshelves I'd ever seen. I was not much of a reader, but this looked like a sacred space for Darvanda.

There was a small portrait on the desk of a woman with silver hair and the most stunning blue eyes.

"Speaking of people who Krait trusts...your sister, the Princess of Phynx? You told me to come back to you when I'd pieced things together—they were in love."

"Aren't you a sly little fox? You get that out of Elsedora?"

I smirked while running my hand over perfectly dusted tomes. "Is it all that hard to get gossip out of Elsedora?"

Ryn laughed. "Fair point. Yes, they were married."

My brows rose. "Married? Someone agreed to a life of eternal grumpiness? She must have been angelic to deal with that."

"You're one to talk," he said in jest. Ryn leaned with one forearm on a bookshelf. "She *was* angelic—our people loved her. She was their fiercest advocate. Yet still somehow the calm in any storm. Unfortunately, she and my father never saw eye to eye. He always pushed me to take the crown, but I didn't want it."

I glanced over at him as I trailed my hands along the rough canvas book spines. He would have made an excellent King, had he wanted it.

"I'm sorry for your loss. It sounds like she was lovely, all jokes aside." I let sincerity carry through my tone, not wanting him to feel as though I took his disclosure lightly.

"I know it's hard to imagine, but beneath all the spiky edges, there is a lot of gentleness in Krait too. I think it is what initially drew them together—that and their Source Match."

I sucked in a breath. "They were Source Matched? I didn't know Origins could *be* Source Matched."

Ryn shrugged and casually crossed his arms over his chest, leaning back against a shelf. "He isn't Desidero. He is still subject to the whims of the Origins just like the rest of us immortal Source-wielders. Source Matches and all."

"How do two Source-wielders know that? That they are matched by the Origins?"

Ryn smirked, but a hint of sadness flashed in his expression. "You feel most powerful when together, depleted when apart. For some it feels as though something has snapped into alignment—like the last puzzle pieces of your souls have been found and placed within you."

Now my heart ached. My friends Asterie and Fenris had recently uncovered their Source Match. They had a strong pull toward one another and a devotion that trumped any example of love I'd ever witnessed.

I'd seen Fen's reaction when he'd thought he'd lost Asterie during the battle at Luz...

A large brown leather chaise sat along one wall; it was covered in plush suede pillows. Bronze ornate sconces hung from the walls, and the whole space felt warm and lived in. Only it was the coldest space I'd felt in Umber House.

Clearing my throat, I voiced that observation instead of lingering on that dreary topic. "It's cooler in here."

Thoughts of a younger Krait in love with his kingdom's enemy still swarmed my mind.

"Right under this are the underground baths, and it helps keep this space a bit cooler during the summer," Ryn answered. "Practically a cave..."

"Or a hole," I joked as Ryn crossed the room and flopped down on the chaise with a flash of a smile and a nod.

I walked around the oval-shaped library, to a rolling ladder that stretched to the ceiling. There were ten or so shelves that I couldn't reach by hand. I stepped up onto the ladder; a particular collection of texts had caught my eye.

"Like a moth to a flame..." Ryn mused as he kicked his feet up on the chaise. "Those would be what you're looking for."

I hummed triumphantly. "What are they?"

"It was said that Isolde, the First Reverist, wrote many tomes by communicating with scribes of her lineage through the years. Legend is that within some of them she hid clues about where her weapons against the Death Origin lie," Ryn answered. "They're hard to decipher though, as she didn't want Caym to find her relics."

I pulled out the far-left tome. "Darvanda can read these?"

"Yes. I can." A deep, smooth voice startled me. "Some of them."

I teetered on the ladder. Krait's Shadows reached out and looped around my waist. They steadied me before recoiling as quickly as they'd come. I shivered at the cool sensation left in their wake.

"*This* is not where I expected you to be," Krait noted while staring daggers at Ryn, who simply rose and crossed the room to us.

I stepped off the ladder and blurted, "We shouldn't have intruded."

Having already pissed him off once today, I turned to leave.

"You're welcome in here," Krait ground out. Despite his tone, the statement rang sincere. He still seemed pissed—though, that was the way he perpetually looked.

I caught Ryn smirking as I asked, "You don't fear that I'll use these texts against you?"

"That would require knowing how to read them," Krait droned without amusement. "And these are not meant to teach you how to kill *me*."

"It seems that you are already a far better teacher than I am," Ryn teased and squeezed Krait's shoulder. "And as I recall, *you* agreed to train our Queen on how to use that wondrous mind of hers."

"Ryn," Krait warned, as though being alone with me would be the worst situation he could imagine. But the silver-haired Prince was up the stairs before either of us could fully object.

Krait plucked the blue text from my fingers and leaned against the bookshelf next to me. His jaw was tense as he leafed through it.

"I shouldn't have questioned you earlier, not in front of your court," I admitted. I'd overstepped. If he'd done the same to me in the presence of my nobles, I would have been livid.

"*Mhm*" was all he offered.

I huffed in frustration and said, "I still don't agree with the ruling. But I handled that disagreement poorly."

He avoided my apology. "This text would actually be a good starting place for our training—you should know where your power comes from." I couldn't even feign annoyance at his change in subject because what he'd said intrigued me. "It's the full texts of Isolde—we call the collection *The Book of Isolde*. But it's actually many prophecies that my family has distilled down to one true guide. Would you like me to read this one to you?"

His anger with my intrusion in the throne room had passed. If the tables were turned, I wasn't sure that my temper would allow me to be so *collaborative.*

I motioned for him to read, skeptical of his altruistic-seeming intent. He pointed for me to sit down on the chaise. I obliged, crossing my ankles and resting my clasped hands in my lap. On the opposite side of the narrow room, he crouched and slid to rest on the ground against a bookshelf.

That somber, deep voice read the text for hours. Occasionally, he'd slip into Brennac instead of translating, and I'd have to ask him to stop and re-read. He glanced at me over the book to ensure I was still engaged.

I was.

But the tomes of legend and lore, full of revelations of my origins, were not what fascinated me. What fascinated me was a man devoted to stopping Death himself, one willing to marry me to keep me here for reasons I didn't understand.

CHAPTER 18

KRAIT

As she entered the courtyard, Sybilla looked tired. Bags had formed under her eyes, and for the past few nights, she'd tossed in her sleep, unable to find comfort. Each night, I would return to my bedchamber to sleep on the cot only after she'd fallen asleep. It felt less intrusive, a way I could offer her some privacy in the evening.

Also, I feared being in the confines of that room awake with her. While Sybilla and I often egged each other on into fury, there was a part of that fury that I found intoxicating—a part that could meld so easily into physical passion. It was evident in the way her breath hitched, the way that even when we argued our bodies seemed to gravitate toward one another.

The weight of Elsedora's judgment had begun to wear on me. Any time we were alone, she reminded me: "You need to tell Sybilla what the prophecy entails. Tell her how she plays a part."

I imagined how that would sound. "An old book says we must have a child, and they'll be the one to end Caym's reign for good."

She may throw actual daggers at me or, worse, whatever weapons she could spew from her mind.

I wasn't ready.

Sybilla greeted me with a raised hand and no words.

"Good morning," I murmured with sarcasm. My grip tightened on the thick leather bag of records we'd collected from those who wished to reenter Henosis.

We approached the Egress, and she cast a skeptical glance at the opening, her lips in a flat line. I offered her my free hand, which she took before stepping in beside me. "East Tower," I directed.

The Egress pulled us from the Sahlms, and we descended into the tower that looked over the city of Laome. From my research of the new maps, the city sat in the coastal jungles of the East Corridor of Henosis.

We rounded many stairs to reach an awaiting carriage. Abundant greenery surrounded us, and sticky air filled my lungs. An unappealing nuisance of buzzing bugs circled overhead.

The neck of my formal red tunic already beginning to rub, I'd have done anything to get this over with quickly. I slung the bag containing the reentry requests into the carriage after helping Sybilla up.

This whole system was ridiculous.

Sybilla wore a blue heavy-wool gown with a ribbed corset tied tight—I imagined it was even less comfortable than my outfit. But the way it pushed up her breasts was overtly distracting.

"You should have El take you into the city to get something lighter than that," I said.

"*Mhm.*"

She was quiet today. Had she taken a page out of my book with the short responses?

I wondered if apprehension about seeing the North King plagued her mind.

We took the carriage up the switchbacks of the dense jungle hills to reach the palace where King and Queen Nadiar resided. Vines cut up the great stone walls, and a swampy moat surrounded the squared structure. A drawbridge was lowered, and after crossing, we finally reached our destination.

King Landor and Queen Edia Nadiar sat side by side at the head of the dining hall table. Sybilla gave a deep curtsey.

"Thank you for hosting us in your home, King and Queen Nadiar," she said and swatted at me to bow, which I did with a low growl. She'd briefed me on the rulers. The Nadiars had ruled the East Corridor together for twenty years and still favored formal, stiff courts.

"Welcome." King Nadiar nodded for us to sit.

King Sheffield entered just after us, and instead of shaking Sybilla's hand, he pulled her in for an embrace. "Queen Sybilla, looking as radiant as always. What's this?" he asked, his thumb hovering over her healing cheek.

Sybilla answered too quickly, "Unfortunate archery incident—all is well. Here to tell the tale." Sheffield was a seemingly good-natured, portly man with round cheeks and a grayed mustache that twisted up at the sides.

Sheffield's gaze rested on the Luz-blue ribbon wrapped around her neck, but he nodded. Sybilla had told me that Sheffield, the South Corridor King, was her easiest alliance. Apparently, they'd bonded over their love of fine port and their hatred for her late father.

The newly crowned King of the West Corridor was already sitting at the table. King Haag Bringham had mussed brown hair and bloodshot eyes. He avoided greeting us. Bringham was the youngest ruler in their ranks at twenty-seven. He had also been the first of Sybilla's father's failed attempts to marry her off—Elsedora had slipped me that tidbit of information.

Queen Nadiar was sitting to the right of me. Her silken black bob, hints of gray at its root, glistened in the morning light. King Nadiar sat stone-faced—his narrow, drooping face showing neither objection to nor enthusiasm at us being there. This was an alliance that intrigued me. The East Corridor's Griffiths were magnificent beasts of war. Hawk-headed but with feline bodies, they were fierce, loyal creatures.

"King Mattock informed me you have appointed advisors for the Central Corridor," King Bringham said across the table to Sybilla. "Are you sure that Source-wielders are trustworthy enough to rule in your absence after all that has happened? The optics of appointing them..." He clicked his tongue. "Questionable."

"Luckily for me, I care less about optics than results, King Bringham," Sybilla said with a diplomatic smile that struck me as unlike her. She wore a mask here. I itched to see her tell him how she really felt.

"That much is clear," a low voice from the doorway said. King Mattock stood with one hand on the pommel of his broadsword and the other running through his hair. My brow furrowed—I'd expected some tension between Sybilla and her former Constable but not outright hostility.

Having two ex-lovers at the table could prove difficult for her. And for me by association.

Yet I couldn't miss the way Sybilla's eyes had lit from within whenever they landed on Mattock. He stopped loitering by the door and sat at the table. "By the next meeting, I will also have appointed advisors in Helos. I apologize for my absence at the last meeting. The battle in Luz took its toll on my strength. But I am here now."

Sybilla's lips turned up at the sides as she watched Mattock like she was observing a bird fly for the first time. "That is wonderful news, Em."

Mattock met her gaze with indifference. "It is King Mattock at this table."

The light in Sybilla's eyes dimmed.

I scowled at Bringham, unable to let go of his slight. "Why would Source-wielders be untrustworthy?" I ground out, holding my posture in a way I knew promised a threat.

"I meant no offense," Bringham backtracked with raised palms. "But the Wasteland wards being down does not mean that Source power is welcome in all of Henosis. The Sisterhood and the Order may have dissolved, but the laws don't change so quickly."

My jaw tightened, and the room grew a bit darker.

"Tea?" Sybilla kicked me under the table.

Before I could respond, she'd reached for the pot and poured it for me. That earned her a pair of raised brows from Queen Nadiar, who motioned for a maid to pour the rest of the cups.

Sybilla cleared her throat. "My new advisors have proven themselves fierce protectors of the people of Henosis. They, along with King Darvanda, saved my Corridor from falling—which would have left each of yours vulnerable to attack. Let us break bread together today and determine the best path *forward*, toward unifying the realms in coming meetings."

King Sheffield gave her a firm nod. "Wonderful idea, Queen Wymark. There is no need to bicker now before the trials have even started."

I gave a nod of agreement, deciding not to bury all of Sybilla's prior alliances in a shallow grave. If she could keep Sheffield's and the Nadiars' loyalties, maybe she stood a chance in helping me win water rights in the North before the canals dried up. If we survived Caym, then my people would need a secured future for their home.

Queen Nadiar whispered to her King who then said, "We will send fleets of Griffiths to help with the rebuilding in Luz."

Sybilla beamed. "Thank you—that is appreciated."

Sheffield cleared his throat. "Have you brought records of the first reentry requests?" he asked me. His tone was respectful. It surprised me to find even one Corridor ruler I didn't despise.

I nodded and reached into the bag to retrieve a stack of paper as thick as a short novel.

"We'll begin reviewing them today, and then make concessions and decisions at the next meeting," King Bringham said.

The word "concessions" made me see red. As though my people had any more to give, as though they deserved having to negotiate their right to return to a land where they'd once lived.

The rest of the dull conversation about the logistics of re-opening Egresses in Henosis and plans for future meetings carried on. Nerves knotted my throat each time Mattock's hardened gaze met Sybilla's pleading one.

He would always be her weakness.

He might be her downfall.

PART TWO

The Origins and my children, the Reverists, lived among mortals in peace. The natural Origins granted their descendants gifts of immortality and magic, creating the first immortal lineages.

But deep in the northern desert lands, near the volcanic shores, a wicked mortal King came to power.

On the first black moon that crossed the realm, the King took a bride.

Drunk on greed and power, the King told his consort that if she did not bear an heir, he would lock her in the dungeons to rot and he'd take another. When no heir came, he kept his promise.

He made four more consorts the same promise.

They each suffered the same fate.

From the damp, cold dungeons, those women cursed the King—upon the next black moon, he would bear children, but they would turn against him. Only death and darkness would befit his lineage.

On the next black moon, the King sired two princes—Desidero and Caym. The babes' essences were tainted by their father's hate and the curse cast by his former consorts. That was the day dark Source magic entered our ranks; the Shadow Origin and Death Origin were born.

I feared for my children and their children and their children's children, for I saw all that would happen in the centuries to come—blood, fire and destruction. The very existence of Death in the realm changed the trajectory of peace. Until Caym's rise, the world had not known disease, war or wrath.

The new Origins grew to adulthood, and Caym overthrew his father, killing him in his sleep. Desidero slunk into the shadows, happy to live an isolated life.

One dreadful day, after having gifted immortality to a young woman who had nearly drowned, the Water Origin, Aquas, sank into the foam of the ocean waves. Pulled back to his Source, he cried, "Death has come for me!"

Thus, the first Source Origin became trapped in the in-between.

Caym claimed Aquas had cheated him of the drowning woman's life when Aquas lifted her from the seas.

The other Origins grew fearful of Death, afraid they would suffer the same fate if they continued to help mortals by gifting their Source power.

Wracked with fear, the natural Source Origins turned against mortals and Reverists alike. The Reverists' mind-altering capabilities were too risky, and the Origins began to condemn Reverists to death.

Caym, pretending to sympathize with my children, offered to help. But it came with a price. Under his guidance, the Reverists did precisely what the Origins had feared. He manipulated them into thinking they needed to force the Sources to give away their immortality and all of their magic.

Every Reverist, except my first child, fell to his deceit, and every Origin fell into that in-between plane at the hands of my children.

He made one exception for his brother, Desidero.

Caym agreed to allow Desidero and his heirs to live. But each heir was only allowed one child, who they passed their Source power and immortality down to. Thus, the Shadow Origin would forever be reborn and never grow strong enough to contend with Death.

When Caym found me, he held the one thing he knew I would bargain anything to protect. Isleen.

She was my first child, the only one to have inherited all of my powers: clairvoyance, compulsion, telepathy, dream manipulation, and projection. My other children supported Caym, but never Isleen.

Isleen was helpless in Death's grasp.

Even all the knowledge in the land cannot stop one from making an unwise decision when the safety of their child is in question. Cunning and persuasive, Caym professed his love for my daughter, and he offered me a bargain. Isleen would get immortality instead of death. My other children would live in peace.

I had to promise one thing in return—my power would be granted to him upon my death. He would be the first full Reverist and Origin in one.

And with my promise, he drove a dagger through my heart.

The peace he promised was a lie. He betrayed my children—made destructive beasts of them.

When he realized Isleen would not bend to his wishes, Caym locked her away.

During a black moon, my cunning daughter summoned the Sources to help her create a trap for Caym and bartered her life for his imprisonment.

But, with my power, Caym will rise again.

I foresee him rising upon the hundredth black moon after his fall.

You must listen, Fifth Heir of Desidero. Find the Last Daughter of my dearest Isleen.

The heir you bear together will be both Origin and Reverist. Your child is the key to ending Death's reign—the key to setting us all free.

CHAPTER 19
SYBILLA

Dusk settled over the courtyard outside Umber House. Night market merchants' tents were rising. Source-wielders cast enchantments to hold the canopies up without posts. The floating lanterns danced above, already lit for this evening's reprieve from the heat.

I waited for Fen and Asterie outside the Egress. The carved opening in the stone wall of the building offered them shade.

Asterie stepped out first. Vangard, her wolf-like beast, trailed behind her in a form no larger than an average dog. His horns were curled back, and his talons scraped against the cobblestone. I'd seen him *much* larger, yet now he trotted at Asterie's side, looking more like a devoted pet than the vicious beast I'd once witnessed fight for my city.

Fenris, draped in a heavily patched thick green cloak, followed, glancing around the darkening streets as though assessing threats. Asterie wore her usual black robe and stone-faced expression. They'd be awfully warm in a few short minutes.

Wanting to be out of my heavy gown, I'd opted for a cream-toned linen dress and woven-leather slip-on mules. Elsedora had taken me to the night market again to pick out attire that suited me and the weather.

"Welcome." I forced a chipper greeting. My voice still rasped, and I longed to be back in bed. I'd push through if only because I wanted to be among friends.

As Asterie and Fen approached, Van headed straight toward a cart selling meats. The merchant shooed him away.

"Van!" Asterie tapped her side to call him before turning to me. "My Queen." Asterie attempted to curtsey, but Van knocked into the back of her legs and threw her off-balance.

"Needy animal," Fen mumbled with a smirk as he grabbed Asterie's arm to steady her. "How are you, Sybilla?"

My resolve for propriety waned, and I reached around and hooked both of their necks to draw them into an embrace.

"I'm alright, but we must speak inside," I whispered before pulling away from them. "It's too warm outside anyway. Next time, dress lighter."

Asterie's gaze slid down to the healing wound across my cheek, and her brow furrowed. At least I was still using my Luz-blue silk ribbon as a choker to hide the bruising—that would have only worried her more.

"Archery accident," I explained with a lump in my throat. I hadn't touched my bow since leaving home. I'd left my weapon in the Luz armory. Telling them about the attack would only distract them, and I needed their attention on my people, on rebuilding the city.

A shadow loomed near the door of Umber House.

"Krait, good to see you," Fenris said.

Darvanda grunted.

He stood at the entry to Umber House, looking both annoyed and imposing.

"That means hello and he has missed you so very much in Dar-van-dick," I teased. Krait glared at me but shifted to allow us to walk ahead of him through the doors. "How is Luz faring?"

Asterie said, while casting a sideways glance back at Darvanda, "It will be a long process to restore things to their former state, but everyone in the city is housed. We are making do. It's moving along; progress would be much *faster* with more magical aid."

"The Nadiars have agreed to send Griffiths."

Asterie squeezed my arm in thanks.

I was in the Sahlms while my people *made do.* That felt wrong, but I could rest assured that my advisors were doing all they could. "Can we send aid from the Sahlms?" I asked Krait.

Asterie's brows rose at the word "we," and my cheeks grew hot. Although we were allied, that did not mean that there was a *we.*

He fell into step beside me but didn't look at me. His jaw tightened before he shook his head. "I cannot let anyone step across that border. Not until I know they can do so in peace, not until their future is secure. You heard the other rulers. There will be 'concessions and decisions' on a case-by-case basis."

I wanted to argue, but I found myself at a loss for a compelling enough reason for him to aid a realm that had so readily turned his people away, a realm that continued to make it difficult for them to return.

I nodded and sucked in my cheeks. "Fair enough."

"Wine?" I asked Asterie. I held out the bottle, and it left my fingers, floating across the table to pour her a glass—a charm I particularly liked for its efficiency in keeping my glass full.

Large serving dishes were brought in. An array of mixed grains and meats paired with decadently spiced sauces graced the table. The flavors were less subtle and often spicier than in Luz cuisine; my palate grew used to the taste.

Elsedora sat next to her brother, chattering about her life in the Sahlms. They'd only briefly been able to speak in Luz before we'd left. The ease between them cut through the tension around the rest of the table as bowls were passed for everyone to serve themselves.

Ryn hadn't arrived yet, and Krait leaned back in his chair, watching us like a predator sizing up prey. Forks scraped plates, and I found myself happy to share a peaceful, albeit stiff, meal.

Van sat beside Asterie's chair with his head in her lap. His wide, begging eyes stared up at her, requesting meat scraps, which she'd happily snuck him multiple times since dinner had begun.

"What has been happening in the Corridors? And do you foresee any threats in the moonstone?" I asked Asterie.

Asterie stroked Van's head between his horns. "All seems quiet. The defectors from the Sahlms and the North Corridor were pushed to the northwest corner of the realm." Asterie glanced at Darvanda. "Not many survived the Warhorses—I no longer think there is a threat of Firose's army rising under new leadership."

"They returned to Sahlmkar," Krait cut in.

Asterie eyed him. "And you condone war criminals hiding out in your realm?" she asked with seeming indifference, but her shoulders had grown tense.

Krait's brow furrowed, matching her challenging tone. "They were detained upon entering the Sahlms. I positioned Sahlmsaran guards along the border. My guards in Sahlmkar already seek out those who Death-wield. Our prison is rather full of those awaiting punishment."

He hadn't told me any of that.

I took a long pull of wine, not showing my ire. "At the council meeting, Emmerick mentioned he is seeking advisors. Has he shared who he is considering?"

Krait's attention shifted to me. I disliked the intensity of skepticism in his stare.

"He has not…" Asterie looked between me and the Shadow-wielding King. "Should we be concerned about him?"

Elsedora cackled at something Fenris had said, cutting through the weight of Asterie's question.

"No, no. I just wish for him to have capable help, that's all."

"We visit frequently, so does Amara—he would tell us if anything was amiss. I'm sure of it," Asterie assured me.

"What are sentiments like in Luz about my alliance here?" I asked.

Asterie's gaze narrowed on Krait. "There is still hesitation about Source-wielders reentering Henosis, even among those in Luz."

Krait let out a "Hmph," resting an elbow on the arm of his chair and his head on his hand. "What else is new?"

Asterie didn't seem deterred by Krait's foul mood. "Skepticism has lessened since your aid during the attack. Word traveled fast that you saved the city. I only hope that we can continue to build that trust."

It was the most polite threat I'd ever heard. *She* didn't trust Darvanda, and she couldn't be blamed for that. Her upbringing had been rooted in keeping magic distant from the realm.

"Do you feel a royal marriage between us will deepen that trust?" I folded my hands on the table.

The table quieted before Elsedora burst out in giggles. I knew Ryn had told her. The two of them seemed incapable of keeping secrets from each other.

As though his loose tongue had been summoned, Ryn opened the dining room door and stepped inside. "What did I miss?" he asked, looking at the mixed bag of reactions around the table.

"Well, I'll be damned," Fenris breathed out, distracted from my revelation. "Rynall?"

The Prince of Phynx cracked a smile. "Shit—El said your notorious ass was still alive. But I didn't believe it until now."

Ryn crossed the room to grip Fen's extended hand. He pulled him by the forearm from his chair into a short, aggressive embrace.

"So, not going to try to kill me then?" Fenris asked.

"Heavens no. If my father hadn't died that night, I'd have killed him myself. His blood would've been on my hands," Ryn said as his eyes dipped to Vangard, who was still gazing up at Asterie, happily wagging his tail.

"But the city..." Fenris trailed off. Four centuries ago, Firose had seduced Fen, her then fiancé, into giving her half of his power. She'd used it to compel Van to fight alongside Brennax and destroy Phynx.

Asterie grabbed Fen's hand and squeezed it.

Ryn shook his head. "That was Firose and Stygian's doing."

I'd gathered that Stygian had been Krait's Commander at the time of the fall of Phynx.

The mood sobered. Fen cleared his throat as Ryn found a seat next to Elsedora.

"Well then," Elsedora said with watery eyes. She seemed over-whelmed to see them all in one room.

I fought the temptation to reach into her head. Seeing two people you loved make amends—that was a feeling I'd never experienced.

Asterie still stared at me, frozen from the casual announcement of my betrothal. I peeked into her thoughts, longing for her acceptance.

"Surely that cannot be a good idea...Has she fallen for the Shadow King?"

Her internal question made my lips creep up at the sides.

I winked at her and said, "I will let you recover your aura of indifference, friend. Rest assured that a strategic marriage is what's best for the future of my reign. We'll discuss the arrangements later and put together a formal announcement."

Asterie nodded and said, "Eager to hear your plans."

Empty plates floated away, and hours passed. Krait remained at the table but barely conversed with any of us. Fenris, Ryn and Else-dora chattered while Asterie and I conversed and nearly polished off a bottle of wine between the two of us.

"If you were an animal, what would you be?" I asked Asterie. The wine had warmed my stomach and blurred the edges of my vision. Being among friends felt like being wrapped in a warm blanket at the end of a long day. The lightness of it lifted me. Gone, temporarily, was the pain in my joints; gone was the fatigue. In pain's place was an escape that would torture me tomorrow but felt lovely in the moment.

"I don't know. What do you think I would be?" she answered.

I tapped a finger to my chin. "Hmm, an owl. Beautiful, wise, and with a constant expression of judgment. Especially right now."

My friend's demeanor softened, and she cracked a thin smile. "I am never judging you."

"I know, but you look like you are." I chuckled. "What about me?"

Asterie said too quickly, "A horse."

I scoffed as her eyes went wide.

"Not in looks!"

"Yes, yes, keep digging a hole for yourself," I teased. "Why a horse?"

Krait dared to stifle a laugh as he crossed his arms over his chest.

"They're such majestic and beautiful animals—but that's not why. Did you know that a horse can hear your heartbeat? They are most comfortable when those around them feel confident. Like how you can feel others' emotions...you are attuned to those near you, and when they are unsure, you're more likely to spook."

"That is profound and utter bullshit. But a decent save, I suppose," I said and swiped at her with a napkin.

"Wait, what am I?" Fenris asked.

Krait cut in and deadpanned, "Tomcat."

Fenris spit a mouthful of wine back into his glass. "Come now, I've changed my ways." He held a hand toward Asterie as though showcasing her as proof of his innocence. Asterie leaned her shoulder into him.

"You two certainly knew each other well in a past era," Asterie noted.

"And you"—I pointed at Elsedora—"are a fox...definitely a fox."

Elsedora did a jig with her shoulders, looking proud to be likened to the curious, elusive animal.

Elsedora turned to Ryn and squinted in thought. "Hmm..." Her expression brightened. "Oh! Wolf."

Ryn rolled his eyes. "Does this have something to do with me howling at the moon?"

"I can make you do that if you'd like," Elsedora said, and Ryn flushed.

Krait stared at me expectantly over his wineglass. My head tilted to one side because I wasn't sure there was an animal in existence that complemented his nature.

"I'll think on yours," I answered his unasked question.

Elsedora said, "I'm surprised she didn't just say what we're all thinking. You're a bear."

With a chuckle, I shrugged. It wasn't the worst comparison.

Asterie stifled a laugh, too, and hiccuped. "I think I've had enough to drink."

Wine was always the answer to stiff conversation.

Feeling triumphant, I smiled.

"Stay!" Elsedora said. "Oh, it would be fun to catch up more. Krait, can they? There are spare rooms by my quarters."

I joked, "Are you sure you want to hear what they get up to at night?"

Asterie's usually pallid cheeks turned crimson. "Is this what friends speak of?"

"I suppose," I said with a shrug.

"Fine," Krait said, surprising us all.

The charmed wine bottle poured another glass of wine for me and Asterie.

Later, Fenris requested a private word with Krait and Ryn. He leaned down to kiss Asterie's temple before he followed the others into the courtyard, and my heart clenched. The silent understanding between the couple reawoke a longing in some depth of me that I thought I'd let harden over.

Royals rarely found love that was so simple and pure. We negotiated a sensible marriage. We produced heirs to take our throne. Then the cycle repeated.

Elsedora stood and placed her forearms on her chair back. "I am going to go check with the maids so a room can be prepared. Asterie, keep Sybilla out of trouble, would you?"

"I have been little trouble," I defended.

"Fine—prevent anyone from causing *her* trouble then." El winked, leaving the room with a flouncing gait.

"She's a handful," I noted.

"She definitely comes from the same stock as Fen."

I huffed into my wine and pushed back my chair. "Come, let's go somewhere more comfortable."

I led Asterie down the hall toward the sitting room. Van walked at her heel, seemingly still searching for food scraps.

After entering the cozy space, we sat on a deep suede sofa. It felt like a cloud against my back muscles, which had begun to ache again as I sobered. Vangard curled up at Asterie's feet and grumbled in contentment on the plush rug. The dim light from the candelabra above and the solid, thick wood doors made for a perfect place for a private conversation.

"Now that we are alone, take off that ribbon and tell me honestly what happened to you here." Asterie cut through the lightness in my mood.

"You're demanding when you drink," I said. Instead of coming up with another excuse, I grabbed one end of the ribbon and unwound it from my bruised neck. My friend leaned forward with a furrowed brow, her glistening brown eyes settling on my neck.

"Sybilla..." she breathed out. "What has he done? Is he forcing you to marry him?"

"It was not Darvanda. I am fine here—truly. Marriage was my idea, and neither of us has any romanticized fantasies. It is a *political* arrangement."

"Then who did this?" my friend demanded. "Because that does not look *fine* to me."

I stiffened. "That is what I hope to discover. You always carry a moonstone, right?"

Asterie reluctantly reached into her robe pocket and withdrew a smoothed iridescent gem. "You owe me more explanation than 'I am fine here' first. Also, the moonstone has been spotty about responding to me recently. My power as an Oracle has waned since that night in Luz. It may help if you channel some of your power with me."

A lump grew in my throat. I owed my friend answers.

Asterie spun the stone between her fingers while I told her about the attack in my bedchamber, about speaking with the prisoners and where they'd claimed to be sent from.

She listened intently as I told her about having full Reverist abilities, being the Last Daughter of Isleen and trying to figure out Krait's fixation on my involvement in destroying Caym.

"Darvanda believes the Death Origin sent them? And that he is in Helos?" Asterie reeled back, her brow dipped into a deep crease. "Do *you* think that?"

"It's a ridiculous claim. There's no proof that the Death Origin has risen...No proof that the Sources are even sentient." Doubt coated my voice. Because I *did* believe in Krait's worries. It bothered me how easily that belief had developed.

My friend shook her head. "I once thought the same. But when I was..." Her voice caught, and I touched her shoulder. "When I died, I met Origin Asterie, my namesake. She told me something peculiar. She said, 'Try not to make Death more than an acquaintance. He is difficult for me to negotiate with.' At the time, I'd been convinced the Lacero curse would summon Death himself. But she'd intervened."

Staring at the hutch across from us, where a dustless collection of ornate clay bowls was displayed, my mind raced. Amara's actions that day in the bailey of the Keep, as my city was being saved by Darvanda's army, corroborated Asterie's story.

"Amara," I mused. "That day, she summoned the Sun Origin too—they must've pulled you back together. The texts say Astros and Asterie were siblings. Do you think they *cheated* death?"

Asterie straightened and extended the moonstone between us. "Maybe...or they bargained with him. That was what the Lacero curse was supposed to have allowed me to do."

My eyes widened as the moonstone between us glowed an iridescent blue. "We need to try to see what's coming," I said and placed my hand atop hers. "I've never done this before."

Asterie put her other hand on top of mine. "Stick with my thoughts. I've only tried taking someone with me once."

I nodded in anticipation, but sweat gathered on the back of my neck and my throat constricted.

Asterie's eyes glassed over in a milky hue, and then she pulled me in. It felt like slipping out of my own consciousness, like being torn from the plane of existence where we sat.

Murky water. I walked, alone, through a shallow pool. Asterie was gone.

Had I failed to follow her so quickly? Darkness engulfed me—like being at the center of a lake at night, with no moonlight or stars.

"Asterie?"

I heard no answer.

"Hello, little Isleen. I've been waiting for you. Watching you," a grating voice whispered, and breath hit the back of my neck. The voice felt familiar, as if it had been guiding me my whole life.

When I spun around, no one was there. "Who are you?"

"You do not remember?"

The hair on my arms stood. "I am not Isleen."

"You are the one they say can stop me. Your blood. But you will not!"
That vicious snarl was ingrained in my mind.

Mattock.

Memories of being sixteen, of slipping into the North King's mind, of being pushed out by another entity flooded my senses. That was the voice I'd heard in Mattock's head all those years ago.

"Yes, you remember now. We've met many times from many faces."

Out of the shadows in front of me, a cruel countenance appeared, shrouded beneath a veil of darkness—featureless yet tormenting, depthless yet sharp. His eyes glimmered green and danced with amber rage.

Death approached me.

I stepped back, but my shoulders met a cold black fluid wall that bound my wrists and ankles. I was trapped—trapped here with the Death Origin. I strained against whatever material was constricting around my limbs.

I couldn't scream. I couldn't plead. "You…you sent men to kill me."

"No. I tested you," he said. "And you are just who I've always thought."

I was taken back to a million moments that should have told me Death sought me.

The moment a rope had wrapped around my neck.

The morning one of my maids had died after testing my breakfast.

The night when northern soldiers had invaded the Luz courtyard.

I had skirted him for so long.

I couldn't free myself with force. There was no way out of this prison of darkness. He held my mind between his fingertips.

The figure was so close that I now could smell the putrid scent of death on his breath.

"You will never fulfill the prophecy. You will be mine and not his. I will revel in taking all those who you love; I will turn them to dust. Surrender to me and save them from suffering. I can spare them, spare you."

He held out a gloved hand.

When I opened my mouth to scream, nothing came out. Then I let go of every ounce of the rage I carried in a silent cry that shook the fluid darkness around me. The wrath, a violent wave, washed away from me and threw Caym back.

I fell through the black viscous void until abruptly landing, a scarecrow hanging on nothing but air.

When I stopped, I came face to face with Emmerick. He looked through me. His eyes were glazed dark green—nothing like the rich brown warmth I knew. There was so much gold around him on the walls. Helos. He stood in the throne room.

He stepped away from me and handed a tall male figure in cream-colored robes a dagger and a rolled piece of parchment. The light caught the blade, and an etched symbol appeared on its pommel—three skulls run through with a triangle.

Then he said, "Take this back to Sahlmkar. It must only draw blood."

CHAPTER 20
KRAIT

Stepping out into the courtyard with my former bounty hunter and the last Prince of Phynx had a nostalgic feeling. The world had been a much different place the last time we'd gathered. Magic had been widespread in the realms. The Sahlms had not existed.

Fen had once frequented the court of Brennax, and for different fees, he'd set out on many missions to collect artifacts and information for me. Unlike his sister, he'd never known what he was truly looking for. That truth had taken many centuries for me to reveal to my dearest friends.

The warlock had no allegiances to my or Ryn's courts. Fen, Amara and Firose had been free agents in dealings with our kingdoms. The Three—as the Old World lords had called them.

I hoped that Fen's leanings remained similarly neutral today, hoped that we might start again on new ground.

Now that Sybilla, the Last Daughter of Isleen, was here, under my roof, it felt like my life had circled around and come screeching to a halt. We were back at the beginning—with two tense realms and more to lose than ever.

"I'm sorry," I said, breaking the silence.

Fen rested his forearms on the bridge railing as we looked over the main canal. "Before I accept your apology—sorry for what exactly?"

"I'd just take the apology. They don't come often," Ryn teased, stepping up to the railing.

"I'm sorry for thinking you would turn on Brennax, that you would choose a path of destruction. I see now I was wrong—and I'm not above admitting when I have been deceived."

Fen blew out a "*Pft*" and shrugged. "It wouldn't be the first time someone thought the worst of me. I don't need apologies, but I do need an explanation of how you two came to be so chummy and why you were so bent on taking Asterie here?" Fenris glanced between me and Ryn. "Because that part, I don't forgive you for."

"This one's yours to tell." Ryn clapped my shoulder. "I need to see a man about a bar tab—I'll be back. Try not to start any wars while I'm gone." Ryn pushed away from the railing.

Fenris eyed me cautiously before I spoke. "After I met Princess Freya, we began to court secretly. It went on for years—sneaking through Egresses to one another, skirting our guards for moments alone during negotiations. Even after my father died and I took his crown, I knew better than to think a marriage would be accepted by *her* father. So we eloped—we intended to tell him after peace negotiations were concluded. Ryn and Freya's dearest friend were the only two who knew."

Fenris stilled and watched me with intensity and pity. That soured my stomach. I didn't need his pity.

I continued, "That friend of Freya's, an advisor to her father's court, told him that we'd been married."

Fen ground out, "Firose. She was Freya's dearest friend."

I nodded. "He took our marriage as a threat to his crown, a traitorous act considering Freya was his heir to the throne since Ryn had refused it."

Fenris blew out a breath. "He killed her," he guessed.

My body temperature rose. I was still unable to talk about it without the sinking feeling of rage. "We were in peace negotiations, but my troops were still stationed along Phynx's borders as a precaution. That night, after he..."

"You chose to attack the city after he killed her."

I nodded as that familiar lump in my throat grew.

It was my fault.

Focusing on the flowing water of the canal and the moonlight reflecting off of it, I admitted, "I lashed out in the only way I was trained to—I told Commander Stygian to prepare for war. He was instructed to provide a warning call so civilians could evacuate. He was to attack only until the throne surrendered. He did not issue any warning, and he did not retreat when white flags flew."

Fenris shook his head. "Did you kill him?"

"We found his decimated body. His war helmet was all that was left to identify him. I wish I could have been the one to kill him," I said with a tight jaw.

"Firose spoke with Stygian that night—she went to the front lines to negotiate with him. I'd thought..."

"We all thought wrong. We were all pawns in a much larger game."

"Pawns of who?"

"Caym. He has risen—was rising then too."

Fen cut me off. "C'mon, Krait. You know that I'm skeptical of the 'Sources walking the lands' legends. It's hard to think of the Origins as anything but balls of energy in the sky—or wherever they come from."

"How can you be so skeptical when your betrothed is in part one of them?"

Fenris turned to me with a scowl and snapped, "You leave her out of this."

I raised my palms. "I apologize for what happened in Luz, but I can't leave her out of it. She *glows.* When was the last time you saw someone with *that* much Source power aside from me?"

"I *like* the glowing." Fen smirked. "Let's say you're right...What does it mean?"

I ground my teeth a moment. "You can't deny that even for Firose, her actions were out of character. So were Stygian's. There had to be an outside influence. I believe what happened in Phynx, and Luz, was Caym's doing. It is just the beginning...We need to be careful."

My old friend shook his head. "All I ever am is careful. But what does this have to do with wanting to take Asterie with you after the attack on Luz?"

I took a deep breath. "All those years I had you searching for something—you remember? I was looking for weapons against Caym. There are supposedly three relics. But I was not only seeking physical artifacts. I also sought a woman with Reverist power strong enough to be linked to the First Reverist's lineage. And I've found her."

Fen began to growl out, "If you think that I'm going to hand over Asterie—"

I cut him off. "It isn't your Star-wielder. I thought so at first, but I was wrong."

At my words, Fen reeled back as though realizing who else I could mean. There was a long silence as he studied me.

Before Fen could react, Ryn returned and clapped him on the shoulder. "Did you get to the part where I groveled to come with him into the Sahlms?"

"Not yet," I grunted out.

"I adored Freya as much as our people did," Ryn explained to Fen. "There was no world I wished to live in that she was not a part of. I wanted her to be happy, and there was never a time when I saw her happier than the day she married this asshole."

Ryn had a way of demolishing my emotions anytime he said his sister's name. He was the only one I didn't bark at to not say it—he was owed his own grief.

"Keep your ears open for rumblings of Caym's influence, and mark my words, Fen—he will destroy any power he deems a threat."

Ryn's brows lifted. It wasn't common for me to confide in anyone, but with the stakes so high, I was left with no choice.

"And you have a plan to stop him?" Fen asked.

I shrugged. "More or less."

You must listen, Fifth Heir of Desidero. Find the Last Daughter of my dearest Isleen. The heir you bear together will be both Origin and Reverist. Your child is the key to ending Death's reign—the key to setting us all free.

That excerpt from *The Book of Isolde* had haunted my life since it had been read to me as a child.

Fen snorted a laugh. "And it has something to do with Queen Sybilla? You've actually convinced the most headstrong royal I've ever met to *marry* you? What exactly does being the 'last Reverist' mean for her?"

"It means she is stronger than any power this realm has seen in centuries." Half of the truth.

Ryn thankfully interrupted. "Speaking of which, we should go check and make sure she and Asterie haven't drunk us dry of wine."

Fenris looked at me with that glint of mischief I remembered so well from when we'd been younger immortals and said, "You're not going to tell me the real answer are you?"

We headed back into Umber House and I grumbled, "Not before I tell her."

The moment I stepped inside, I was met with a high-pitched screech.

No, not a screech—a shriek. I couldn't tell where it came from.

Sybilla.

Thinking she would be safe with the Star-wielding enchantress suddenly felt like the most foolish choice.

Following the screams, I burst through the Shadows and up to the sitting room. Asterie knelt beside Sybilla, trying and failing to calm her. Sybilla writhed against the sofa, letting out agonized sounds between screams that barely sounded human.

"What have you done?" I shouted.

A moonstone rested on the floor beside them.

My Shadows wrapped around the Star-wielder and pulled her away, knocking her backward onto the ground.

She squeaked out in protest. "Nothing—we tried to conjure a prophecy about her attackers. It-it was as though she was ripped from me."

That wolf-beast of hers snarled at me with raised hackles, but Asterie called him to her arm and the ink reappeared there.

Panic seized me.

Sybilla stopped screaming as Fen, Ryn and El burst into the room behind us.

"What the fuck?" Ryn said and moved to help Fenris pick up Asterie off the ground. Fenris then put himself between my Shadows and Asterie. Elsedora lingered by the door, wide-eyed.

"Wake up, come on," I commanded Sybilla as my knees sank down on the sofa beside her. Gripping her shoulders, I pulled her into an upright position. Sybilla's eyelids popped open to reveal dark irises where striking green should've been—like the murky water at the depths of a lake.

Sybilla leveled a dark glare at me. "She will be mine in the end. I will take everything from you again, Desidero," she said, but her voice was gargled and strained.

I didn't balk. Instead, I barked back, "Over my dead body, Caym."

Sybilla's expression turned predatory. "I'm counting on that."

Her eyes fluttered closed again, and I cradled her neck with my palm, tapping her cheek as gently as my panic would allow. "Sybilla, wake up."

A hand grasped my shoulder. "Krait," Elsedora warned.

"Get away from us," I snarled.

The next time Sybilla's lids snapped open, I was greeted with emerald and a cold relief washed down my spine. She flung herself back against the sofa's armrest.

"It's okay. You're okay," I breathed out.

"Asterie?" She searched for the enchantress.

"I'm here, I'm here." Asterie approached, despite my threatening Shadows snapping around her ankles. "Where did you go? You slipped away so quickly."

"He took me. The Death Origin, Caym. He..." Sybilla's breath quickened as she trailed off, and Elsedora pulled me back by the shoulders. Sybilla looked like an animal trapped in a corner, disheveled and frantic.

El said, "Give her *space*, Krait."

Asterie crouched beside Sybilla. "You're with us. Breathe, my Queen. Breathe. Count with me," she soothed but didn't attempt to touch her.

Sybilla mouthed the numbers along with Asterie. "Ten...nine... eight...seven..."

"I hate to ask you this. But while the memory is fresh, tell me, what did he look like?" Asterie asked.

Sybilla answered, "He...he was veiled in gray, but his eyes...they were the worst shade of green—with flecks of amber. He felt *wrong* to his core. It is hard to explain."

Asterie turned to Fen. "I've seen him once too. In the orchard, when I had the vision of what happened to my mother—Firose's face contorted into his. Fen, I know you don't believe us, but—"

"I do," Fen cut in. "I believe you, my beauty. I'm sorry I ever doubted you." He moved to her and wrapped his arms around her shoulders as she rose.

Sybilla stared at them with tear-soaked cheeks. Every impulse in me itched to comfort her. It had been a long time since I'd soothed anyone, and my boots froze to the floor.

"I need to be alone. Please, everyone, go." Sybilla pushed up off the sofa. She circled behind it to put distance between herself and the rest of us.

"No," I answered more gruffly than intended. Despite whatever fire she wanted to throw at me verbally, there was no way I would leave her alone, especially when she looked that fucking terrified. "Elsedora, take our guests to their quarters. Ryn, go make sure the house has a full staff of guards around the perimeter and dismiss all of the maids. I don't want a soul in this house other than those in this room."

"What will swords and shields accomplish?" Sybilla snapped. Her whole body shook as she steadied herself, white knuckles on the wooden frame of the sofa. She glanced at Elsedora and said, "Bring me the dagger that the men in the dungeon used to attack me."

Elsedora nodded and jogged out of the room without question.

"We'll be just down the hall," Asterie assured Sybilla. The enchantress' hands shook, too, and the expression of remorse written on her face gave me some confidence that she had not done this intentionally.

They all exited the room, leaving me and Sybilla alone. The click of the door cut through the silence.

"We should stop meeting like this," Sybilla said, but I was not amused by the situation. This was the second time she'd been attacked while under my roof.

"Agreed," I snapped back, immediately hating my tone.

"I'm going to need you to be nicer or leave me the fuck alone."

"Charming," I gritted through my teeth. My posture relaxed only slightly. Our gazes met over the couch—I couldn't think of a nice thing to say or do. How pathetic was that? El had been right. I definitely owed this woman more than flowers.

Adrenaline ran hot in my veins. Slowly, I stepped around the couch to stand next to her. Breath ragged, she watched me approach.

I flinched as she flung her arms around my middle and squeezed. She whispered, "Don't say anything. Please."

Wrapping my arms around her shoulders, I ignored the tickle of her curls against my nose and felt her relax into me. The warm condensation of her breath wet my tunic, and the rise and fall of her chest slowed. The scent of lilac, tea leaves and fresh linen enveloped me—so distinctly her.

"Am I allowed to say anything yet?" I asked.

"No."

She clung to me for a few more minutes before she straightened and released her grip. Unraveling my arms, I plucked a stray curl that had gotten stuck in my tunic button so it wouldn't snag. She still looked so damned shaken. I wanted to wrap my arms around her again.

"Thank you," she said as she pretended to wipe dust off her linen dress.

"Mhm," I answered, unable to think of a single coherent thing to say that would ease her fear. "Why is Elsedora bringing you that dagger?"

Tears welled in her eyes; my teeth ground when one slipped down her cheek.

"Because I think I know where it came from."

There was a knock on the sitting room door before Elsedora entered with the blade. She crossed the room and handed it over, still without question, as though not wanting to break thin ice.

Sybilla turned the blade. I followed her gaze to where a symbol was engraved on the pommel—three skulls run through with a triangle. It looked oddly familiar...

The air was knocked from her lungs in a quiet gasp. She bent at the waist, unable to stand against the weight of whatever she'd just realized.

"I'm going to bed," she said breathlessly, as she quickly handed the dagger back to a very confused Elsedora. "Destroy this. Immediately. It is how Caym found me."

My fists clenched at my sides. What did that symbol mean to her and why did I feel like I'd seen it before?

"I'll walk you to bed." It wasn't a question, and she flashed a watery glare at me but didn't argue. It wasn't the time to pry into why she'd needed to see that dagger...but I had my guess as to what she'd pieced together.

That dagger had come from Helos.

I motioned for her to walk first down the hall and then up the steps. We came to the bedchamber door, and I reached around her to open it. Unsure of whether she truly wanted to be alone, I didn't follow her through the frame; instead, I leaned there.

"If you need anything, I'll be right out here." I pointed to a bench across the hallway. I'd stare at that door all night.

Answering too quickly, she said, "No. Stay. On the cot." Her voice wavered. "I...don't actually want to be alone."

She kicked off her leather mules and walked toward the bed. Looking defeated, she slipped under the covers without changing.

Seeing her spit fire was a royal pain in my ass. Seeing her vulnerable was cracking parts of me I'd thought had more stable foundations.

Sybilla had encountered Caym tonight and lived. It doubled my resolve to help her prepare to face him.

I kicked off my boots and laid on top of the cot's covers. The silence stretched between us until her breathing turned into a low whistle. Only then did I close my eyes.

CHAPTER 21
EMMERICK

Since that awful day when I'd faced Sybilla in the council meet-ing, I kept replaying her hurt expression when I'd told her to call me King Mattock.

That was what she'd wanted. She wanted me here, to rule, to learn this role.

It was the middle of the night. I sat by the crackling fire in my bedchamber in a big leather chair. Despite it being late spring, in Helos the nights still grew cold, the city less temperate than Luz.

A creaking sound from the hallway caught my attention. A cross between the feeling of being watched and a sense of dread scraped down the back of my neck like fingernails.

I grabbed my dagger, lovingly named Angeline after my mother, and slipped quietly out of my bedchamber. My gaze scanned the hallway—a window had blown open at the end of it, and I breathed a sigh of relief.

Reaching the end of the hall, I found a gaping part in the stones...a hidden passageway. The stones, where there had been a wall, were pushed in, creating a space perfectly sized for a man, even one of my size, to slip through. A dark stairway descended.

The only thing I knew lay below the castle were catacombs.

I gripped the dagger. "Angeline—something feels a little off here, eh?" I whispered to my weapon. There were plenty of logical reasons the passage could be open. Maybe maids lit candles in the tombs below. Simpler yet, maybe the passage was used for quicker access to other parts of the castle and someone simply had forgotten to close it behind them.

I didn't yet have my bearings on the traditions of this Corridor or the layout of this colossal estate.

I stepped down the stairs and held my free hand out, creating a small orb of golden light in my palm. It took so much concentration. The first time Asterie and Amara had taught me how, I'd nearly passed out. Wielding my Sun Source was coming to me quickly, but it was taxing. They'd said it was normal to feel that way.

The light cast on the stone walls as I descended into the belly of the Castle of Helos. Candles lit the walls, but they didn't look intentionally placed or meant for commemoration.

"What are you doing in the crypts at this hour?"

I jumped a foot in the air and spun with my dagger pointed, only to meet a lithe auburn-haired adversary.

Elsedora raised a brow at the dagger. She wore a dark tunic and dust-coated leather breeches. Her hair was in a loose braid over her shoulder, disheveled and cobweb coated as though she had just been rummaging around the crypt for something.

"What are *you* doing in the crypts of Helos? Who the hell let you in?"

"I followed the wind," she said, glancing around the space. When she stepped away from me, I followed her.

This night was starting to feel very strange.

"So did I," I admitted. "Well, from the window."

"Hah! The wind is intuitive...Sometimes it puts you exactly where you're meant to be, doesn't it?" she mused. "So that means you did not open the passageway—hmm."

Fantastic. She was now speaking in riddles.

"Why are you here, Elsedora?"

She shrugged and approached a large stone tomb, where she bent down to collect a leather messenger bag. She slung it over her shoulder, and I wondered if she was here to steal valuables. How much gold had she stuffed into that bag?

"Did you notice this one has been cracked open?" she asked, avoiding my question. She pointed to the large stone top that was split down the center and pulled aside. It would have been far too heavy for her to move alone.

"I've never been down here before."

She assessed me, looking me up and down like she was sizing up an animal at a market. "You sure about that, puppy?"

"Quit calling me that."

"But you have the saddest eyes, and I've witnessed your guard dog skills firsthand—such a good boy." She let out a playful '*woof*' over her shoulder as she swaggered toward the stairs.

"You didn't answer me," I challenged. "Why are you here?

"I already told you—I followed the wind." She turned back to look at me from the second step. "And we got word that a threat might have come from the North...I am here to check that all is well—magically and politically speaking."

"Next time, get permission. Egressing into another ruler's home against their wishes *is* a threat. It is an executable offense."

She smirked. "You going to kill me then, pet?"

I tilted my head. What about that did she find so amusing?

"Ah—see, there it is," she said and mimicked my head tilting.

Before I could respond, she trotted up the steps, her feet silent against the stone. She'd make a terrifying assassin.

I followed, not ready to let this conversation die, taking the steps in twos. By the time I reached the top and glanced both ways, she was gone.

CHAPTER 22

KRAIT

I'd begun to watch the Central Queen more since that night when Caym had slipped into her head.

I'd begun to pick up on her small idiosyncrasies. She held her hand to her neck when she grew nervous. She picked berries out of muffins to avoid eye contact when she wasn't in the mood to talk. She rubbed at her wrists often—I couldn't pinpoint the trigger for that.

She whistled quietly when she found a peaceful depth of sleep. The sound soothed me as I fell asleep on the other side of the room on that too-small cot.

I hadn't asked about the dagger, but part of me wished she would confide in me. Every day, I woke before she did and left the bedchamber to afford her privacy.

This morning started like any other. After lighting the candles in the bell tower and scratching my head as I attempted to add marks to my running list against the Queen's character, I headed down to my library.

Since she couldn't read in Brennac, she'd taken to lying on the chaise, stomach down, and fiddling with the tassels of a pillow as I translated aloud. I knew she was listening because she stopped me to ask me questions or catch me if I slipped into Brennac.

Yesterday she had lain there with her legs kicking in the air behind her as I read sections that had set the hairs of my arms on edge.

"You must listen, Fifth Heir of Desidero. Find the Last Daughter of my dearest Isleen. She is the key to ending Death's reign—the key to setting us all free," I'd told her, and conveniently *omitted* some details. She'd accepted it as fact.

Eventually, I'd be ready to face her with the truth.

Our heir was destined to prevail against Caym.

Today we'd try something different than reading. After setting a game board down on a low table at the center of the library, I placed colored stones on it. Tugging two large cushions over to the table, I prepared for her arrival. Like clockwork, Sybilla would show up soon to let me read to her before we visited the amphitheater for physical training.

I knew she was capable of compulsion, but it wasn't coming easily to her. She'd revealed through subtle details that as a child those around her had convinced her that her power was a weakness, something to conceal, something to be ashamed of.

"Good morning," Sybilla chimed from the foot of the stairs, pulling me from my thoughts.

I hummed a response, hating to admit that the flutter of eagerness to see her.

Our second council meeting with the rulers of Henosis was scheduled for later that evening—concessions and decisions. Then tomorrow we were introducing Sybilla as an ally to my people.

"Ryn let you in?"

"I always let myself in," Sybilla answered. "Ryn taught me your little passphrase."

Impossible...

I narrowed my gaze as she stepped further into the library. The bruising on her neck was now a light purple and had nearly faded. She wore dark-green linen breeches and a white tunic, looking more casual than I'd seen her. Her curls were tied up atop her head with that stupid blue ribbon. She was barefoot, having kicked her slippers off at the bottom step.

"What are we reading today?" she asked as she stepped onto the library ladder and leaned far to the right, taking in the titles of the texts.

"No reading." I sat down on one of the cushions cross-legged.

"What are we doing then?" She spun on the ladder, leaning against it and gripping the rung over her head to balance.

The sight made my mouth dry. I imagined her up there, just like that, only wearing far less clothing...

Enough.

It might not be the worst thing to find her attractive. It would certainly make parts of the prophecy less dreadful.

I cleared my throat. "We're going to play a game."

"That seems like a waste of time," she said as she teetered precariously on the ladder rung. "How exactly will games help strengthen me against Caym?"

"If you come down from there, I'll explain."

She rolled her eyes but stepped down from the ladder. After seating herself across from me, she said, "Fine. Get on with it. How do we play?"

Sighing, I reminded myself to add:

IV. Impatient.

"It's like checkers, but instead of pawns, there are five different colored stones. None of the pieces belong to either of us until you jump stones of the same color and collect them. You can jump multiple if empty space between them allows it. I'll go first and show you."

"Do you often *go first?*" she asked me with one side of her mouth curving up.

I sighed, pushing away the mental image she'd conjured. I wanted badly to say "never" but she was baiting me with that lewd comment. Instead, I ground my teeth and reminded myself to add to the list:

V. Vulgar.

I focused on the board and made my first move. Blue jumped blue, leaving an opening for her to jump a green stone. She would probably miss the fact that moving that stone would allow me to jump two yellow stones. I collected my blue stones and waited for her to take the opportunistic move.

"Your turn," I said.

She found the green and took the short-term gain as I'd expected.

VI. Shortsighted

Smirking, I jumped two yellow stones and collected all three of them.

"By the way, I'm good at this," I noted.

"Clearly," she huffed out. She looked tired again today—still breathtaking but the color had faded from her face. There were signs of a rash on her cheeks and chest. Her eyes didn't hold the same fire they usually did.

"Focus on the game, and then when you're feeling your most focused, try to reach out and get me to do something. Maybe you being in a different state of mind will help you to get past my mental shields."

"What do you want me to make you do?" she asked skeptically.

That statement thrilled me in ways it shouldn't have.

"You could make me get up and do a jig if you wanted to," I grumbled.

"Oh the things I can think of…" She trailed off with wistful theatrics. "Why in the world would you want to teach me to control you?"

"Because despite what evil you think of me, I would prefer you survive your next encounter with the Death Origin," I answered. "And I'd much rather *you* control my mind than he control me."

"You are not so evil." Her lips pursed as she concentrated on the board, leaning over it. The collar of her tunic dropped off one shoulder. My mouth went dry again. I dragged my eyes away from where the seam met the tops of her breasts and down to the board.

"You sound so sure."

She'd lined up a triple jump of yellow and squealed as she hopped the stones. She made a dramatic show of pulling her winnings to her side of the table.

Served me well for getting distracted…

Her eyes met mine. "I am sure. You're infuriating, but the people here respect you. You have kept them safe from Death, kept them fed and happy for centuries…You have friends. You cannot be so horrid if people choose to be in your company…"

She trailed off as she watched me jump two blue stones.

Air escaped her lips in a raspberry sound of frustration. I was beating her at this game, even after her small victory. Concentration furrowed her brow.

"I thought about what animal you would be."

"Did you?" I drawled in a dull tone.

"You are not an animal at all…You're a tree."

I scoffed. "A tree?"

"Yes…unyielding, stuck in your sways and rooted in your beliefs."

I lifted a brow.

When my gaze met hers again, she was smirking, and she continued, "But you're also strong. Reliable. You've created a home here for people to nest. It is not so bad to be a tree."

She looked back down at the board with a deep flush across her cheeks. That eager flutter in my stomach stirred again.

Then my hand rose against my will, and I slapped myself across the face. Hard.

The fuck?

I hadn't felt a caress against my mind. I'd felt nothing. She'd gotten past my mental blockades.

She gasped as my mouth hung open in surprise.

"Oh, fuck! Krait, I'm so sorry—that was meant to be a *much, much* lighter tap! I swear it."

Sybilla crawled around the table and leaned over me. Cupping my cheek in her palm, she knitted her brows together and her lips slightly parted. Her gentle touch against the stubble of my cheek smoothed away the sting.

A laugh rumbled in my chest.

"You sadistic prick. Why are you *laughing*? I could have snapped your neck!" she exclaimed.

Dramatic.

Her shoulders collapsed forward, her head almost knocking into my chest.

"You made me slap myself," I said. My cheeks hurt from the stretch of a smile that was wider than I'd worn in a long while. "I asked you to make me do something, and *that's* what you chose?"

The rise and fall of her shoulders indicated she was fighting laughter, too. "I did," she choked out through a laugh. "I'd do it again too." When she lifted her head, our eyes met.

"Do you even understand how much my friends would pay to have been able to do that?"

Something shifted in her expression—softened. Her hand still caressed my cheek, which no longer held any sting, and her touch was intoxicating in a sobering way.

The humor of the moment faded as she held my gaze with a need that I tried my hardest not to match. Our noses were so close, and her hand dropped from my cheek to my chest.

She shifted and crawled over me. I fought a groan as she lowered onto my lap. Though the air had been light with humor moments before, it now felt heavy, with no reprieve from my lust.

I should have pushed her away.

Every instinct screamed at me to stop her. She didn't have all of the pieces of the prophecy—to let her act was to take advantage of her.

I thought myself better than that.

Until her hand trailed up my chest to my neck and her gaze followed, seeming fascinated. As her fingers traveled over my pulse point, a shiver ran down my spine.

This was a good thing, wasn't it? Let her desire me. Let her want more.

She leaned forward and replaced her fingers with her lips. Her mouth grazed my throat, traveling up to the sensitive spot just below my earlobe. Every fiber of my control begged to be snapped. "Fuc k..." I whispered as my head fell to one side.

My hands stayed planted on the ground beside her knees, but my Shadows weren't behaving. She sucked in a breath as they snaked around her waist and teased the skin on her lower back, climbing beneath her tunic.

My hips gained a mind of their own and ground upward to meet her warm, welcoming core. The sound of her gasping into my ear nearly undid me.

She moved, and her lips brushed against mine, open, alluring. I longed to taste them more, longed for a kiss less sweet and more exploratory.

"Enough," I ground out between our breaths.

I could not let her carry on without knowing the full weight of Isolde's prophecies.

At once, she seemed to surface from her desire, sliding down my knees. It might have once brought me some pride to have a woman this worked up without even having to take her clothes off—without even really kissing her. Now, it just made the empty feeling inside me grow.

"Shit," she muttered before lifting herself up in one swift motion. "Shit, shit, shit."

"Charming," I groaned as I adjusted myself in my breeches.

"What the fuck was that?" she spat.

"I believe *that* was all you."

"*All you,* my ass—I felt those Shadows creeping up my shirt, you pig." Her hand rose to meet her throat. "That was a lapse in judgment because it has been a while, and you were being nice to me and...and...it won't happen again."

"What, missing your Sun King? Ready to fill that empty feeling with something meaningless?" Those words weren't for her though—they were for me. I kept digging a hole for myself and said, "What is it that you learned from that dagger, Sybilla? Is he not still your devout lover?"

What did I even care? And why was that symbol still tickling something in the back of mind?

"Fuck you," she growled. She rose and crossed the room to pull on her slippers. "If I want pleasure, then you are the *last* person I should consider."

Her actions hadn't matched those words. Yet still, it stung, which made me even more pissed.

"It seems you've considered me plenty. You were *all* too quick to scheme up a marriage of convenience when it suited you."

She huffed, fists clenched and cheeks pink, then stormed away with a growl of frustration.

Maybe I truly was the sadistic prick she thought me to be because she looked all too alluring when angry. As the door slammed shut, I cursed beneath my breath and fell backward against the cool tile.

Feeling guilt had no part in my plans.

CHAPTER 23
EMMERICK

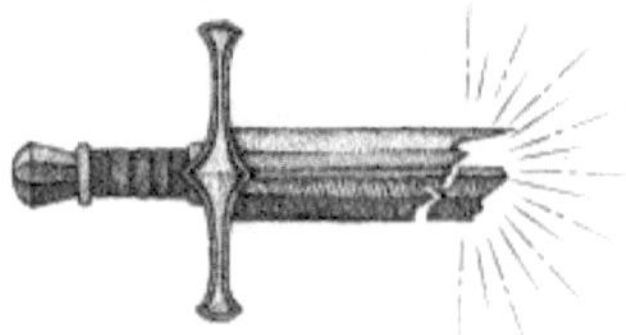

*S*o much blood on the floor. It was everywhere, all over the walls,
dripping from the crystal chandelier.

Where was I?

*The fire in the hearth lit the cramped space. There was a peculiar
heart-and-key emblem carved into each door, and an array of women's
coats hung from hooks at the entry—the wools and furs now splattered
with crimson.*

*My heart thundered as I realized I'd been here before. Back when
I first joined the ranks of the Luz guard, the men had taken me to
a "pleasure hall" while we were traveling through Helos. I'd already
gotten too drunk at a pub and so had spent the evening throwing up
into a pail while a pretty redhead rubbed the back of my head. It had
been humiliating...But this scene now? This was horrifying enough to
make me sick for a different reason.*

*A dark-haired woman was at my feet, her throat slit. I dropped a
blade.*

*Then amber smoke seeped from my fingertips, mine? Screams
wrenched from upstairs before they were cut short.*

Everything went dark, and then I surfaced in the throne room of Helos Castle. A new vision, this one more blurred at the edges. Firose Van Gran approached me and kneeled, taking my hands in hers.

"It was not you, my King," she said. "He will bend your will; you must try to fight it."

"Kill me," I pleaded. My voice sounded deeper—it was not my own.

Firose swallowed hard. "Corric, you know I cannot. He will only take another—we must try to fight this together."

I looked up, but when Firose's gaze met mine, my blood ran cold and my grasp tightened around her wrists.

I spat back at her, "My flame, how soft you have grown."

Firose began to convulse, and everything went cold and dark.

I sat up in bed. A hand held my cheek. I grabbed the intruder by their dainty wrists too aggressively.

"King Mattock," Lady Ryssa whispered. "It is me—Ryssa. You were yelling—and it's noon."

I loosened my grip.

"You startled me. Can you get the curtains, please?"

"Of course." Ryssa's airy, distorted voice returned. "I'm sorry to intrude. No guards were outside and...I'd worried that someone might be harming you."

"No, no..." I winced against the light cast in from the window. "It was just a nightmare." Regaining a normal rhythm of breath, I tried to convince myself that I was here, in bed, and not at that brothel. Not in the throne room.

What had those been? Not dreams...they were too real.

I sat up in bed, letting the blankets pool at my waist. This room felt wrong with its golden arches where I still expected silver and marble, black where I expected Luz blue. The ceilings were too high, and the air was too cold and dry.

I missed home—especially the laughter around my parents' quaint dinner table each week. My mother had returned to Luz, and I'd promised to visit soon yet hadn't.

The world of my past life grew so distant from my new life, even if the Egresses made it simple to visit.

The only people who constantly surrounded me were nobles with questions I did not have answers to.

Ryssa stared down at me through that gauzy, charmed maroon veil before glancing away toward the window. I became acutely aware of my state of undress.

"I'm sorry," I said, pulling the covers up. Thankfully, I'd at least left on my breeches. "I take it this is not how you expected your day to begin."

Nervous-sounding laughter came from behind the veil. "Barging into my new King's bedchamber? No, that is not how I imagined it—and also my day started hours ago. I'll step out and give you a moment."

As soon as she left the room, I couldn't help but smirk as I ran a hand down my face. At least she was good-humored.

My humor faded when I caught sight of my fingertips...They looked as though they'd been stained by coals from a fire. I sucked in a breath as all the blood in my body went cold.

I put on gloves, new breeches and a light tunic before leaving my bedchamber and telling a maid in the hall I intended to go for a ride. She agreed to have the grooms prepare Bishar, my horse.

Asterie and Fenris had frequently checked in for tea since I'd moved here. Their concerned countenances had grown exhausting to see. Amara also visited often; she seemed always to be searching my face for the ghost of a man I'd never known. It was a lonely feeling being in the presence of my old friends.

I hoped no one would come by Helos today before the council meeting.

My only solace was my afternoons spent with Lady Ryssa. Every day, she arrived at noon for tea.

I stepped down the gaudy halls to find her, hoping she hadn't seen my now-concealed hands. The men who'd attacked Luz with dark magic had had coal-covered fingertips too.

I found Lady Ryssa in the sitting room, and she poured me bluebell vine tea and stirred in sugar. I'd picked up an acquired taste for it from Sybilla. At times, I longed for my former Queen's company, and yet I had grown too stubborn to forgive her.

A question haunted me—why would my dearest friend have kept the most life-altering secrets from me for over a decade? The Source magic in my veins, the throne I was heir to. It was unforgivable.

"Good morning. Again." Ryssa's muffled voice greeted me as she handed me the tea.

"Morning," I returned and sipped the floral brew.

"You look distracted. What are you thinking about?" Ryssa grabbed my attention.

"Oh, just..." I paused, taking her in. "Just an old friend."

Despite the fact I never caught a glimpse of Ryssa without her hood or gloves, there was still something in her demeanor that drew me in. I felt like more than a flailing new King when she was near. She felt *right*.

I was grateful for whatever wisdom she provided on how to do my dealings with landowners and farmers. She'd been instrumental in repairing my relations with the lords of the North Corridor, who'd distrusted the late King Mattock. She'd praised my wise choices and gently questioned my not-so-wise ones.

I didn't sit down with her on the sofa; instead, I said, "Would you like to take a ride with me?"

I needed to pass the pleasure hall—to see it with my own eyes and know it had just been a dream. I wore a cloak with the hood up as we rode into the southern part of Helos.

When my eyes landed on the establishment, a woman was on the steps with her head in her hands, crying, as a Helos guard loomed over her. The questions he asked made me pull up on my reins, steer into an alley beside the hall and come to a halt.

"You say you couldn't see his face?" the guard asked.

The woman sniffled. "Yes, sir. He was tall and broad-shouldered and wore a cloak. I...I woke to screams and when I came downstairs, they were all...they were all dead..well, dying. He killed them all. All of my girls, every one. His back was turned when I came down the stairs."

"Forgive me, it would be hard for one man to kill ten women at once. Are you sure it was just one man? And if they died, where are their bodies, miss? There is only one dead courtesan in there."

I gritted my teeth against the guard's callous response.

"It was...there was smoke consuming them. It smelled terrible, and it was a pale, horrid yellow. Then...they turned to dust before my eyes. I swear it."

The guard didn't believe her, but I did. A lump grew in my throat. I'd recognized my hands in that dream, and yet I'd never been in that pleasure hall after that first time.

Ryssa pulled up beside me. "Is everything alright, my King?"

I swallowed hard. "Yes."

Ryssa looked toward the madam and the guard. "Would you like me to ensure her business is funded to recover from this tragedy and any damages?"

The way she asked with such eerie recognition of what had transpired made me turn my head abruptly her way. She couldn't have known...what was there to know? I'd been in bed. I'd been dreaming. I'd been nowhere near this part of town.

Staring into the void of Ryssa's faceless cloak, I nodded. "Yes," I said again. "And find out who that guard is and remove him from his position."

It left me feeling helpless and numb. It left me wondering if the evil that grew within me had always been there.

CHAPTER 24

KRAIT

When I came down for an early dinner before the council meeting, Ryn and Elsedora were sitting beside each other in the dining room. Sprawled across the table was a stained and filthy vellum that looked older than me. It was a map with Brennax and Phynx cities inked upon it.

They were bickering about something and pointing to parts of the world.

"This would be where Helos sits now," El said.

When the two of them put their heads together, they made a good team. There were also moments of catastrophic disagreement that made me want to send them to opposite sides of the realm.

I mused, "Those are hopeful faces."

Elsedora blurted, "Caym has someone new doing his bidding."

"Explain," I ground out, still in a piss-poor mood after having pushed Sybilla away in the library—in an even worse mood because the moment replayed like a tune stuck in my head.

"Well, we always suspected Mattock and Stygian were under Caym's influence—Firose too. But we've never found evidence to link them all together. We think that the envoys bear a mark. Look."

Elsedora gently spun the ancient map in my direction. She pointed at a familiar symbol—three skulls with a triangle intersecting them. The hairs on my arms stood.

"It moves..." Elsedora's eyes followed as the mark moved very slowly through what would be the city of Helos.

I narrowed my gaze on the page.

"It was on the dagger those men used on Sybilla," El continued.

I nodded. She'd been so cagey about that damned dagger.

"I recognized it immediately. It was also carved into the belongings of those we suspected to be harvesting Death for Caym," El said. "When Firose grabbed me in the fray at the battle of Luz, I saw *this* symbol engraved on a golden ring she wore. I thought it odd because—"

It snapped into place. I knew where I'd seen that symbol. I cut in, "Stygian had this inked on his arm."

Mentioning my former Commander, the man who'd betrayed me and led my troops on a Death rampage through Phynx, made me grind my teeth. I hoped he rotted amongst the worms.

"Then it *is* connected to Caym. I saw it on Corric Mattock's crown as well. Which was what I was *about* to say before being interrupted," El huffed.

Isolde's tomes were infuriatingly vague, but they had mentioned Caym often acted through others—envoys. With Isolde's Reverist power, even while trapped and most of the power out of his reach, Caym could influence those most vulnerable. Those angry or seeking purpose...

Like a North Corridor King who wore a crown he seemed not to want and who had been jilted by a Queen he had been loyal to.

Elsedora's leg bounced, and it wiggled the table. Ryn grabbed her knee and rubbed it to calm her in a way that was far too familiar. I would ask about that development later.

"If they are all dead, then there must be a new envoy...one in Helos," Ryn concluded, pointing at the mark on the map.

It seemed we were all avoiding saying Emmerick's name.

"Could Caym be controlling more than one envoy again?" El asked. She looked down at the single symbol on the map with a furrowed brow. "It seemed that both Firose and Stygian were under his influence at once...maybe the late Mattock, too."

"Possibly." I sighed. "*Where* did you find this? And how do you know the symbol was on Corric's crown?"

"I saw it in a tomb beneath Helos; that's where I found this. Obviously. Keep up," Elsedora answered. "There was also a memorandum, but I'll need one of you to use an opening charm on it." She retrieved a smoothed triangle-shaped black stone with gold etchings of the sun carved into it from her pocket.

I stifled a growl of frustration. "What were you doing in the catacombs of Helos?" El had a habit of going above and beyond on her information-gathering missions. She'd taken many detours through the years.

"Do you just pay me to look pretty?" she retorted.

I scoffed. "No, but being paid requires that you keep living."

"Don't question my methods." El flipped her dusty braid over her shoulder and waved away my concern.

"You really are going to get yourself killed someday," Ryn said. "We won't always be there to Source-wield you out of things."

"Quit dreaming of getting rid of me," El said and stuck her tongue out. Ryn attempted to grab it, and El tried to bite his finger.

I reached up to squeeze the bridge of my nose, amazed that two of the brightest minds in the realm could default to acting like children when put in the same room together.

El sobered and looked past me as I placed my palms on the table.

"Asterie thinks that the Sun and Star Origins bargained with Death," Sybilla cut in from the doorway to the dining room, seeming unsure about whether to enter.

We'd been too busy bickering to hear her footfall. She hovered there, now dressed in her heavy finery, ready to attend the next council meeting.

Elsedora pointed to Sybilla. "See. *The Book of Isolde* warns that Death will rise through such bargains."

"That tells us nothing. We always knew he would rise," I said, losing my patience.

I eyed Sybilla, motioning with my chin for her to join us. She wore an impractical Luz-blue velvet gown, and a flush from the heat had already spread across her chest. The dress hugged her body in a way that held my attention. Though it seemed anything she wore did that.

"Good afternoon." Ryn rose to pull out a chair for her and then took one of her hands to plop a kiss on the top of it as he helped her sit. *Kiss ass.*

Sybilla seemed grateful for it. "At least one of the men in this residence has manners. What's with the dusty old map?"

Ryn straightened and scratched his head as Elsedora filled in the gaps of what Sybilla had missed—of the map and the memorandum. As Sybilla's eyes landed on the symbol, her shoulders tensed.

"Are you going to tell me now why that symbol makes your skin crawl?" I asked.

Sybilla held my gaze. "Because when Caym infiltrated my mind..." She swallowed hard. "I saw King Mattock give that dagger to a cloaked figure, instructing him to bring it to Sahlmkar. It had that symbol on it. I think the blood it drew allowed him to pull me away from Asterie." Her fingertips traced the healing cut on her cheek.

My jaw grew stiff. "The late Mattock?"

She shook her head, and it infuriated me to see her blink back tears. But there it was—she'd finally confided in us, and yet it still burned to see her distraught over what her former lover had done.

Ryn carefully said, "If Death truly bargained with the Sun and Star Origins, if he is gaining strength, we have to find a way to slow him down. It seems he's using the envoys to harvest Death—he has been since the Great Wars." As Ryn spoke, Sybilla grew more tense.

"To do what exactly?" Sybilla asked.

I drew in a deep breath. "He *could* take his true form through the Death harvested from his envoys. If he has done that, which is likely, he will have years to walk among us and gain momentum, to kill, before he gains Isolde's powers back as the prophecy says he will."

I shifted in my seat; we danced dangerously close to truths I hadn't yet told Sybilla.

"The same prophecy that includes me?" Sybilla asked.

Elsedora narrowed her gaze on me. "Yes, Krait. How *is* Sybilla involved in Isolde's prophecy again?"

I could've let my Shadows wring Elsedora's neck.

"I've already told her. *The Book of Isolde* names the Last Daughter of Isleen as a key to ending Death's final reign."

Ryn's mouth narrowed into a line. This wasn't how I'd wanted to break the full meaning to her.

"Ah yes, *that's* what it was." Elsedora's voice dripped with sarcasm.

Sybilla's brows knitted as she homed in on Elsedora with a tilt of her head. I held my breath, realizing that without Source magic, Elsedora was a living, breathing liability to my withheld truths.

"You are singing limericks internally, which makes me feel like you're keeping something from me," Sybilla mused as she patted Elsedora on the hand. "I'll make you tell me later."

I breathed a sigh of relief.

"Can you two open this memorandum now?" Elsedora asked.

She set the obsidian stone down on the table. Glancing at Sybilla, I explained, "A memorandum is created by someone, usually before death, to document last words or wisdom or a message for their loved ones."

Sybilla nodded. "I've heard of them from Asterie but have never seen one."

"I've got it." Ryn cut the tip of his finger and let his blood drop into the engraved sun symbol that adorned the stone. He then whispered a Phynnic charm. As soon as he'd finished, a ray of light shot straight up from the stone, like shimmering gold dust.

"I do not have much time," the late Mattock rasped; his weak voice filled the room. His face, suspended in golden light, shone above us. "My dear Amara—you are my light on the darkest days. Keeping you and our boy afar has destroyed me.

"I must warn you. The Death Origin rises. He is within me. There are three of us who do his bidding. He grows stronger with every death at our hands. Firose is also in his grasp—do not blame her, my dear. She tries to ward him away when he overtakes me, but she has grown weak against him too.

"When we're gone, he will replace us. None of us can kill the other. It is a hopeless web he has woven. You must find them all and kill them all at once to deny him a chance to take another."

Mattock senior coughed and cleared his throat. "I hope it is not too late. Knowing you are safe has kept me strong, but I fear fighting Death has taken its toll on me. I'm so sorry, my love."

The light flickered out. My hands trembled from how tightly I clung to the edge of the table. When I looked over at Sybilla, tears were falling.

We could delay the inevitable, but our time ran thin.

"I must tell Emmerick," Sybilla said.

"Not a chance. He sent a weapon that nearly *killed* you. He is likely an envoy, Sybilla."

"It cannot be him...Maybe Caym tricked me. Maybe Em is in danger," she tried.

She could justify it however she wanted—I wasn't going to see her killed over puppy love and a false sense of loyalty. I turned to El and said, "Continue to pay the North King visits until we know where the threat comes from. All signs point to Helos being a hub for Caym's envoys."

Sybilla huffed indignantly, eyes darting between us.

El kicked back in her chair. "Gladly. He's fun to look after." She offered Sybilla a playful wink, which I loathed. Sybilla seemed too distraught to react.

Sybilla's head snapped in my direction. "Emmerick would not send those men."

Ryn was the one to reach across the table this time. I wanted to let my Shadows pry his fingers away before he could touch her. He took Sybilla's hand. "My Queen, *he* would not. But if Caym has infiltrated his mind, he may not know what he is doing...We are only trying to keep you safe, to take precautions"

She pulled her hand from his and placed it at her throat. "That implies that I am unsafe with Emmerick, and that cannot be further from the truth." She shook her head. "He cannot be. He—"

"We hope he is not an envoy, but you aren't to step foot in that city until we know for sure," I commanded. "And if you see that symbol on any person's belongings, you run or prepare to fight because your life will depend on it."

I hated the callous command to my voice, hated how Sybilla grimaced and glared because of it. Ryn and Elsedora nodded in agreement, though they, too, looked unsure.

"Do you think this map tracks where they are? It's suddenly in the South Corridor isles. Maybe they traveled through an Egress?" El speculated.

"We could hunt them down," Ryn added. I desperately wished my advisors were less good at their jobs.

Sybilla eyed me and spat, "You will *not* kill him. None of you." Her tone turned more pleading than I'd ever heard it before. "Promise me."

Ryn glanced at me. "We cannot promise that."

Sybilla pushed out her chair and stood. "Then at least promise you will wait until there is *actual* proof that Em is an envoy. Not some fucking symbol from a piss-stained map and the word of a dead man."

"If all must fall at once, we'd need to know who the others are first," I cut in. "No one is being killed today. *We* don't act on impulse."

She looked slighted and flushed. I'd done my best to repress our earlier encounter in the library; now I'd gone and revealed it still lingered in my mind.

"How could I forget," she said and then stormed out of the dining room.

Ryn asked, "What was *that* about?"

"None of your damned business," I retorted.

Before we left for Eros, I headed up the bell tower to light the candles, only after having checked our bedchamber door. Locked.

VII. Willful

CHAPTER 25
SYBILLA

Some time after our tense interaction in the dining room, I met Krait in the courtyard, ready for the council meeting. Wordlessly, he motioned toward the Egress. What had I been thinking in the library? Something about the levity of the moment, of him laughing and smiling up at me, had made me convinced there might be something good in him.

I'd been terribly wrong.

I needed to ask Emmerick about the dagger, needed to tell him of his father's memorandum and the risk to his life. What I'd seen in that vision must have been distorted by Death's manipulations.

Krait wore the same dress robe that I'd first seen him in on the wall of the Palace of Luz. The golden embroidered rattling serpent coiled across his chest and up the shoulder of the rust-red fabric. His dark breeches were tucked into brown buckled boots.

I stepped into the Egress beside him.

"South Tower," Krait commanded.

We were pulled away—weightless, like the sensation of falling just before drifting asleep. Traveling by Egress was still disorienting to me. I fought the creeping nausea.

We exited the Egress into the South Tower in the Southern isles. Krait's hand hovered at my shoulder as though contemplating whether to help ground me.

He leaned down to whisper into my ear. "It gets easier."

"I'm fine," I snapped back.

"I never said you weren't."

I hated that he'd noticed I was out of sorts.

Maybe it wasn't only the Egress travel making me ill. In all the commotion of Asterie and Fen's visit, I'd forgotten to ask her to have Healer Mortag make more of my tonics. My mind and body felt at odds with one another. Every joint ached. It took all my energy just to put one foot in front of the other.

Lashing out came more easily than being vulnerable. Showing any form of vulnerability to King Darvan-dick seemed foolish. Krait raised a brow at me before we stepped into the hallway of the South Tower. A tense energy greeted us. Dozens of guards with shell-shaped shields surrounded us at the Egress.

"Announce yourself," one commanded.

"Queen Sybilla Wymark of the Central Corridor."

Krait sized up the guards. "King Krait Darvanda. Sahlmsara."

Sighing, I glanced to my side. "Play. Nice."

"This *is* nice," he muttered. The guards lowered their shields and allowed us past.

Two walls of open windows that overlooked the sea framed the hallway. The tower was built onto a narrow peninsula of salt-soaked cliffs of the South Corridor.

Asterie and Fenris waited outside a light wood door with Amara—this tower was still her residence even though it held the only Egress in the South. She must have invited them.

"Ah, my advisors." I smiled.

Fenris reached me first, and he took my hand and kissed the top of it. Krait didn't greet them at all.

"Queen Sybilla, you're doing well since our visit?" Fen asked.

"As well as I can be," I said.

"We need to prepare you for negotiations today," Asterie's placating voice said, putting me on edge. "Amara called us here."

Krait stiffened next to me. "Why?"

"The North has taken a stance against negotiating with the Sahlms," Fenris carefully said as he turned his attention to Krait. "Don't lose your temper."

"What temper?" Krait asked, but his fists clenched at his sides.

Negotiating with the Sahlms, and holding trials to allow reentry of the Sahlmsaran people, had *always* been part of the plan—a fair and just plan.

My former lover was never one to act selfishly.

"That can't be true." I dismissed them with a shake of my head. Yet worry plagued me...what if it was?

"Sybilla"—Asterie stepped before me as I tried to walk around them and enter the room—"something is wrong with Emmerick."

No. I still refused to believe that.

"Then let me speak with him," I bit back. My friend only stood taller, not letting my ire deter her.

"Listen to your advisors, Sybilla." Krait's voice made me see red.

I spun on him. "This isn't any of your business."

"Is it not? *My* people face persecution. Again."

I deflated. Despite the sting of Emmerick's betrayal, in the end, the outcome of these meetings held less weight for my people than they did for Krait's. The Sahlms were running out of resources, and water could only come from the mountains under Emmerick's rule. Or they would have to leave, which also couldn't happen without

Emmerick's cooperation. He was playing political cards that he had no idea how to manage.

Hating that Krait was right, I crossed my arms. The long billowing sleeves of velvet bunched between my arms, and his gaze flickered to my neckline just long enough to deepen my glare.

"I'm listening"—I swung back to face Fenris and Asterie—"to you two."

Fenris had taken Asterie's hand. The way her arm was positioned showed off the ink where Van rested. I was surprised the wolf-beast was not roaming the halls of the South Tower. Things must have been tense in there if she'd put Van away.

A lump grew in my throat as Fenris drew Asterie to his side. The gentle comfort between them was something to aspire to. I never considered myself a romantic, but the way they supported each other with such care made me question whether that type of companionship would ever be within my grasp.

No expectations.

No secrets.

No resentments.

They looked at each other. Fenris returned his gaze to me and said, "There is talk of unseating you."

My blood went cold. "*Unseating?*"

"The people in Luz are receptive to my and Asterie's presence since they've experienced how Source-wielders can help them," Fen answered. "But the nobles outside the city have not witnessed it firsthand. Lord Haward is rousing support with surrounding regions that would rather see the Order be maintained, and now, with Emmerick's backing, Bringham is leaning that way too."

My friend would not send a dagger to harm me. He wouldn't turn against me.

"You still have the Nadiars' support, and Sheffield has sung your praises," Asterie added. "We hold the majority. All isn't lost, Sybilla—we'll see this through, but we need to be cautious and not cause a stir."

She squeezed my arm reassuringly.

"Not yet, at least. We don't have the law on our side. Regulation still prohibits Source-wielders, prohibits any use of magic...They have a case for unseating you should we continue to use it in Luz."

"Fuck that." I pushed past them and burst through the double doors of the dining hall. I'd had enough of men deciding the fate of my Corridor.

Met with a bright sunlit room that would have been cheery if I wasn't so pissed off, I squinted. The tall domed ceilings were painted with creatures of the sea, and a driftwood chandelier hung above a large pine table that had maps sprawled across it.

"Queen Sybilla." Sheffield greeted me with a smile.

"One moment, I must address my former Constable," I gritted through my teeth as I walked past Sheffield and straight to Emmerick. He stood on the far side of the room, speaking with Haward and Barden. They shouldn't have even been involved in these proceedings.

Their backs were to me, and they faced a large window that overlooked a small sand beach below the sea cliffs.

"Look at me," I growled. Emmerick turned to meet my gaze with a sigh.

Haward wore a smug expression that I wanted to slap from his face. "Cousin," he greeted.

"Queen Wymark," I corrected him with a pointed finger, but my eyes never left Emmerick's.

When had the boy I'd once confided in become the man who now sided with those who opposed me?

Haward chuckled and whispered, "Not for long, I hear."

It took every ounce of restraint not to shove him away from us. Instead, I found my mind reaching out to Haward—searching his infuriating thoughts.

Surely Caym had made Haward an envoy. It had to be him. But all I felt from my cousin was his usual greedy desire to see me fall, his envy and his insecurity.

Keeping my attention on Emmerick as my cousin continued to stand stone-still, I finally asked, "Why?" It came out in a whisper.

Emmerick shrugged. He looked too nonchalant, too unbothered.

My gaze narrowed.

"We decided that the Central Corridor needed a stronger ruler should the North Corridor remain its ally. And we will put one there through force, if necessary."

"Are you *hearing* yourself, Em?" I spat back, my voice rising.

Emmerick seemed devoid of emotion.

This was not him.

He rested his hand on the sword I knew he'd named after me, and something inside me snapped. "You don't mean this."

In my despair, my mind slipped from Haward's, and he finally surfaced, glancing around as though startled.

"We don't all get the luxury of doing things for ourselves, Sybilla. My people *require* a more powerful Central ally, and I will have to compromise to obtain it." Emmerick stared me dead in the eye as he spoke my own words back to me.

Motherfucker.

I wanted to claw at his face and pull out his hair.

Haward interjected, "You still have a chance. You could always marry King Mattock and join your Corridors."

My cousin wasn't even trying to steal my crown...He just wanted to see me leashed.

Emmerick tilted his head, but his gaze...it was predatory. The golden shimmer to his irises faded to dark depths.

This was all that I'd feared.

I scanned him, trying and failing to find the symbol. "I will not marry the man who stands here now. If it's hostility you want, prepare to fight me every step of the way. You know better than anyone that I will go down in flames with my Corridor—kicking, screaming, *burning*. I will *never* hand it to anyone. Not even you, King Mattock, and certainly not you." I pointed at my traitorous cousin.

Barden lingered nervously behind Haward. All other conversations had stopped in the room.

No matter how hard I pushed and tried to break through to Emmerick's mind, I could not. All that I could feel was a cold, hard wall. The other rulers' feelings trickled in.

King and Queen Nadiars' discomfort was palpable—a dull taste on my tongue.

King Haag Bringham was amused. *"Boy, she really knows how to throw a fit."* His condescension tickled my throat like an allergic reaction.

Sheffield felt helpless—the poor man had just wanted to host a *peaceful* negotiation session. *"Oh dear, maybe we are not ready for such negotiations."*

My advisors and Darvanda stared at the scene I'd created.

Asterie's thoughts bled into my mind. *"There is something wrong with him."*

Drawing in a deep breath, I stared at Emmerick. He stood with his hand on his sword like he might use it, looking down at me with that dark, mile-deep stare.

"Please step back..." Krait's thought entered my mind. Uninvited.

I didn't want to stand down.

"We won't convince any of them if we cause trouble."

He was right.

I fucking hated that he was right. We wouldn't be able to make any headway with the other rulers if we didn't play this right, but all I saw was red. I stepped away from my lost friend.

Turning to Sheffield, I said, "I apologize for the disturbance, King Sheffield. Next time King Mattock and I will resolve our conflicts privately. In the meantime, my word and the words of my advisors are *law* in the Central Corridor. I don't care what was written in the Order. It has been abolished."

King Sheffield nodded reassuringly, but he was not who I was worried about.

When I heard the rumble of Krait's voice, it came as a relief. "Will we be discussing 'concessions and decisions' pertaining to the list of Sahlmsarans who still await reentry into the Corridors today?"

I returned to Krait's side.

Sheffield glanced nervously at King Mattock and King Bringham.

Queen Nadiar nudged King Nadiar who said, "The East Corridor requests that we postpone those discussions until all leaders of the Corridors agree upon terms."

Krait let out an impatient growl. "If there will be no negotiations, or trials, then we will be leaving. But not without a reminder." Krait stared down Emmerick and Bringham as he spoke. "To wage war on Queen Wymark is to wage war on the Sahlms. My Warhorses have already cut down the North's previous attempt to bring Death upon her Corridor. That battle was child's play."

The way Krait turned his attention back to me and extended his hand heated something inside me. I didn't know if I'd ever had that reaction to someone speaking on my behalf before. Usually, I'd have scoffed at it.

I'd never allowed another soul to speak for my Corridor.

He had defended my rule.

It solidified my belief that Krait had no interest in my crown. He had his own people to serve; he had his own problems to solve. Yet the look of fear that crossed Bringham's face, and the way Queen Nadiar straightened made me feel as though I'd chosen my ally wisely. Insufferable as he may have been—they all feared him.

I took his hand and then gasped as he pulled me to his chest and wrapped his other arm around me. We descended into Shadows. It was disorienting and dark. The thrill of making such a dramatic exit went straight to my head.

When we surfaced from the Shadows, we were back in the halls of Umber House.

The man didn't even need an Egress. We'd just traveled across a whole realm.

"You could have given me some warning." I tilted my chin up to meet his gaze. He still held me drawn to his chest with one hand while the other held my side. He huffed and slumped into me, appearing dead on his feet. For a moment I thought he might fall into me, and I braced us both with my free hand on his chest.

He shrugged and said through labored breath, "I like seeing you surprised."

"You're a sadistic prick. Does traveling like that drain you? You look dreadful."

"Immensely. Especially that far. But I wanted you out of that room, that realm...The risk was too high."

"What risk?"

His grip on my fingers tightened. "Mattock had a hand on his blade the whole time. I will not let a lover's quarrel be your end, Sybilla."

I shook my head. "Why? Because of some old prophecy in *The Book of Isolde?* What does that make me to you? Are we Source Matched?"

Krait stared at me as the silence dragged on between us. I wanted to scream—answer me, you stubborn ass.

A lump grew in my throat because standing there so close, leaning together, reminded me of how good he'd felt beneath me. My gaze slipped down to his lips, and my mouth went dry.

"That would be impossible. You don't have Source power, and I've already found my Source Match," he finally said, only answering my last question.

His words should have sounded like a clear rejection, yet he licked his lower lip when he looked down at mine, and my body felt molten.

The fall of hurried footsteps sounded down the hall. I sprang away from Krait as Elsedora rounded the corner. She cast us a mischievous smile that told me I must have been as flushed as Krait.

I'd just been sizing the King of the Sahlms up like a delicacy on a dessert table. My decision-making skills were in ruins.

"What did I miss?" Elsie cooed.

"Nothing," Krait grunted before running his hand through his hair. "Search the King of the North for anything with a deathmark."

Elsedora's amusement faded. "We were right?"

"We don't know," he answered. "But she's not allowed within a foot of him until we figure it out." He pointed to me in a way that made all the heat leave my body.

"You cannot order me around."

He ground out, "I just did."

"If he is in trouble, I can't sit back and do *nothing*," I huffed.

He turned his back on me, ready to walk away. That prick.

"Would you have just left Freya to fend for herself against Death?" I spat at him.

Elsie's eyes widened as though I'd just stepped off a cliff, and her hand hovered over her mouth.

Krait's whole body stiffened, but he still faced away from me. "Don't speak of her." His low snarl raised the hairs on my arms.

It was clear I'd rubbed salt into his deepest wound.

I'd never been particularly great at stopping while I was ahead.

"Answer the question. It isn't complicated."

When he glanced over his shoulder, every hard line was taut. While I wasn't afraid, the Shadows snaking off him and onto the tile toward me made me step back. His expression was that of an enemy, not an ally.

"That is where you're wrong," he said before storming off.

Elsedora blew out a breath. "I think you might have the largest testicles that I have ever seen. And I've seen a great number of them."

Even her jokes weren't enough to set my mind at ease. Not when the Death Origin might have my dearest friend in his grasp.

"You'll visit Helos again? You will check in on him?"

Elsedora nodded. "Of course. After all, now I have orders to *search* him..." She wiggled her eyebrows, and I slapped her arm.

"Please, be careful."

Krait did not come back to the bedchamber that night, to my relief. Or disappointment?

The moment his late wife's name, his Source Match's name, had left my tongue, I should have begun apologizing. I hadn't realized that until he'd walked away.

Emmerick's words the day I'd left Luz came back to me. Maybe I did always have an angle. Maybe I would never consider anyone else's desires but my own.

Once again, I'd only been thinking about my problems when I'd spat that venom. The weight of remorse crushed me.

It was growing late, and I'd climbed into the massive, unbelievably comfortable, delicious-smelling bed. As I leaned over to blow out the bedside candle, a piece of parchment slipped under the door and skated across the tile.

I got out of bed and crossed the room to pick it up. The penmanship was neat and tight, yet the still-wet smudges told me the note had been hurriedly written.

Queen Sybilla Wymark,

The alliance between Sahlmsara and the Central Corridor remains strong. I have decided it best to see you back to Luz. I regret to inform you that I also rescind my agreement in regard to our pending union. After presenting you to the people of Sahlmsara as our <u>ally</u> tomorrow, and providing my people assurance, I will arrange for your departure.

King Krait Darvanda

I crumbled the too-formal letter in my hands.

That dick hadn't even had the respect to tell me to leave his city to my face? That our agreement to marry was null and void?

I quickly altered my plans.

If Krait's court was up against the Death Origin, and I could somehow help them, help keep Emmerick safe, I wasn't going to piss away that chance over an argument with their King.

No matter how much I missed home, I needed to find a way to extend my stay. At least for a little while.

I knocked on Elsedora's door. She came to it with a robe draped around her.

Her brow furrowed. "What is it?"

I handed her a folded piece of parchment and a sack of bronze coins. "I have a few requests for a seamstress and jeweler for my presentation tomorrow to the Sahlmsaran people."

Elsedora opened the parchment, and her brow rose. "It will be difficult to get these on such short notice...but, lucky for you, I spend quite a good deal on garments and know someone who can help. Is that all you have planned for tomorrow, *an outfit?*"

I huffed a laugh. "Of course not. How much do you want to know? If you stay in the dark, you can still plead innocence."

That roused a wicked smile from her. "Oh, now I'm intrigued."

"Krait's trying to send me back and has broken our engagement," I blurted. "But I'd like to make him reconsider."

El's eyes widened. "He wouldn't."

I handed her Krait's crumpled note and said, "He would. So, help me?"

She opened the door wider and ushered me inside—I was thankful for a confidante and someone to talk my plans through with.

I needed to make a statement to the people of the Sahlms.

Their King could loathe me for it. The risk was worth the reward.

Chapter 26

Krait

"**W**hat a shit idea, Krait."

Elsedora was fuming. I'd never known her to be riled so easily.

"She's manipulative and naive," I tried. Sybilla's words had crept under my skin yesterday and uncovered a sore of festering guilt that I'd not realized was still open.

"She is the Last Daughter of Isleen—the person you have, for centuries, had me scouring the realms for. Why are you trying to send her *away*?"

"I'm not trying. I *am* sending her away." I shrugged. "We'll find another option. She is useless to us if she can't help us secure water rights."

Speaking the lie made my jaw tighten, and I knew that El of all people could see through me.

Her eyes narrowed, and a gust of wind blew back my silk cloak. The breeze was a welcome reprieve from the sweltering heat. We stood on the main balcony of Umber House. The courtyard bustled with people preparing for our formal announcement of an alliance between Luz and Sahlmsara.

"You know well that what you just said is utter horseshit."

It was. I didn't know of any other way—my whole life I'd been led to find her. Why did she have to come in such a provoking package?

Ropes were being strung between stakes to prevent anyone from getting too close to the balcony. We needed Sybilla unscathed when she left my realm tomorrow.

El sighed. "You've come too far to give up now."

"It will be alright," I reassured her. *It wouldn't.*

Freya's name on Sybilla's lips had felt wrong, like a disrespect to the memory of my late wife. Maybe I wasn't willing to face that closure yet, or maybe Sybilla had just reminded me that I'd done too little to protect Freya.

Either way—after a few glasses of amber liquor and hours of seething, I'd wanted Sybilla far away from here until I could piece together what could be done. Her two advisors in Luz seemed capable of keeping her alive. I'd made my decision, and I doubted retracting it now would matter.

Sybilla was bullheaded and proud. She wouldn't have taken kindly to my written rejection. I'd committed to sending her back into a viper's den in Luz. My throat constricted at the thought of it.

"I can assure you that you won't fulfill the prophecy any faster by sending her away and calling off your betrothal. Are you confused about how heirs are made? Do you need a lesson?"

"Elsedora." My voice cracked. "I can't. Alright? I can't."

Her eyes widened. "Oh, Krait..."

Fuck. I didn't want her pity.

I shook my head and tried to flee, but her arms snaked around me, and she pulled me into a squeezing embrace that was more suffocating than comforting.

"I can't breathe, El."

"I know."

"Let go," I grunted.

"No, not until you stop this self-loathing bullshit," she shot back.

"'Self-loathing bullshit'?" I asked.

"Yes! You can blame yourself forever for what has happened in the past, but it won't change a damned thing for your future."

"What future?" The attempted joke didn't deter her, and she squeezed me tighter. I groaned. "Fine, please let go of me. I'll think about it."

"You'll think about what? I need specifics."

"I'll think about letting her stay," I answered. "If she even wants to."

"Oh, she'll want to." As El released me, I faked a cough. "I support whatever decision you make. But have you *seen* her? Even Ryn wouldn't blame me if I ended up in bed with her, and he's growing awfully jealous when I sleep with others."

"We need to talk about that, by the way." My two officers warming each other's beds would spell disaster at some point. Or worse—dramatics.

She shook her head and waved me away. "I am not the chosen one with the magical seed to sow to save the world. I owe nobody an explanation for how I spend my intimate time. You need to talk to her."

I grimaced. "Please don't say *magical seed* ever again in my presence."

She laughed before reaching up to squeeze my shoulder. "I mean it. I support you—no matter what. You know that, right?"

My heart swelled.

I didn't deserve friends like El. When I'd found her, she'd been a scared seventeen-year-old without direction who had just lost everything. Now, she'd grown into a force that never shied from fighting for me or kicking me when I needed a kick. She'd never once doubted me...

I nodded. "I know that."

Elsedora smiled before heading toward the balcony door. "I'll go make sure our Queen is prepared."

Hours later, people were gathered in the courtyard below; the bustle of chatter coated the air in excitement. Rust-colored flags had been handed out to the crowd along with Luz-blue ones. The balcony was adorned with both crests—the Sahlms' coiled rattling serpent and Luz's crown of thorns and acorns.

"I can't find her."

Ryn's whisper to Elsedora halted me before I could step out onto the balcony.

"Tell me you don't mean who I think you mean," I growled.

Ryn had one fucking job—get Sybilla from her room to the balcony.

My officials straightened, Ryn looking all too wide-eyed and Elsedora looking all too unconcerned. She knew something.

I pointed at El. "What did you do?"

"She's safe," Elsedora answered. "I promise."

I clenched my teeth. In just moments, I would address my people with the reassuring message of unification with the Central Corridor. I would tell them that we had allies in Henosis. And my said ally was unaccounted for.

Her safety mattered to me for many logistical reasons...but a different type of worry twisted in my gut.

A frustrated groan escaped my lips. "She better be alright—now, go get her."

"Well, I can't do that right *now*..." Elsedora grimaced.

I had an awful feeling that I would hate whatever happened next.

All the noise in the courtyard began to die down. The eerie quiet of whispers below made it easy to hear the thunder of my heartbeat. I stepped up to the balcony railing.

No one noticed me there. The crowd had turned, looking away from Umber House to the opposite side of the long courtyard.

At the back of the crowd, people began parting for someone on foot. I could have recognized that head of honey-blonde hair anywhere, and my chest clenched. Mumbling spread across the courtyard as they realized the Queen of the Central Corridor was on the ground among them. I gripped the railing.

Sybilla continued to walk through the parting crowd. She wore a rust-colored silk gown that left little to the imagination. Black embroidered thorny vines trailed their way up the train. The dark embroidery looked like my Shadows.

Meanwhile, two charmed bronze rattling snakes trailed her on the ground, lazily circling her whenever she stopped.

Every few feet, she approached members of the crowd, offering them her hand or crouching to allow smaller children to hug her.

Every person she interacted with seemed enthralled and taken with her—as though she were the sun and they basked in her attention. *Clever.* But I also knew it to be the most genuine part of this grand gesture. She *liked* speaking with them.

I'd have never approved of her entering the crowd, but the effect was overwhelming. Her show of trust, her calculated choice to be unarmed and unaccompanied, it all left my people in awe. With a mind like hers, she did not need weapons. It still made me nervous to see her down there alone.

"I'm very pissed off at you," I mumbled to Elsedora, who'd reached my side on the balcony.

Elsedora shrugged. "You don't stay mad long. Plus...it's the entrance we needed to sell this alliance. Look at her."

"I am," I answered.

Sybilla stopped in the center of the courtyard before glancing up at me.

I tilted my head down, watching as she turned to address the crowd in front of her.

"You do not know me," she yelled over the buzz of voices.

A wave of silence rippled around her.

"You don't know me," Sybilla repeated. "But you will. I am Queen Sybilla Wymark of Luz. I would like to tell you a story about the night your King saved my land. Would you like to hear it before I head up there?" She pointed to me on the balcony, and the people of my city let out a cheer of approval. She waited until the roar died down to speak again.

"I thought you might," she said, smiling in a way that, even from a distance, told me I was in deep trouble. I found myself stepping down onto one of the balcony steps just to get a better look at her profile.

She recounted the night in Luz like I was her hero despite having thought me the villain at the time. The captivated crowd remained silent. I held onto every word because in a different time, a different context, maybe I could have been everything the spun story made me out to be.

"And so, I fell in love with your King. It happened the moment I first set eyes on him. He appeared there on the wall of my palace as his men rescued my city from inevitable demise."

My head tilted, and a twitch started in my eye. What the fuck was she doing?

But the crowd was entranced—women swooned and men puffed out their chests and hollered up at the balcony with pride.

Sybilla motioned with her hands for them to be quiet. "Now, I prepare to give this realm my whole heart. You deserve every assurance that the Central Corridor will long remain an ally to the Sahlms. As part of our wedding vows, I promise to be as much your Queen as I am theirs."

She was a beautiful liar. I wanted to be upset, but no anger found me. A sense of terrified awe settled over me.

"Elsedora," I whispered, still not fully understanding what I was meant to do while she addressed my people about wedding vows I'd rescinded the offer of.

El's grip tightened on the railing, and she stepped beside me. "*That* part we hadn't discussed," she said with too much amusement. "But I can't pretend I'm disappointed."

"Now, although it has been a joy to spend time with you all, I will join my betrothed on the balcony," Sybilla called out before she was on the move again and cheers cut through the air. Ryn trotted down the stairs to help Sybilla past the guards at the bottom. Too stunned to think straight, I retreated to the top step.

Once Sybilla began to ascend, I could take her in fully. She looked good in Sahlms colors, and Elsedora had been right about one thing—she would be willing to stay. I hardened my expression, not wanting to acknowledge the flood of relief that brought me.

The bronze serpents slithered up the steps next to her, rattling and hissing at any guards that came too close. The snakes circled their way up her legs. One rested around her waist as a belt, the other kept slithering past her neck and then up to her head, coiling itself into her curls to become a crown. That one kept its eyes on me. Its tongue tasted the air as Sybilla approached.

A dark, terrible thrill washed over me.

She'd made a memorable entrance.

She wore our colors.

Our symbolic serpents adorned her.

And she claimed to be in love with me.

That last part turned my lips down into a frown.

When Sybilla reached me, she grabbed onto my arm before standing on tiptoes to kiss the side of my mouth. I closed my eyes, imagining that she meant what she had said, imagining a life where this wasn't all a facade.

The crown serpent rattled as her soft lips met my skin. I didn't move away. The charmed metal posed no threat, though it was quite the visual effect with them wrapped around her.

"What in the realms are you doing?" I asked softly against her cheek.

"You tried to send me away," she whispered back as she peered up at me like I'd offered her the world. For a moment, I believed that expression.

She said through the teeth of her demure smile, "Now stop looking constipated."

My brows rose at that.

"Better. Look at me like I'm the most beautiful woman you've ever seen, even though we both know I am not. I respect that, and I am truly sorry for what I said about her. That was unfair and unkind."

I let out a low growl of acknowledgment. Reluctantly, I let the hardness peel away and smoothed out my frown as much as possible. Taking in the curve of her neck where her hair met the gown's straps, my imagination wandered to pushing those straps down. I could manage lust. But I couldn't handle the warm flutter in my chest that her apology elicited.

"Not bad," she said as our gazes met. Her hand moved up to rub a gentle circle on my chest before she turned to face my people with a smile. The crowd had erupted—the Central Queen of Henosis, here, ready to be their Queen consort.

I'd barely noticed the commotion.

Sources, she was good. She'd outmaneuvered me, yet I couldn't bring myself to feel threatened.

"This is a lot of trouble to go through to marry a man you find insufferable." My words came out gruff as she took my hand and followed me to the center of the balcony.

There, she waved down at a small child who sat atop his father's shoulders. "You are one of few eligible men in the realms who seems both repulsed by the idea of marrying me *and* uninterested in taking anything away from me. Plus, you at least look more age-appropriate than Sheffield would."

I huffed a laugh at the last part.

She was built of contradictions—hardness where you expected something soft, softness where you expected something hard. Where some might have seen weakness, I saw a keen sense of self-preservation. The challenge of her had become exhilarating.

At least that's what I tried to convince myself of.

I liked verbally sparring with her.

I enjoyed her company enough that it wouldn't be a terrible match.

If only she knew all of the prophecy.

"I hope you realize what you're doing," I mused.

She'd left me little choice but to agree, at least while in public. Her choice to wear my colors, our public display of affection, our standing hand in hand now. The maids talked. It was likely already known around my court that we shared a bedchamber.

Turning her down here would only win me criticism from my own people for having offended a valuable ally.

I raised both of our hands. The crowd below bellowed, and flags waved wildly—a sea of rust and royal blue. I gently tugged her into Umber House.

I hadn't thought this day would end with me presenting a Queen consort to my people.

"The snakes were a nice touch," I noted as we slinked away from the bustle of the balcony and down a hallway.

Elsedora and Ryn remained behind to help the guards usher the people away from the estate in an orderly manner. Maids scattered about the halls, seeming to want both to eavesdrop out of curiosity and to flee at the sight of me. We needed somewhere quiet to speak.

"You told me the rattling serpent was your symbol because, unlike other snakes, they are typically docile and warn you before they attack. I identified with that."

I pulled her into an alcove for privacy, kicking the clay-potted citrus tree that was displayed there aside. My gaze searched hers for a clue as to where this rambling would go.

She continued, "I have lived in a city of snakes for a long time, Krait. My snakes just never gave me any warning before striking. So I've learned to adapt and do what is necessary."

"So what? You want to stay here indefinitely? Hide from your problems in Henosis?" I challenged.

She huffed a laugh. "Fuck no. I'll stay only until we have worked out the details. But this is my rattle of warning for *them*. If Emmerick and Bringham would like to unseat me, then I will make it harder for them."

I sighed. "You cannot spew venom at me and expect my kindness."

"I know. I misstepped—my words were horrid—but did they change anything you said in the South Tower? Did you mean it when you said you would fight for my Corridor?"

I clenched my fists, fighting against the urge to touch her. If she knew the true extent of her own power, she wouldn't be shackling herself to me for some false sense of security.

"Why marry me? I'd wage wars with you without a marriage contract," I said.

She swallowed hard. "Because the rulers in Henosis fear making an enemy of you. I'd like them to fear making an enemy of me, too. Also, I'm running out of time. If the central lords are leaning into old laws, then my right to rule ends in less than two years *if* I am unwed. If they don't find a loophole sooner."

"So you thought you'd just force my hand?" Blood pumped hot in my veins.

She glared up at me. "Admit it. It's the perfect arrangement. Neither of us has the petty desire to marry for love. You need me. I need you. That's all."

"What about heirs? Do you need those too?" I moved closer to her, shielding her from a few passing maids as she slumped against the stone wall of the alcove.

"Do *you*?" She turned the question back on me.

My jaw tightened. I caught her rubbing her wrists as though they bothered her.

With one hand resting on the wall beside her head, I leaned my weight into her space and studied her.

"I asked the question first."

She tilted her chin up. Shadows were cast over her features, but those emerald eyes could light up a room.

I longed to hate this idea, but it was growing more appealing by the minute.

"What type of breeding fantasies do you have, Darvanda?"

I scoffed. "Answer the question."

"Your heart belongs to another, and my heart belongs to no one," she continued. "Whatever physical *reaction* we have to one another does not need to be complicated but could be *helpful*. When the time comes." Her tone remained unaffected, but the way she bit her lower lip as she scanned my face gave her away.

That still didn't answer my question fully.

"Would you like to act on those *physical reactions,* Sybilla?" The question was too suggestive and expectant.

One's heart and one's physical desires could walk two separate paths and never meet. I could separate the two.

My lust for Sybilla grew into a thick, palpable weight in the air; it tore at my resolve to stay away. But my heart had long ago melted down into the wax that lit the candles around Freya's statue. It couldn't be reformed into anything worthwhile.

I focused on the way that silk dress hugged her hips.

"That would be irresponsible until you've agreed to keep your promise to marry me." She did not move away, and our foreheads felt drawn together by a string.

"It would be," I whispered into her mouth.

She'd forced my hand. But how perfectly had the pieces fallen together? I was skipping all the stones on the board at once.

One hand clenched at my side, the other against the wall. My Shadows had ideas of their own—they reached out and tangled around her as though cocooning her. Typically, they only touched to hurt, destroy or ruin. But, once again, they skated gently across her lower back, and she shivered and arched against their touch.

"What happened to 'no man setting his hands on me without my permission'?"

"Those aren't my hands. And what I said was, 'No one lays a finger on you unless you want them to.' Something tells me you are conflicted about what you want."

She finally broke eye contact, stifled a laugh and pulled away from me. The darkness that had begun to vine around her released and slithered back to me, seeming dejected.

"Well." Her tone returned to demure indifference. "You're wrong. There is no conflict. When the time comes for heirs, we'll discuss it. Because I do not just need them, I want them. Someday."

She made her way toward our bedchamber.

Sleeping on that cot was becoming more torturous each night. I'd tried to send her away. Now, I was accepting a marriage to keep her close.

I'd be a wreck before she was through with me.

CHAPTER 27

EMMERICK

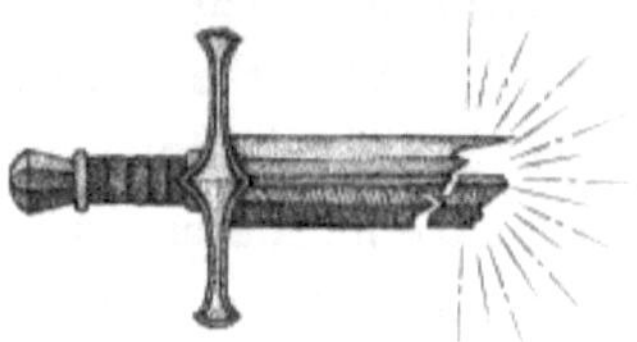

"**W**hat is on your agenda tonight?" Ryssa asked.

We were in the drawing room, and the light from the windows had begun to dim. Nighttime was a reprieve from the way that all the gold in the castle glistened in the sun.

"Ale," I answered easily.

She tilted her head as though she disapproved.

"Wine?" I tried again.

She motioned to the veil over her face. "Can't, I'm afraid."

"I can face away." I stood and grabbed two crystal glasses from a side table as well as a dusty bottle of wine. After uncorking it, I poured two glasses and handed her one. "Put your feet up that way," I said, instructing her to face away from me.

A waterlogged-sounding chuckle emitted from beneath the veil. "Fine...fine."

I sat next to her on the sofa, kicking off my boots before lifting my legs in the opposite direction and pulling my knees tight to fit there. We sat back-to-back. She was much shorter than I was, and her head rested between my shoulder blades.

As her weight pressed against me, I felt the rise and fall of her breath growing quicker. She shifted, and the veil caressed the back of my neck. My eyes closed at the friction of the fabric.

"Cheers," I said as I lifted the glass to my lips.

She took a deep breath and whispered, "Cheers, my King."

Her voice was hauntingly beautiful—velvety and strangely familiar. The temptation to turn, to see her, was so strong. I was certain that no burns or scars would prevent me from finding her breathtaking.

"You sound beautiful," I hummed.

I could feel her silent laugh. "Don't waste your energy charming a broken woman."

Using my elbow, I gently poked her rib cage. "You feel plenty whole to me."

She was quiet. We both sipped our wine and relaxed against each other. She finally cut through the silence. "Sometimes it isn't just the outer parts of a person that can be broken."

I sighed. "That is the saddest thing I've ever heard. But I understand."

Broken didn't quite cover how I felt. My sense of self withered. Where was the person who loved cooking dinner with his mother? The person who would stand by the people he loved unconditionally? I couldn't find him.

He'd been replaced by a wicked King who woke with ash-tipped fingers, who may have been capable of the murderous acts I'd witnessed at the pleasure hall...

Ryssa must have drained her wine because her voice was wispy and muffled when she spoke again. "The world is often a sad place." She shifted away from me.

Instinctually, I followed, turning forward and letting my socks hit the dark wood floor. Something possessed me to take her hand.

The warmth of her gloved palm in mine filled me with something—hope? Affection? I wasn't sure.

"I know the things that have broken me. What has broken you?" I asked.

She hesitated a moment and then said, "My upbringing was not what you might imagine of a noble woman's formative years. I wasn't born into a prosperous family—I had to work for my position, to rise through the ranks of this realm. All of the things I have done to get here..."

She paused, and I ran my thumb up and down her gloved knuckles. She wore a ring under the glove, which made me wonder—how much had she once lost? To my knowledge, she'd never mentioned a husband, and she seemed to own her own estate.

She cleared her throat. "I've made enough mistakes to fill a book—a thick one. I deserve every scar I wear. Sometimes the life you wish for leads you to places that later bring you shame."

"I'm sorry that life dealt you that hand. But I don't believe for a moment that you deserved it." The maroon void where her face should've been turned and stared at me. "Maybe things don't have to be so dreary forever."

I lifted her hand to my lips and placed a tender kiss on her palm. I imagined being able to look into her eyes.

"Doubtful," she answered. She abruptly pulled her hand away, stood, and headed for the door to the sitting room. "Beneath the veil, I am monstrous. I should be going, King Mattock."

Too forward, you idiot. My heart pounded, and I desperately wanted to take back the last thirty seconds.

"Wait, Ryssa," I said before she could get to the door.

She peered at me over a cloaked shoulder.

"Whatever is under that veil—it doesn't matter."

She stiffened.

"Forgive me for my advance," I continued. "But I have spoken to you enough to know that no person can be so kind on the inside and be anything but a joy to look upon."

She shook her head. "You are wrong. Goodnight, my King."

With that, she left the room, and I felt empty.

CHAPTER 28
SYBILLA

*D*ear Sybilla,

Sheffield and the Nadiars have sent letters agreeing to open their cities as a haven for Source-wielders to reenter, effective immediately. They state: "We do this in support of Queen Sybilla Wymark of the Central Corridor's long reign; we do this for unity and a prosperous future for our realm." All that will be required is proof of identity upon entry for appropriate record keeping. The use of magic within their borders is still, unfortunately, illegal under Henosis law. Changing that will require the agreement of all ruling parties.

It seems that not all is lost—but I brace you for the next news.

In response, Emmerick and Bringham made hostile moves this week, positioning troops along the northeastern and central borders. They have decreed that anyone from the ~~Wastelands~~ Sahlms setting foot on their land would be an act of war. The only safe travel routes are by Egress to the East, South or Central Corridors directly.

I hope you are well. I apologize in advance. Van dug up your rose bushes.

With love,

Asterie

I stared at the documents she sent along with the letter that committed to allowing Source-wielders access to more than half of Henosis. It wasn't enough. Why shouldn't they be allowed to use their powers within our realm?

I set Asterie's letter down. With a wince, I pulled on my leathers and a thin cream tunic. Inevitably, when Krait heard this news, there would be that clench in his stupidly handsome, chiseled jawline.

When I opened the bedchamber door, Ryn stood outside, fist raised as though he were about to knock. "Ready to get your ass kicked, Princess?"

I greeted his mile-wide smile with one of my own and nodded. "*Today* is the day I best you, friend."

My body felt like an unoiled metal gate, and I doubted my words.

My training sessions with Ryn and Krait had done nothing to help my growing pain. They'd begun drilling me on disarming them with my mind. Ryn ruthlessly teased me about my swordsmanship, which, admittedly, was not my greatest strength.

We were in the amphitheater, a place on the northern edge of the city where theater productions often put on shows. The space was empty today besides us. Thousands of marble seats towered around us as we stood in the "pit," an oval dirt arena below the upper stage.

I'd gotten Ryn to drop his sword twice out of my countless attempts, and Krait not once. There had been no moment of clarity like I'd felt over the gameboard, just roiling wild power that I had little control over.

While my body revolted, my mind felt *strong*. If I could just pinpoint how to wield it, then I'd be devastating.

"Again," I panted and lifted the wooden sword at Ryn, preparing to block.

Ryn shook his head. "That's enough—you look like you'll fall over if I strike again."

I probably would fall over. It was becoming my new go-to move, and my whole body trembled from the day's effort and the heightening heat of the late morning sun.

Krait watched us from a metal gate, where he was leaning with one foot up behind him on the steel. He scowled, and I couldn't help but wonder if he noticed how my legs wobbled beneath me. As predicted, the news from the Corridors had not sat well with him.

I growled a curse under my breath, but kept the sword raised. "Come on, Ryn. Will Caym or his envoys give me breaks just because I am tired?"

"She has a point," Krait chimed in. "How about you Source-wield at her instead?"

I glared at him, and he responded with a slight lift at the corners of his mouth. *Prick.*

Ryn blew silver hairs from his eyes, and pointed the wooden sword at my head. "I am not Caym," he responded. "And if I were, you'd be dead by now because you are shit with that sword and shit at disarming us."

The Prince formed a white orb in his palm, bright as the moon itself, only condensed and ebbing. He threw it up playfully once before chucking it at me.

Using my moment of distraction as I ducked, he charged, his sword outstretched.

His diversion worked to set me off balance. But I channeled my rage and found the thread of his mind that would allow me in.

Weaving around the places I knew he could detect me, I struck at the back entrance to his thoughts.

"Sources!" He braced against it, but his weapon fell from his hands and every muscle in his body froze mid-charge. He grimaced, trying to escape my mental attack. I had control over *everything*. Every one of his senses and actions.

Light formed in his palms. Ryn's eyes widened as he turned toward Krait and threw two beams of white light toward him. Krait straightened and quickly outstretched his hands. Shadows consumed the moonlight. Ryn's power surged through me. I felt drunk off it—a fun sort of wine drunk.

"The fuck, Ryn?" Krait growled.

Ryn managed to cut through my hold on him enough to say, "It wasn't me!"

I smirked. "I don't need to be good with a sword." When I dropped my mental hold on Ryn, he sank to his knees, and I stumbled to mine next to him.

Sources, that took so much out of me, but it felt divine.

Krait approached us as Ryn looked over at me with labored breath.

"You're terrifying." Ryn shook his head with a smirk. "I tried my hardest to fight you."

"Good," I said, shifting my weight to one side, wanting to lie down right there in the sand and sleep. Fatigue tugged at me. I felt like a rag doll. But without the tonics and mind-clouding remedies, my mind's abilities thrived.

How long could I maintain this without breaking?

If anyone had noticed my movement growing stiffer, no one had said anything. Some days, it hurt just to put weight on my feet. On other days, my finger joints felt like rusted hinges.

"You wielded another's Source power," Krait drawled, finally seeming impressed.

I nodded and took a swig from the canteen I kept at my waist before sitting back on my heels.

"It offends me that you seem so surprised." I finally let my ass collapse into the sand.

Ryn did the same beside me, and my head fell onto his shoulder. "Carry me back to Umber House?"

Ryn chuckled. "No way—I don't want to be Shadow pulp."

I waved up at Krait. "Him? Why would he care?"

Krait crossed his arms, glaring down at us like we were an inconvenience despite the fact he chose to be here.

"Because of *that* look," Ryn teased.

I snuck into the King of the Sahlms' head. His thoughts wandered to carrying me back to Umber House himself and then down into the underground baths. He imagined flashes of peeled fabric and revealed flesh.

For once, the heat offered me a reprieve; there was no way in the realms I wasn't deeply flushed from having intruded on the fantasies in that man's head.

So he wasn't as unimpacted by that encounter in the library as he'd been pretending. I could use that.

"You look like shit," Krait said. *Pleasant.* "Take tomorrow off from training. I have business to attend to with the lords and will be back late."

I searched his stare and then lifted my chin toward Ryn, who shook his head, unwilling to disobey his King's order. "Fine...I will occupy myself then. Maybe with a *nice, long* soak in the bath. *Alone.*"

Ryn appeared, rightfully, confused, but Krait's brow quirked up with interest.

"You do that," he grated out.

CHAPTER 29
EMMERICK

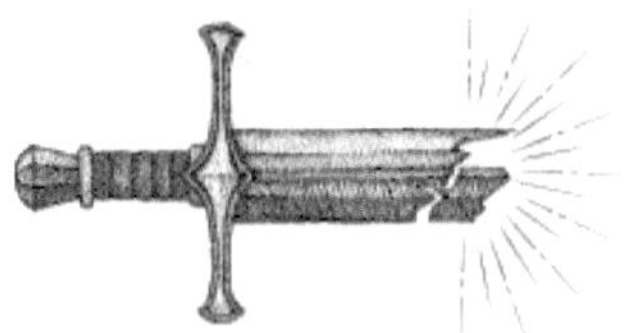

It was late. I couldn't sleep, so my hands busied themselves, polishing Sybilla's blade as my mind wandered.

I needed to rename this fucking sword. It seemed awkward to own a weapon named after a former lover while my mind thought so frequently of someone else.

A crown that I didn't want lay on a velvet cloth on the desk before me. Of course, it shined gold and was lined with gaudy black gemstones—the most hideous thing I'd ever seen. It mirrored the one that the late Mattock's ashes were entombed with.

A knock came at the door.

"Come in," I said as I palmed the hilt of my soon-to-be-renamed sword. Maybe I would name it Bryanna, or Chrysteen, or Thorne, or...

"Elsedora?"

"Shoo!" Fenris' sister swatted away a sniffing Lynx as though it were merely a house cat. She swaggered into the room and touched countless priceless things as she entered. I swore she might have pocketed something.

"Hello, puppy."

"Would you stop calling me that?" I ground out.

She smirked. "Sorry—*Your Majesty*."

I ran a hand down my face. Fenris' sister was bold and too much like him. She lacked a certain subtlety that I liked in a woman; today, her leather corset was laced in the front with nothing beneath it, exposing her down to her navel. I tried not to let my eyes wander.

"Fine. Call me whatever suits you."

Wondering why she was here, I nodded to the chair across the desk from me. Her visits were becoming worrisome.

Whatever she'd come for today couldn't be good news. I'd angered Sybilla at the last council meeting. It had been as though the words were both mine and not, and I was falling into alliances I'd never expected or *wanted*. Yet I couldn't retake the reins.

I waited for Elsedora to tell me that the Sahlms would wage war on the North, but she didn't say anything. Instead, she kept looking around and running her hands over things as though searching for something.

"Who let you in this time? I assume you used the Egress."

Instead of sitting in the chair, she rounded my desk and sat on it, right in front of me. "Your Egress guards are easy to distract. And *incredibly* horny. You should let them out more. Panting dogs—the lot of them."

I snorted and pushed my chair back to put distance between our thighs. "Who do I owe thanks to for this visit?"

"King Darvanda."

My jaw tightened. "Sounds like a lie."

"Only in part. Queen Sybilla sent me, too. She is worried about you after that...*display* at the council meeting and your decision to position troops at other Corridors' borders." She reached out to touch the tip of the blade I'd retired from polishing and had set on the desk.

"That's also a lie—she's pissed, and she sent you to scold me."

She smirked again; her eyes shined with mischief. "No scolding. Unless you'd like that. But you may want to remain seated for this next part."

I sighed. "Try me."

Elsedora picked up my sword and spun the hilt in her hand, assessing the weapon with eagle-like intensity.

"Queen Sybilla is betrothed."

I swallowed hard, wishing I'd misheard her. It wouldn't be the first time I'd heard similar news. Sybilla had almost married three times. She had a reputation for never making it down the aisle.

I shrugged. "Who agreed to *that*?"

Elsedora continued to stare at the blade in her hand.

Maybe letting her remain armed was unwise, but a self-destructive instinct had taken over me. It might be for the best if she ran me through the heart now, before whatever evil there grew.

"My King," she answered.

"Quit joking," I scoffed.

"I'm not. It's a wise alliance, and they know it. None of the other royals will side with you if the Heir of Shadows could come knocking on their door."

I shot up from my chair and began to pace. "She wouldn't."

"She would. She is," Elsedora said gently.

My breath heaved out of me, hands shaking.

I'd pushed Sybilla too far.

"She could not love me one moment and marry *him* the next."

"So you think it was love." Her eyes narrowed on the hilt of my sword, at the pommel, before she added, "Love is a sacrifice of freedom, one you are happy to make. Do you feel like you both thought each other worthy of such a sacrifice?"

"That's an awful way to view love," I answered.

"Is it?" She offered me a pitying smile. "What are you willing to sacrifice for your Queen?"

"She isn't mine," I ground out.

"And whose fault is that?"

I glared at her. "That's complicated."

She took my sword by its blade and handed me the hilt.

"It isn't really," she said. "Love doesn't come with the freedom to choose when it is convenient. Love defies logic and complexity. There isn't anything you could do to stop it or dull it or walk away from it."

"Leave my castle," I growled. Elsedora stilled, her palms planted on the desk.

"Have I hit a nerve, puppy?" she asked.

I was seething—not at her, but at the underlying cut of her words. Sybilla had always kept me at arm's length when it had suited her and close when she'd needed me most...Was love a series of convenient distractions alone in the dark where no one else could see us? I'd wanted more than that.

"What makes you an authority on love?"

She smiled weakly. "My parents had that kind of unconditional love. You only dislike what I'm saying because there is some truth in it. It's okay to dislike me for that. Eventually, you'll find someone that turns your world upside down. Someone who you would walk through fire to stand beside, no matter the circumstance."

"You don't know me at all."

She tilted her head, assessing me. "No. But I know me, and you don't seem so different. Fenris has told me your parents—the ones who raised you—are very much in love."

A chill crept over me. Admitting that I didn't love Sybilla felt like a betrayal. But to whom?

Elsedora jumped down from my desk.

"What's in it for him? Why does he want to marry her?" I asked—not knowing whether I could handle the answer.

Elsedora shook her head. "My King rarely reveals his motives. He isn't going to hurt her, though—that much, I assure you. He isn't the monster this realm makes him out to be."

I hated the parts of me that wished he *would* hurt her. Anger had been boiling inside of me ever since I'd taken the northern crown. What kind of person wished harm on their best friend? Threatened to take their crown by force?

I stood and stepped beside Elsedora, sheathing the sword at my hip.

"Your eyes..." Elsedora noted, watching my face too closely. "They were a very pretty shade of gold when I arrived, but they are a dark green now."

That cool, dark feeling began to envelop me. "It's time for you to leave."

"But—" she tried.

"Go!" I shouted, and Elsedora flinched—seeming startled for the first time. Her nonchalant mask cracked as my face curled into a scowl.

"Very well," she said, before pulling an expensive-looking golden egg that had been on my shelf from her pocket and dropping it on my desk. She quickly left the room.

I kneeled on the floor and closed my eyes. Then, the darkness descended and whisked me away.

Visions visited me. Memories.

But they were not mine. I saw through someone else's eyes.

We were in the gilded Helos throne room again. Amara was before me, her stomach round and cheeks glowing under the golden lamplight.

Me—she carried me in her womb.

Then she said, "Why must it be this way, Corric? Please...Do you not wish to know our child?"

"Amara," a voice not unlike my own answered. "It isn't safe for even you here..."

"But why? Please tell me why."

"I cannot."

Light footsteps drew near the throne room door.

"King Mattock, are you in there?" Firose sang from the hall.

Amara's eyes widened, the whites showing all the way around.

"Go," Corric said to her. "Hide the child—from her, from me. Do whatever it takes. I am lost, Amara. I am lost."

I was lost.

So very lost.

CHAPTER 30
SYBILLA

Dusk darkened the bedchamber. I hadn't seen Krait all day. Begrudgingly, I'd taken the day off from training, but his absence had done nothing to clear my mind. Krait and Ryn were right about my needing rest—I felt weighed down by bricks and had been unable to get out of bed until well into the afternoon.

After the announcement of our engagement, the maids had removed the cot. I stared at the two leather chairs, now returned to their spot in the cot's place.

I'd agreed to let Krait sleep in the bed rather than on the floor. With pillows between us.

It hadn't mattered. He refused to enter the room while I was awake. The only evidence of him this morning had been a rumpled pillow.

It was for my own good.

I'd been mentally undressing the King of the Sahlms since having arrived here. Part of me wanted to get the inevitable over with. We'd eventually fall into our marriage bed, and I wanted to be headed back to Luz with an heir on the way sooner rather than later.

That was what I wanted, wasn't it?

A lump grew in my throat at the thought, unable to imagine a child growing inside of me, unable to picture myself holding a swaddled babe in my arms. Stuck between an ache for that future, and my anxiety toward it, I was glad for the time alone.

I needed to get out of the bedchamber, so I decided to spend my evening scouring the tomes in Krait's *hole*. Still in my robe and slippers, I carried on down the hall and into the cool, dim library.

I'd never been bookish, but something about putting together pieces of a puzzle appealed to me.

There were three envoys.

Killing them could delay Caym's path of destruction...

Not an option.

Not if Emmerick was one of them.

Trailing a finger over the leather and canvas spines, I sighed. I spent time leafing through texts. The floor became littered with dusty tomes.

I could read a bit of Phynnic, but most of the books were in Brennac and therefore useless to me. One Phynnic volume caught my attention. I stepped up on the library ladder and reached for the dust-saturated green linen cover.

Stepping down to sit on the chaise, I opened the volume in my lap. As soon as I did, the pages began flipping themselves. I gasped and raised my hands away from the book.

The pages came to a halt as though something was guiding my reading to a specific section.

The Sethe Curse

To curse any soul to wakeless sleep. When cast, one must premeditate a length of time for the cursed to rest. The cursed must be awakened before their time expires, or they will remain forever asleep.

Glancing around, I wondered what magical interference had just occurred, but sensed no threat here.

My mind reeled with the possibilities. What if we could trap Caym with this curse? My chest clenched. That might mean subjecting Emmerick to the same fate.

The bell tower above rang eight times.

I hugged the text to my chest and carried it back to the bedchamber.

Entering the empty room, I ground my teeth as I kicked off my leather slippers. The cool, multi-colored terrazzo tile against my swollen feet was a relief.

Why was I disappointed Krait wasn't waiting here?

I hid the tome beneath my side of the bed.

***

After tossing for hours, I gave up on sleep.

I swiped a bottle of port and a chalice from the desk and padded out of the room. The ache in my hands and feet needed dulling.

I could push through...

The hallway was dark, but sconces lit the tile walls just enough to allow my vision to adjust. Umber House was much quieter at night than the Palace of Luz. Outside of a few guards, most staff here did not live in the residence and returned to the city at night. I wandered, poking my head into the drawing room, the kitchenette, the throne room.

I passed the door to the bell tower quarters. Surely it wouldn't be easy to unlock.

I backtracked—testing the doorknob. Locked.

Surely Krait would be in here. "In the Shadows we trust." At my whisper, the deadbolt clicked, and the door creaked open.

"Krait?" I called. No answer.

Curiosity won out, and I slipped inside the room.

There were so many candles. That was the first thing I noticed. I saw a spiral staircase to my right, which I assumed led up to the bell. Then my gaze landed on a platform to my left with hundreds of dancing flames around it. A fire-lit form hovered over me.

I jumped, spilling some wine from the chalice, before realizing the form was made of bronze.

Just a statue. I breathed a sigh of relief.

The craftsmanship captured every detail of her delicate hands, which reached out toward a crescent moon. Her hair was braided back at the crown and the rest hung loose over her shoulders, catching the non-existent wind.

Freya.

I recognized her face from the portrait in Krait's library—also it so resembled Ryn's.

A pang of grief settled in my chest. If she'd been anything like her brother, then the lands had lost a ruler worth mourning. A candle beside her foot had blown out, so I set down the bottle and picked up a candle to relight it.

"It's no wonder you won the heart of such a surly asshole. You're breathtaking," I whispered to the woman in brass. There was a foot-stool that looked meant for kneeling. Groaning, I lowered myself onto it and straightened the cream-colored robe around my knees.

I tipped the chalice of port up toward Freya in silent acknowledgment before taking a drag. The flicker of candles held my attention. What would she have accomplished by now had she not been beheaded?

It was known that the last Princess of Phynx had fallen out of favor with her father just before the attack on their kingdom. Likely for some bullshit reason or another—that was always the way with royal men.

I didn't know what compelled me to say, "My mother was beheaded too. I was there when they—"

This was the silliest fucking thing I'd ever done—talking to a dead woman as if the spirits cared about our living struggles.

I sighed and continued, "I was fourteen. I've never spoken of it. It seemed easier not to mourn her when everyone else was so angry with her. To show sympathy would have just turned their wrath toward me. It was rumored that she had committed adultery."

I took another gulp of port; the drink meant to be sipped was being thoroughly chugged.

"I knew they were wrong."

Freya seemed to gaze down on me, egging me on.

"The last words she ever said to me were 'Don't have children, Sybilla,' which I obviously took as an insult. But then she said, 'The world will only serve them disappointment.' Funny, isn't it?"

Even still, part of me longed for a palace full of laughter, full of love. Yet each time I had been presented with a suitable betrothal...I couldn't go through with it.

"That's the furthest thing from funny that I've ever heard," a grave voice answered from the darkness behind me. Fucking Shadow traveler. My veins were so warm from the port that my reaction time was lacking—his presence hadn't even startled me.

I huffed and set the chalice down on the ground before leaning back on my palms. "Why?" I challenged.

"Because true or not, that is a shit thing to say to a child."

"Now we're berating the dead?"

He grunted and crossed the room to relight another candle that had blown out. "No—I just mean that you shouldn't have had to hear, or see, any of that."

"Ah, so you've been eavesdropping the whole time then." I shrugged, watching the muscles of his arms as he set the candle back down on the mantle. "Life is not all rainbows and sunsets, is it? My mother wasn't wrong. Bringing children into the world is to hold confidence in the future. She held no such confidence."

Krait was silent, his hand still held the candle. He seemed uncomfortable with my being here, yet he didn't ask me to leave.

"She was beautiful," I said.

He hummed, but glanced away from the flames. "She was."

The room was rather dreary, with thick drawn curtains. There was minimal furniture aside from a desk on the far side, which had a glass case on top of it that housed a large tome.

It was no place to honor the dead.

I wished for more light for her, for her to see the moon that she'd once commanded.

Krait cut through my thoughts. "You speak of children as though you've made up your mind against them. Yet you told your cousin that you'd have a dozen children to keep him off your throne—is that what you actually want?"

I wondered why he was asking and tried to slip through the back door of his mind. Either he really wanted to keep his thoughts to himself, or I was too exhausted to push through.

"Nice try." He confirmed my latter suspicion.

I let my head rest on my shoulder. "I want to secure my Corridor's safety—to know that there is someone to rule when I die. But that seems like a terrible reason to bring a child into the world. Sometimes it sounds nice. Marriage, children, grandchildren, a palace full of laughter for generations to come...but that laughter isn't guaranteed, is it? Any heir of mine would be born shackled to a crown they may or may not even want."

Biting the side of my cheek, I realized I'd never voiced that fear before to anyone.

He remained guarded and hard to read.

"Is that how you feel? Shackled to your crown?" he asked.

"Am I being interrogated for something?" *I was too tired for this.*

He sighed. "You're in a quarter you shouldn't be in, drunk, chatting with my dead wife—I'm not interrogating you. I'm trying to understand you."

When he put it that way, I knew I didn't have the moral high ground in this argument. "Fine—yes. I have often resented my position, resented my parents. That does not mean that I don't love my people or that I will not continue to do everything in my power to protect them."

He made a sound that resembled a grunt of agreement. "We have that in common."

Thinking that was the end of this bizarre conversation, I grabbed the bottle of port and the chalice and poured another glass. Rising and stepping up beside him, I extended it to him.

"Does marrying me change your view on having children?" The question came out blunt as he took a long sip of the port I offered him.

With wine-loosened lips, I answered, "Here we go with the breeding fantasies again."

He smirked.

"Any children we conceived would be both Reverist and Source-wielder, would they not?"

"Reverist and Source Origin," he corrected.

My brows lifted. "How could that be? I thought *you* were the Origin."

The candlelight warmed his otherwise cold gray irises as he met my stare. I wasn't sure when my hatred for him had begun to melt away. Something about being under his gaze now made my stomach flutter in a stupid, reckless way.

"When Caym led the Reverists to betray the other Origins, his brother, the Shadow Origin, Desidero, bargained with him for his life. Caym agreed, but he didn't want Desidero to ever grow strong enough to be a threat to him. He let him live but under a curse."

My head tilted as he backed away from Freya's altar and motioned for me to follow him to the desk, where the glass case sat, a giant text within it with frayed binding.

"That curse meant that Desidero and his descendants would each only have one child. Upon doing so, they pass the role of Origin and their immortality down to their only heir, and their power slowly transitions to their child. It was my twentieth birthday when my father wielded his last Shadow."

I balked. "You will become mortal if you have a child? That...that is..." I stammered before shaking my head.

"That is what is necessary," he mused with a sad smile.

I shook my head again, unwilling to believe what he was saying. "That is quite a sacrifice. And if it makes you feel better, it is not one I would require you to make. I can find another way—someone willing to..."

His brow knitted and his fists clenched as though I'd misstepped.

"There is another caveat..." He looked down at the glass case. The tome beneath it was leather bound, and the cover was carved in a language I did not know. "This is the true *Book of Isolde*, the one that names you in its prophecy. My ancestors long ago discerned meaning from the texts that I've been reading you."

Stepping up to the glass, I instinctually raised my fingers to the cool pane. "What does that have to do with anything?"

He opened the glass and carefully flipped to a page he seemed to have memorized. "This here, it reads: 'You must listen, Fifth Heir of Desidero: Find the Last Daughter of my dearest Isleen. The heir you bear together will be both Origin and Reverist. Your child is the key to ending Death's reign—the key to setting us all free.'"

It didn't immediately sink in. I could feel the crease in my brow as I stared at the section he pointed to, unable to read it. My arms crossed over my chest. I searched my thoughts for why this sounded familiar.

His words when he'd told me he was the Shadow Origin. He was the fifth heir of Desidero.

I gasped out, "You? And me?" Taking a step back to put distance between us, I looked him up and down. "You have read me this passage before, and that is not what you said."

He stood there with his arms at his sides as my composure evaporated. Between the port and my growing fatigue, I could barely stay standing. The whole room spun.

He said nothing—no denial, no remorse...

"You knew...you brought me here knowing."

He shook his head. "I didn't know at first, didn't think it could possibly be you."

"What did you intend to do?" I couldn't help the hurt from creeping into my voice as I backed away from him. "Did you...Were you going to force me to—"

"No," he growled. "I told you—no one touches you if you do not want them to. Including me. I have never lied to you."

My back hit the door, and I reached for the knob.

"Lying and withholding important truths are two of a kind. So urces...you have played me for a fucking fool."

It felt like a dagger in my chest was being twisted. I hated that this was what I'd done to Em—I'd withheld so much for far longer.

Krait looked up at the ceiling for a moment before pinching the bridge of his nose. "I was scared."

Krait being scared of anything seemed like a ridiculous concept. "*Scared?* You can't expect me to believe that. Scared of what?"

"I lost everything," he said and waved his arm toward Freya's statue. "From birth, I was prepared for this. But it was always supposed to be with her. Then she died, and I couldn't imagine carrying out the prophecy without her. We'd always planned to raise my heir together."

It was preposterous. I'd walked right into it...

He'd intended to raise his heir with Freya regardless of who I'd been.

I reeled for balance and white-knuckled the doorknob.

"And what of this heir now, what would we do? Raise them together and split their time between Luz and Sahlmsara? When were you planning to discuss this?"

The only thing that kept me hovering at the door was my desire to believe Krait was better than all the horrible assumptions of him running through my mind.

He took a deep breath. "Until meeting you, I'd never considered your involvement."

My free hand impulsively found its way to my neck—visions of what had happened to my mother surfaced.

Disposable.

Removable from the situation.

A husband who grew tired of me.

An heir who resented me for the heavy crown they wore.

I'd heard enough. I stepped out and slammed the door behind me. What he'd admitted was a gut-wrenching reminder that he could not be trusted.

Krait Darvanda may not have been the enemy I'd once imagined him to be, but he'd intended to use me and that crumbled my prior confidence that his motives were altruistic.

Bile rose in my throat as I thought about the ways I'd opened myself up to him already. I'd agreed to marry the bastard before knowing he'd deemed me a broodmare—before knowing my fate fully. And he'd *let me*.

With shaking hands and a drunken gait, I forced myself down the hall.

I didn't know where to go. Halfway back to the bedchamber, Elsedora found me.

She wasted no time with pleasantries and grabbed my hands. "The deathmark—it is on King Emmerick's broadsword. Right on the pommel," she gasped. "I saw the light leave his eyes, and the transition happened right before me. Something is *very* wrong in Helos. King Mattock no longer acts entirely of his own accord."

"Did you hurt him? Did he hurt you?" I sputtered.

"No, of course not. I'm fine. But Sybilla, you cannot go near him. Promise me. Not until we figure out a way to rid him of Caym."

I grew dizzy. El held my shoulders to steady me. Maybe the swaying was from the port, or my waning health, or the shock of having my worst fears confirmed.

Every stone of a carefully built tower was coming crashing down around me. Yet the puzzle was snapping together.

I was a daughter of Isleen.

Krait was the fifth heir of Shadows.

Our child could stop the Death Origin.

The Death Origin had his grasp on Emmerick.

I swallowed hard.

I should have insisted we went straight to Krait...but propriety was lost to me now. After what Krait had told me, my respect for his boundaries had worn thin as glass.

He expected a child? I expected safety for all of my loved ones.

We needed to help Emmerick. We needed to stop the Death Origin before it was too late.

I knew my friend. Even angry, Emmerick would not betray me without outside influence. He would not turn on me the way he had in that council meeting.

But was it already too late? That was a doubt that I didn't allow myself to linger on. The King of the Sahlms might have deceived me, but he could still be useful for the time being.

Strong strategies could sometimes take root in soft soil. I didn't trust this realm or its ruler. But I did trust that he would keep me safe...until I gave him what he wanted.

Tears rolled down my cheeks, and El squeezed my arm with raised brows. I crumbled, bending at the waist. "Maybe we should ask King

Darvan-dick what to do. He seems to have *plenty* of plans I have not been privy to."

"He told you."

Elsedora's thoughts raced. *"Oh shit. She's going to leave."*

"I'm not leaving. *Yet,*" I said, answering her internal worry.

El's whole body slackened in relief. "I told him to tell you weeks ago." She sighed. "You must understand—we have been searching for you for so long. It killed me not to be able to share the truth with you sooner, but as you know, he's a dick when his mind's set on something."

I smiled weakly through tears. "For the time being, can I please stay in your quarters? If not, I may smother him in his sleep."

"Of course," she answered while brushing a tear from my cheek with her thumb.

We walked through the halls arm in arm. Fenris' sister could be flighty, but one thing she wasn't was cruel or scheming. The hope in her voice when she'd spoken of searching for me warmed my cold shock.

I may have been part of some grand plan for Krait, but Elsedora cared about some of the people closest to me and that was a link in a chain I wouldn't easily break over a man's dishonesty.

Other people's lives were at stake.

CHAPTER 31
KRAIT

A note had been slipped under the bedchamber door when I arrived back that night.

Sybilla is safe but shaken. She's sleeping in my quarters tonight. I'm proud of you for telling her—she'll come around. I know it.

-El

It felt wrong not to see the Central Queen curled up in my bed. Most nights, I slipped in after she'd fallen asleep. The rise and fall of her breathing and her little nose whistle had begun to be what lulled me to sleep, and it was hard to drift off without her here.

The look on her face when she'd realized what I'd kept from her had been like a punch to my gut. Before leaving the bell tower quarters, I'd grabbed my list from the drawer, and I scanned it now as I sat up in bed.

The distance between her strengths and faults had shrunk. She came off bullish, but there was a vulnerability to her I'd seen time and time again. There was only one thing that I could possibly add to the list.

VIII. Not ready

How could she be? She'd been failed by the people meant to protect her, by a system in Luz that expected her to marry, and by me, who'd kept the truth from her for far too long. There would be no way she could overcome that. I'd broken the thin layer of trust I'd built.

After shuffling out of bed and crossing the room, I pulled open the bottom drawer of the vanity and shoved the parchment inside. My fists clenched, and I wanted nothing more than to storm into Elsedora's chamber and make Sybilla talk to me. But that would do no good for either of us.

Instead, I returned to bed to lie on top of the sheets and let the musky, sweet scent of vanilla, tea and lilac envelop me until my eyes grew heavy enough for me to doze.

Sleep was only a temporary reprieve. Hours later, I stared at the dark wood beams of my bedchamber ceiling, trying to will myself to go back to sleep before the sun rose and woke me.

No use.

Groaning, I swung my feet out of bed and ran a hand over my face. After dressing in a brown tunic and dark breeches, I combed my hair and kicked on my boots.

Dawn could only be a few hours away, so I decided to start my day early. The candles in the bell tower wouldn't relight themselves, and Sybilla's accusations weighed heavy on my conscience. "Would you have just left Freya to fend for herself against Death?"

I had let Freya die.

My selfish desire to marry her, to deviate from the prophecy, to build some delusional life had killed her.

By pulling Sybilla into this web, I'd endangered her too. That made my throat constrict.

It wasn't the same.

Freya could have risen to power in Phynx. She could have changed the realms for the better if I'd only left her alone.

Not letting myself linger on those thoughts, I exited my bedchamber and headed toward the east quadrant stairs. Before I'd reached the bell tower, I heard the patter of someone jogging down the hall.

"Krait!" Her tone jolted me. With a robe haphazardly pulled over a nightdress, as though she'd been torn from sleep, Elsedora reached me.

"What happened?" Panic spiked through the dullness of my exhaustion.

"It's Sybilla."

My stomach dropped.

El continued, "She is burning up. I woke to her whimpering—I already called a healer; she is on her way up."

"Sybilla's alone?"

"No—I found Ryn first. He is with her now. But hurry." She pushed me down the dark hallway. The distance to El's quarters felt miles long, even though it was only a few yards away.

Elsedora rambled. "I shouldn't have told her about Emmerick, about the deathmark. I found it on his sword's pommel. What if the stress was her undoing?"

"El," I grated out. I didn't have time to react to the confirmation of Mattock being an envoy. "Mortals get sick. She will be alright." Despite my justification, my heart raced.

By the time we got to the door, Ryn was speaking with the healer. "What is that for?" he asked, gesturing to a vial.

"This will help bring down her fever," the healer answered.

"Why does she have a fever?" I growled out as I entered the room.

Elsedora couldn't help but prod me with, "What happened to 'mortals get sick—she will be alright'?"

Sybilla lay asleep—if whatever her restless, trembling and labored breath state could be considered sleep. Dark circles had formed under her eyes, and her hair was slicked back with sweat at the temples. Just by looking at her, it was easy to see she was far from *alright*.

"Why is she so sick?" I demanded.

The healer, a shorter woman with thick blonde hair and brown eyes, grimaced at my words.

I needed to work on my tact.

"There are many reasons a mortal can fall ill. Most of her symptoms are completely normal of a common fever. Did Queen Wymark arrive with any records of health? Was she taking any remedies or tonics?" she asked.

It wasn't something we'd ever thought about or considered. *The vials.* Remembering the green liquid spilled across the floor when she'd been attacked caused me to curse.

"We don't have any records." The fact I'd missed something so obvious made me want to throw something. "She'd been taking something. It was a green liquid. She didn't mention what."

The healer nodded. "Right now, she needs rest, fluids and tonics to control her fever. Do you have a way of tracking down what she was regularly taking? It could have been helping her ward off illness if she's prone to spells like this. She could recover more quickly if she started taking it again."

Elsedora added, "When she was awake, she said she hurt and needed Emmerick. It was mostly incoherent, but I caught that much."

Shaken, I clenched my fists and said, "I'll be back."

"Krait, where are you going? Please don't say Helos."

I hummed a response and stormed out of the room.

The sight of the sweat on Sybilla's brow, the paleness of her cheeks aside from the rash across her face, and her miserable expression pulled me apart.

But I wasn't the comfort she wanted, and if she'd asked for Emmerick, it meant he would know how to help her.

I only hoped that enough of him remained to see reason and that he'd tell me what she needed.

I didn't want to risk draining my energy by Shadowing the full way to Helos, not with the risk of Caym controlling Mattock. When the Egress dropped me into Helos Castle, guards flocked the hall, but I traveled through the Shadows too quickly for them to get a look at me. Lynx snarled and tried to leap at me, but I skirted them too.

Despite it being before dusk, I found the North King at his desk, writing a letter. Even though I was already in his room, I knocked on the door behind me to announce myself.

Mattock's head snapped up; his gaze hardened, but there was a gold ring in his irises. A good sign. He abruptly got to his feet.

"Entering my Corridor uninvited is an act of war, Darvanda" he barked. "I have already told your officer that."

I raised both palms to reveal I had no weapons. "It's Sybilla. She's sick. Who am I speaking with right now?"

His expression turned from indignation to concerned confusion. He assessed me. "What are you talking about? And how sick?"

"Fever, chills—she can't stay conscious."

Mattock nodded but did not seem shocked. "For how long?"

My arms dropped to my sides as I said, "It came on quickly...so metime through the night."

I glanced around for Mattock's broadsword. I wondered how near it needed to be for Caym to reach him, or whether it worked like that at all. We didn't understand enough about how Caym was infiltrating his envoys.

"She asked for you," I ground out. "What should we do for her?"

Mattock grimaced. "Has she been taking Mortag's tonics?"

My posture slumped. "No. What does she take them for?"

Mattock breathed out as though exasperated with me. He had every right to be. I'd allowed his former Queen to grow ill. I hadn't known what to look for. Those broken vials had been important, and I'd failed to piece it together.

"She struggles with ongoing pain and inflammation. She takes tonics to help reduce it. Go to Healer Mortag in Luz. He has cared for her since she was a girl. He'll have the right tonics," he sighed out. "She gets sick frequently. Her body isn't as good as others' at fighting off common illnesses, especially if she's been under any stress. It isn't something she likes many people to know. She views it as something that could be used against her claim over the Central Corridor."

At each revelation, the knot growing in my throat thickened. He knew so much about her—so much about how to care for her. He hadn't even sounded smug as he'd unveiled her deepest anxieties, only downtrodden.

I'd been so careless.

Part of me wanted to strike him for contributing to her stress. But in the months she'd been under my roof, she had been confronted by one obstacle or piece of bad news after another. His being an envoy—it wasn't even his fault.

I could only grow angrier at myself.

"Thank you," I ground out and retreated toward the shadows.

Emmerick's jaw tightened. "Congratulations on your betrothal. If she's let you anywhere near her while she's sick, there must be something redeeming about your character." The sentiment was clipped but seemingly sincere.

It burned at my sense of pride that she hadn't come to me at all. The straightening of his posture and the light dimming in his eyes told me his next words might not be his own. There were footsteps outside the door.

"We'll be back to deal with you..." I said to Caym as dark-green smoke and amber flecks filled Mattock's irises.

At my parting words, a chilling smile spread across the North King's face. He nodded and said, "Until the next black moon, nephew. I will enjoy your death the most."

Holding my breath, I sank back into the shadows and parted without another word to visit a healer in Luz. I didn't bother returning to the Egress; instead, I Shadowed through the breaking dawn.

The guards at the gates of Luz barked orders for me to tell them why I was there. I'd used the entry, out of respect for Sybilla's new advisors.

"Your Queen requests I speak with her advisors, Fenris and Asterie," I told them, tapping my boot against the stark marble.

They checked me for weapons before they led me inside.

Only after Asterie had descended the steps did the guards back away, seeming to understand that her power far outweighed their ability to protect her.

"What's the meaning of this?" she asked.

Judging by the thick purple velvet robe she wore and the hair astray from its braid, they'd pulled her from sleep.

"It is Sybilla," I said.

Asterie's brow furrowed. "What's happened to her?"

"She's sick—Mattock says a healer by the name Mortag usually helps her."

"He has not returned. Let me fetch Wyeth. She helped me draw up tonics before Sybilla left. Is she out of them already?"

My heart sank as I realized I'd been right. The green vials were what she needed.

Asterie walked over to one of her guards, quietly giving him orders, and he ascended the steps. She stepped down into the main hall of the palace. Silver-accented sconces and royal blue rugs were laid out down the hall. The marble had been patched, and much work had been done since I'd last seen the space.

Something about being in Sybilla's home while she lay sick in mine didn't sit right with me.

"How bad is she?" Asterie watched me like a hawk.

"Bad enough that I visited the North King—bad enough that I am here."

Her gaze narrowed. "Was there foul play? Poison?"

"No, of course not," I grumbled.

Asterie's head tilted.

"Can you go tell your healer we don't have all night?"

Fenris trotted down the steps in an open robe, wearing trousers but no tunic. He paid me no pleasantries, which I appreciated. "What happened?"

Begrudgingly, I told them of Sybilla's fever, of our healer's prognosis—that she would be fine, but that we needed to provide her with the tonics she was used to taking.

It wasn't long before a petite woman with neat shoulder-length black hair appeared at the top of the steps. She was dressed in a light-green robe and thick black nightdress.

"Nice to see you, King Darvanda," Wyeth said as she descended the stairs, and her hair flashed green. I'd heard of a kingdom in the East Corridor whose lineage had been cursed with such a truth charm—I had no time to be offended.

Wyeth sized me up and then held out two bright green vials. "I only had enough supplies for a few doses. This should get Queen Wymark through tomorrow, and I can prepare more to send Asterie with after I gather the ingredients."

Asterie chimed in, "Sybilla mentioned that the tonics she usually takes are blue—do you know of anything anti-inflammatory that would be blue?"

Wyeth tapped her chin and shook her head, "Only garrot root, and that was banned from medicinal use *long* ago. It's impossible to find now. Maybe her healer was using bluebell vine tea to lace the healing tonic and make it taste better? There is plenty of that in his quarters."

I ground my teeth. Garrot root had been one of the magic suppressants used during the Great Wars against my people—the Phynnic had polluted the water with it.

Palming the vials that Wyeth handed me, I looked between the three of them. "Thank you. I'll send El in the morning to give you word on how Sybilla is feeling."

Asterie offered me a quiet nod before I Shadowed away from the realm of Henosis and swirled through the darkness toward the Sahlms. I'd be beyond tired tomorrow, but every minute away from Umber House made me grow more anxious.

CHAPTER 32
EMMERICK

When everything went cold and dark, I'd been considering the nerve it took the King of the Sahlms to ask for my help. Almost valiant.

The more infuriating part was I'd happily provided answers, unable to fathom the idea of denying Sybilla comfort. I'd pushed her into a corner, and she'd lashed out by planning to marry that asshole, and yet...the thought of her sick or suffering still felt like having my chest ripped open.

Darvanda's worry had seemed genuine, which bothered me more—that he cared for her when it should've been me. Yet she'd rarely let me in the room for longer than a few minutes when she'd experienced bad days despite how well I knew her.

Sybilla never showed vulnerability in front of anyone. She'd sooner die alone than let another soul in her bedchamber when a flare-up was occurring. Yet she let him see tender parts of her. My anger always seemed to be a gateway to my vision blurring, the room chilling, my control waning.

When I came to, I was standing in the throne room of Helos. Something wet and warm coated my hands. Looking down, I saw blood dripping from my fingers. Beneath the crimson, my fingertips were charred like they'd been smeared in coal.

Dark magic...

Again.

The hairs on the back of my neck stood tall.

My vision tunneled. Someone entered the room.

"King Mattock?" Ryssa's shadow-logged voice whispered from behind her veil.

"Don't come near me!" I held out a blood-soaked hand. "Go..."

Ryssa's cloaked form approached. She seemed to look down between us, and I followed her gaze.

Haward.

A flash of him saying, "My brother is not made for royal life. He will need to be handled."

So callous, so calculated. And then I slashed his throat. Amber smoke surrounded him, removing the color from his face, causing his cheeks to sink in. Then the tendrils of it ran up my nose, and the evil within felt fed.

My mouth turned dry to see the repercussions of my actions—the stiff look of shock written on Sybilla's cousin's face. He lay in a pool of murky scarlet, which seeped into the gray grout between the black marble tiles.

"King Mattock, is it you?" Ryssa whispered.

Eerie how her words nearly matched Darvanda's.

My hands shook. "Yes? Who else would I be?"

My broadsword lay next to Haward's body, and I reached for it.

"Don't," Ryssa ordered. I'd never heard that tone from her before. "Let me take the sword. I'll hide it. We will smooth this all out."

What atrocious loyalty.

I deserved to be in a prison cell.

"I killed him?" I asked. Just like I'd killed those women in the pleasure hall, just like I'd killed countless others whose faces haunted my dreams.

"It was not you," she answered before she picked up my broadsword. "Go clean yourself up. I will handle this, my King."

With shaking hands, I said, "I can't...You can't."

Her cloaked head tilted. "Trust me," she said. "Go."

On trembling legs, I left her there to clean up a mess that was not hers. I deserved worse than a dungeon...I deserved the gallows.

CHAPTER 33
SYBILLA

I woke up groggy and weak. My sweat had soaked the sheets—pooling at my hips. Wait...

Oh Sources. No.

The blankets around my bottom were *far* too wet to be from sweat alone. There was a brooding warlock snoring quietly in the armchair beside the cot. Those infuriatingly thick, dark lashes lifted as though he'd sensed me wake.

No, no, no.

"Get out!" I croaked.

Krait leaned toward me. "You're awake."

"Out!" I demanded again, mortification setting in that, at some point in my fever-riddled sleep, I'd wet the bed like a fucking child. I wore a different nightdress than I remembered having put on. That heated my cheeks—had he *changed* my clothes too?

He glanced down and seemed to notice the source of my embarrassment. "Oh."

"Leave," I groaned. I could feel the rash on my chest grow hotter.

Rising from the chair, Krait stretched his forearms behind his head. The flash of tight muscles of his abdomen was torture in my current state.

How dare he look attractive while I lay here, feeling like a sack of piss and sweat?

I was angry with him about something, but my thoughts were too jumbled to catch up. I took inventory of my surroundings—pretty landscape paintings of the Hussa mountains in the North Corridor hung from the walls, and a gilded vanity with lots of baubles and gems atop it sat in the corner. I thanked the Sources that the maids had brought up a cot and I hadn't soiled El's bed.

My curls had plastered to my forehead, and I felt too dizzy to rise. I probably *looked* as weak as I felt. And he had to go and look all...sleep-tousled and dreamy.

I definitely still had a fever.

It began to come back to me. I hated the King of the Sahlms. He'd intended to impregnate me and then discard me once he had his heir. He was an insufferable prick.

Yet I was too exhausted to discuss any of that.

"Sybilla, you are sick. There's nothing to be—"

I cut him off. "Just let me clean up, okay? Go, please." There was no fight left in me.

He shook his head again. "No," he grunted as he drew closer. He pulled back the covers—his eyes never leaving mine—and I groaned. "You can't even sit up. I'm taking you to the baths."

I didn't have time to argue with him before his arms were beneath me. My humiliation heightened as he drew me into his chest.

"You don't have to—"

"Can you shut up?" he retorted.

I mumbled back, "Well, that's more in character."

"It's just piss," he noted as he headed for the door with me.

When I wrapped my arms around his neck to steady myself, he looked down at me with an expression that I couldn't place at first.

Then it hit me. He was afraid.

I'd watched fear strike people thousands of times. But it was an odd reaction from a man I was convinced didn't *have* feelings.

Letting my head fall between his neck and shoulder, I let him carry me through the halls. For as long as I could remember, no one had ever held me like this. I'd never have let them—not even Em.

We passed someone in the hall who he quietly instructed, "Bring some fresh towels and clothes down to the baths. And let the kitchen know to prepare some broth."

My cheeks were now an inferno. I didn't look up. Only when Elsie replied did I know it was her. "Of course. Is she alright?"

"I'm fine," I groaned into the crook of Krait's neck, wanting this mortifying interaction to end. I felt Elsie's hand brush my back before she carried on away from us. I didn't need everyone in the realm knowing that I could barely lift my head and that I'd soiled the bed.

Krait carried me down the steps to where the scent of bath salts and soaps coated the air. I could feel him kick off his boots before stepping into the lukewarm water.

I asked, "Why are you being so nice to me?"

"Because I'd like you to stay healthy enough to keep fighting with me."

"I can take you now," I said, although it humored even me.

He let a throaty laugh escape him. "Is that so? I'd love to see you try."

When I reeled back to look up at him, that hint of fear remained etched into his brow. He stepped down into the pool of water, soaking his clothing and my nightgown.

"Why are you afraid of me?"

He scoffed but avoided meeting my gaze. "I'm not afraid of you."

"Then what are you afraid of?"

He sat down on the stone seat that was designed to bask on, with me across his lap. "I'm afraid I got too used to you running your mouth at me. And when you were too sick to do so, I felt helpless. Helpless enough to go to Mattock in order to understand what to do for you."

I straightened. "You had no right. He doesn't need to know the status of my health."

Krait drew in a deep breath. "You were asking for him. I hated doing it as much as you hate me for it."

I swallowed hard. Emmerick was often who I'd made the maids fetch when I needed to see Healer Mortag.

"I don't hate you." I desperately wished that I could hate him. "I need to wash off...away from you."

"Let me help you," he said as his hands moved toward the buttons on the back of the nightdress.

"Trying to undress me, Darvanda, like in your little fantasies?" I instigated, hoping for a cutting response.

"You just pissed yourself, Sybilla. A tryst is far from my mind."

"What happened to 'it's just piss'?"

"Just stop moving already." He worked on my buttons, and I slumped forward into his chest. The stubble on his chin tickled my temple.

It was possibly one of the most intimate things I'd ever let someone do for me—yet not an ounce sultry.

"All undone." He helped me stand upright in the water, and I held the nightdress up to my front—not that it did much to conceal anything with the way it clung to me. His eyes didn't wander; instead, they scanned my face as I stepped away.

Once I dipped deeper into the water, he lifted himself out of the pool. Pulling his soiled shirt over his head and tossing it into a sopping heap beside the bath, before he walked to the pool beside mine.

Then he stripped off his soaked linen pants.

My mouth went dry at the sight of his bare ass.

Absolutely shameless.

I tilted my head at the work of art that was the back of him—sculpted as though an artist had chiseled away meticulously to craft the perfect man.

Before he sank down into the water, he glanced over his shoulder, catching me staring. "Should we commission a portrait for you?"

My cheeks heated as he sank into the bath and then floated to the edge of the pool to rest his forearms on the colored tile between us.

"I must be gravely ill because it almost sounded like you had a sense of humor," I bit back.

He smirked as though my cutting words brought him joy.

I turned away from him, pulled the soaked nightdress over my shoulders, and threw it down with a wet slap beside his discarded tunic. The small walkway between our pools created enough distance that my breasts weren't visible below the water. I was thankful he couldn't see me. In this state, I felt anything but alluring.

When I submerged my head, the salt and sweat leaving my face felt divine. When I reemerged, Krait's hair was wet, too, and slicked back. I stepped to the edge between our baths and peeked over it.

Krait lifted himself onto his palms for a moment, snatched a square of soap from a basket and offered it to me across the divider. The wicked V-shaped dip of his hips made heat gather in my core.

I happily took the soap, distracting myself from my scandalous thoughts, and scrubbed myself from head to toe with the mint-scented bar. Maybe if I scrubbed hard enough, it might remove the grime of all my mixed emotions about the King in the next bath.

Ignoring the handful of hair that came out as I scrubbed, I relished the feeling of my fingers against my scalp. I'd made such a mess of everything—forcing his hand to uphold our betrothal, playing political games that now felt too large for me to carry.

"You said to me once that you didn't understand who made me think they could put their hands on me without consequence."

Maybe the ebbing fever had inspired me to speak. Or maybe I needed more clarity from him as to what he wanted.

If I went through with this marriage—what would it be like?

How would he treat me once he had everything he longed for under that prophecy?

He seared me with his gaze, forearms flexed on the edge of the bath, a thin wall of stone between us.

I continued, "My father was a merciful ruler in public affairs. He did not extend that mercy to his wife."

Krait's brow furrowed as he focused on my mouth, seeming angry at it. "And did he extend that mercy to you?"

"I was his only child, the future of his kingdom," I tried to justify.

"That doesn't answer the question."

I sighed. "He never hurt me the same way he hurt her. At some point, he accepted that I would need to rule—and that prevented him from leaving marks where others could see them."

Krait's fingertips dug into the smoothed tile. His mouth drew into a flat line. "That isn't acceptable."

"Acceptable or not, he felt it justified. My parents tried and failed for the son that my mother hadn't given him first. Each year that went by without a male heir, my father resented us more. I was never blind to the fact that he treated my mother poorly. He'd always implied that she had done something to deserve it—that she let other men into her bed, that she was not worthy of my respect either."

For a time, I believed him.

Until the night before her execution, when he'd claimed to have caught her with another man. I knew she hadn't left her room because she had been there with me and Healer Mortag. I'd been sick, much like I'd just been. My mother had urged me not to share my physical ailments with my father, so I'd said nothing.

Krait licked a droplet of water from his lips, drawing my attention. Damn him. His stare hooked mine with such intensity that I kept rambling.

"I look so much like she did. There were times I wished I wasn't hers. Maybe if I'd been his bastard, then he might have loved me as I did him."

Krait let out a frustrated sigh. "Some men aren't worthy of their daughter's love. If he was incapable of loving you, then he was a damned fool, but you were never the problem." He turned his gaze away from me and ran his hands through his soaked hair, seeming nervous. "You understand that, right?"

I nodded. "I know that now. He was ill for nearly a decade before dying. I used to wish that his death would come faster. But when he finally died, it was still a blow to realize that I had *no one* left. My uncle wanted to crown one of his sons—Haward. So they, too, became my enemies."

Standing taller, I unfurled my arms from where they'd instinctively wrapped around my top half in order to grip the pool's edge.

I leveled a determined look in Krait's direction. "I've been obsessed with securing the best alliances, leading me to agonize over every decision. It is particularly exhausting trying to convince every noble in your own court that you are better off alive. But I couldn't fail. My father's prophecies told of how Luz would fall, and I waited until the day came when Asterie wrote to me to act."

Krait focused intently as I explained the prophecies I'd shown Asterie in the Luz crypts—the mad scribblings of my father's final visions.

The Wastelands will be known to you...

He will rise and Death will reign...

War will be fought with shadows and light...

"Your father was an Oracle—was your mother also gifted with any Reverist abilities? Someone of Isleen's blood would not *only* be an Oracle."

"No. Just him."

He hummed a response that was neither positive nor negative—a solid, comforting neutral that kept me talking.

"Hearing the thoughts of everyone around me helped me make calculated decisions and smooth over hard conversations. For a long time, my mind was just a useless cacophony until I figured out how to wield it."

"Your mind is a beautiful thing."

My brows rose at his words.

I expected him to be finished at that, but he continued, "And you are cunning and terrifyingly relentless."

I scoffed. "Most men would not consider those good qualities."

"Then you've been surrounding yourself with the wrong men," he said as his gaze met mine across the pools.

"Are you implying that *you* are the right man? That I should roll over for you—bear the heir that you so desperately need and then be put down like a retired bitch afterward?" I argued. I couldn't help it, even as I revealed my greatest wounds.

"You think I'm a monster, don't you?" He shook his head, and only then did I notice the dark bags beneath his eyes. "Ask yourself—how much of that manifestation is truly about *me*?"

It had only taken a short time for me to find myself infuriated with him again. I snapped, "Maybe I wouldn't think you such a monster had you been upfront with me."

"Right. As though that would have gone any better." He ran a hand down his face as though I knew nothing. I knew a great deal about the workings of Kings who cared not for their consorts. I wouldn't fool myself into thinking that a happy life by his side awaited me; we had a duty to the realms, not to each other.

Too tired to handle that line of conversation, I let myself submerge under the water again. All my breath left me in bubbles that tickled my cheeks as they rose. I stayed there for as long as my body would allow.

When I surfaced with a gasp, he had stepped out of the pool and was wrapping a towel around his waist already. Pity. I'd missed a good view.

He exited the baths momentarily before returning with divinely soft-looking clothing and a towel, which he set on a bench by the door.

"I'll be outside," he said with ice in his tone. The click of the door separated us.

Whatever fabric the breeches were made of *was* splendidly soft—it felt like butter against my skin as I slid them up my legs. The tunic Krait had left behind was loose-fitting enough to billow off me and smelled faintly like his pillowcases. I wouldn't have been caught dead in such an ensemble in Luz.

Clothed and clean, I padded barefoot to the door. He was waiting on the stairs—well, napping. I studied him. Leaned back against the stone wall, in a black tunic cuffed to show strong forearms, and his skin still dewy from the bath, he looked like a fucking deity. The most peculiar thing was that his Shadows were cocooned around him like a shield.

Something warmed inside me to see him waiting there, too sleep-deprived to stay awake—all shadowy and sleepy.

I was definitely still feverish.

One wisp of a Shadow stretched out toward me. At first, I flinched, but then it wrapped around my hand and gently lifted my arm. It felt like a cool breeze over my wet skin.

I watched the darkness loop between my fingers.

"They like you—that's unusual."

I pulled my hand away abruptly and met Krait's bloodshot eyes. "You fell asleep?"

He nodded. "I Shadowed across the realms last night. I'm still recovering."

The thought of him depleting his energy tugged at my will to stay angry with him. "You didn't have to take care of me. There are healers for that."

He grumbled, "You scared mine away—she said you tried to bite her."

"I would not!"

He smirked. "You didn't. But I wouldn't put it past you."

I half-heartedly glared with a shrug. "I don't think I'd put it past me either."

He cleared his throat and said, "They're having a fresh cot brought up to Elsedora's room, if that's where you'd prefer to rest."

My cheeks heated. "Your bed is more comfortable," I said as he offered me a hand to walk up the stairs. I reluctantly took it before muttering, "Darvan-dick."

He leaned down and whispered into my ear, "You use the word dick around me far too frequently."

I shot back, "You almost sound like that excites you."

"Masochistically, it does."

His fingers entwined with mine felt warm and steady. I wanted to keep thinking of him as my enemy, wanted to hate him for his intent to use me, and wanted to keep fighting him. But I was so damn tired, and the light of morning when we hit the landing reminded me that I needed sleep.

We rounded the hall to the bottom of the main staircase. I stared up, feeling hopelessly run-down. Those steps seemed equivalent to climbing the Hussa mountains.

I bit my lower lip, contemplating what would be worse—the stairs or admitting defeat. "Tomorrow, I'm going back to being livid about what you told me in the bell tower."

"Yeah?" he asked with an intensity that unnerved me.

I nodded as we began climbing the stairs.

"What about after tomorrow?"

Why were there so many stairs in this house? "Then you'll keep teaching me how to use my Reverist abilities against Caym. He has Em in his control, and I will consider whatever it takes to release him."

Each step felt like a hammer against my skull, and I couldn't help but wince and stop halfway up.

"And what are we to do now?" He steadied me as I wobbled.

"Now, if you've got the strength to, you're going to carry me to bed because every part of my stupid body feels like it is swollen and has been run over by a carriage ten times and walking up the bath steps felt like three miles."

He looked at me with a deep intake of breath. When he exhaled, it was as though all the hard lines of his face softened. He scooped me up like a child being carried off to bed, and I closed my eyes, trying not to revel in how good the weightlessness felt.

It was foolish.

Krait set me down just inside his bedchamber. The balcony door was open, letting in fresh air through the curtains.

"I'll be right outside."

"No," I urged him.

He tilted his head, staring down at me with a creased brow.

"You have been up all night—sleep. It's your bed."

"I don't think that—"

"Oh, shut up and get in bed," I demanded before crossing the room and pulling the sheets down. I slipped beneath them and patted the place next to me. "You'll need your rest for the fight we're having tomorrow."

He smirked. "I am only listening because you nearly died on me. *Tomorrow*, we are back to you not telling me what to do in my own house."

Wrapped in soft silk sheets, I rolled over to face him as he lay down over the covers. Despite the growing heat of the morning, I'd never felt more comfortable than I did spun up in the cool fabric.

Krait lay on his back, but he looked toward me. I should not have felt safe, but lying there next to him, I did.

Still—he was the Shadow Origin. He had been plotting long before the moment he knew I was the Last Daughter of Isleen.

It would benefit me to remember that none of his intentions had ever been pure. When he finally closed his eyes, mine followed. While we weren't touching, the rise and fall of his breath lulled me to sleep.

I awoke to the sound of clattering dishes. A form in a black robe with long dark hair poured tea into a cup at the desk across the room.

"Asterie?" I croaked before sitting up. My head pounded.

"Stay there, my Queen," she said as she brought over a tray and set it across my lap.

The smell of fresh jam and bread made my stomach churn with hunger. An untouched bowl of broth that was no longer steaming sat on the bedside table.

"They searched me extensively. You've found quite a protective friend in that silver-haired warlock."

Offering a weak smile, I added jam to a piece of bread. But my smile faded as I thought of the reason why my newfound friends had searched her.

"Emmerick—he is an envoy..."

Asterie nodded before taking my free hand in hers and sitting beside me. "They told me. He has not returned any letters from me, Fen or Amara. He lets no one in that castle to visit him. Not even Angeline or Leo."

He wasn't even letting his parents see him. My heart clenched, and my eyes snapped shut for a moment as I tried to settle the dizziness.

"Is Haward still advising him, and is he still allied with Bringham?"

Asterie nodded before she patted my hand. "Put that out of your mind for now. You need to rest—get strong for us. I brought more remedies from Luz."

"How did you know I was ill?"

"King Darvanda came to us after visiting Emmerick. How long have you struggled with these spells?"

There was no use hiding from my all-knowing-owl friend; she would root out my truths one way or another.

I squeezed her hand. "I've always struggled with pain and inflammation. It began in childhood and worsened through my teen years. The healers...no one has ever been able to determine what it is exactly. I've been told my body doesn't ward off illness the way others' do. So, I've taken to ways of keeping the swelling and pain at bay. I'm fine—really. I just sometimes need a bit longer to get back on my feet."

Asterie's posture slackened as I revealed one of my most closely kept secrets to her.

"I've written to Healer Mortag's family home in the South Corridor, asking him to send back instructions on how to make the usual tonics you take." Asterie rubbed the ink where Van rested on her forearm. "You are *sure* you are safe here?"

I nodded. Surprisingly, there was no place I felt safer than under the surly King's roof despite the truth he'd withheld, despite logic begging me to find more reasons to distrust him.

Asterie licked her lower lip, thinking, *"I shouldn't worry her now."*

"My friend...I am *already* worried that you are keeping things from me."

Asterie sighed and said, "Fine...King Sheffield is missing." Her unease leaked out of her. "He went for a morning ride along the beaches and never returned."

I balked and tried to get up, but Asterie's hand settled on my shoulder, pushing me back down.

"You have to *rest*. Let Fenris and I worry about this for now. Trust us to handle matters and keep you apprised."

The South Corridor King was missing, and she wanted me to sit back and relax. With a huff, I let myself collapse against the pillows. I winced. My head throbbed, and I realized, much to my disappointment, that she was right. I'd be useless if I did not let myself regain strength. Being run down and incapable of holding my own head up wouldn't do anyone any good.

"What have we heard from the Nadiars? Are they safe?"

Asterie smoothed the sheets at her side and said, "Yes, they have increased their flying guard at the East Palace. They are still steadfast supporters of Luz and your rule. With *or without* this betrothal. Sybilla, are you certain about this?"

"What better prospects do I have? Haward will come storming in for my head soon. And...there are other complications with ending the arrangement." I still didn't understand how I was supposed to wrap my mind around the prophecy—around Isolde's wishes. Old hag, haunting me with a maternal expectation that was both alluring and terrifying.

"All I beg you to consider is that there are other ways we can remain allies with Sahlmsara—I need to understand that you know that."

I sighed. "Not everyone finds their soulmate. Not everyone marries for love. You and Fen are a storybook example of something many of us will never find. I have a duty to the people I've sworn to protect...So yes. I'll marry for political gain. I have very good reason to believe the King of the Sahlms will not harm me."

My friend's gaze narrowed. "If that is what you wish."

It was what I wished for. Oddly enough.

"Let's talk about how to address the troops on the borders of the East and Central Corridors."

Asterie shook her head. "Absolutely not. *Rest.* Cassidee is working closely with the Nadiars. She has deep expertise with the East Corridor fleets, and the Nadiars respect her. You drink that." She pointed to the bluebell vine tea.

My heart sang. She'd brought my favorite—I could kiss her. "Yes, ma'am."

She rolled her eyes, but a hint of a smile cracked through her usual stone facade. "We'll come to you if anything changes. No war has been declared. You have one of the strongest Constables looking after Luz. Restore your health. Think not of any of this until we meet again."

"What else would I think about?"

I sipped my tea; it didn't taste as full-bodied as I remembered. My illness must have taken my sense of taste.

My friend's brow rose, and I could feel her bubbling amusement. "You'll think of something," she answered, crossing the room to the door. "Maybe plan your very *real* wedding? Maybe set a date?" Her tone was dry, but I knew she spoke in jest.

I grumbled a slew of curse words as she reached the door. There was nothing I hated more than being told to stay in bed. "Fine, but if anything changes in the realm, or if Sheffield is found, you are to come here with news immediately."

Asterie nodded. "Of course."

I waited for the soothing effects of the bluebell tea to take hold as they usually did and for my mind to quiet. No such luck struck me though, and I let the drink go cold in my hands.

Tea would not bring me clarity under these circumstances.

Chapter 34

Krait

With the appropriate tonics, Sybilla appeared less and less tired each day, and she refused to allow us to hold off training any longer. She'd only been recovering for a week, but she'd strong-armed me into taking her to the amphitheater.

The Star-wielder and my old bounty hunter visited nearly every day, bringing word from the Corridors. There'd been no movement of troops, but it was clear that Bringham and Mattock were unwavering in their refusal to cooperate.

So be it.

Their actions seemed to give Sybilla a newfound tenacity toward our training.

So there we were—back in the pit. This time, she insisted it be me that she dueled with.

She'd cracked through my mental shields and disarmed me twice already but was growing fatigued. I could tell by the way her chest rose and fell without reprieve, by the way her hand found her throat when we rested between maneuvers.

Her combat skills still left much to be desired. As soon as a weapon graced her hands, she could no longer disarm me. It seemed she couldn't master the art of fighting with her body *and* her mind.

The sun rose over the amphitheater. The echoing sound of the wood-on-wood of our swords carried through the empty domed space.

"Stop me," I grunted as I swung the hollow wooden sword at her shoulder again.

She didn't block. "Ouch! You ass!" She glared. "This is foolish. I'll have a dozen bruises."

She was absolutely useless with a sword.

"Again. Stop me. You don't only have that sword to use, Sybilla. You can disarm me *while* moving."

I swung, and she jumped back out of the way. "Prick," she gasped out. "Just give me a bow and then you'll see what I can do with moving objects."

Loose curls stuck to her temples, and the rest of her hair was piled on her head with that blue ribbon. She gripped the wooden sword with two hands and charged.

I smirked because the memory of her with an arrow pointed at my head, on that palace wall in Luz, did something wicked to the blood flow in my groin. "I remember," I said and blocked, which caused her chest to slam into mine with a strained growl. "But you're still shit with a sword."

"Well, I was never trained with a sword." *Clunk.* She winced against the vibration of the wood clashing.

"We're making excuses now?" I asked. *Block.*

This time, when I swung, the hollow wood hit her hip. She yelped, and my resolve broke at the sound. I dropped the wooden sword to my side for a moment.

She'd finally agreed to see our healer. They could fix a common bruise—she'd be fine. But every time she failed to stop me, it heightened my anxiety.

If she couldn't stop a wooden sword—what would happen if she faced a steel one?

"You can't stop me, can you?" I instigated before lifting and pointing my sword between her eyes.

"I can." She grabbed the wooden blade of my sword and pushed it away. "These swords are made for children. Swing a real one at me, and I *can*. I just heard you thinking it."

"No," I shot back.

"C'mon, Krait, this is ridiculous," Sybilla huffed. Elsedora strolled into the ring, flipping one of her throwing daggers in her hand. *Sources*, she had a way of sneaking up when you least expected her.

"She's right," El said.

A frustrated groan rumbled in the back of my throat.

Great, they'd teamed up against me.

Elsedora pointed the dagger at Sybilla. "You want to stop a real blade, my friend?" she playfully asked.

Sybilla's stance widened—there were only a few yards between them. El never missed a mark.

"Don't!" I shouted at Elsedora, but there was a mischievous glint in her eyes. Sybilla's sword rose, and she charged forward as Elsedora took aim.

Please let her not be aiming at any vital organs.

Just before the dagger left El's fingertips, her torso bent forward. She cursed and flung the dagger at the ground. It landed inches from the toe of Sybilla's boot.

She'd really intended to throw it at her.

I seethed.

Elsedora held her stomach as though she'd just been punched.

"Sorry!" Sybilla called out. She ran to El's side. "I just...reacted. Instead of stopping you, I...diverted you."

Elsedora winced. "What *was* that?"

"Pain..." Sybilla answered. "I think."

"It was fucking awful. Is that what you did to those prisoners?"

I approached them. Elsedora had disobeyed a direct order, and Sybilla had encouraged her. She could have been struck with that blade. It had come so fucking close. "You." I pointed at Elsedora. "Out!"

"Krait," Sybilla reasoned. "I stopped her! *While* moving." There was a wild, widening grin on her face that made me lose steam.

"She isn't going to learn by being coddled," Elsedora said before pointing another throwing knife at me. "You want her safe? Let me and Ryn handle her physical training because you have done a piss-poor job today. Your feelings have gotten the better of you."

"That's enough," I growled out before throwing my wooden sword down between them and walking toward the amphitheater's exit.

I could hear Elsedora whisper, "He'll calm down. Don't worry."

The thought of Sybilla in harm's way had become a mounting source of anxiety. Finding her had always been my destiny to resent. Now that she was here, sleeping beside me, letting me still train her despite knowing all of my ill intentions, I couldn't find a single damned thing to resent about her.

The fight she'd promised? It hadn't happened.

And I'd never been more angry about *not* having had an argument.

If she didn't care enough to confront it, so be it. Wanting to keep her around had not been in the plans.

Yet Elsedora was right.

My emotions were too deeply involved.

Sybilla Wymark refused to leave my mind in more ways than one.

If it was a political arrangement she wanted, then she'd get one. So long as we were allied in defeating Caym, we couldn't afford complications.

CHAPTER 35
SYBILLA

"He'll calm down. Don't worry," Elsedora assured me.

Strong rays of afternoon sun beat down on us—summer here was oppressively hot, though my body was adjusting. I'd grown to love the lighter fabrics of the fashion here and the way all the clothing billowed off my body. Much better than the tight cuts of heavy velvet, wool and corsets of Luz.

Krait was nowhere to be seen after his temper tantrum over El throwing a knife at my face. So touchy.

"What is his issue?" I mused to Elsedora.

She smirked. "He knows we are running out of time, and you are not near ready to face Caym if his Reverist power returns on the next black moon. I suspect that scares him."

I crossed my arms over my chest. "*Whose* fault is that? He has me playing with toy swords and then holds back if I wobble even a bit. I saw him hesitate after hitting me."

He hadn't faltered every time. I had the bruises to prove it. But every other.

"I do not disagree," Elsedora said before she took a swig from her canteen. "But we hoped to find you sooner—not with only a few years to spare. We know so little about what the prophecy actually means. He's anxious."

"That makes two of us," I mumbled.

Since I'd been sick, Krait had returned to that frowning, clipped-conversation asshole that I'd first met. Whatever softness and warmth I'd witnessed the morning he had carried me into the baths had melted away.

He'd only need to be my husband, not my friend.

It seemed he was setting his line in the sand.

I still hadn't decided what to do or say about the prophecy, and his failure to bring it up made my blood boil. As though he'd just changed his mind after four centuries. It was his immortality to sacrifice—his power to give up. Maybe he *had* truly changed his mind. In his situation, I might have. I shook away my empathy.

All I could do was keep getting stronger, keep preparing for whatever threat came first.

"What is happening in Helos?" I asked Elsedora as we exited the amphitheater and I adjusted my silk scarf to cover my shoulders from the sun.

"Mattock has lost the support of many lords in the rural regions around Helos—most were excited about the return of magic and its impact on their crops and livelihoods. His own people are turning against him. He is alone up in that castle of nightmares."

Since Emmerick and Bringham had decreed that no Source-wielders could enter their Corridors, Elsedora had acted as an easy loophole. She was from the Sahlms but not a Source-wielder. And so she kept dropping in unannounced, hopeful that she'd learn something about how the Death Origin was controlling Emmerick.

"Has force been considered to unseat him?"

Elsedora stopped short and turned to me. "You want to take the North by force? Go to war with your Emmerick?"

"Whoever sits on the throne right now is not *my* Emmerick. That *isn't* him."

My friend might be angry at me—but he wouldn't turn against Asterie and Fenris for no reason like that. He would not use a grudge to drive a wedge between himself and the rest of the realm, and he would not jeopardize the safety of the people of any court.

My Emmerick was good to the fucking bone. And that death-mark and Caym's influence tore away at that goodness.

"There's been another development."

"What is it?" I raised a brow.

"Your cousin Haward...he is missing."

My hand found my throat, trying to ease the constricting feeling there. "For how long?"

I tried not to let the indifference I felt show. No one should be excited to hear of their cousin's potential demise and yet...he'd never given me a reason to *not* be excited about his demise.

"It is hard to say—the Castle of Helos isn't exactly keen on sharing."

"He could be an envoy," I mused as we veered down a narrow street bustling with mule-led carts of produce from the greenhouses. It seemed every vendor was preparing for the night markets, and the streets were a maze to navigate.

Elsedora nodded. "He could be. Until we know where our threats come from, you must understand—it isn't safe for you to attend any more meetings. Not even with your sworn allies. Fen and Asterie are handling things beautifully, trust me."

"Trust you?" I asked with a smirk.

Elsedora huffed a laugh. "You don't?"

"I would have trusted you more had you told me your King wanted me to bear his heir and then leave me for dead."

I did trust Elsedora—Luz was in good hands. I even trusted her not to kill me when she threw daggers in my direction. But she was biased when it came to her King.

"That isn't what he wants, you know," Elsie said. "He is a broken man, but he needs you just as much as you need him. The fact that you two haven't figured that out yet is painful to watch."

What an amusing point of view.

I snorted as we passed a bustle of people decorating doorways with colorful fabric banners and setting out large barrels.

"I need no one. But speaking of needing things, it's grown so dry. One of the maids told me this morning that it looks like the first summer rain is on the horizon. Is that what these preparations are for?"

"Oh, yes!" Elsie took my hand and bounced over to the bridge's railing to look out at the main canal outside of Umber House. We had a good view of the sprawling city of Sahlmsara, and it was lined with colorful banners and people setting up tents all the way down to what I assumed was the riverbed area Krait had led me to that first night in the city.

"We celebrate by the river and collect as much rainwater as possible," she continued. "Hopefully the rain will fall soon. The first storm marks the beginning of monsoon season. There's a festival—it's a good time. Lots of wine. Fun clothing with *lots* of fun ties." She winked.

I rolled my eyes. "Your mind only thinks in terms of its next romp, doesn't it?"

"When you've lived as long as I have, you have to work really hard to entertain yourself." Elsedora pulled me along to show me the other side of the canal, where tealight candles lined the edge.

Despite the growing threats, the buzz of eagerness for something to celebrate filled me.

I knew Krait would be in *his hole*—likely there to brood.

There would be no apologies because El was right. He *was* coddling me. It didn't matter if I wobbled; it didn't matter if I was tired. I needed to be pushed to my limits.

The Death Origin would not go easy on me, and someday, I would go up against him.

Approaching the small door beneath the eastern stairwell, I whispered, "In the Shadows we trust."

Met with dim light and cool air wafting from the underground room, I let out a sigh. I pulled the silk scarf off and tossed it over a coat hook at the top of the steps.

"What are we reading today?" I called down before descending into the book-lined room. Our first day back to "normal" and he was already annoyed with me, but I hoped that he would still read to me from the texts. With the full prophecy revealed to me, there was more I longed to know.

"I thought you might like to skip reading today." Krait was stretched out on the chaise. I crossed the room and sat beside him at his hip. Pulling one leg beneath me, I faced him. His personal reading choice caught my eye, and I plucked it from his hands, turning over the leather-bound book.

"Are you reading...*The Great Romances of the Old World*?"

He met my question with a scowl and a grunt as he quickly snatched the book back. "Love is often used against rulers in war. Why not study it?"

Which story was it? I peeked over the spine.

Ah, the one about a princess in endless sleep and the knight whose true love's kiss woke her.

I'd read those stories as a girl. They were nothing to study—pure unabashed and unrealistic tales of love at first sight. Who was I to judge him?

"Of course," I mused, too politely it seemed because it earned me another scowl. "We need to discuss my training—"

"Sybilla," he warned as he ran one hand down his face and sat up on his other elbow.

"I'll be hunted..." I said, and his hand dropped to his side, inches from my fingertips. "Caym knows I am a threat to him, that our *future child* will be a threat to him. So I will be hunted for the rest of his days. He's already gotten to me once here. What happens when he grows stronger, when we come face-to-face? It is bound to happen."

He shifted to give me more space, and a crease formed in his brow. He cleared his throat. "That's fair. But you were bedridden a week ago."

"It doesn't matter. I am fine now, and you need to push me harder."

Our gazes locked.

"No," he said.

Sources be damned, I couldn't win with this man. "Elsedora said you'd say that. She also said you'd see reason eventually, but I've got my doubts on that part."

"The two of you will be the death of me."

The death of him. I very well could be.

"Who wants to live forever anyway?" I teased.

"You have something against immortality?"

I tilted my head, thinking about that. "Well, yes, I do. It sounds like a shit way to spend your life. What is the meaning if there is no end? To have all the time in the world and yet little motivation to live to the fullest—it's ridiculous. What inspires an immortal to do today what they can do tomorrow? Or a hundred years from now?"

He laughed. It shook the chaise below us, and I couldn't help but match his smile.

"What is so funny?" I squinted as the dim lamplight illuminated every hard line of his face. His facial hair had grown out a bit. Sources, when he smiled, he was even more attractive.

"I agree. I've just never heard someone put it so beautifully frank before." He flipped the book face down in his lap.

I smirked. "Here lies Sybilla Wymark: She was *'beautifully frank'* with a grumpy King."

His expression sobered as his eyes traced my face and then fell to my lips.

"You're beautifully something," he said and swallowed hard.

I became acutely aware of how close I was to him.

"What?" He raised a brow.

"Well, I just about died from you paying me a compliment again. You better be careful. I may start to think you actually like me." I mockingly fanned myself with one hand.

"I've complimented you plenty."

I snorted. "Oh, yes. Ever the romantic," I teased. He grunted a reply and folded his hands on top of the book.

"What will it be like...being married to you?" I asked.

"I don't want to talk about this," he ground out.

"Well, we are. So answer the question."

"I'll make shit company."

"Obviously," I replied.

"I'll be no comfort to you."

"You don't need to be good company or good comfort to be good at conceiving an heir though. Do you?"

His jaw tensed in that telling way—I'd pissed him off already. "What exactly are you worried about, Sybilla?"

"Are you…" I could feel my face growing hot as I spoke. "Are you interested in the physical side of our marriage?"

His distance since having told me of the prophecy, his shortness and his abrupt departures from the bedchamber each morning as I lay pretending to still be asleep—had he changed his mind?

Why did that disappoint me?

He took a deep breath before he carefully said, "I am…"

The prick trailed off.

"Why do I feel there is a 'but' following that?" My eyes narrowed at him sprawled there on the chaise, looking far too comfortable, while my cheeks grew hotter and hotter.

He lifted further up onto his elbows and drew nearer. I hadn't realized I'd leaned down toward him. "*But* that would require you being ready for such a tryst," he said, his eyes going dark but his face remaining all hard lines and tension.

My temper spiked. "You drop the news on me that I'm destined to have your child and then avoid me—avoid fighting me about it. Now you're questioning my readiness as I proposition you? You really are a—"

"Sybilla," he snapped.

Instead of pulling away, I leaned further down, bracing one hand on the shelf behind his head. The book slid from his lap and fell with a thud. Warm spice tickled my nose, and the mingling of our breath made my arm tremble. Before I could think of another insult, his Shadows wrapped around my torso.

I gasped out, "What are you—"

"Sybilla. Shut up."

How endearing.

Then cool Shadows tugged, and I was drawn up to straddle his waist. All my anger melted into a molten feeling in my core.

"I've thought about taking you just like this since you climbed onto my lap here over that game board."

His lips were inches from mine, our bodies touching in the most torturous places. I'd allowed myself to wonder what he'd be like as a lover more times than I was proud of.

A good husband and a good lover were two separate things. I only needed the latter. I desperately tried to convince myself of that. I knew what he needed from me, and while it scared me senseless, the act of taking Krait to bed? That part didn't seem at all horrid.

"I never imagined sharing anything more than a child with the Last Daughter of Isleen. I'd married another—she was my destiny, even she would have allowed me that. I never considered anything else. I never considered that *you* would be at the end of this prophecy. I don't fear mortality. I don't fear giving up everything." Krait breathed out between us.

Another inch closer.

"I fear that you'll regret it." The words he didn't say out loud snuck into my head as he added, "I fear the way that I can't sleep without hearing your snoring."

"I don't sno—"

He cut me off. "I said shut up. You question the wrong things. I see the way you look at Fen and Asterie—and that isn't a life that I can ever give you. I had that life. Sex is easy. I'm plenty willing for that. But would that be enough for you?"

Another inch closer, and now our noses touched.

I opened my mouth to speak again, but I didn't trust myself. I'd tell him anything he wanted to hear to keep him exactly like this—hungry, wanting, between my thighs.

"If you say one more word, then I will have my Shadows set you aside," he warned. "I'll walk right out of here. No questions asked. We can go back to pretending like we don't want to rip each other's clothes off. The choice is yours—you're the one who 'propositioned me' after all."

I sat there, silent.

Staring at the hard lines of Krait's face, I internally scolded myself for the slick anticipation between my legs and the desire to close the distance to kiss him.

My mouth fell open but no sound came out. Krait's gaze seared me as he waited for me to break the silence.

I didn't say a fucking word.

Because if I did, he would stop, and I very much did not want him to stop whatever we were doing.

I closed the last inch between us. His Shadows pulled me flush against him, and his lips met mine in a hard kiss that felt like the heady buzz after the burn of amber liquor slid down one's throat.

Fury. Bliss. Rage. Pleasure.

I honestly didn't know where one emotion began and the next gave way.

His fingers dug into my thighs, and I couldn't help but roll my hips against him. It felt frenzied, like we were both trying to keep up with the other. The chaise knocked up against the shelf—books fell with heavy thuds. When his tongue ran along the inner seam of my lower lip, I was so lost in the moment that the ground could have crumbled beneath us and I wouldn't have noticed.

All of his hard edges melted into passion.

Cool wisps of dark vines surrounded me. They snaked over my back, around my stomach and between my thighs. I gasped into his mouth, and he swallowed it with a groan that made my toes curl.

He was touching me in so many places that I *almost* didn't notice his hardened length pressed against the thin silk and linen between us. He pushed my hips down against him and thrust up against my core. The sensation elicited a moan.

Fucking blasphemy. A King shouldn't be that well-endowed. I'd thought his badder-than-all personality was merely compensating for something.

I was *wrong*.

I hooked a thumb in the waist of his pants and tried to push down. I would let him take me.

"Tell me to stop, and I will," he groaned between us.

I shook my head and tried to recapture his lips. I would tell him no such thing.

One moment I was above him, the next I'd been flipped onto my back. Dark vines peeled my breeches from me, and I gasped. I felt exposed and my hands moved to cover myself, but his Shadows were faster. They pinned my arms to the chaise cushion.

"Open your legs, Sybilla," Krait commanded.

I'd never followed an order so fast in my life.

He hooked a finger in my undergarments and pulled them to one side and let out a satisfied hum when he saw the evidence of my arousal, slick against my thighs. I panted and watched him kneel in front of the chaise before he placed my legs over his shoulders.

My brain no longer had the reins. Instead, every nerve hummed for his touch. I saw his intent to taste me in his eyes as he took me in and pushed up my tunic with one hand. His gaze roved up to my breasts before trailing back down to where I burned for him most. He licked his lower lip.

"Krait," I gasped. "That isn't how heirs are made."

He smirked and said, "This is exactly how heirs are made. And if you insist on opening your mouth still, then all I want to hear is you screaming all those filthy words you love so much."

Then his mouth was on me. His tongue parted my seam and worked against my sex as though it were an instrument he was skilled in playing. I cried out, unable to stop my hand from grabbing a fistful of his dark hair.

No duty to the world edged me onward now. All I could think of was how good I felt as he pressed two fingers inside of me, how frantic I was to have even more of him.

My back arched, and my hands clawed at the leather cushions as he continued to work me until I was cursing as he'd told me to.

Sources. I'd never reached a peak this quickly.

"Fuck, Krait. I'm going to…"

Krait answered by curling his fingers and sucking, and then my eyes snapped closed, head thrown against the chaise. The noise that left my body didn't sound human as my release reached a crescendo.

I felt light. I could've floated to the ceiling as I pulsed around his fingers. He returned my feet to the floor with gentleness and nipped at the skin just above my navel. The weight of his head rested below my wildly beating heart, and I felt a contented growl rumble in his throat.

A feminine gasp from the stairway interrupted us, and I crashed down from the height of my pleasure.

"Sorry, sorry, sorry, sorry," Elsedora repeated with each hurried footstep she took back up the stairs.

"She saw us…she saw. Oh, fucking Sources. Get up," I demanded, though my body made no move against him. He didn't budge at first, remaining still with closed eyes and a feral sort of drunken expression. When he moved off me and sat on the chaise beside me, I quickly pulled up my breeches. He leaned back against the bookshelf and gently banged his head a few times as though scolding himself.

"Fuck. Fuck. Fuck."

The weight of his internal panic and guilt alarmed me.

Elsedora had already ascended the steps, and we were left there alone—panting, wanting. He was still aroused; the evidence of his need bulged in his linen pants. And he hated himself for it.

Finally, he stood and looked down at me. "How many filthy thoughts have gone through that head of yours in the last few minutes?"

Too out of breath to answer, I gaped up at him. He roiled with self-loathing over what we'd just done, and that caused a shameful feeling in my gut. What did he blame himself for? Then it hit me.

Freya.

He felt responsible for her death and being intimate with me was eating away at his conscience.

I was too stunned to speak.

"You do not need to worry about whether the physical parts of our marriage are something that I want," he concluded.

And then he walked up the stairs like nothing had just transpired.

I stood there, feeling so tightly wound that I could snap.

Sources save me.

CHAPTER 36
KRAIT

Elsedora's hands were clasped in front of her. "What was that?"

She'd followed me up here and now she paced the bell tower quarters. I needed to repent, or sulk, or blow off steam. Without company.

My physical reaction to Sybilla was natural. It was normal to feel attracted to a beautiful woman with whom I could prospectively have a child. Whom I would marry. It pissed me off that she had doubted *that* part.

"*That* was both nothing and none of your business."

El winced, looking hurt. "Not my business? You *are* my business, Krait. I have spent my life working for you. Most of it searching for her." Elsedora motioned toward the direction of Sybilla and my bedchamber, and a lump grew in my throat. "How long has that been happening?"

"El, it is *nothing*."

Pink flushed between the freckles on her cheeks.

"You need to stop saying that. Do you not think it could be something?" Her voice grew an octave higher as I reached the desk and slumped onto the desk chair. "Have you two—"

I stopped her. "We are not discussing that."

El smirked and said, "Fine. But Ryn owes me a hundred coins."

"For what?" I asked.

"We made a bet. He thought you had already but that doesn't look like a satiated expression."

Please let this line of conversation end.

"It is good that you like her, though, is it not?"

I knew what she wanted to hear, and I wasn't ready to say it. She liked Sybilla. I knew by the way she was prodding me. Her questions came from a place of care and not just for me.

"There is nothing to this, El. I can never offer her what she wants—don't romanticize it."

Elsedora hopped up to sit on the desk next to me and nudged my knee with her foot. "What exactly do you think she wants?"

"Comfort, safety, a family, halls full of laughter." I twisted my hand in the air, trying to make light of it.

"And you don't?"

I sighed. El could be so tiresome. "I had my chance for all of that once. It's not something you come across twice."

"Says *who?*"

I glared at her and grunted, but that didn't deter her.

"Kraiiit, get this through your thick skull—that woman has the weight of two realms on her shoulders while also facing a shit decision. And for some reason, she's still even an ounce interested in your insufferable ass. Loving each other in the end? Wouldn't that be a karmic reward for both of you?"

I groaned with a hand over my face before my gaze landed on the bronze statue in the corner.

My heart sank.

"No one said a thing about love. Stop building a life for me in your head. We need a child—those can be made without the novelty of parents who love each other."

Elsedora reached out and grabbed my shoulder, with an irritating, condescending expression. "Know that when you ruin this for yourself, and it comes crashing down, I'll be here for you. But I will not refrain from saying that I told you so. Because with that attitude...you are undoubtedly going to ruin it."

She hopped off the desk and headed for the door. "I'm off to see a King about a sword." Her airy voice carried over her shoulder.

There was no point in telling her not to go. "Be careful," I said uselessly as the door shut behind her.

She couldn't have been more wrong.

You could not ruin something you never intended to have.

I'd let desire win in the library. I couldn't allow that to happen again until I pulled myself together. I needed to stay indifferent to her.

I entered the bedchamber that night only after Sybilla had fallen asleep and *intended* to rise before she woke.

But when my eyes snapped open at sunrise, Sybilla was awake—facing me. I nearly jumped from the bed.

She'd propped herself up, with her head resting in her palm and elbow on the pillow beside me. Her hair was tied back with that silly blue ribbon, and she'd already dressed for the day in a light linen dress.

"I already relit the candles that burned out in the tower."

My eyes widened. She'd been to the bell tower. Again. I wondered what conversations she'd attempted to have with the dead this time. I wondered whether she'd spoken ill of me.

"You didn't have to—"

She cut me off. "I know. I wanted to. And there is something we need to discuss, so I couldn't afford you running off before I woke up."

Lifting myself onto my elbows, I scooted up so my back rested against the wooden headboard. "Alright," I answered, looking down at her there in my bed. She stared at me like she was about to begin negotiations.

I'd been ambushed at the crack of dawn.

"I once wanted to marry for love...My father tried to arrange three perfectly suitable political matches. Bringham was one. There were two others—a noble from the East Corridor, then another from the Southern isles. Each engagement failed because I was too stubborn to recognize that love didn't need to be a part of the equation." She swallowed hard.

"What about Mattock?" I asked, my teeth clenching against the subtle pain in my chest at the thought of her with the North King.

"I asked Emmerick to marry me once. It was long before my father died. I wasn't yet eighteen. But I didn't ask him to be my King—I asked him to run away with me. To live a life away from the courts of Henosis. He refused, obviously."

My brow furrowed. "Why *obviously*?"

I wanted to let my Shadows tear apart any other man who'd touched her.

She gave me a dry expression. "That would not have been the life he deserved. He made the right choice for both of us. I was young and naive. My people didn't need a fool in love. They needed a Queen willing to sacrifice whatever she must."

She met my eyes with an intensity that was like poisonous flames ready to engulf me. I missed the heat in her stare, the gasps and moans I'd summoned out of her, the way she'd tugged at my hair. This cool and calculated alternative spelled disaster.

"I don't need love in a marriage," she concluded.

"Did Elsedora put you up to—"

"No, she didn't. I see the way you war with your physical desire for me—I've now *felt it*. And I understand. Our lapse in judgment was just that. I don't need your heart or your love. And your internal struggle is a distraction we cannot afford."

My heart was pounding. "What are you saying?"

She answered, "I'd like to remove that conflict for you—a physical relationship between us is off the table."

My jaw tightened. That was it, then. "You've decided against fulfilling the prophecy."

"No. I've decided that a child born from friendship would be better than one born from whatever we'd become after letting anything turbulent happen between us. I need an uncomplicated marriage arrangement; you need an heir. So I would like to set the conditions for you."

A lump grew in my throat. I'd told El I couldn't offer Sybilla love, a family, or the comforts she desired.

So why did her acknowledging that suddenly feel so wrong?

"A child born from friendship?"

"We are friends, are we not?" she asked.

"We are." Wrong. Wrong. Wrong.

"Then it can be simple. We keep preparing to face Caym upon the black moon with the hope that I can keep him at bay until we figure out what our heir requires to end his reign."

She sat up now, with her legs pulled in and her linen dress stretched over her knees. Light crept in from the window, accentuating the lines of her heart-shaped lips and making her pale cheeks glow gold. It was no mystery why two men had been willing to roll the dice on an engagement with this woman even after she'd left another jilted.

I didn't fear being left. But her always being there but an arm's length out of reach? A creeping sense of dread overtook me.

She offered me the easiest sort of forever, and I was left disappointed. My mouth hung open at the sight of her—honey silk curls escaping at her temples. A monument of beauty.

Beauty that shouldn't be shackled to a man who would never love her the way she deserved to be loved.

"Why are you willing to do this?"

"Because Death has no place in my realm. Or yours. Despite what a prick you are, I feel our intentions are still aligned, and I don't want you resenting me later." Sybilla leveled a contemplative look at my mouth. "Now for my conditions."

There was a lump in my throat as I said, "Name them."

"I am never to be cut out of any decision made on behalf of myself or our child. They will be raised between the Luz and Sahlmsaran courts. Once they are born, you're welcome to take other lovers and I—"

A low growl left my throat involuntarily.

Fuck. I couldn't listen to her diplomatically tell me that she would warm my bed only until an heir was born. She was about to say that she'd be free to take other lovers, and my mind screamed at me still. Wrong. Wrong. Wrong.

It would never be enough to offer her a husband who didn't love her, a child forced upon her, a life of fighting that she never imagined for herself.

Her gaze narrowed on my mouth, glaring at it like she could wish the growl away.

"I know *exactly* what you can offer me," she answered my internal worry with an air of finality that struck me as sad. "I've known many women whose love for their children outweighs their romantic indifference for their husbands. It *will* be enough."

She'd reversed and echoed my concerns back at me.

"Very well," I ground out.

What she offered was a selfless gesture—she'd protect my sense of loyalty to Freya. She'd honor the prophecy.

She began to rub her palm. Impulsively, I took her hand in mine and then massaged the back of her knuckles where I'd noticed she often applied pressure. Her eyes closed as though the sensation brought her relief.

"Is this somewhere that you usually hurt?" I asked and pressed the meaty flesh between her thumb and palm.

The least I could do was offer her small comforts.

She nodded with a contented hum, and I sat up and pulled her hand closer to me, massaging in pressured circles. She attempted to fight back a delicious groan of satisfaction that made my cock twitch.

"Yes," she answered. "You don't have to do that, though." But the look of relief that flattened the lines that usually formed between her brow egged me on.

I couldn't offer her love, couldn't offer her the perfect marriage, couldn't even promise to be a good father. Mine had been shit at it. But I knew how to be a good friend—mostly. I could help carry the burden of some of her pain.

"I want to. If it's friendship you wish for, then let me be a friend. Friends don't let each other suffer when they can do something about it."

Sybilla straightened with a grimace—I'd struck a nerve.

Shit. I'd forgotten the sole reason she was agreeing to this. Mattock. The man she loved was possessed by a monster, so she would make do with another for the possibility of his safety. She pulled her hand from mine.

"No, they don't," she mused quietly as she slid out of our bed.

I watched her cross the room to her trunk of belongings and pluck out a vial of green tonic. She downed half the vial in one delicate swallow, with an almost imperceptible wince.

"I have one final condition," she said from the foot of the bed. I couldn't gather my thoughts to rise or answer. "We will not *come together* the traditional way to conceive…" She blushed between the words.

Though I was confused, all of my blood went to my groin to hear her speak so freely about sex.

"I'd like to handle that as professionally as possible."

That felt like a bucket of cold water to the head. "I see," I said, not fully understanding.

"I've talked to your healer here. There are ways that they can time my cycles, collect from you, and well—it would just be simpler if we involved a healer and kept things…"

"Professional," I repeated, hating how the word tasted on my tongue.

"I don't want you to feel guilt or regret when you look at me or our child. Given our desires to remain emotionally independent, it seems a good option," she noted. "So, I'm glad we could reach this agreement."

Had I agreed?

Stuck between the right thing to say or do and my desire for self-preservation, I let her slip on her leather slippers and exit the room without saying a word.

CHAPTER 37

EMMERICK

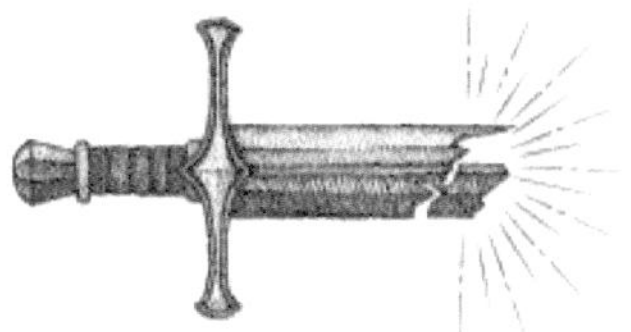

Ryssa hadn't come for tea. Maybe she was as disgusted with me as I was. Tapping my foot against the sitting room floor, I took a deep breath and stared into my cold cup of tea.

It had been a week since I'd come out of the darkness to find I'd committed another unspeakable crime.

One moment that ass of a King from the Wastelands had been here talking about Sybilla being sick. Then, I'd been standing over Haward's body.

My own heinous actions shook me.

I should write to someone—confess. But what if it happened with my friends and family nearby? What if I let them into this castle and then tried to hurt them too?

Even if I didn't harm them, the idea of pulling them into whatever web of evil plagued me felt wrong.

They couldn't possibly understand.

Ryssa had taken my broadsword that morning a week ago and handled hiding Haward's body in the garden crypts. I couldn't

307

imagine how she'd done it alone, and when she'd returned, that shadowy void in her robe had stared at me.

"It wasn't your fault…" she'd reassured me. But how could it not have been? Then she'd asked the most peculiar question. "King Emmerick, have you taken a map from the crypts below the castle?"

I still had no idea what she'd been referring to.

We'd told Barden that Haward would be traveling to the West Corridor to negotiate land contracts on my behalf with Bringham. He'd seemed unworried until no word of Haward's arrival had come.

Our ruse would not hold for long. Barden had already begun asking me questions and word had started to spread about the missing lord.

My foot kept tapping, and I gnawed on my lower lip.

There was a light knock on the door before a familiar flash of auburn hair bounced into the room and Elsedora sat beside me on the sofa.

"Who let you in this time?"

Elsedora kept appearing unannounced and sniffing around the castle. I'd told my guards to ban her, but she kept seducing them or skirting them; she was frightfully fast and lethally quiet.

"Again—I am quite good with guards. They tend to like wild redheads with no moral compass."

"So you're still propositioning my guards to get into my castle? Remind me to fire them all." I huffed, not having the energy or patience for her today.

"Only the pretty ones," she answered. "The brunette with the dimples is quite taken with me. Her name begins with an 'S,' but I forget what it is."

"Do you prefer women?" I sipped my cold tea, wanting her to leave me be. Though for some reason, her presence kept the dark thoughts from creeping in. So instead, I engaged her.

"I prefer *people*. Soft things," she said as she leaned over me and trailed a finger down the buttons of my jacket as though she was searching them for something. "*Hard* things, too."

The insinuation in her voice made me choke on the tea I hadn't realized was still in my mouth.

She smirked and continued, "Speaking of hard things, where is your blade today?"

"Being repaired by the blacksmith," I lied.

"Really?" She placed an arm over the back of the sofa behind me and crossed a leg beneath herself to face me.

"Is it unusual for a sword to require maintaining?"

She smirked and asked, "Do you know why I'm really here, puppy?"

Curiosity was a beastly inconvenience. I sighed, not wanting to admit that I did, badly, want to know.

Her visits had become something of a comfort—a poorly timed, confusing comfort. But if she came without bad news, it meant Sybilla was safe.

"No. But something tells me you're going to tell me even if I do not ask."

She shrugged. "You would be correct. The Death Origin, Caym, has risen. He is using envoys to do his bidding. Done any of his *bidding* recently?"

My shoulders tensed. I'd never been much good at lying. "What would make you think that I have?"

She hummed for a moment. "Well...for one, there is a mark of Death on the hilt of that broadsword you usually carry. I hope you trust whomever you gave it to because we don't know exactly what it does. And also, I have seen the change occur in you more than once."

I held my breath.

I'd put Ryssa in danger.

My heart rose to my throat. "I have never seen anything wrong with my sword. And what change?"

"It could be charmed so its wielder cannot see it," she answered. "Your eyes grow darker—hollow and callous. Nothing like the warm gold they are now."

I shook my head. "That is a ridiculous accusation."

"Oh, pet. I do like you. It would be a shame to see you die." Elsedora trailed a finger down my neck and to my collar and then flipped it as though inspecting it, too.

"Elsedora..."

Her expression brightened far too much for the nature of this conversation. "Yes?"

"Stop trying to turn me to putty after delivering information like that—I am not the Death Origin," I ground out.

She hummed, "No, you are not. But he's sank his claws into you. You've wielded Death, haven't you? You seem to always be wearing those gloves."

"I've done no such thing." The lie felt sour on my tongue. *I had.* She continued to touch the space where my stubble met my neck, tickling me. "And stop touching me like that. For Sources' sake, you're Fen's sister."

"So what? You are owed a bit of fun before your likely demise."

I leaned away. "He's my friend. He would burn me alive where I sit. And you're just trying to distract me like you do with my guards."

I scanned her face. She was pretty—wide hazel eyes and freckles across a dainty nose that made her appear softer than I knew her to be. Under different circumstances, maybe my interest would have been piqued.

But I'd never been one for trysts, and my damned heart always latched onto only one woman at a time. I'd made a habit of taking an interest in emotionally unavailable women who held my secrets.

But Ryssa held my secrets *for* me, not *from* me.

Elsedora stood and said, "What a shame. Something tells me you could use a bit of distraction."

As she headed for the door, my heart thundered.

"Wait." I stopped her. "Did you take a map from the crypts?"

Her lips turned up and she nodded. "Care to tell me what it does?"

"I don't know, actually," I answered. "I'm not confirming that I believe you, but hypothetically, if I am one of these envoys...how do I stop it?"

Leaning in the doorway, she crossed her arms and something akin to sadness crossed her features. "You don't," she said. "At least we have no reason to believe that Caym would let you go in any way other than death. He will keep killing through you, building his strength until then."

She hovered there as though wanting to say more as I swallowed hard. I'd killed innocent people. I'd "*Death-wielded,*" as she'd put it.

My shoulders collapsed; my elbows rested on my knees as I tried to absorb what she'd told me.

Finally, she added, "There are two more like you. Sybilla suspects Haward and Bringham. Be careful who you allow into this castle...for their sake and yours."

I nodded as my stomach dropped, and then she was gone.

As soon as Elsedora's footsteps were far enough down the hall, I leaped up and moved for the door.

Lady Ryssa had mentioned once that she spent most afternoons in her gardens. Suddenly, I felt ashamed that I'd never visited her before. It was a prominent estate just a short ride from the castle, and I took a carriage.

I stepped up to the front door and flexed my gloved fingers in anticipation. I knocked, and there was a commotion inside like someone was fumbling to get to the entry.

A gruff male voice said, "Who's it?"

Had she mentioned a husband? I knew she wore a ring beneath her gloves. Why did that possibility bring out an ugly possessive streak in me?

"It is—" Before I could finish my answer, the door swung open.

A man, seeming to be in his late eighties, greeted me. "What do you want?" His white hair was wiry and untamed atop his head.

He seemed to look past me and didn't bow—that much I liked about him. "It is King Mattock. I'm here to see Lady Ryssa. This is her residence, is it not?"

At that, the man let out a hearty, condescending laugh. "Yeah, boy, you're King Mattock. And I'm the Prince of damned fools."

I was taken aback, but then I realized the man still wasn't looking at me.

"This is *my* residence, boy. That Ryssa girl has been a big help to an old blind bastard like me. Come in."

Help. His residence. I stood there confused.

If Ryssa wasn't the lady of this house, then Haward and Barden had been duped. I had been duped.

I followed the old man inside.

"Name's Rivolt."

"I truly am King Mattock," I said, for the first time wanting someone to believe it.

He simply scoffed at me.

"And Lady Ryssa, she's not here?"

"She is no lady of this house. That isn't what we call housemaids. If you were King Mattock, you'd know that much. She's out in the greenhouse—likes to tinker out there when she gets a break from helping in here."

I glanced around. Dust coated most of the surfaces, and the rugs looked as though they hadn't been beaten in years. Texts reminiscent of the ones in Asterie's tower library were stacked high atop the dining table.

I'd been allowing Ryssa to help me with administrative tasks for months. She'd always seemed privy to noble matters.

Always helpful.

Always insightful.

She may not be the lady of this house, but judging by the state of this house, she also wasn't a housemaid.

"Might I go and have a word with her?"

"She doesn't talk much, but sure. Out through the terrace, down the steps, take the path to the pond."

"Thank you, Rivolt." I moved through the cluttered estate and out the windowed double doors into a manicured garden. She'd said she spent most of her free time in the gardens at *her* estate.

One truth. One lie.

I'd get to the bottom of this. There must have been some mistake. The man was old; maybe he was a relative she'd taken in. He was confused.

I carried on down the path until a sprawling pond came into view, and beside it sat an overgrown greenhouse. When I stepped inside,

I found Ryssa bent down by a row of newly planted rose bushes, plucking weeds from the soil around their roots.

Her burgundy robe hood was down, and she faced away from me. All I could see of her were petite, scarred hands pulling at roots in the soil, a gold ring on her left ring finger, and a long tousle of straight wheat-blonde hair tied back at her nape.

Of course she had to be a damned blonde.

She was just as gracefully beautiful as I'd imagined her, and I longed to see her face—to know the woman I'd grown fond of.

As I approached, deep scarring around her neck became visible. I grimaced, thinking of how painful whatever had put it there must have been. Drawing closer, I wanted a glance of her profile, to confirm what I knew—she'd be beautiful.

My boot hit a metal bucket.

Ryssa startled and turned toward me, rising.

No.

Backing away, I tripped over the pail and came down on my ass, hard.

Firose.

"What have you done with her?" I shouted from my vulnerable position, splayed there on the ground. "How are you—you're dead!"

Firose's face dropped—as did the weeds from her marred hands.

"King Mattock," she gasped.

Though she made no move to strike, I slid back and rose to my knees, searching for the sword no longer at my hip.

"You shouldn't be here."

"Where is Ryssa?" Self-preservation made me ask the question. Because I knew the truth. Ryssa had never existed beneath that veil. The cloak she wore was wrapped around Firose's petite frame.

She stepped forward and extended one hand toward me. "Listen, Emmerick, please."

I pushed to my feet, pulling my dagger from my boot. Holding the blade between us with a shaking arm, I stepped out of her reach.

"Please. Don't strike until you've heard what I have to say."

Blood pulsed in my ears, and cold sweat ran down my back. The scarring at her throat formed a ring all the way around her neck, purple and gnarled. Her face looked like cracked marble, with scars running from her temple to the peak of her full lips.

Lips that had once kissed mine roughly over wedding vows in the Central Tower on a night that I'd hoped to forget. The Divine who'd conducted our ceremony had worn gray robes and a gray veil—his voice had been grave and commanding. It'd seemed as though he held an investment in our marriage and wanted to put Firose on my throne. Poison-soaked memories blurred into the reality that she had never truly died. Seeing her face again was all I'd needed for the memories to return.

Our union had not been nullified. My lawful Queen consort stood before me.

My heart shattered. This woman before me was not the soft-spoken Ryssa that haunted my dreams. She was my worst nightmare.

"You," I growled.

Firose's eyes brimmed with tears. *Fake. She's incapable of remorse.*

"How?" I shouted and lunged for her. She didn't attempt to fight—no fire formed in her palms.

She gasped when I slammed her against the iron-framed glass of the atrium. "Please," she said through tears. "I beg you. I've tried to help you, to stop you when he takes control. I had been tracking him with a map, but it was stolen from me. He kept reaching you before I could. I was your father's friend once...I tried to help him then too."

With my body pressing hers to the glass, I brought my hand up to place the blade against her throat. "You have thirty seconds to convince me not to bleed you out right here."

I should just kill her.

Firose winced against the feeling of the blade at her throat. "It was real...our time spent together. It was real. At first I only wanted to ensure you did not Death-wield, that he couldn't harvest more through you. But then I enjoyed your company."

I shook my head.

Closing her eyes as tears streamed down her pallid, cracked cheeks, she continued, "Caym found me a week after Fen asked me to marry him. He was in Commander Stygian's body then. I was in the Temple of Light in Belray.

"I had everything I ever wanted. I was about to be the happiest woman alive. Caym took the worst of me and set it aflame. At first, it was infatuation. Then fanaticism. Within weeks, he could control me fully. He takes your anger and uses it to kill, destroy, maim, and when he bleeds you dry of your will to live, he simply takes a new envoy in your place. There are three of you he's infected." Her voice cracked.

Elsedora's words circled back to me about the Death Origin rising, about me being an envoy. Sybilla suspected me, Haward and Bringham.

I lessened the pressure of my dagger, too appalled with myself to hurt her. Not when she looked so damned helpless, not with tears burning down scarred cheeks. She breathed a sigh.

"How do I know you are not him now? I assume he can still control you?" I demanded.

"I am no longer an envoy," she answered. "He cannot control me any longer."

I scoffed. "How?"

"I don't know," she answered frantically. "One moment I was being torn apart in the throne room of Luz. The next, I woke in a field of flames on the West Corridor shores. It's as though the Sources melded me back together."

"Can he hear us now?" I should let the blade sink in. On one hand, she'd deceived me; on the other, she'd also been at my side for months. Every emotion grew at odds with another. I hesitated.

"No, he can only move between envoys when you are close. It's why he relies on his relics—the deathmarks. The marks do not control you; they *track* you. That is what the map in the crypts tracked too—the active deathmark. I knew when he neared. But I could only stop him so many times without risking him finding me." She reached up to place a hand on my chest. "I'm sorry...for lying, for it all."

I growled at the memories darkening my thoughts.

"Marching us into battle with me chained like an animal...you or him?"

She winced. "Me. I so desperately wanted to die. The late Mattock, your father, fought him, but over time he weakened, and fighting Death only leads to death. He had chosen Asterie as his new envoy. But when you killed her—"

He'd picked me instead.

I let my arm drop to my side with a fist clenched around the dagger's handle. In those awful visions that haunted me, I'd seen her there helping my father.

"And who are the others?" I asked.

"I have good reason to believe Barden is one—he was always near where the map showed the mark. I never found the other. He only needs envoys until the next black moon, when his Reverist power will return to him in full. Then anyone and everyone is at risk of coming under his influence."

I reached down with my free hand and raised her chin to force her to meet my gaze. Crystal-blue irises greeted me—like the prettiest blue skies. I wished their beauty brought me the joy I'd thought seeing Ryssa for the first time might. "How do I know you're not lying?"

She rasped out, "You don't."

I scanned her face while running my thumb over the scarring that ended just above her cupid's bow. Flatly, I said, "You died. Asterie saw it."

Why did I pity her?

A lump formed in my throat.

I was one of Caym's envoys. If he could truly hop between us, then it was imperative that we avoid Sybilla's cousin like the plague, and anyone else for that matter.

"Are you loyal to him?" I demanded with inches between our noses.

She shook her head. "No. He ruined me. He ruined everything...I don't want to see you meet the same fate."

Those clear skies began to well with tears again. I had to think. I had to do something.

We had a chance to get away.

I had a chance to get *her* away. I wasn't entirely sure when that had become important to me.

"Do you know if the deathmarks are exclusively on his envoys? Could he be tracking others or other objects?" I asked.

She swallowed hard. "It's possible. They are crafted with a dark charm. The envoys cannot see them. All those books in there I've collected for centuries—I've scoured every page, every line. These are uncharted waters."

I slipped a finger around one of the buttons of her cloak and undid it.

"What..."

Her mouth hung open as I undid the next button.

"What are you doing?" she breathed.

"Undressing you. Take every bit of cloth, every pin and piece of jewelry *off*." We would take no chances of being marked by Death wherever we traveled next. "I have been seeing memories of you. He might have realized you were near. It seemed that subconsciously…I knew you were near."

In that moment, I might not have been possessed by the Death Origin, but surely something possessed me. For months, Firose had loomed in my shadow-filled nightmares and Ryssa in every moment of light. Somewhere between the two planes, she stood before me, embodying the truest forms of love and of hate rolled into one.

"If it is the relics he uses to track us, then you need to be rid of any before we go," I said.

"Go?" She stilled. "With you?"

"Yes."

I stepped back to allow her room to undress herself.

I couldn't put the pieces together fast enough. But I knew that I wouldn't leave her there. After dropping her robe, she pulled her tunic over her head. She discarded the golden ring from her finger, and it fell with a metallic ping on the stone of the greenhouse path.

I stared at it. A memory flashed of me slipping it over her knuckle.

Firose could have challenged my crown or forced her way next to me as Queen.

She hadn't.

She could have run from it all.

Yet she'd stayed to help me.

She pulled the ribbon from her hair and dropped it. "He could have placed more than one on you," she said as her fingers hooked into her breeches. She pushed them down her legs, which were scattered with deep white blotches of scarring. "You should change clothes too."

Watching her undress shouldn't have excited me, but I'd once told Ryssa that I would find what was hidden under her robe beautiful no matter what.

Somehow, I still did find her alluring.

Her blue lace undergarments made my mouth dry, and I averted my gaze.

I nodded and dropped my dagger to undress, too. Since I wore only a tunic and breeches, it was quick work. Leaving only my undershorts on, I asked, "Where did you put the sword?"

"I've mostly been carrying it since I found you that day. I left it in the Temple of Light this morning. It will just look like you are having a day of prayer."

She struggled with the laces of her corset.

"Let me?" I asked.

A pile of clothes and unsaid words lay between us as she nodded and turned. I found the clasp at the top before pulling at the dainty laces far less gracefully than I'd like to admit. She leaned into the touch of my fingers at her lower back.

At the sensation of her soft skin, need sank heavy in my stomach and blood rushed to my groin.

She was flushed when she spun around, and I watched her slip the corset straps off and let the garment fall. My heart pounded as Firose placed her hand on my chest over one of the burn scars she'd given me that night in the tower.

"This," she whispered, "wasn't me."

I desperately tried not to stare at her body, but failed. My resolve to be a gentleman ran thin.

She licked her lips before she spoke again. "You're a kind man, and you will be a great King. You deserve none of this, but he will warp what you are. It is what he did to me—I didn't start this way either. It doesn't mean I don't deserve your hatred for what I became."

"Why did you decide to help me? Why not just run?" I ground out, trying to ignore the heat of her palm on my chest.

"It felt right. I thought maybe if I could save you from falling too, then it might redeem some of the pain I'd caused. That it would redeem not having been able to save Corric."

I examined her face—the pinch between her brows, the way her mouth hung parted as she gazed up at me. I should kill her, loathe her. She'd tried to destroy my city, tried to kill my friends, and forced me to marry her for my crown.

It hadn't been her. At least not all of it.

Could we be broken down and sorted neatly into the good and bad parts of ourselves?

I'd killed more people than I could remember—him.

I'd gone against my dearest friend and threatened to take her crown by force—me.

I'd visited King Sheffield, found him on a ride and knocked him from his horse, letting Death crawl into his veins—him.

I'd stationed troops along the borders at Bringham and Haward's recommendation—me.

I'd become a vessel. Unveiled before me, a woman stood who understood how helpless that felt.

My voice grew lower. "I don't know what to think of you. I don't know if I hate you or want you."

Her fingers traced the burned handprints on my bare chest as though mourning them. She looked up at me again and said, "Then think nothing of me at all."

The sapphire flames in her eyes made me grow brazen. "Do you want me?" I asked.

"Yes," she breathed out. "But your favor isn't something I deserve."

There was a half-naked woman before me who had become the object of so many of my desires these past months. They blended together in a fog of hate, and lust, and a heady sense of having too little time to make my own choices.

My resolve broke.

"Then I'll think later," I groaned as my mouth crashed down onto hers. Her fingers dug into my shoulders, breasts pushed to my chest with nothing between us.

In one swift motion, I lifted her and pressed her to the atrium glass. My mouth moved down her neck, eliciting a gasp. Tracing the lines of scarring there with my tongue, I groaned as she hooked her thumbs into the waist of my undershorts and pushed down to free me. I pulled the lace of her underwear aside.

As her hand found my length between us and positioned me at her entrance, I groaned into her shoulder.

"Take what you need, my King," she whispered into my ear.

Obliging, I pushed into her, and she cried out. I gave her no time to adjust to me before driving in again, reveling in the feel of her tightening around me.

Nails dug into the upper plane of my back. I grabbed a handful of her hair. In urgent fury, we both chased releases we didn't deserve—retreating and colliding in a frenzy of need. The way she felt writhing against that glass was freeing.

I'd only been with one other and sex had never felt like this. Raw. Hungry. Mutually selfish. Wrong in ways that felt unjustifiably right. It was life and death, punishment and revival, passion and ruin.

Firose met my pace until we both cried out, and I spilled into her with a satisfied groan. Her head fell to the center of my chest, between the marks she'd left on me that terrible night when neither of us had control over our fates. We both panted.

Something snapped into place as she looked up at me, still coiled around my waist. The lust of the moment faded with the setting sun, but an aching sense of recognition settled in my stomach that I wouldn't admit to myself or her.

The Source power in my veins felt fed.

Her irises were dancing with red flames, and in their reflection, I saw a glowing ring of light in mine.

After having come together, we didn't share words or tender moments. Instead, we both walked silent and naked as the days we'd been born to the main house. It would be impossible to verbalize how incredibly reckless this all had become.

Guilt settled in my gut—I'd turned away Fen's little sister out of respect earlier that day and then ended up pressing his ex-lover against a greenhouse window and taking her in an impassioned frenzy.

What in the Sources' names had gotten into me? The answer to that question was a dark truth.

Rivolt was snoring in a chair in the sitting room. With a finger over her lips, Firose motioned with her other hand toward a bedroom door. Inside, she approached the wardrobe and opened it.

After tossing clothes that were far too small my way, she pulled on an oversized tunic and loose breeches.

As I slid up my breeches, I stumbled into a chair.

Firose responded by shushing me. Mussed and flushed looked good on her; she appeared naive even—at odds with the centuries-old scheming enchantress I knew her to be.

The tunic uncomfortably hugged every muscle of my torso, but luckily, the breeches fit without crowding spaces they shouldn't have. Firose had to lace too-big boots tightly before she passed me a pair.

We slipped out the back doors without an inkling of where we should go to hide from the Death Origin. He would undoubtedly search for us once he noticed my relic hadn't moved for some time.

Where would he be the least likely to look?

CHAPTER 38
SYBILLA

The market bustled with anticipation for the first rainfall. The gentle rumble of thunder could be heard in the distance. No droplets had fallen yet, but I looked forward to the cool reprieve that the rain would hopefully offer tonight.

"Isn't this marvelous? Why would you *leave?*" Elsedora said as she spun around me once before taking my hand. She'd hugged me when I told her of my agreement with Krait and promised to be there whenever I needed. However, she wasn't subtle about her dislike of my conditions.

It only seemed right to return to Luz. I could continue my training with Cassidee, and my advisors were more than capable Source-wielders.

Darvanda and I could see a healer each month until the prophecy was fulfilled. It was my plan—my terms. It removed my heart from the matter.

A marriage of convenience didn't require cohabitation, and I knew that if I stayed, I'd only desire more from Krait than he would ever be willing to give me.

Happy for a day of distraction, I let El pull me through the crowds. The vendors were setting up for the night festival—what I'd been told was the biggest celebration of the season.

"I need to go back to my people," I reasoned. No one else knew yet, not even Krait, and something made me hesitate against writing Asterie.

The tonics were barely keeping my pain at bay, and with no certain path forward, it was hard to stay in the moment. If we had until the next black moon, then it was a few years before Caym was at his strongest...We had time. But would my body allow me to carry on at this pace?

We moved through the street parallel to the main canal. The thoughts of the people around me swirled in a frenzy of happy sensations and a few surprised exclamations. One such thought I picked up repeatedly.

"Renai." It was always followed by a gasp. Some kissed their fingers and extended them to me, a gesture that I returned.

"What does 'renai' mean?" I whispered to El.

"It's Brennac. It means 'lovely,' or when used as a proper title, 'Queen,'" Elsedora explained before getting distracted by some shiny baubles and jewelry in a charmed floating tent. "How much for these?"

My heart tugged. These people accepted me as their Queen and soon I'd leave them.

The street grew darkened by the overcast of clouds. Colorful banners flailed in the wind, backdropped by the mixed tilework of a row of arched buildings. Balconies draped with both the Luz and Sahlmsaran flags lined the canal. Awe and hope flooded me.

Leaving this realm would be bittersweet.

"Are you about to cry, Sybilla?" Elsedora asked as she put on a pair of gold dangling earrings.

"What?" I wiped at the corner of my eye. "No, don't be silly. It's the dust."

"Riiight." She exaggerated the vowel in her breezy way.

It had grown dusty since the winds had begun to kick up this morning, bringing dark clouds in their wake.

"Oh it *smells* like rain," El said with glee. The vendors' tents flapped around, and thorn-like bushels of vegetation tumbled down the roads.

Elsedora carried on to the next booth, where beaded clutches too vibrant for my taste were piled atop a wood table. She tried one that suited her.

A small group of children formed a circle around a spigot of water on the street's corner. Their attention was held on a boy wearing tattered linens. A clay bowl lay in front of him to collect coins. He faced the others, away from me, but looked familiar. I stalled while El continued through the market.

The boy reached into the pail below the spigot and took a handful of water. He lifted the water toward a young girl who giggled as the liquid suspended and moved in a circular motion just above his hands. He spun a finger, and the water began to ebb and flow, settling into the shape of a single butterfly that flapped toward the young girl. Her eyes went wide with disbelief—mine matched.

A Water-wielder right here in the Sahlms. This could solve Krait's drought problems.

While none of the texts of Henosis acknowledged the Sources as entities, some of the texts that Krait had since read to me claimed that Origin Aquas had been the first to lose his mortal form. Water-wielders had been rare for centuries, and it was thought none had survived the Great Wars.

I made my way through the crowds, catching attention as I bumped into leisurely shoppers. When I'd nearly reached the boy, the other children looked up, and one gasped, "Renai!"

The Water-wielding boy turned to me with a panic-stricken expression.

Hurley.

It was the young groom who had sold out my location to those men from Sahlmkar. The butterfly fell with a splatter. Hurley took off running down the street.

"Not this time, you little shit," I muttered, sprinting after him.

"Sybilla, wait!" I heard Elsedora call from behind me as I turned down an alley to follow Hurley. He'd slammed into the chest of a man there and ended up flat on his back.

"Watch it, kid!" the man growled, kicking at Hurley as the boy scrambled to his feet and continued to outrun me. My ankles ached, every step feeling like a sharp jab.

Fire formed in my throat, and my legs burned.

"Stop!" I commanded. A rippling feeling shot from my mind, and suddenly Hurley froze.

I needed to start thinking of that first.

Finally catching up to him, I grabbed Hurley by the shoulder and spun him around to face me. He was lanky and had a boyish roundness to his cheeks.

"You..." I gasped for air. "You brought those men to attack me."

"I didn't know." Tears streamed down this face. "I swear to the Sources. They told me they wouldn't hurt you. They said they needed to deliver a message and that I'd make twenty coins."

"They delivered a message, alright," I grumbled as Elsedora's footfall landed behind me. We were in the shade of the alley, with buildings stretched up above us.

"Sybilla, what the—"

"It's okay," I reassured her. "This is Hurley."

"The groom boy? The one who—"

I interrupted her again. "Yes, yes. He's harmless and potentially *very* useful to us."

Hurley's eyes widened. "I'll do anything. I owe you whatever debt. Please, please don't hurt me."

"Hurt?" My brow scrunched, and I shook my head. "You listen. If I wanted to hurt you—I wouldn't have let you run off and escape that night. Now, if I let you go, will you *promise* me not to run?" Holding his feet there was surprisingly fatiguing.

Hurley nodded through his tears.

I looked at Elsedora. "You'll take him to Luz."

She balked. "Luz? Why?"

"Because...he's a Water-wielder. And if we bring him back to Umber House, then Krait will have his head." I reached down and ruffled the boy's brown waves. "And you wouldn't be able to pay off your debt without a head, would you?"

"I can only do stupid tricks. I can't do anything to help..." Hurley tried to deflect.

Elsedora cut in, "Water-wielders could once part oceans, wield rivers at their fingertips, and make rain fall even when it wasn't due." She seemed to be catching up now.

I added, "You could help us, Hurley. In fact—that is your punishment for nearly getting me killed. You owe your Queen a debt. I'd say that a comfortable life learning how to use your Source magic in Luz is a better punishment than the gallows. No?"

"Okay, yes, yes." Hurley finally breathed out, wiping away his tears on a dirty sleeve. "Please don't send me to the gallows."

"Do you have family here?" Elsedora asked.

My heart clenched when he shook his head. The toes of his boots were broken through, his feet outgrowing them, and his clothing looked as though he hadn't changed since he'd been working in Umber House.

I put one hand on the boy's shoulder. "Promise me, then, when my advisors, Asterie and Fenris, teach you all they can—you will come back here. You bring the rains; you help this place remain habitable. Do you accept that duty?"

"Yes, my Queen." Hurley nodded.

Elsedora eyed me. "I will take him to Luz before Krait catches wind of him. Head back to Umber House and get ready for the festival," she said as she glanced up at the threatening sky. "What should I tell Asterie and Fen?"

"Tell them he is their ward until I return."

Elsedora kept her promise and delivered Hurley to Fen and Asterie and then met me to get ready for the first rain festival. She'd brought a note back with her, which I set down on the desk in the bedchamber that I still *platonically* shared with Krait.

Sybilla,

At your request, we will teach young Hurley everything we can about wielding his Source power. I only ask that the next time you drop a child on our doorstep, you give us a bit of warning. And wash them first.

Your friend,

Asterie

I smiled at the familiarity of her cursive. We'd written often, with me providing guidance on everything from the sheep trade to land disputes between nobles in the Central Corridor. With her keeping me so well apprised of the goings-on in my Corridor, it was as though I'd never left.

Yet my heart yearned for home.

"Hold still," Elsedora said, feigning annoyance as she tied the fabric around my body in ways I couldn't imagine ever repeating.

I glanced down at the rust-colored dress she had wrapped me in. It was a too-sheer silk ensemble that gathered into a flowing skirt and showed off far more skin on my torso than I felt comfortable with.

"Dancing skirts!" El exclaimed and spun me around by my hand. Her own golden wrap dress caught the wind as she twirled too.

My Luz-blue ribbon lay across the bed. Instead of pulling my hair back with it, I left my curls down over my shoulders. It didn't match this particular ensemble, and wearing the Sahlms' colors for their annual celebration seemed more fitting.

A rap at the door startled us. I called, "Who is it?"

"It's Ryn—are you ready, Princess?"

Feeling guilty about not carrying the Luz color on me, I stuffed the silk ribbon into the bust of my dress. Elsedora burst out a laugh, watching me.

"Yes, come in!" I called out.

Ryn pushed the door open. He stilled and gave me an appreciative once-over. "You are absolutely bewitching. Are you sure you want to marry this grump?"

Krait stepped up behind him. "I suppose swapping out a King for a Prince is still on the table. What dowry do you come with, Ryn?"

Elsedora stifled a giggle, and Ryn glanced her way with a sheepish shrug but the lines around his eyes pinched when they landed on her.

The brooding King looked entirely unamused with the ribbing as he shouldered Ryn. Krait was dressed in a deep-red formal tunic that had gold-threaded seams; the way it hugged his shoulders and tapered at his waist caught my attention.

Source-damned man with his Source-damned muscular build. Everything he wore suited him. Yet I'd bet a good number of coins that he looked divine in *nothing*. I'd only gotten a good view of the backside…

It was time to leave this place because lust made me a damned fool.

"I'd like to keep my head," Ryn said. "And I make a better tryst in the dark." He winked but it wasn't at me. He was dressed similarly tidy—a cream silk tunic and dark breeches tucked into leather boots.

"Enough," Krait grunted at his friend, which only caused Ryn to give me a wide-eyed, knowing smirk. He wanted me to listen.

I obliged. "*It really is too easy to get under his skin when it comes to you.*" Ryn's thought slipped into my head.

I smirked back and curled one brow up.

Krait observed us and let out an exasperated huff of air. "First Elsedora, now you too? Can at least one of my officers remain loyal to me?"

"With an attitude like that, I wonder why," I teased before meeting Krait's stare.

The slow drag of his gaze down my body felt like a hot brand over every inch of bare skin. Which was quite a lot of skin since I wore one of Elsedora's dresses.

"Is it too much?" I asked, picking at one of the fine crystals that lined the seam at my bust.

"No," Krait answered too quickly.

"Told you," Elsedora mused as she marched out of the room.

Ryn cleared his throat and before trailing after her, he said, "We'll make sure the carriage is ready for us."

"Why are you looking at me like that?" I snapped as soon as Ryn and El rounded the corner.

"Like what?"

"With…heat."

The corners of his mouth turned up, and I placed my hands on my hips, which only seemed to ignite his interest.

"I'm serious, Krait. That better be a 'filet me' stare. We discussed this."

"Did we?" he asked with one raised brow.

"Yes," I shot back.

Things were about to get complicated enough in the upcoming years. Yet Krait made me feel safe, protected, heard, and wanted in his own toxically grumpy way. I hated admitting that I'd miss him.

He sighed and said, "You are ravishing—you can't expect me not to notice. Your terms never stated I couldn't appreciate the sight of you."

Fuck.

I was falling for the King of the Sahlms.

We had no time for heartache or petty, girlish crushes. Not when our realms were at stake, not when my people were at the fingertips of the Death Origin if we did not succeed. Not when we would have a child that deserved a stable upbringing. I knew the limits of what he could offer me.

While my mind rattled, he'd drawn his eyes up to catch mine again.

I needed to change the damned subject.

"I sent Hurley to Asterie," I blurted.

"What is a 'Hurley'?" he asked.

"The boy—the one who led the men from Sahlmkar to my room...when I was attacked."

All of the steam in his gaze evaporated. "You did what?"

Now, that was a tone I could work with.

"He is a Water-wielder," I explained.

"He should be a *dead* Water-wielder along with his company that night."

Popping a hip out, I said, "He is a scared boy—one that may solve your drought problems when I send him back to you. I believe you were looking for the words 'thank you.'"

He ground out, "Thank you." When I slipped into his mind, he was roiling with distaste for what I'd just revealed. *"Stubborn woman."*

Fighting a triumphant smirk, I took his offered arm. As he led me down to the carriage, I wondered if I'd ever find another man with whom I so enjoyed arguing.

CHAPTER 39
SYBILLA

Hundreds of tents were pitched along the riverbed Krait had brought me to that first night, just outside the city. Tealight candles were set on the rocks that speckled the banks of the too-low river. Heavy clouds still gathered and had turned dark purple in the setting sun.

Children flew charmed flaming kites in the turbulent wind, and the smell of fried bread wafted past. I'd had it once during a night market with El—the fluffy bread had been topped with hot peppers and various mouthwatering sauces.

Beside the water, musicians played for coins, and those who had gotten an early start on celebrations were already dancing with bare feet through the tall brown grasses of the riverbanks. Here in the wash, the thin tree coverage created flickering shadows on the ground.

The humidity added a chill to the air, which left goosebumps on my arms. I could understand why the people of the Sahlms gathered to celebrate—I'd never thought I'd *miss* feeling cold.

I hadn't seen an ounce of rain since arriving and longed for the sound of pattering on rooftops that so frequently occurred in Luz.

I'd return soon.

Lightning struck in the distance, and thunder rumbled overhead.

"This way." Ryn guided me with a hand between my shoulder blades. We passed an enchantress selling love charms and another selling everlasting seedlings. Magic spread through the veins of this land—so common that I almost forgot that my realm was completely devoid of it.

Only when Ryn shot me a sly look did I realize I'd pursed my lips involuntarily.

"What?" I defensively retorted.

"You're thinking yourself in circles."

I rolled my eyes. "Are *you* the mind reader around here?"

He huffed a laugh and continued, "El told me you plan to leave us this week."

I glanced over my shoulder at where Krait trailed a few yards behind us, feeling self-conscious about this line of conversation so near to him. It felt important for me to be the one to tell him I'd go.

"Well—I can't stay forever," I said. "But I appreciate your help these months. I am not an easy student."

Ryn smiled. "You will turn these realms upside down for the better, Princess. Wherever you choose to do it from. Though there will be many here who miss you."

I offered him a sad smile. "How do you stay so positive all the time when so much has been taken from you?"

He shrugged. "You can choose to be pissed off at the world or you can choose to embrace it in all of its injustices."

He guided me toward a tent with open flaps flailing in the wind. Wicker rugs had been laid down inside, and wood-framed seats with lush cushions offered a quaint sitting space. Elsedora was already lounging there with a bottle of wine in hand.

She held the bottle out to Ryn without a verbal greeting. He took a swig before offering it to me. I looked around for a chalice.

Ryn shrugged. "It's the first rain. Live a little, Sybilla."

At that, I put the bottle to my lips and pulled from it. The decadent richness of the burgundy fruit warmed my tongue. I'd been limiting my consumption since having fallen ill, but the tonics and rest now had me feeling well enough. For now.

The scent of warm spice and smoke enveloped me. Krait stepped up behind me, reaching around my waist to swipe the bottle with playful ease. It slipped from my fingers as his front brushed my back, and I suddenly hated my own condition to put him off. He stepped away from me, and I missed his warmth.

It needed to be a clean cut.

We needed to remain allies.

He got to keep his realm out of Death's grip and his people from losing their land. I got the same. I would not be his guilty pleasure to resent as his heart yearned for what he'd lost.

I took the seat beside Elsedora. This would put a safe distance between us. It had been hard enough to share a bed with the man while keeping my hands to myself with the way he looked like a Source-damned statue sculpted from women's fantasies. It didn't help that his tunic sleeves were rolled up onto his forearms. My weakness.

Elsedora reached over and grabbed my hand, squeezing it tightly. "I'm so glad you can experience a first rainfall before leaving."

Krait had sat across from us and taken another swig of wine. He passed the bottle to Ryn as his brows knitted together. "Leaving?"

My posture straightened.

Elsedora and her big fucking mouth.

"Yes. I'm returning to Luz at the end of the week. Now that we've reached an agreement, I'd like to be seen by Wyeth through the process. I'll write to you when you're needed."

The words sounded callous, and I wished I could retract them.

Krait clenched one fist around the wood armrest of his seat, his jaw pulsing. Ryn passed the wine to El with a sideways glance.

Krait waved his hand as though trying to dismiss his own anger. "Ah, yes. Keeping things professional. How could I forget your intent to use me as a stud?"

Elsedora covered her mouth to prevent spitting out the pull she'd just taken from the bottle. Ryn crossed one ankle over his thigh and stifled a chuckle.

Prick.

"We both agreed upon conditions," I snapped back.

He grunted a response and averted his gaze toward the darkening river.

Ryn's thoughts pushed through. *"So that's why he's been so moody. You've hurt his pride."*

I wanted to disagree with him, but that would draw attention.

Going back to Luz was the right thing to do. My people were faring well under Asterie and Fen's rule, but that was meant to be temporary. With the threat of Caym rising, my Corridor needed to remain my priority.

"You two are welcome to visit me anytime," I directed at El and Ryn, not acknowledging Krait's piss-poor mood.

Krait remained cagey as he said, "So glad you have it all figured out then."

It grew dark, and candlelight from the tents around us lit the surrounding area in a golden glow. Thunder cracked overhead, and the first patter of rain hit the top of the tent, sweetening the air with a loamy musk. As the drizzle of rain turned into a downpour, the crowds of Source-wielders, immortals and mortals alike hooted in celebration.

Some lit colorful charms into the air that crackled in shades of red and orange above us. The river below became spotted with heavy droplets, and the tealight candles were extinguished in tiny spouts of steam as the rain persisted. Music from the bands grew louder, picking up the tempo, as though the rain fueled the need for song.

"Krait, you know the drill." Elsedora stood and extended her hand to him. He reluctantly reached up and let her drag him out into the rain. El was barefoot, and Krait carefully maneuvered his boots around her feet as they danced through the muddying grasses.

"She typically gets his first and only dance before he slinks off to a corner to watch others celebrate," Ryn explains.

"Why am I not surprised?"

Krait was a stiff dancer. While coordinated, he lacked all of the energy that Elsedora more than enthusiastically compensated for as she spun around him like a graceful sprite.

I'd drunk just enough of the shared bottle for frolicking in the pouring rain to sound fun. "Do you want to dance, Ryn?"

Ryn's smile widened, and he wiggled his brows. "You're sure? Are you trying to get me killed tonight?"

I laughed and nodded before dragging Ryn out into the slick grasses, feeling light and carefree for once. Thankfully, the leather slippers I'd chosen had a good grip on the soles. The heft of every worry within me washed away under the first warm downpour of the Sahlms' summer. The rain weighed down my curls and slid over my cheeks.

The moment my body fell into rhythm with Ryn's movement, his features began to distort...

Shit. No, no, no.

I'd forgotten this particular charm of those Source-wielders of the night sky. Suddenly, I felt guilty for having paraded Asterie around the Luz courtyard, making a party trick of revealing my nobles' true desires. Under the moonlight's trickery, Ryn's features would change to mirror those of the person I most desired.

Ryn's pale skin grew darker and his frame taller. I expected in the next moment for Emmerick to stare down at me.

But instead, gray irises met mine. Beneath the hard lines and stubble, he was almost unrecognizable without his brooding expression.

"Who is it that you see, Sybilla?" Ryn's tone was entirely too mischievous. He'd set me up.

He was manipulating this enchantment. He had to be.

I swallowed hard. "Darvan-dick." My voice was barely above a whisper. The people surrounding us became interested and crowded around to watch. "How are you doing that?"

I could hear the internal whispers surrounding us.

"It's true—she loves our King."

"When will they marry?"

"Our realm will have a little heir in no time."

Their awestruck thoughts only fueled my anxieties. Every gaze felt like hot air from a hearth glazing over my skin.

"I'm not doing anything, Sybilla. You are." The lines of Ryn's brow softened as though only now did he regret putting me in such an awkward position. He shielded me from the crowd, drawing me closer. While he looked like the brooding warlock that my heart felt conflicted about, he didn't smell like him—Ryn smelled like lemongrass and musk.

Past Ryn's shoulder, I saw the *real* Krait, still holding Elsedora's hand, but having gone stone-still. They stood outside the crowd that had circled around us. He stared at us with an unreadable expression before dropping El's hand to approach me.

I was a fawn caught in a hunter's lamplight—caught off guard and too exposed to fight.

So, I did the next natural thing.

CHAPTER 40

KRAIT

As soon as Ryn led Sybilla out into the rain, Elsedora stopped spinning around me like a water-logged fairy. Wet red locks of hair slapped me in the face, catching me right in the eye, as she came to an abrupt stop.

"El," I groaned. A wild grin spread across her face. This was the one day a year I *tried* to allow myself to have a bit of fun. Or at least let others have fun. The news of Sybilla's impending departure had already soured my mood.

"Should I remind her?" El asked. "She knew of the enchantment when Asterie visited her court. Surely she remembers that—"

"No," I grunted at the ground. "Let her see. It's best she remembers."

Elsedora squeezed my hand as the band nearest to us picked up a new song, this one slower.

So what if Sybilla saw the reflection of her own desire in Ryn? So what if it was the young King Mattock?

"Kraiiit." Elsedora attempted to soothe me in anticipation.

Under the moonlight, Ryn's Source power would bring out truths I'd rather not face on a night meant for joyous debauchery. I stared at the ground, not breathing.

"Sources," Elsedora exclaimed. When I dared to raise my gaze, a crowd had formed around Sybilla and Ryn as they swayed awkwardly through the dead, rain-soaked grass.

Seeing a version of myself there, gazing down at Sybilla with a smile, made me grow hot. It struck me—we looked *right* together. I'd spent all of my time with her trying to convince myself it would be wrong.

I couldn't read her lips but could tell she was being contrary.

She didn't believe the illusion.

I didn't believe it either.

Then, Ryn brought her in closer, seemingly to guard her flushed cheeks and surprise from the crowd. When her gaze met mine, her posture went rigid, and she backed away from Ryn.

After dropping El's hand, I took one step forward.

Sybilla searched the crowd for an opening and ran as soon as she found one. Ryn didn't try to stop her. I pushed through to get to him as his features shifted to his own.

"What the *fuck*, Ryn?" I quietly growled, trying not to draw the crowd's attention. "What stunt are you pulling?"

Ryn sighed and threw his hands up. "I love you, Krait, but this is getting ridiculous."

My brow furrowed as my usually jovial officer tried to walk away from me. I grabbed his arm. "Ryn. Tell me, please...tell me you didn't manipulate what I just saw."

He turned to me. "No, you raging ass. You know I can't manipulate that reaction. She desires *you*. And judging from how quickly I shifted...it isn't some dalliance or crush, you lucky bastard. Now, instead of berating me, go after her before you botch your second chance at happiness."

She wanted *me*.

I squeezed his shoulders and said, "Thank you."

He rolled his eyes with a renewed smile and nodded toward where she'd fled. My boots hit the ground, and I sprinted toward the trail up to the city.

Glancing around, I found an older woman who pointed up the slope of the riverbank. "Your Queen went that way, my King."

After I had ascended the riverbed, jogging over rocks and roots, more of the citizens in the streets of Sahlmsara joyously pointed me in the right direction until, minutes later, I was at the front entrance of Umber House.

Had she gone back to Luz?

A cart vendor called out, "Looking for your betrothed? She went inside."

The heavy weight on my chest lifted. She had not used this opportunity to Egress away.

She'd run to my home.

I didn't give my mind enough time to question whether finding her tonight was the right choice. The only choice that made sense led me straight to her. And I knew exactly where she'd be.

CHAPTER 41
SYBILLA

The air in Umber House was sticky and humid against my hot, flushed skin. Running up the riverbank had left me out of breath, with a hammering heart. My knees felt weak, and my head spun. Egressing home to Luz had tempted me, but I didn't want to worry Asterie and Fen by showing up at this hour.

I needed a private place to think—not the bedchamber, which smelled of sultry smoke and spice. Not the bell tower, where Freya would stare down at me in judgment.

Refuge would only be found among old leather-bound books and cool air. I whispered, "In the Shadows we trust."

The door to Krait's *hole* unlocked for me. Sconces lit the stairs and guided me into the belly of the house. The library, where a surly King had read me stories, legends and prophecies, hummed with silence.

I'd been so stupid. I'd let my desires out in the open; all of my vulnerabilities had been laid on the table for him to dismiss or reject.

I kicked off my mud-covered leather slippers; they made a wet, sopping thud on the ground where they landed. Finding a wool blanket slung across the chaise, I used it to dry my face and then wrung my hair into it.

The silk of the dress clung to my stomach and thighs, but I wouldn't dare try to remove it here without a change of clothes. With so many ties, and how many times Elsedora had wound it around me, there was no way I'd ever get it back on the same way again alone.

Blowing out a raspberry, I leaned against the library ladder and let the blanket fall in a damp heap at my side.

"Fuck. Fuck, Fuck, Fuck," I whispered to myself.

"Charming." Krait's voice echoed from the shadows before I saw him. He appeared from the darkest corner. It was *his* private library—suddenly, it felt foolish to be there. He looked flustered, like he'd been running, his breathing elevated.

With an exasperated sigh, I asked, "Don't you have some candles to light?" Maybe if I poked his deepest wound, he'd leave me alone.

One corner of his mouth inched up. "Don't deflect." His voice lowered as he crossed the room toward me. "It doesn't suit you to pretend you didn't want to see me."

"I'm not deflecting—there's a brass statue upstairs that will make far better company than me tonight," I shot back, but he took a step closer.

"She did make amazing company. The best, really; she never dressed me down or slung curses at me."

"Fuck you," I spat. I didn't doubt that any woman who could capture the heart of this man had been excellent company. I didn't resent her—I resented the fact that she'd had his love before she met her end. Whose love would I have before meeting mine?

"Does that bother you?" he challenged, drawing a step nearer. All the perfectly sculpted edges of him were accented by rain-soaked silk, and his dark brows knitted together as he stared me down. He looked so damned delectable even when being a prick.

"It doesn't bother me a bit, so I'm telling you to go."

He smirked as droplets of rain fell from his wind-whipped, dark hair onto his forehead. His tongue ran across his lower lip, as though contemplating me, and it sent heat down my chest. "You want me to walk up those stairs? Leave you here wanting?" Another step, and I was backed against the ladder.

"Wanting what? *You?*" I scoffed. But my heart fluttered, and I hadn't had enough wine to blame it on that.

He reached down and took my chin between his fingers. When he tilted my head up to meet his iron-gray stare, I held my breath. His lips parted, and at first, I thought he might kiss me. A glint of realization shone in his eyes.

I did want him. All of him. And he couldn't be stupid enough not to know it.

"Climb up," he commanded and nodded to the ladder.

"Don't tell me what to do," I shot back. My traitorous bare feet were already on the first rung. Goosebumps formed on the flesh of my arms as he steadied me.

He hummed his approval. "It seems what I consider good company has changed over the years."

"I can't imagine a soul ever finding *you* good company," I snapped back. Though my blood boiled, my body could have melted through the rungs of that ladder. Verbal daggers made the best shield against bad decisions.

"You know...I've grown fond of you running that pretty mouth at me."

"Sadistic prick." My words were cutting, but the momentum of my anger began to dissolve into lust.

He leaned forward and whispered into my ear, "You're just making me harder."

I bit my lower lip, reveling in his nearness. He had to be able to hear my heart racing as he braced himself with one arm on the ladder over my head.

"You drive me to the brink of insanity. You make me want to be selfish. You make me want to abandon reason," he continued to whisper into our mingled breath.

My chest touched his with every inhale. "Then go ahead—I dare you. Abandon reason," I challenged.

He searched my gaze as if looking for evidence that he should stop. I gave him none—desire had overrun my ability to have one clear thought. No matter how hard I tried to think of another insult, none came.

Then, his mouth met mine, and his weight pressed me against the ladder. It felt part kiss, part reckoning. Our bodies took over for us. I wrapped both hands around his neck; my thumbs found his pulse point, and I squeezed.

"There would be no going back." He'd let his guard down, let me slip into his thoughts. *"Why does she have to be so fucking beautiful?"*

When we broke for air, he looked mussed and delicious as he slid his tongue over his lower lip again. This time I leaned toward him, craving more. He tasted of sweet red wine and warm spice. He leaned out of my neck's reach as though to scold me, and I huffed.

"Up another," he said as his expression shifted to a smoldering one that should be downright illegal. As I fumbled up the ladder, one of his fingers found a loose end of a silk tie at my waist. "May I?"

Elsie's words came back to me about the Sahlms' fashions—about it being fun to be unwrapped like a present. "Yes," I breathed out.

"If you don't keep climbing that ladder, I'll tie you to it and leave you here without ever getting to the good part."

Then he tugged the knot loose and exposed my torso.

My feet found the next rung, and my hands returned to the rail for balance. This was unwise—I'd set all the right conditions. I'd given him the perfect, uncomplicated arrangement.

The room sizzled with humidity. The air was charged by both the storm outside and the aching sense of need that buzzed across my skin.

It took a moment before I realized that the sensation was coming from him. The barricades of his mind were down completely. I could *feel* his desire mixed with mine—the anticipation, the wanting.

Three ties held the remaining rain-soaked silk to my body—two at my hips and one at my breasts.

I'd climbed high enough now that Krait's eyeline was at my chest. He surprised me by leaning down and taking my pebbled nipple into his mouth through the sheer silk. The warmth of his tongue against the cool fabric caused a moan to build in my throat. Letting my head fall against a ladder rung, I tried my hardest to think of why we shouldn't do this.

No reason or sensibility was within grasp.

I wanted to object when he drew back his head. Then he picked up the silk tie at my breast.

Seeing him pissed off was one sort of attractive, seeing him both pissed off and drunk off his own lust was fucking irresistible. He watched me, waiting, with a quirked eyebrow.

"Take it off," I demanded, and he rumbled with a satisfied groan.

When he pulled the tie to unravel the bodice of that awful contraption called a dress, my Luz-blue ribbon that I'd stowed there fell to his feet.

On his way down to pick it up, he sucked my other bare nipple into his mouth for a fleeting, torturous moment, and my toes curled against the bar. When he righted himself, he held the blue ribbon in one hand and said, "Up another."

Swallowing hard, I stepped up again, hands white-knuckling the railings.

I was afraid of what he'd do next—not of him, but of how intensely he was taking in my body, exposed to him from the waist up. The way his gaze lazily drifted over me, taking his time to catalog every detail of me, was intoxicating.

"Now," he said with a tone of fiery challenge. "Keep things professional and stop me."

Before I could think, breathe, or question what he meant, his Shadows descended on me. They wrapped around my torso, between my breasts. Cool vines slipped between my legs and made me gasp against their cold touch.

Krait climbed the ladder, pushing a knee between my thighs to replace the sensation of the Shadows. "I *said,* stop me," he repeated as he reached down to grab my wrists and pin them. "Come on, Sybilla..."

"I don't want to stop you," I admitted. Heat built in my core—and the friction of his leg had me grinding against him as he pushed my arms up over my head. No, I wasn't going to stop this.

"What am I going to do with you?" he whispered into my mouth before kissing me again. It was an all-consuming kiss—a kiss where the world spun around us.

Between our next kiss, I retorted, "Tying me to the ladder is still an option."

He pressed his knee up against my core again and lifted me onto my tiptoes. Meeting my gaze, he said, "You'd like that, wouldn't you?"

I wanted so badly to deny it, just to be contrary. Instead, I nodded. He knew as well as I did—I could stop him anytime. Something about giving myself over to whatever he had planned appealed to the worst of my instincts.

Krait wrapped my blue ribbon around my wrists and tied them with a deft knot to a rung above our heads. I pulled down to test the knot's strength. He'd truly tied me there. Up on tiptoes, dangling. My lips curled into a smirk.

Despite being bound, I felt like the most empowered woman on the planet to witness this feral, wanting side of him. My wrists would hate me for this tomorrow. My body hummed in anticipation despite the pain where the silk pinched, and it felt indulgent that he was not coddling me.

When he stepped back, his Shadows retreated. He tilted his head, assessing me and swiping his thumb over his lower lip in thought. Then, he began walking toward the stairs with casual ease and said, "Well, this has been entertaining—"

"Don't you dare fucking leave me here!" I screeched. "You get back here. Right now, Darvanda."

He glanced over his shoulder with amusement. "Make me."

The bastard was going to make me use my power on him.

My mind opened up to him and pushed past every barbed barrier he set in front of it. The sole of his boot squeaked against the terrazzo floor as he came to an abrupt stop and stiffly turned toward me.

Dealing pleasure was the opposite of dealing pain. Instead of draining, it was rejuvenating. Krait's head fell back a moment with a groan as I let my thoughts caress him.

"You're going to need to stop whatever *that* is, or we'll never get started," he said, sucking in air between his teeth.

"Then strip and come here."

"Yes, my Queen." His words were his own, but the frantic movement of his fingers on his shirt buttons was all me. He kicked off his boots before unbuttoning his trousers. A deviously handsome smirk graced his lips—seeing him wear anything but a scowl was jarring in the most alluring way.

"Are we in a hurry?" he asked, throwing his belt aside.

"Don't tempt me to make you leave. Everything *off*," I demanded.

Once his tunic was tossed to the floor, he thumbed the waistband of his trousers and pushed them to the ground. With him standing bare in front of me, my mouth dried. I drank in my fill of his exquisite form, letting no detail go unobserved.

After mentally egging him on to cross the room back to me, I finally dropped control of him. He placed his palms against the ladder on either side of my head and stepped up a rung to catch my lips with his.

Not close enough.

Wriggling against my restraints, I breathed out, "Please, stop teasing. If you still want this—"

"Shut up, Sybilla." He shook his head. "This is all I've wanted for months."

That couldn't be true. The longing that stretched between us had turned desperate, and I was not above pretending in the moment that he could want more.

He knelt against the ladder before drawing my knees up over his shoulders, which eased the strain on my wrists. With his teeth, he bit down on the tie that held the dress at my left hip and yanked until it was undone.

When he ducked his head toward my core, my mouth fell open. His hot breath against my thigh left gooseflesh in its wake. I could only watch in wonder as he did the same on the other side, baring me to him completely. Watching this man unwrap me like a present with his teeth was going to live on forever in my mind.

Shadows snaked up my stomach and braced me against the ladder before he parted my core with his fingers, and his mouth followed, tongue delving into my now exposed center.

"Fuck," I cried out as my hips ground against him and my thighs scrapped against his stubble. I wanted to reach down and pull his hair, push him down off the ladder, and take him there on the floor.

He brought me toward a desperate peak, and every muscle in my body tensed.

Then he abruptly pulled away and left me whimpering without any relief. My core clenched as he trailed kisses up my navel.

"Keep going," I demanded.

"No," he growled into my stomach. He continued to trail kisses up between my breasts. "Better idea—this time I want to feel you tighten around me when I watch you come undone." He stepped up between my legs, positioning his length right where I needed him. He lingered there a few moments, dragging himself through the evidence of my yearning.

"Do you need a map?" I gasped out impatiently.

"No—I need to take my time."

After sliding into me an inch, he stopped and drew my chin up to meet his gaze again. My hips sought more of him, but his Shadows braced me like vines, binding me to the ladder.

My body turned to putty—hanging by that Luz-blue ribbon, hanging by a thread of my own desire.

I craved the fullness of him and gasped as he pushed in another inch. My vision was spotting white with adrenaline-fueled pleasure. "Krait, all of you. Now."

"You don't get to tell me what to do while I'm inside of you," he said, in between biting at my earlobe. As if I got to tell him what to do when he *wasn't* inside of me.

Just when I thought he might make me wait forever, he thrust himself into me to the hilt with a satisfied groan.

Pulling my wrists against the restraint, I longed to dig my nails into something other than my own palms. He stayed there, completely still, his forehead pressed against mine for a moment too long. I grew impatient, overtaken by the heat that filled my veins.

"*Move* now, or we are done," I commanded. A terrible bluff.

A gruff, dark laugh escaped his lips, just inches from mine, before he said, "We will never be done, Sybilla."

The blue ribbon gave way above me as though his Shadows had untied it. I fell into him, wrapping my legs around his waist. My fingers dug into his silken, wet hair as they'd so desired. The rungs of the ladder might leave bruises, but I felt no pain.

The sounds our bodies made against one another were a vulgar symphony that I'd gladly listen to until the end of time. He'd lied—he did bite. The skin of my shoulder held proof of it.

"Fuck," I gasped.

"Such a foul mouth," he answered before he grabbed my lower lip between his teeth. "I'm learning to love it."

With my head thrown against the ladder, I crested over the edge of my desire with the intensity of cannon fire. Screaming out, I clenched down around him.

"Yes, Sybilla," he breathed out before a guttural sound escaped him, too. He slammed into me to the hilt once more. Then, just as I thought he'd spill into me, he abruptly pulled away. Warmth hit my inner thigh and ran down my leg.

Surfacing from my desire-infused fog, I reeled back out of his arms and found my own footing on the ladder. "What are you doing?" I demanded.

With his lips swollen and hair mussed, he looked boyishly confused.

"Why would you do that? Why pull away?" I asked.

"It...it is a habit. And I didn't know if you were ready to—"

"Oh. So then you *do* know how heirs are made—well, *that's* a relief," I snapped. "Why would you not take the opportunity? What did you think we were doing here?"

The harshness of the words felt wrong, but they'd already been said and they eased the hurt of his admission.

I didn't know if you were ready.

This was still about an heir, about a prophecy, to him, wasn't it? His doubt in me made my blood boil.

To my surprise, he looked dumbstruck and bashful, but my anger didn't allow for recognition of humility. "You were adamant about keeping things 'professional.' Were you not?" he justified. "You've put up so many conflicting smoke signals it's hard to tell what in the realms you want."

"Since when does it matter what I want? You are the one who told me I'd never have what I want from you." That statement shocked him enough that his mouth hung open a moment.

Climbing down the ladder, I pushed past him to pick up the blanket I'd discarded earlier. After wiping off my inner thigh, I slung the too-complicated dress over my shoulders and tried to tie its impossible fabric around myself.

Out. I needed out of this library before I admitted more to him.

All the pleasure he'd dealt me crashed away with the realization that I'd just done something so incredibly stupid. He may be able to separate desire from caring, but I couldn't do the same. Entangling myself with him more than necessary served neither of us any purpose.

"Wait, please," he said and held my wrist, drawing closer to me. His scent nearly broke my resolve to be angry—his sweat mixed with spice, smoke, and desert rain.

He carried on, "*Stop*, Sybilla. Just slow down." He released my wrist to push a stray curl behind my ear.

Fighting had been my go-to defense for years. Vulnerability wouldn't rear its ugly head now even when he offered me that soft expression.

"It matters what you want—greatly," he continued. "When I saw you dancing with Ryn and realized what it meant, it excited me more than it should have. I expected it to be the North King, expected to be in a piss-poor mood the rest of the night because of that."

I crossed my arms over my chest since the dress did nothing to cover me after my frantic attempt at assembling it myself. "So, you came after me to treat me like some illicit tryst?"

"Did I?" he snapped back.

There was the bite I needed.

"Yes!" I huffed out. "I know what you have to offer me."

His voice grew rasped and his expression pained as he retorted, "Oh, I see. So, you were just filling *your* time with another rollick with a prospective husband. How many notches are on that list again? Am I simply another one? Because I don't want to be."

My mouth hung open. "Oh, fuck you, you arrogant bastard. That's especially rich coming from a man who still hasn't gotten over his late wife. Who is too guilt-stricken to consider any other. What in the Sources were we thinking? We're not fit to be anything more than—"

"Stop that!" he barked.

His outburst caused me to take an outraged breath.

He growled, running his hands through his hair. "Stop shooting daggers at me. Sleep on this, Sybilla. A good friend once advised me not to make rash decisions without sleeping on them. I've lost enough by not listening to him."

My arms fell to my sides as he backed away. Disappointment settled in my stomach that he would not keep sparring with me. He dressed without another word before he ascended the steps. My cheeks were hot, and my mind battled itself.

It occurred to me I wasn't even sure what I'd been mad about or what we were fighting for.

I didn't know if you were ready. His concern echoed in my mind. My anger stemmed from the truth in his fear.

I'd always considered an heir a necessity—always imagined children. Without any good model to act as a benchmark, it seemed impossible to know if I'd fail at the role. My throat constricted at the thought.

Even if the realm depended on it, I didn't know how to prepare. Krait's doubt left me reeling.

The ground seemed to shift beneath my feet, changing the paths I'd once seen myself traveling. Yet it had been unfair to throw the weight of those expectations onto him in the form of snide comments and insults.

I'd just properly squandered my fourth betrothal.

CHAPTER 42

KRAIT

Sipping amber liquor, I sat in a supple leather chair by the fireplace, watching Sybilla as she slept. She seemed so at peace, tangled up in my red silk sheets—no signs of the fire she'd been breathing in my direction just this evening.

What in the Sources were we thinking? Her jabs wracked my mind.

But other words did too—her admission that she wanted something more than I offered her. I had myself to blame for that frame of thought.

I'd leave before morning. Hearing her sleep was torturously tranquil and comforting. The faint whistle of a snore calmed me because, despite her anger, she was there. She had not left. Yet.

I pinched the bridge of my nose, trying to dull my restless headache. I clenched my eyes shut, taking a deep breath.

I'd bedded the Last Daughter of Isleen. That had always been the plan.

She'd agreed to marry me and fulfill the prophecy. That should be enough.

She wanted to leave me. That was where the panic stemmed from.

Sybilla had rewritten things I'd thought were set in stone. I hadn't wanted to soften to her. Yet the way our breath had hitched and hurried, mingled together, would haunt me. I would not be able to eat again without thinking about how she tasted or breathe again without desiring a faint scent of lilac.

Now that I'd had her, all I wanted was more. Desire spread through me like a toxin beneath my skin, crawling through my veins. We hadn't savored each other as I would have liked to, and a sense of yearning that I'd thought was buried beneath centuries of self-loathing overwhelmed me.

She was a cruel growing obsession, and everything I wanted was the furthest cry from keeping things "professional."

"Krait?" The sound of my name in her sleep-soaked voice surprised me.

When I opened my eyes and glanced at the bed, she didn't sit up but was squinting at me through the dark.

"It's me," I mumbled.

"Come to bed," she demanded.

My head tilted. "You're sure?" I asked while swirling the amber liquid in the tumbler.

"Mhm," she hummed and scooted over to give me space on the right side, where I usually slept. I set down the glass, knowing that this was a bad idea. I'd told her that I'd give her time to think, yet here I was, hours later, at her bedside. My bedside.

"Is this a trap to suffocate me in my sleep?" I whispered.

"Would it work?" she asked, and I huffed a silent laugh. She could be so infuriatingly stubborn, and yet my heart warmed at the idea that she was still willing to let me near her.

I stood and kicked off my boots and pulled my shirt over my head. She watched me move about the room in only the moonlight that peeked through the curtains before rolling onto her side. Rounding the bed, I slipped behind her, under the sheets. Staring at the back of her head, I grew certain she wouldn't turn toward me. At least she wasn't spitting venom at me any longer. That was a start.

Then she rolled over and met my gaze.

"I made a mistake with you," I whispered.

I'd put up so many emotional barriers that I'd always thought the mistake would be loving another. But now that there was a chance of it, I thought the mistake might have been not trying.

I'd dragged her into a mess of my tangled past and my even more tangled future.

"Just shut up and hold me," Sybilla whisper-barked at me. Her sleep-glazed stare didn't hold any more fire.

My brow furrowed. "Why?"

"I don't know. I want to see how it feels. Just try it," she answered with a tired sigh.

I swallowed hard, not giving a damn how humid the night air was from the rain. Wasting no time, I wrapped my arms around her middle and pulled her to me. Our legs tangled, and her head tucked into my chest. As she nestled in deeper, I unraveled one arm to brush her unruly curls out of my stubble.

"I wasn't a mistake," she whispered. "You don't feel that way. You're just scared..."

"I know," I answered. I wouldn't deny her that truth here in the dark of the bedchamber we shared, here when she seemed ready to be gentle with me.

Maybe she was simply flying a white flag until she could reinforce her troops.

"Can I tell you something?" she asked.

I swallowed hard. "Yes."

"I'm afraid too."

I tightened my grip around her, finding her wrists and massaging where she seemed to suffer, hating myself now for having tied her up because this soft tenderness felt worlds more intimate than how I'd taken her in the library. "I don't want you to be afraid of me."

I'd always been shit with words, but that sentiment seemed to cause her to melt into me. "Then stop being such an insufferable ass."

Muffling a chuckle into the nape of her neck, I lazily rubbed her back.

She surprised me by continuing. "I'm not scared of you. I fear that all my weaknesses will stack up against me. That I will fail and be alone when I do."

"I see no weaknesses," I whispered.

She drew in a deep breath and, after releasing it, said, "I can tell the tonics Wyeth prepares aren't as strong as my old healer's. I'm starting to have to triple the doses."

A knot formed in my stomach, thinking about how hard it must be for her to reveal this to me. The woman had gone weeks without remedies simply to not draw attention to her waning health.

"We'll track him down and get you what you need then."

She hummed into my chest as though sharing the weight of her concern had lulled her to sleep. I still didn't know if I could offer her the life she may have dreamed of, but maybe there was still enough left of my heart to try to be there through good days and bad.

CHAPTER 43
SYBILLA

Hundreds of people crowded around the temple steps. The guil-lotine was set and ready as they led her out in nothing but a canvas nightdress more fitting as a potato sack than clothing. They wouldn't even take her head by the sword, the honorable way. People watched with quiet anticipation as their adulterous Queen was pushed forward.

I tried to look away—anywhere but at her face that so resembled mine.

"Watch, Sybilla," my father commanded from his place on the temple balcony beside me.

It all blurred together at the seams, but this time, I saw someone in the crowd. A man shrouded in a gray veil. He watched as the blade came down upon my mother's neck. Then he looked up at me.

I gasped awake.

Krait stirred but didn't open his eyes. Breaking free of his arms without waking him proved difficult; I had to wiggle from his grasp. Luckily, he was sleeping soundly. The lines of his face were all soft and unworried as his arm reached out in the direction of where I'd just been.

I shouldn't have felt warmed by that.

Remaining angry with him grew harder and harder.

Still reeling from the vivid nightmare, I stepped silently around the room and pulled a blue duster over my nightgown. Glancing back at the sleeping King, I wondered if he could ever be the type of man to force me to my knees before a blade.

My heart told me no.

I was sure my mother's heart had told her the same, too.

I needed to put my hands to work on something so that my mind would stop pinwheeling. My comb was missing from the vanity—I'd left it in Elsedora's room. Thinking maybe Krait had one to spare, I opened the top drawer, then the middle, then the bottom. The edge of a piece of parchment caught my attention.

It bore my name.

I held it up to the golden sunlight from the window.

I. Phynnic idealist

II. Stubborn as a bull

III. Has little control over her own power

IV. Impatient

V. Vulgar

VI. Shortsighted

VII. Willful

VIII. Not ready

My blood flashed cold. The handwriting was familiar—I recognized it from the letter Krait had written me when he'd tried sending me away.

I should have left then.

He'd been keeping a tally of my faults. A night of passion and softness would not change the things he thought of me that were inked on this page.

The guillotine dropped.

Instead of my head rolling, my heart split in two.

Krait shifted but didn't wake. Swallowing hard, I made no sound as I stepped to the foot of the bed and dropped the parchment down at his feet. To think I'd been contemplating opening myself up to him, building a life with him, letting myself fall. My tongue felt two sizes too big, and heat pressed on the back of my eyes.

Krait had been clear all along that he didn't see love or affection as necessary for us to have an heir, but the sting of seeing all my written defects hurt no less.

Especially that final entry.

Not ready.

I was not prepared to take on Death, not ready to marry, not ready to be a mother, not ready to love. It didn't hurt that he'd written the list; it hurt that it was all true. There was no use even waking him to be angry—he wasn't the realm's biggest fool. I was.

Slipping on a pair of leather mules, I left the bedchamber. I needed to find Elsedora. While she would never speak ill of her King, she would at least be a welcome distraction. And was likely to have wine.

Knocking would have been wise.

In a flurry of emotion, I'd entered Elsedora's bedchamber only to be met with the sight of a *very* well-sculpted pale ass, tensed and driving. Ryn held Elsedora's ankles over his shoulders, and their sounds could only be described as animalistic.

Squeaking, I stumbled back, closing the door, before shielding my eyes and fumbling for the handle. Once out of there, I slammed the door. Holding one hand to my forehead.

At least that shock had staved off the tears that had swelled in my eyes for a brief moment. My feet were stuck to the spot. I did not know where to go next. Every instinct screamed—the Egress. Go home.

There was loud shuffling and an "Ouch, Ryn!" before the door creaked open. Elsedora stepped out with a silk robe haphazardly pulled around herself, her red hair mussed.

"My Queen, if you wanted to join us, you only had to ask," she teased with a smirk.

My face burned hot, and I shook my head. All words escaped me, and my eyes brimmed again. Source-damned tears.

"Oh no..." Elsedora's face fell.

"I'm sorry. I didn't mean to interrupt. Get...back to it." I staggered backward, turning to spin on my heels.

El caught my forearm. "Hold on," she said. She cracked the door and commanded, "Ryn, get dressed. Out!"

Thankfully, Ryn was clothed when he appeared, looking not at all sheepish. He smiled until he saw the tears streaming down my cheeks and then glanced between me and Elsie, wide-eyed. "Right then. I'll leave you two."

Elsedora pushed him out of the doorway before dragging me toward her bedchamber.

"Come back later," she called after him.

Ryn just huffed a laugh over his shoulder and said, "Only if she does agree to join us."

A watery laugh bubbled from me, but I didn't respond to Ryn's crude joke. I watched him go, knowing exactly how good he looked out of those breeches now.

"Hush, you'll get yourself killed if he hears you," Elsedora warned him before dragging me inside and shutting the door. She spun me and sat me down on the sofa below a gallery wall of paintings depicting the Hussa mountains and Belray. It had never struck me that maybe Elsedora might be homesick. Her chambers were a tribute to the North Corridor.

"Here." El plucked a handkerchief from her wardrobe and handed it to me. She sat beside me. "What happened? If you tell me that Krait is the reason you're crying, then I will go castrate him right now. Prophecy-blessed seed be damned."

"He isn't. Well, not entirely. I honestly have no idea why I'm crying. This is ridiculous."

Elsedora's posture softened, and she secured the tie of her robe. "It does not make your emotions any less worth feeling if you don't know where they're coming from."

Somehow, that brought me comfort.

No one had ever told me it was okay to just *feel*. I'd spent so much time under a facade of strength, holding myself together. Now every loose seam had unraveled at once—my body ached, my mind was fatigued, and my feelings were wounded.

"There are so many unknowns. I don't know what's right or wrong, or up or down. What if I'm not strong enough to keep Caym from overrunning the realms? What if we can't save Emmerick? What if I *can't* conceive as the prophecy requires? It isn't always easy—many women struggle. What if I have an heir with that insufferable man and still fail to be the mother our child needs? What if I do deserve the same fate my mother received? What if I've—"

"Woah, woah, woah." Elsedora placed her hands on my shoulders. I couldn't find the energy to be embarrassed by the amount of snot I was blowing into her handkerchief. "Slow down and breathe. I'm afraid if your head spins any faster with what-ifs, then it may very well fall off. Have you talked with Krait about any of this?"

"No. That would be pointless," I said, letting out a laugh at her suggestion. "It could all fall apart. All go up in flames just like that." I snapped my fingers.

Elsedora hummed and nodded. "It could," she plainly said. "But it won't. Because even if everything goes up in flames, there are no two people better suited to fight through the fire together than you two. Stop carrying all that weight alone...It will all happen as it will."

I drew in my first deep breath since waking up and nodded. Not because I believed her, but because no single answer to my many what-ifs would have prevented any of our fates.

"What happened, Sybilla?"

For the next few minutes, I confided in her about my and Krait's time in the library, our bickering and our reconciliation. When I finally told her about that dreadful list I'd discovered in Krait's drawer, her lips pursed.

"That man is his own worst enemy. He doesn't mean those words. He's spent so long alone that he's just trying to find reasons to continue that course. I'll talk to him."

Shaking my head, I answered, "Please don't. It isn't worth the breath." I cleared my throat, desperately wanting to ignore the tears still streaking down my cheeks. "I truly am sorry that I interrupted."

El smirked and waved her hand. "Ah, it wasn't so great anyway."

"*That* is a lie."

Elsedora winked. "It is, but I am trying to make you feel better, not worse."

I laughed and asked, "How do you separate the physical from the emotional? You...have other partners, no?"

Elsedora shrugged, but her face fell slightly. "Don't mistake promiscuity for heartlessness. My mother and father were Source Matched—so sickeningly in love. I always longed for that as a girl. That feeling in your soul that connects you with another. Even with no Source in my veins, sometimes I still wonder if that match exists in other ways. So I throw myself at every opportunity for affection, thinking, maybe, someday, someone will surprise me."

"That is…self-aware."

Elsedora chuckled. "It took me a couple of centuries to figure out what I was doing. Everyone always considers Fen the hopeless romantic and me the impulsive one, but romanticism may be a family trait, I fear."

"And is Ryn the one?" It intrigued me to think of Elsedora's airy and light personality as a coping mechanism.

She shook her head. "I don't imagine so. But he has known me nearly my whole life. I trust him. He's my dearest friend, and he would never betray me. That may need to be enough."

"Bullshit."

Elsedora laughed. "Oh, now you are suddenly a romantic?"

"No—but if you are, you deserve nothing short of a fairytale. And I don't think for a minute that you'll settle for 'enough.'"

She nodded and said, "Maybe you should take a dose of your own tonics on that one."

While annoying to admit, I knew she was right. I'd put up so many obstacles between my heart and others that even those closest to me never truly understood what I desired.

Not even Emmerick, and he'd spent over a decade protecting me.

Elsedora pursed her lips with a soft, narrowed gaze and nodded before squeezing my hand.

"Can I stay here a while?" I asked.

"Of course. I'll go grab some tea and pastries. Nothing baked goods can't fix, right?" She got up and bounced to the door.

I wished my problems were simple enough that sugar could solve them.

CHAPTER 44

EMMERICK

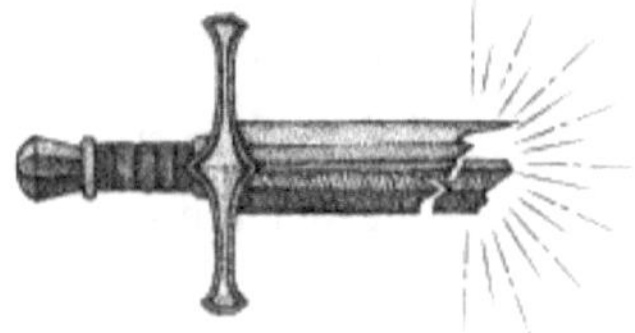

Firose and I avoided being seen in any major town as we headed north. We procured packs with over a week's worth of water and a meager supply of food. The beating sun of the Wastelands had become insufferable once we'd descended the Hussa mountains. While we could see rain in the distance, we got no reprieve.

"Tell me again why this is a good idea?" I asked her as I wiped the sweat from my brow, glancing at the rising sun. We'd encountered seven rattling serpents and numerous skulls on the trail already.

"Because if anyone has found a way to defeat Caym, it would be Darvanda. It is personal for him. There was an ancient scripture called *The Book of Isolde*—it holds a prophecy thought to be the only way to rid the world of Caym's presence. He's to find the Last Daughter of Isleen, and their child is said to be the key to stopping Death. So, let us hope the old book is right and he's found her."

"Why is it personal to Darvanda?"

"Because Caym once held the body of his Commander...Stygian was at first an envoy—until he *wasn't*. It was as though he *became*

368

Death when he betrayed Darvanda. He capitalized off of Krait's anger after his wife was killed, and that is partly how Phynx fell."

Firose's brow wrinkled, and her face dropped as though she'd remembered something that she was not sharing. Something about this particular memory haunted her.

I couldn't bring myself to ask—I knew her part in that story. She hadn't been an innocent bystander.

"So, we show up at Darvanda's doorstep and say what, exactly? That you're sorry for tearing a realm apart and setting it in flames? But he should forgive you because Death made you do it?" I asked, unable to hide my skepticism.

Even outside the range where Caym could reach me, I felt him in my veins like poisoned blood coursing through me.

"Would you rather do the talking, my King?" she asked.

"No," I admitted, stopping to catch my breath and take a swig of water.

Her gaze trailed down my body, which shouldn't have excited me, yet it did. My sense of honor had been thoroughly stomped on.

I pulled at the too-tight tunic that chaffed my neck under the early heat in the desert.

"You can control it, you know," she said.

"Control what?"

She pointed up at the sun, and I scoffed. "Right," I grumbled. No part of me wanted to let my Source power out, even here where the laws of Henosis held no weight.

"This trip would be worlds easier if you harnessed it. You can wield your power to hold on to the rays and create a shield around you—sort of like pushing the sun away. It's a simple charm."

I assessed the angle and position of the sun. The heat would only get worse as the morning continued. She was right—this would be more pleasant if the heat couldn't assault us.

"Fine," I sighed. "Teach me as we walk."

She spent the next twenty minutes explaining what to do, and after three failed attempts, I felt a cool breeze for the first time. Our surroundings ebbed and flowed like a mirage, but there was an immediate reprieve from the harsh rays. She breathed a sigh of relief.

"You can likely hold that for a few hours before becoming fatigued. When you drop it, do so slowly to avoid backlash."

"Backlash?" I questioned, worry creeping into my voice.

She pursed her lips in a tight smirk and nodded. "It feels awful, like being crushed."

The hairs on my neck stood up. There was so much about my magic that I didn't understand. Now, the woman who had once tried to kill me, kill Sybilla, capture Asterie for Death's use, and destroy my city was teaching me how to wield it.

We hadn't discussed what had happened in the greenhouse, nor had it happened again. The exhaustion and grime of travel made any thought of repeating our intimate slip of judgment grow distant.

Every once in a while though, she stared at me with a spark of flame behind those blue eyes that tugged on my heart.

That pull was built on mutual turmoil, yes.

But it was also built on our magic's ruthless draw toward one another.

Firose Van Gran was potentially my Source Match. The Sources were cruel and unjust beings.

We'd gotten little sleep and rose with the sun. The land seemed cut from red rock, covered only in dust, dead grass and spiked vegetation. I hadn't expected to crest a hill and find a sprawling city built at the center of a deep canyon, extending beyond where the eye could see.

Firose and I both stopped to gape at it before we descended.

"Well, Darvanda sure has been busy," she breathed out.

After a grueling trek, it was nearly mid-morning when we reached the city center. People bustled around us, vending from carts and tents.

"Think of slowly reeling in your magic as though you're coiling up yarn," Firose reminded me.

I'd lowered my ward the night before but still felt nervous. I followed her instructions and raised my palms to the Sun ward that I'd created. Focusing intently, I pulled it back to me and the last rays of sunshine reached us.

It felt odd that no one balked or stared at the use of magic. Instead, townsfolk cleaned up damp confetti and discarded wine bottles as though there had been a celebration of some kind recently. We reached the city square, surrounded on three sides by large canals.

A pit grew in my stomach as I realized how peaceful this place seemed and what an oasis Darvanda had built here for his people. I hated the thought that maybe the King of the Sahlms was truly fit for Sybilla in ways I would never be. A true King, one that had accomplished all of this.

Plus, *he* wasn't currently possessed by the greatest evil the realm had ever faced.

The weight of losing her wasn't at all lessened, even knowing she might've found happiness with another. I longed for that to be enough and wanted to rip the ugly, jealous feelings out and cast them aside.

"There, that looks like where we should go." Firose nodded toward a great estate stretching toward the cloudless sky. "Don't expect a pleasant greeting," she warned as we approached the entrance.

I approached one of the guards and said, "I am Emmerick Mattock, King of the North Corridor. And I request an audience with Elsedora Lamoreaux."

CHAPTER 45

KRAIT

"**W**ake up, asshole."

My eyes shot open.

"You made a *list* of her faults?" Elsedora scolded. She stood at the foot of my bed with a scowl that could peel the bark off a tree. By Sybilla's definition, I was a tree, so I stood no chance against whatever berating El had in store for me.

Sources, I hated people sticking their noses in my business. El picked something up from my feet—a familiar piece of parchment. Dread sank down into my stomach. *Why hadn't I torn that fucking list to shreds?*

I groaned. "Tell me you are the one who found that." I covered my eyes as she flung the curtains open, casting sunshine over me.

"Afraid not." Her clipped tone confirmed my fears as she read the words on the page aloud with haughty dismay. I winced harder with each slight, imagining Sybilla reading that page.

"Where is she?"

"Rightfully avoiding the likes of *you*."

Glad to have gone to sleep with my breeches on, I stood quickly, found my tunic on the floor and threw it on. "And where might she be avoiding me?"

"You stay away from her today—she's hurt, and you've done enough to make any woman run for the hills. This is the part where I get to tell you...I told you so."

I shook my head as I pulled on my boots. "I haven't ruined it. I didn't mean any of that."

"It doesn't matter if you meant it. It matters that she believes you did, Krait."

I needed to make this up to Sybilla somehow—get through to her that despite all my hesitation, there was no better way to wake up than by her side. I wasn't too stupid to understand what budded between us.

Only fear prevented me from calling it love.

A loud knock against the door made us both flinch.

"We've got trouble, Krait," Ryn called in. "Is El with you?"

I went to the door and swung it open in an instant. "What trouble?" Ryn's brows lifted as he looked past me at Elsedora.

"Visitors from Helos. King Mattock is here asking for El, and he told the guards to keep Sybilla away."

My legs faltered, and I took a step back before glancing at El.

"She's in my chambers still," she reassured me.

I nodded and returned my attention to Ryn. "Go, distract her. Where is Mattock?"

Ryn seemed uncomfortable. "He was cuffed and brought to the cell"

I stilled. "Is he under Caym's influence?"

Ryn winced. "No...but he is with Firose Van Gran."

My blood ran cold.

She was supposed to be dead.

A murderous ring of Shadows stretched around me.

"Krait...you can't kill *either* of them, not until we have answers. The two of them might have valuable information," Ryn warned. "They surrendered willingly. Let them talk."

A low growl built in the back of my throat, and while I knew he was right, I certainly didn't feel like being patient when the woman responsible for Freya's end sat under my roof. She had been the only person who knew of our marriage aside from Ryn. She'd been Freya's dearest friend...and when she'd revealed our nuptials to the Phynnic King, it had condemned my first love to death.

I would let her talk.

And then I'd let my Shadows tear her apart limb by fucking limb, like I thought she'd been by that wolf-beast.

"You should really let me talk to them first," Elsedora mused.

I responded with a displeased grunt. We reached the bottom step, and El sighed.

Mattock and Firose were being held in the cell below Umber House. The dust caught the light from a sconce, but it was otherwise bewilderingly dark down there for midmorning in the Sahlms.

Our visitors from Helos faced one another, chained to opposite walls with their hands above their heads.

"Why are you here to speak with Elsedora?" I directed my question at Mattock, not wanting to look at Firose. To look at her would be to face my wrath and I was not ready yet. My fists clenched at my sides, and my body felt stiff with the urge to end this the easy way.

"Because I had nowhere else to go, and Elsedora has been kind to me." He glanced past me to Elsedora who tsk-tsked lightly.

"Oh, puppy, you've stepped right into the lion's den now. What is it that you wanted to say to me?"

"That you were right. I am an envoy. It's like he's split me in two, and I've done horrible things..."

I let a low growl leave my throat. "And you decided to bring yourself *here*, to my city?"

Firose cut in, "Caym can only move between minds when he is near. He uses marks to track envoys."

"Silence!" I barked at her. Elsedora flinched beside me.

"The map." El grabbed my arm.

Firose gasped out, "*You* have it?"

I chanced a glance at the traitorous enchantress. Her face was cracked by scarring—a ghastly one across her neck. "Then you know of the deathmarks. You know Caym has risen and—"

I lost control and let my Shadows stretch across the cell and wrap around her throat. "I said...silence."

When I returned my attention to Mattock, his expression hardened as he watched Firose writhing against the wall, unable to breathe. *He cared for her.*

"Don't kill her. Please," Mattock pleaded. "Let her go; she is not to blame—Caym is."

I scowled. They might know how to stop Caym. It was the only thing stopping me.

"Why are you two here?"

When Mattock's eyes met mine, they were bloodshot and accompanied by dark circles beneath them. "I want to be free of him. Before he can hurt anyone else. We seek your help."

Maybe in another context seeing Sybilla's ex-lover look this desperate and exhausted would be satisfying, but it only put a pit in my stomach now. If I hurt him, if I killed him...she'd never forgive me.

"Who are the other two envoys?" I ground out the question as Firose gasped for air. I motioned towards her. "I assume she is one?"

El squeezed my shoulder. "Krait, as much as I'd love to see her dead, too, please stop. We need to hear them out…"

My Shadows craved Firose's blood. I didn't want to let her out of their grasp. Listening to El's better instincts, I reeled the vines back to me, but it took all of my strength. Firose heaved in a breath.

"Barden is one, but we do not know the other," Mattock answered, looking relieved as Firose regained her composure.

A lump formed in my throat to see him so invested in her life.

"How is she not an envoy?" I refused to ask Firose the question, keeping my eyes trained on the North King.

"We don't know," Firose gasped out, and every muscle in my body tensed. "You don't look a day over thirty. You haven't found the answer to that prophecy, have you?"

I approached her, this time without my Shadows, and shouted, "Do not speak of that!"

"It was not me who told your father, Krait. I told you this then, and I will tell you again now. I loved Freya, dearly. Caym used her to get to you, to me. He wanted you in a rage; he wanted me broken. He wanted to make it as hard as possible for you to find the Last Daughter of Isleen. Please tell me you have found her…"

Every word she said made me want to tear her apart more and more. My Shadows whipped in the air around us, like they had minds of their own, reaching toward her. I wouldn't let her speak of Sybilla.

I low growl rumbled out of me.

"Krait," Elsedora warned from behind me.

Firose's eyes widened. "You did," she gasped. "Who?"

"It's Syb, isn't it?" Mattock's voice sounded devoid of all hope.

His eyes had turned watery, which cooled the wrath in my veins.

It brought me no satisfaction to see the turmoil on his face when I said, "Yes." I watched the man who had kept Sybilla safe, who cared for her, who had long been by her side, crumble, as I heard footsteps behind me.

CHAPTER 46
SYBILLA

When Elsedora didn't return with tea and pastries, I grew worried she'd gotten sidetracked. It was so very like her to flit around the estate and forget what she'd intended to do.

With my mules pulled on, I opened the door just as Ryn was about to knock. He offered me a smile that seemed weaker than his usual beam.

"Good morning, Sybilla."

"El's gone to grab us tea," I said, answering his assumed question of where she'd snuck off to.

"No, no." Ryn rubbed the back of his neck, looking a bit disheveled. "I came to see you. How are you doing?"

My eyes narrowed on the Prince of Phynx. Something felt off with this drop-in. It was almost as though he was intentionally distracting me.

"Oh, I am just rainbows and butterflies," I drawled. "Why are you really here?"

He shook his head. "I can't just care about how my friend is faring?"

"You *can*. Has Elsedora abandoned me and sent you up to compensate?"

Convinced that he was hiding something, I moved into that place of Ryn's mind I knew to always be left open even when he was shielding his thoughts. When I sank into his mind, his emotions unsettled me; he was shaken.

I pushed deeper.

"What in the realms could Mattock want so badly he dared step foot in Sahlmsara?"

"Emmerick is *here?*" I gasped, and Ryn's brow furrowed.

"Sources, I hate that. Sybilla," he warned, "Krait will kill me. I can't let you near Mattock, not while knowing he is an envoy."

"You wouldn't be letting me," I breathed out. "Where?"

He grimaced. "The holding cell."

I could feel his anger bite at my mind for taking away his will to obey Krait. Guilt gripped me. But the worst hadn't yet been done.

"I'm very sorry, Ryn." Then I forced his feet to stick to the spot where he stood, and I slipped past him through the doorway and ran.

When I reached the stairs down to the holding cell, there were three guards waiting.

"Move aside," I commanded

"My Queen," one said. "We've been told not to let anyone down there. King Darvanda is—"

I silenced him. At my will, the guards stepped aside. It had become so easy to bend those around me to my whims. That intoxicating and terrifying feeling enveloped me.

"He will not punish you for your disobedience," I assured them as I stepped past. I closed the door behind me and took the steps in two, not knowing how long the hold on them, or Ryn, would last. It was fatiguing to use so much of my power at once.

My eyes adjusted to the low light as I entered the holding cell.

I heard my dear friend's voice. "It's Syb, isn't it?" he questioned with brimming tears.

"Yes." Krait's voice sounded grave. That prick had no right to talk about me without my being present.

"Em," I gasped out, and Krait stiffened before turning to me. "Why is he chained up like an animal?"

Then my eyes landed on the High Enchantress of the North. A ghost. No, not ghoulish—whole and in the tattered flesh.

I pressed my back against the bars of the holding cell.

"You." It escaped my lips as a feral snarl.

"Sybilla." Elsedora approached me. "You shouldn't be down here."

"For fuck's sake, I need everyone to stop telling me what I should or should not do and explain. Now."

"Syb," Em breathed out and stared from his place there, arms over his head—*how could they have done this?* Envoy or not, he was a King. Logic told me that they were only taking precautions, but fury told me they were about to disregard my wishes to keep him alive.

"Leave us..." My teeth ground.

Krait's hard, murderous stare didn't deter me.

As he spat back, "No," I moved his feet *for* him. He looked more pissed off than I'd ever seen him before—a scowl crossed his face as he left the holding cell and walked up the stairs.

I glanced at Elsedora and said, "Don't make me do the same to you." She bowed her head. "Keep Darvan-dick and Ryn up there until I am through."

"As you wish, my Queen...but be careful." She didn't want to leave, that much I could feel. But she respected my request and followed Krait up.

Alone with my greatest friend and my greatest enemy, I reeled—dizzy with power, with shock, with confusion.

"Are you him, or are you, *you*?" I asked Emmerick.

"It's me...but they're right, Sybilla. I am not safe for this world if Caym has any chance of reaching me."

I looked over at Firose momentarily. "And the traitorous scum that you dragged with you...what is she?"

Firose's nostrils flared, but her lips pressed together.

"She has helped me a great deal, and for that, I owe her a great deal. She's not an envoy."

I scoffed, not for a second believing that. "I don't know how you regrew a head like the worm that you are, but I'll have it off again soon," I said to her, finally willing myself to approach the woman who'd inflicted so much chaos on my city.

She finally spoke. "I can assure you that your hate for me is mutual, Queen Wymark. But we seek the same outcome. Caym bent my will for centuries, and he will do the same to King Mattock should he not be stopped."

I glanced at Emmerick briefly. "I don't see any use for you alive. If you could have stopped Caym, you would have done so before bringing Death to my doorstep."

"Sybilla." Emmerick's voice sounded desperate, which made me pause and look between them. They wore kindred haunted expressions.

I focused, reinforcing my hold over Krait at the top of the stairs and Ryn floors above him. Both were likely seething by now.

Just a little more focus, a little more strength, was needed. Digging deep into the well of magic I possessed, my mind pushed into Emmerick's, needing to understand for myself how he'd come to be here with Firose.

Was this all an elaborate trap?

Peeling back layers, I closed my eyes as his emotions and memories began to flood me.

Flashes of their time spent together with her in a burgundy veil flew past. Every conversation. Every revelation. Every memory and nightmare in the months that had passed, some tinged in a dark amber glow.

He trusted her.

He'd *bedded* her.

My heart sank, and my desire to see what other stones I might be able to overturn grew. I delved into Firose's mind next, wanting to know if she was truly helping him without ulterior motives.

When her emotions hit me, I had to bend over at the sinking weight of them. Her pain, her suffering, her torture at the hands of Caym.

Her thirst for vengeance was so strong it felt like hot iron against my mind, sizzling into the fibers of my soul. But she was so very tired of carrying on.

Years of warring with Caym's will.

Her hands being forced to do unspeakable things.

Betraying Fenris, who she'd loved.

Watching the demise of Freya, who she'd cared for deeply.

Centuries spent hiding that Asterie was not truly bound to her.

Watching her friend, the late Mattock, wither away in his battle against Death.

Being torn to shreds in the Luz throne room.

Waking, scarred but alive, in a field of flames.

I abruptly shut her out, gasping for air.

"What has he done to you?" I wheezed.

It would've been easier if I'd still wanted to put Firose's head on a stake and ride through my city with it. But now my conscience fought against that thought. Her memories were more like nightmares.

"He's like a parasite. The deeper he digs, the worse it is..." Firose explained. "Until you believe yourself incapable of good."

My eyes welled with tears. Emmerick's stance against me in those council meetings, his newfound anger—it all grew clearer.

Em swallowed hard. "He's doing the same thing to me. I needed you to know that I am not your enemy—not yet. I never want to be, and that is a weakness he so easily wields against me."

None of this was right. None of this was fair...I wanted to throw something. My hold on Krait and Ryn grew thin.

I crossed the room to find the key that lay on the steps and returned to where Emmerick was bound, standing on my tiptoes to undo the chains from the wall.

"Sybilla, that isn't wise," he tried.

"We'll leave the binding cuffs to prevent wielding. But I'm not leaving you chained up like this."

"No," he commanded, and I stilled as the key slipped into the lock above our heads. His gaze met mine, pleading. "I couldn't live with hurting you. You know that. Let Darvanda keep us here."

"You know that telling me 'no' has never worked. I won't let Caym hurt me and neither will you."

The lock clicked, releasing him from the wall. I left the thin cuffs around his wrists, but they were no longer attached to those dreadful chains.

Maybe it was foolish, but my resolve strengthened as his arms lowered and he embraced me. I slumped there against his chest. "I still have to stay down here, Syb."

"Fine," I answered. "But I'm having cots, food and supplies brought down for you."

I backed out of his arms before stepping over to Firose. She'd stayed quiet through our exchange but appeared altogether as wary of me as I was of her.

I'd felt the hatred within her—anyone who loathed Caym that much was an asset, whether I wanted her dead or not.

My mind was growing tired, the stacked layers of magic I was using weighing down my body. It felt like moving through mud.

Her eyes widened when I reached above our heads and undid the chains binding her to the wall as well.

"Should you ever betray me...I can promise you that what he did to you will pale in comparison to what I shall do," I said through clenched teeth.

Firose nodded as she lowered her scarred arms and rubbed at her wrists where the cuffs remained. She appeared almost girlish—broken and tired. I wondered if that was how I sometimes looked. It felt odd to find kinship with her.

"Read into the Sethe curse," Firose offered. "If we can trap Caym in one of the envoys, we may be able to cast the curse and delay him. Until an heir can be had...assuming our guess about you is correct."

Recalling the excerpt I'd read in the library, my heart clenched and my jaw tightened. I glanced at Emmerick and said, "We will not cast it on Emmerick."

"That we agree on," Firose said as she slumped back against the stone wall.

"So we find Barden and get him alone," I mused, recalling their conversations about him being an envoy from Emmerick's memories.

As I crossed the cell, toward the stairs, one of her memories made me halt. She'd loved Freya; she'd felt betrayed and heartbroken over her friend's death.

I turned on my heel. "If you did not tell King Toth about Freya and Krait's marriage, then who did?"

Firose swallowed hard before she said, "I always suspected Rynall Toth, her brother. He was the only other one who knew."

My gaze narrowed on her. "That is quite an accusation."

"I assume it was not without interrogation from his father."

I drew in a deep breath. I couldn't deny the truth in her memories. I'd seen her do such unspeakable things—why lie about this?

"It could have been the Divine that married them."

"It could have," Firose said dully, as though she didn't believe her own words. "You can use the map that Elsedora stole to track Caym's active envoy. Pray to the Sources that the envoys are not together. It will be harder to trap him if he can move between their minds. Don't approach him without reinforcements."

I nodded, glancing at Emmerick. He stared at the two of us with a furrowed brow as though watching us work together was not something he'd ever expected to see.

"I'll be back this evening," I told him.

Then I stepped out of the holding cell and locked the iron gate behind me.

"We are going to settle this," I promised through the grates before ascending the stairs. My feet felt attached to weights with a mile-long mountain to climb. Each step filled me with more dread as I released my hold on Krait and Ryn.

CHAPTER 47

KRAIT

El had been pacing in front of me for the past twenty minutes. I stood frozen to the tile, grinding my teeth as anxiety built in my chest.

Sybilla was down there with one of Caym's envoys and the woman who'd brought war upon her city. And she'd cast me out of the cell so damned easily.

"She'll be okay," El reassured me. "She's stronger than the two of them combined..."

My greatest fears crashed down on me. Descending those stairs to see her limp and lifeless. Having to step through her blood to kill anyone who had dared to hurt her.

Mourning her.

I couldn't fucking breathe.

Sybilla's hold on me slipped just as the heavy door down to the cell swung open.

"I need everyone here, immediately," Sybilla barked at Elsedora as soon as she appeared. "Asterie, Fen, Cassidee, Wyeth, Amara...all of them."

"You cannot give my officer orders," I snapped as the door slammed behind her. Upon seeing her alive in all her stubborn beauty, I let out a breath. Every muscle in my body relaxed in relief.

Sybilla glared at me as she stepped out of the doorway. "I don't see why I cannot. I will be your Queen, your equal—list of shortfalls or not. And you were right—I *am* willful. I *am* stubborn. So go ahead and try to stop me."

My whole body tensed again as she referenced that damned list, and I shook my head. "You could have been hurt, Sybilla. Or worse." My voice cracked.

"Yes, and?" Her hands found her hips, fingers digging in there in such an alluring way.

I no longer feared being with her.

I feared being without her.

"Fetch that map you found in the Helos crypts too. We need to show the others," she instructed Elsedora, who glanced between us, mouth agape.

"Go, do as she says." I waved her away. El looked relieved to oblige and hurried down the hall.

Sybilla's eyes possessed no shine, and her shoulders slouched. Had the way I'd fought that mental hold fatigued her?

I approached her and she didn't retreat. My Shadows trailed the ground before they rose to create a shield that engulfed her in soft darkness. They wrapped around her, seeking out any injury, any scratch.

"You have no reason to be pissed. I do," she said. "You tried to keep me from matters that concern me—that concern someone I care for."

"I wasn't pissed, Sybilla. I was terrified."

Her posture slackened slightly, as though she'd anticipated an argument.

I was too relieved that she was okay. "I don't care what you think of me but know this—I don't want you to ever have to face danger alone. Sources, I felt helpless…I refuse to lose you; I refuse to lose everything again."

One of my hands wrapped around the back of her neck, drawing her gaze up to mine, and the other held her at the torso. I lowered my head, desperate to seek out her lips. Our breath tangled in the Shadows between us.

Her brow furrowed, hands still on her hips, and she said, "Krait. I do not wish for your hands to be on me right now. Remove them, or I will do it for you."

Swallowing hard, I pulled my hands away from her, longing for the warmth of her skin beneath my fingers.

My foolhardy sense of hope hinged on her caveat of "right now." She took one last look at my lips, which I dared to think seemed tinged with longing, before stepping away from me.

"Emmerick is truly an envoy, but Firose is not any longer. She was reborn from fire. I know that sounds impossible, but I sank into both of their heads…"

"The Origins work in ways even I can't fathom."

Ryn's heavy footsteps rang down the hall. He reached us with labored breath and a scowl that I'd never seen him wear before. "Sources, woman," he huffed. "If you'd asked nicely, I would have brought you down here."

Sybilla stiffened. Ryn looked confused by her sudden cold front.

"It is not my truth to unfold for you," Sybilla said to Ryn. "But I could not find anything in Firose's memories that suggested she was the one to tell your father about Freya and Krait eloping."

Her words were like a blow, and air escaped my lungs.

That couldn't be.

"I need to go find someone to send down supplies. For now, both Emmerick and Firose are wards of *Luz*. Any harm that befalls them is an act of war against me. Also, they're unchained."

I fought the impulse to scold her. She didn't look at me before she headed off stiffly down the hall.

Ryn stood stone-still as I listened to Sybilla's receding steps.

"Firose told him," I insisted. "She told your father that Freya and I were married. She is the reason I lost my Source Match, and she'll suffer for it."

Ryn shook his head and said, "You're wrong, Krait." His eyes glistened, and my heart stopped.

"What do you mean?" My tone grew so grave that Ryn's face fell. The Shadows that had protected Sybilla grew like angry vines above my head.

"It was me."

I stalked toward him without thinking. "*What* do you mean?" I repeated, in a snarl.

Ryn's cheeks glistened with tears that now rolled freely.

"Krait..." My longest-standing friend and officer of my realm held up his palms. "The night you were married, I tried to kill my father. Freya deserved to be on his throne...but my plan backfired. I was caught."

I couldn't control my breathing or see through the Shadows growing around me. They reached for him, ready to tear—to destroy.

"Please, Krait...My actions killed her. My father immediately suspected something was amiss. He knew that so long as she lived the people would reject him. I was interrogated until I cracked, and her life was the price of my attempt on his. I live with that the guilt every fucking day." Ryn was spitting through his own tears when I threw the first punch.

I expected him to fight back.

He didn't.

Hit after hit, he groaned but did nothing.

It took every ounce of control I had to not let my Shadows descend, rip and tear.

My vision blurred as I knelt over him, panting—all my anger spent and thoughts tumbling into despair.

My knuckles were bloodied. "Four centuries. You lied to me for *four* fucking centuries."

Ryn spat blood to the side and didn't try to rise. "I have been loyal to you just as long. I deserve whatever beating you'd like to deal me—but know that there hasn't been a day in these past four centuries that I haven't spent trying to repent for what I did. She was as devoted to that prophecy as you, and I was trying to make it right in her place."

I shook my hands out. They were cramped and bruised. Standing and looking down at my dearest friend, I knew the guards could easily lock him in with the two downstairs. He wouldn't fight it. It was what any ruler in my place would have done to someone who'd so wholly broken their trust.

Now that I'd expended all of the violence in my veins, my thoughts felt clearer. There was no way Ryn would have cracked easily. The Phynnic methods of torture might have been enough for me to crack, too. His father was a fucking bastard.

"What did he do to you?" I asked through a tight jaw.

Ryn winced with each breath and held onto his ribs, which I'd undoubtedly broken. "I'd prefer not to relive that," he answered. "But I broke. I didn't believe he would kill her, only me—I still have a hard time believing it. It should have been me." His hair was a tangled silver mess, bloodstained at the temples.

"Get up."

Ryn did what I said and staggered to his feet, holding his side. It would take a day or two, but he'd heal.

"I should kill you," I growled.

"You should," he agreed.

I heaved out a ragged sigh. "But that isn't what Freya would have wanted."

"I'm not so sure about that," he said.

I shook my head. "She wouldn't. She loved you. We were all foolish. One way or another, your father was going to find out. I've tried to stop blaming myself for his actions. You two were his children...and he brutalized you like you were war criminals."

Only now did remorse start creeping into my veins, making my blood run cold.

What would I have done to him if he'd told me a century ago? Two? He'd been loyal to me for so long and imagining the friend before me dead in Freya's place tugged at my heart.

"The one constant behind it all is Caym. He tore us all apart then, and he is trying to again." I wiped my bloody knuckles on my breeches. "Go clean off your face...We are apparently expecting company."

After a visit to the baths to rinse away the grime and betrayals of the day, I dressed in a formal silk tunic and dark linen breeches, and followed the loud hum of conversation into the dining room.

I avoided thinking of who was down in that dungeon, avoided thinking of the heartbreaking revelation I'd uncovered about my dear friend.

Focus would be needed to determine a path forward.

When I stepped inside the dining hall, our guests sat around the long oak table—all but Elsedora and Ryn. I suspected she was helping to clean him up. My heart sank and my stomach soured a bit at the thought of what I'd done to him.

Wine bottles floated into the room, along with blown glass chalices. The tile shone, and a golden sunset glistened through the wall of windows on the opposite side of the room.

Since I'd awoken with that horrid list at my feet, everything had gone to shit.

Sybilla sat at the head of the table.

I'm afraid too. The sensation of her in my arms had felt more right than anything I'd experienced in centuries, but her willingness to open up, to trust me with her vulnerabilities? I'd work hard to hold on to that.

Sybilla looked so natural there as she passed a bottle of wine to Amara. My two worlds collided as I watched them chatter.

Amara and Freya had been friends. Long ago, for a short while, the enchantress and I had enjoyed each other's company. Until a young cousin of the Toths', the late Corric Mattock, had thoroughly distracted her. Feeling disheartened, I had snuck into a Phynnic masquerade ball one evening, looking for Amara. Instead, I'd found a young Princess hiding in the garden away from prying eyes. At that moment, I, too, had become thoroughly distracted.

I now found myself similarly preoccupied with a certain Queen, who I'd so recklessly underestimated. When Sybilla glanced up at me, the glimmer of her weak smile faded. A chair was left for me on the opposite side of the table.

Between us, Fenris and his Star-wielder sat with their chairs bumped together, arm-in-arm.

The healer from Luz, Wyeth, sat opposite them beside a tall brunette wearing dusty war leathers—Cassidee, I presumed from Sybilla's descriptions of her new Constable. The two of them were teaching a mop-headed boy with a missing front tooth how to move water from one glass to another with his Source power.

It was the boy Sybilla had found before the festival, the one who'd nearly gotten her killed on her first night in Sahlmsara. The same boy who could very well be the only hope to solve my realm's endless droughts. I suddenly wished we'd included more context in our invitation because this was no conversation for a child's ears.

Before sitting, I crossed the room to where Sybilla sat. I bent and placed a lingering kiss on her brow. She couldn't hide her expression of surprise as I lowered my lips to the space just below her ear and said, "Be angry as long as you'd like. You know what it does for me."

The icy smile she offered as I righted myself made me smirk. "Oh, I will," she answered through clenched teeth.

"Where is Elsedora?" I asked her quietly.

Sybilla tilted her head and narrowed her eyes. "Likely helping Ryn dress himself," she said with a knowing glare. "You broke *four* of his ribs..."

"It could have been more," I drawled under my breath as I crossed the room to my seat.

Asterie sat to my left, a black robe slung over her chair, and she fanned herself with a handkerchief. Fen's signature patched green cloak had been discarded on his chair as well, and the sleeves were rolled up on his cream tunic.

I leaned over to address Asterie quietly. "Sybilla's dosage of tonics isn't enough—has Healer Mortag returned?"

Fen's eyebrows rose as Asterie turned her head to me and said, "No, but he finally wrote Wyeth that he is on his way to Luz. I'll send him here right away when he arrives. She didn't tell me she was struggling."

Twisting a cloth napkin in my hands before placing it in my lap, I hummed an acknowledgment. Since Sybilla had told me she was tripling her doses, it had grated on me. "She's been under a lot of stress," I answered, hating that I was a contributing factor to that stress.

For the first time, the former High Enchantress' gaze softened when she beheld me.

If only I could get a very stubborn Queen to stop staring daggers at me now.

CHAPTER 48
SYBILLA

"Care to share what you two are whispering about?" My eyes narrowed on Krait, who had leaned over and been speaking to Asterie.

Krait's brows rose. "I will tell you later in bed," he said without an ounce of sarcasm.

Fenris appeared entertained. Even Wyeth, who was usually reserved, stifled a laugh. I pursed my lips, biting back a retort. It was not the time to show any division.

I hadn't told him about Firose's accusation against Ryn so that he would go and beat his friend to a pulp. Yet his reaction told me that the enchantress had not lied.

Fighting my growing sympathy, I tapped my foot beneath the table. Elsedora would be here any minute with the map.

"How are your studies progressing, Hurley?" I asked the young warlock, trying to distract myself and the others from whatever tension was strung between me and the infuriating man at the other side of the table.

Young Hurley's cheeks reddened at the attention. "Good," he croaked out.

Fenris chimed in. "He's a natural. He'll be shaping rivers in no time."

"Resourceful." Krait's thought caressed my mind. I chanced a glance at him. *"I'm working on a new list."*

I hadn't been trying to hear his thoughts, but it seemed my mind was open to compliments.

It felt oddly good to have found those tally marks against my character.

I'd been a fool to grow too intimate with him.

I should not trust him with my heart.

Krait had the right intentions for our realms, for defeating Caym—that I could trust.

Cassidee leaned her elbows onto the table, turning to Krait. "It's nice to formally meet you. Those Warhorses back in Luz were really something." She whistled in approval and added, "They cut through that attack like butter."

"Forgive her," Wyeth cut in. "She has a penchant for only talking about war."

Krait only hummed in acknowledgment.

Cassidee carried on, "So, why were we searched and stripped of our weapons at the door? If it's a matter of safety in Luz, we need to know what we face."

I cleared my throat, catching her attention. "We'll tell you as soon as Elsedora and Rynall join us."

Cassidee smirked and relaxed back into her chair, seeming eager to get to the dangerous bits of the conversation.

"Was King Sheffield found?" I asked Amara.

"I was waiting for the right moment to tell you. His body was found on the south coast of Eros," Amara said with watery eyes and a wrinkled brow.

She had served the King of the South Corridor for many years. I'd always longed for advisors like her, ones who cared about my well-being.

"It was hard to determine his cause of death...too much time had passed." Her shoulders deflated as she stared into her wineglass.

"I'm sorry for your loss," I said. "He was an honorable King. Did you know he used to send me letters on my birthdays with pressed flowers between the pages?"

Amara offered me a sad smile and shook her head. "That does sound like him. It's a great loss for the Corridor. He has a young nephew—school-age. His father, Sheffield's brother, died years ago. It will take a great deal of training to fill the King's shoes."

I had no doubt she would be an excellent guide for the young royal.

I liked Amara. Elsedora had let it slip out over wine one evening that Amara had once been Krait's lover, just before Freya. We had too many threats looming for me to stop and consider that awkward—plus, he was not mine to feel possessive of.

We were all so tightly interconnected to each other; it was something Caym could prey on if we let doubt or hatred guide our decisions. "What's Bringham to say about it?"

"He's calling for a noble from the West to usurp the boy," Amara answered.

I sighed. "Of course he is."

The doors opened, revealing a tender-stepping Ryn and a worried-looking Elsedora, who led him by the crook of the arm into the dining hall. The rolled-up map was tucked under her other arm.

"What did we miss?" El asked.

"We'll catch you up later. Come, sit," Krait instructed. "And roll out that map."

Amara stilled beside me when her gaze landed on Ryn. "Fenris told me that you lived, Rynall—but it was hard to believe until now."

"Beautiful as ever, Amara." Ryn greeted her with a quick squeeze of her shoulder, then he took his seat beside Krait.

Elsedora unraveled the old parchment, careful not to rip it, and Cassidee and Wyeth pitched forward in their seats to observe it more closely.

"What do we have *here?*" Fen asked with great interest, turning the old page toward him and Asterie. He appeared lit from within with intrigue.

"A map," I answered dully. Fen leveled a look at me that read, *You don't say?*

I added, "Of where the Death Origin's current envoy is."

Amara's fingers trailed over her mouth. Asterie's brow furrowed. I took a deep breath and chanced a glance across the table at Krait.

"*Strong, so strong,*" he thought. "*I'm adding that to the list.*"

I rolled my eyes. Forced compliments wouldn't win my favor.

Elsedora rounded the table and leaned down to whisper something to Amara that made the enchantress' eyes grow dewy. Then El placed Mattock's stone memorandum down on the table. Amara quickly grasped the stone and brought it to her heart.

Krait addressed everyone around the table. "The Death Origin is rising. I believe he gained strength the night you were saved." He nodded toward Asterie. "Whatever bargain was made, we need to discuss it now."

Amara spoke first. "I summoned the Sun Origin—but that isn't what saved her. Astros said *they* made a bargain with Death."

There it was.

"Who is 'they'?" Ryn inquired—his curiosity piqued. It bubbled on the back of my tongue.

Amara sighed. "The other Source Origins. But it's long been thought that the Death Origin had been laid to rest."

Asterie gripped the edge of the table, looking forlorn. "I cast a Lacero curse on myself. I thought it would bring me to bargain with Death, but it did not. My namesake intercepted me."

Cassidee tapped her fingers on the table. "What exactly did Origin Asterie say?"

Asterie cleared her throat. "When I asked her if I was an Origin she said, *'In part.'* And then she said my place was with the fireling and sunling and that I should 'Try not to make Death more than an acquaintance. He is difficult for me to negotiate with.'"

Ryn cursed under his breath, and Krait stared down at the table, as though bearing the weight of that news on his shoulders.

"Then it is true...the Origins intervened. They bargained with him." Amara sighed. "But why?"

The Sources could have been bored of watching us from whatever middle plane they were stuck in. Or maybe Death had promised them their return should they allow him to reign...We could wonder for eternity.

Poor Hurley's eyes were wide as saucers as he listened. I nodded to him and said, "Why don't you go play in the sitting room?"

He brightened. "I brought the marbles that Wyeth gave me." He was out of his seat and fleeing the room before the unsettling news had time to sink in.

"What do we know about Caym's whereabouts now?" Wyeth chimed in. She glanced at the map.

We explained everything we knew.

The three deathmarks.

Emmerick and Barden being known envoys.

The prophecies of Isolde and the Brennac legends, which I'd come to believe in.

Krait told them of the prophecy naming our child as the key to ending Death's reign—Asterie's brow rose.

With all our truths on the table, I sipped a bit of wine and held the sweet burgundy liquid in my mouth.

Cassidee kicked back on two feet of her chair and pointed to the deathmark on the map. "Looks like an envoy is in Helos now, likely in Mattock's body. Why not just ambush him and then hunt the other envoys down?" She winced as soon as her gaze landed on Amara.

Amara grabbed my knee below the table and squeezed. My jaw tightened, and I sloshed the wine through my teeth, likely staining them. If they knew Emmerick was here...

Krait stared across the table at me for a long moment before he said to Cassidee, "You're talking about killing a King and a noble of Luz."

I finally swallowed the now-warmed wine.

"So what do we do?" Fenris asked, glancing between Krait and me.

"Outside of fulfilling the prophecy, I don't know," I said, drawing in a deep breath. "Even then, if Caym rises to his full strength, we are doomed."

"You need time," Wyeth said. "To figure out what that prophecy actually calls for and to stop Caym from growing stronger through the Death-wielding of the envoys."

Asterie added on, "*Without* killing them."

My stone-faced friend wouldn't allow for any plan that harmed Emmerick either. I offered her a weak toothless smile.

"What about the Sethe curse?" Asterie spoke up again, seeming uneasy. "We could find the envoys and use it on them to slow Caym down, no?"

It was the third time the idea had been put into my head.

Amara snapped, "That is too risky for the envoys. It is basically the same sentence as death."

It would be too risky to Emmerick.

I bit my cheek in thought, before I said, "Tell me how that would work. What are the risks?"

"The Sethe curse puts the subject in a deep sleep for a predetermined amount of time that the caster chooses," Asterie explained. "It cannot be an *unreasonable* amount of time or the curse won't take. And it needs to be specific—moons, years, days. It is likely what Isleen used to bind Caym in the first place. If not awakened before that period ends, then...well, they are thought to sleep forever. It seems Caym's true form has awoken before his time was up. That is likely what he bargained for."

"And how would one wake someone under this curse?" I asked.

"There is no known way to lift it," Amara blustered at Asterie. "Are you suggesting that we use Emmerick's body to trap Caym and put him to sleep potentially forever? Let the Origins decide his fate?"

"That is exactly what I'm proposing if it comes to it." Asterie grew taller in her chair and pursed her lips. "Because it is exactly what Em would want us to do should all else fail. He would not deter us from this option, and I urge you not to either."

My heart raced and swelled simultaneously. I wanted to reach across the table for Asterie's hand and squeeze it.

She was right. And this would give him a chance.

Amara grew withdrawn. She swallowed and shook her head.

"Right now, Caym's ability to control the envoys seems limited to just them," Ryn warned. "We don't know what form he has taken, but he's likely still weak. Imagine the damage he could inflict if able to control anyone near him. He's raised an army of Death-wielders once already—who's to say he isn't doing the same right now in the North or West Corridors?"

I shivered.

Cassidee nodded. "We need to prepare reinforcements before we approach the active envoy. What do we have?"

Elsedora noted, "We have the East's fleets of Griffiths and our Warhorses, but they won't be enough."

Krait hummed in thought. "We could wake the beasts of Sahlmkar."

Ryn balked. "They've laid in stone for thousands of years. And doesn't legend say they were Caym's creations?"

"They were. But that does not mean they will answer to him." Krait stared across the table at me.

"What are they exactly?" Asterie seemed skeptical. I was too.

"The souls of Isleen's children," Krait answered. "It is thought that when Isleen cast Caym away, their magic coiled together, and he turned her and her children into beasts. That is why none of her lineage was thought to have survived."

"So they may answer to the blood of Isleen," Amara noted.

"Which means Sybilla will be able to control them," Krait said with too much confidence.

I was meant to control *them*?

Fenris' eyes went wide. "What if they don't answer to her?"

"They will." Krait relaxed back into his seat.

"Then we prepare for all options," I said. My arm hair stood on end, but I would not deny us any chance to be rid of Caym.

Krait's lips curled into a smirk. Something like adoration burned in his eyes. It made my heart beat faster. "*Brave,*" he thought. I sat up a bit taller in my seat.

We would wake beasts of nightmares.

Lay Death to sleep.

Try for an heir that may someday rid us of Caym for good. However unprepared for that option I felt.

To save us all, I would compromise everything.

PART THREE

Isleen stopped Caym once. While she was in his grasp, she cast the Sethe curse on herself, and with her, Death was locked away. But not before he turned all but one of her children to stone. He will find a way to wake.

Under the hundredth black moon after Isleen's demise, he shall walk again with all my power. Those who worship him will give their lives to become his vessels of destruction.

And so I write this book of prophecies through whatever Reverist scribe in my lineage can still hear my voice. I beg you to listen.

I failed you. But there is still hope that Caym can be stopped.

Three relics are hidden for the child of Isleen's Last Daughter, the sixth heir of Desidero, to wield. I've left you all you need to awaken the highest power.

Death knows no justice or meaning in life. For the sake of all, never bargain with him.

To the kin of my Isleen, when you read this, remember:

When time needs to be borrowed, look to the light.

When all seems lost, trust in the shadows.

CHAPTER 49
SYBILLA

Ve dispersed to make preparations to approach Caym with
reinforcements.

Asterie, Wyeth and Fen returned to Luz, bringing Hurley along
with them. Cassidee set off for the East Corridor to consult King
and Queen Nadiar. Amara Egressed to Eros to oversee the crowning
of the young heir to the South Corridor and to keep things there in
order.

Krait, Elsedora, Ryn and I lingered in the dining hall, wordless
and tired.

Krait finally broke the silence. "We'll leave for Sahlmkar tomorrow. Ryn, I'm sending you ahead of us to prepare the flat." Giving
no further context, he rose and stepped out of the room. He took a
left. Undoubtedly, he'd go to the bell tower.

I squashed my urge to follow him.

Ryn stood and stepped around the table before planting a kiss
on top of Elsedora's head and exiting. I'd forced him to tell a horrid
truth, yet his dismissal still hurt.

El released a deep breath. "I want us to be right about the Sethe curse—that it will be enough to delay Caym, that he won't get hold of Isolde's power again."

"But you don't think we are right?"

She grimaced and shook her head. "Something feels unsettling. Like we've missed a crucial detail."

I rose from my chair, suddenly feeling the weight of the day's events. My joints ached, my head hurt and my heart felt like a heavy, useless weight in my chest. "You'll watch over Emmerick—make sure that he is treated well while I'm gone?"

Elsedora offered a sad smile. "Of course. Your guard dog is safe with me."

"And don't kill Firose. There is more to her than her actions against Fen and the realms."

That sentiment was met with an eye roll and a reluctant nod.

When I unlocked the cell door, Firose was sleeping fitfully in a cot. Emmerick sat on the ground with his back resting against the wall, facing her, sipping from a wooden cup of water. They both looked cleaner in their fresh linen tunics and breeches. Buckets and rags sat discarded in the corner.

Em's attention caught on me. I walked with tender steps and lowered myself, with a grimace, to sit shoulder to shoulder with him.

With a frown, he watched me rub my wrists.

In my youth, we'd used to sit this way atop the palace walls when I'd skirted my guards. Peeking over the edge, we would joke and make up stories about people in the bailey below. Now, together we faced the inside of a dark cell and the woman who'd once tried to kill me.

"I'm sorry you must stay down here," I whispered.

He shook his head. "It's for the best."

I let my head roll in his direction against the stone. "Are you alright?"

The corners of his lips turned up. All the light in his warm brown eyes had extinguished. "I've been better," he answered and rubbed the magic-binding cuffs on his wrists. "You look well."

I stifled a laugh. "No, I don't. But I appreciate the lie."

He shrugged in a downright playful manner and said, "I'm happy to see you, nonetheless."

There he was.

I breathed out, "I'm so sorry, Em."

"For what exactly?"

He was going to make me say it. Damn him. "You saw me through everything—always protecting me. You were my person for so long that, somewhere along the way, I forgot to let you be anything else. It was easier to keep you. I have been a selfish, terrible friend."

His brow furrowed. "I wanted to be there for you. I loved you."

Loved.

The word shouldn't have cut.

"I wasn't worthy of it. I let you watch as I almost married others, as I banished my feelings for you to the confines of privacy. I resented and punished you for not agreeing to run away with me when it was in neither of our best interests..."

"I think we were too young and inexperienced to know *how* to put each other's best interests first," he said with a sigh.

Then, he leaned down to touch his forehead to mine.

His body tensed slightly when he asked, "Do you love him?"

I held my breath.

Yes.

"Maybe." Admitting it to him first felt wrong.

He rubbed my shoulder. "I have only ever wanted to see you happy, Syb." Tears swelled, slipping down my cheeks.

As he backed away and dragged his thumb across my wet cheek, he added, "I hate to admit that, of all the matches I've seen you almost make, this one seems the most genuine. Even if it means losing you."

"None of it is real. We'll have an heir and then be mostly estranged. Love wasn't on the table for me."

He met my gaze with a hard stare of disbelief that made me question my own words. "When you were sick, he came looking for a way to help you. I have never seen a man more frayed at the seams. If that isn't real, or love, then I don't know what is."

I reached for his hand and squeezed it. "I'm sorry."

"You don't need to apologize for where your heart is, Sybilla. I've held onto an idea of you that was unfair." He ran his thumb over my stiff knuckles. "Is he good to you?"

It took all my self-control not to snort. Yet when I looked ahead, I couldn't imagine life away from Krait. "He is good *for* me. He challenges me—infuriates me—so much."

Em nodded. "Stop giving him reasons to infuriate you so much."

"Rude," I huffed out. "And completely unrealistic."

He smirked, and Firose stirred but did not wake.

I wished that I could still love a man like Emmerick—loyal, bighearted, open with his emotions. Instead, I'd fallen for a man who thought the worst of me, guarded his emotions and remained elusive.

"I am going to be traveling to acquire some new resources against Caym. Our hope is that we can find one of the other envoys alone and put them under the Sethe curse...but if we cannot, or if he gets to you first..."

He nodded. "Then you have to place it on me."

"Yes. We will only resort to putting you under it as a last resort. Because there is no known way to reverse it." My voice cracked. "We'll need to specify a timeline to break the curse."

"Then promise me something."

"Conditions?" I whispered with a raised brow. "Have I rubbed off on you?"

"Yes. This time I have one." He offered me a weak smile and said, "If it comes to it, don't let them curse me to sleep longer than my parents' lifetimes. If I had to wake up without them..."

At that, I embraced him, burying my face in his fresh tunic.

"I promise, Em."

Maybe it made me a fool to trust a man who had shown me nothing but betrayal in the past few months. But I knew Emmerick's heart was still in there, somewhere behind Caym's treachery.

The boy I'd climbed trees with, the Knight who'd protected me through my formative years, the Constable who'd stood by my side—*he was here.*

So long as he breathed, I wouldn't believe there wasn't a way to break through the darkness to get him back.

CHAPTER 50

KRAIT

"Do you have enough water?" I asked from atop my horse, beside Sybilla's.

She hummed a yes. This time, I hadn't made Sybilla ride in a cart or on a mule. She was armed to the teeth, with a sword sheathed in her saddlebag and bow across her back. A blacksmith had fitted her with an everlasting quiver and arrows of charmed iron capable of penetrating even the toughest of stones and metals.

There had been a time when I would have done anything to get her to be quiet. That time was not now.

"Are you feeling well?" I tried again.

"Yes," she sighed out.

I let out a grumble of frustration.

It was less than a day's ride to get to Sahlmkar if one covered ground briskly, yet I fretted about her strength. We had deliberately not built an Egress there. The region just south of the volcanic shores held a decent amount of industry—textiles, masonry and blacksmithing. It also held the highest concentration of prisoners in the Sahlms.

We'd locked away Old World war criminals and those unwilling to keep the peace with our neighboring realm. Like the ones who'd attacked Luz.

Due to the lower altitude and harsh climate, Sahlmkar was even hotter and drier than Sahlmsara. The travel was treacherous enough to warrant a party of thirty soldiers. The wind whipping the air was a welcome reprieve from the heat, though it brought dust with it.

Elsedora was staying in the Sahlms to manage affairs and maintain communication with Henosis while I was gone.

The way Sybilla held her reins in one hand and massaged her wrist with the other told me she'd lied. She was hurting. My jaw tensed. I wanted her to confide in me the way she had when I'd held her in bed.

Sybilla glanced over. "Elsedora told me what to expect in this region," she noted. So she was willing to talk—about geography, at least. *It was a start.*

"Did she tell you its history?"

"It is thought to be Death's land," she said. "Is that true?"

"It is," I answered. "It's where Caym and Desidero were born."

While I was the King of Sahlmkar, and while the industry there served all of the Sahlms, there were still many in the old city who prayed to both the Death and Shadow Origins. They accepted me only as one half of the whole.

We could be walking into a trap. I suppressed that fear. "The people of Sahlmkar respect me as their ruler—but most still worship Caym, believing him to be the superior Source Origin. It may be unwise to bring you there, and if there is any indication of unrest, then I'm Shadowing you out."

She made a *"Pfft"* noise between her lips. "As if I am not used to living among those who want to see me dead."

Elsedora's earlier suggestion of flowers paled in comparison to what I truly owed Sybilla. Ryn would at least ensure that our arrival in the rough lands was a pleasant one. It had been a long time since I'd tried to convince a woman to entertain the idea of my company.

Taking her into the underbelly of dark magic seemed incredibly foolish, but we were running low on options.

"The people there are not inherently bad," I reasoned.

She snapped, "I never said they were."

I sighed against my impulse to bite back.

Her renewed coldness made it impossible to prove that my feelings had grown beyond what was required of us. *That damned list.* I still hadn't formed a compelling argument against my own written words.

One of my soldiers trotted from the front of the party. He yelled, "Trouble ahead, my King. The river is running deep from the first rainfall. We'll need to ford it carefully—there's a shallow point, but the current is strong."

"Understood," I barked back.

We approached the river. Its rush was more rapid than I'd seen here before. I watched the first soldiers attempt to cross. The water nearly reached the horses' bellies, even at the shallowest point. Sybilla's small mount might be withers deep.

"Would you like me to Shadow us across?" I asked.

She turned her chin up. "The soldiers ahead have crossed fine."

"We'll go slow," I grumbled as my mount's hooves splashed into the water. Sybilla's horse stepped in beside mine and flared its dish-shaped nose with a snort. The current tugged at the horses' legs, and they strained against the rushing water.

"Easy." I urged my mount onward as we fell into a single file line with Sybilla behind me.

I shot a worried glance back just as the blue ribbon that held Sybilla's hair caught the wind and pulled free. Her lips fell open as she tried to snatch it from the air, but it blew forward and hit her horse's ears. I could see her mutter a curse. Her horse spooked, leaped forward and then stumbled.

"Sybilla!" I called back as her horse collapsed to its knees—the steed's head disappeared below the surface as he thrashed and tried to regain his footing.

"Woah, woah!"

She tried to pull up on the reins, but her mount began to roll sideways.

"I can't swim!" she called out. The wind blew her hair across her pale, panic-stricken face.

Sybilla was knocked free of the saddle with a yelp. Her mount fled, swimming toward the bank. Sybilla's hands grasped at the water, trying to grab onto something, anything, to keep herself afloat.

The rushing river began to carry her away.

No.

She gasped before being pulled under.

No, fuck, no.

"Sybilla!"

My horse's hooves hit dry land, and I sprung off and raced down-river.

Three of my men, who had already crossed, rode ahead and looked for her. The hooves of their wet mounts pounded against the riverbank. I could hear the men calling to each other. She hadn't resurfaced, and their panicked shouts only heightened my fear.

I continued sprinting down the bank. I couldn't see her in the muddy water, and the faster the current moved, the faster my heart pounded.

I couldn't lose her too.

Her head popped above the water a few yards from where I stood.

I dove into the cool, murky water toward her. The current fought to drag me away from where I wanted to go.

Seconds felt like minutes, and my lungs burned. My hands finally met something soft—her arm or leg. I couldn't tell in the tumble of the river. I pulled her to me, getting a good grasp on her. She clung to the front of my shirt, and a wave of relief rushed through me. She was still conscious. Wrapping my arms around her, I Shadowed us to the bank.

She coughed and sputtered up water. I unclasped the buckle holding her bow to her, and let it and the charmed quiver fall to the side. She was soaked in mud, and trembling; her brow pinched tight as she gagged and coughed. I pounded on her back.

"Sybilla? Talk to me," I demanded. How could she not have told me sooner that she couldn't swim?

"Stop. Fucking. Hitting me," she choked out.

They were the most beautiful words she'd ever said while lashing out at me. I sat on my heels and stopped pounding.

Unable to help myself, I reached out and drew her into my lap, collapsing onto my ass and cradling her head against my shoulder. She regained her breath as I rocked her there. My men scrambled to go catch her mount, shouting at one another to catch mine as well.

My hands shook. Why hadn't I just insisted on Shadowing us across the river from the start? Then, all the energy to be angry left me.

There wasn't a single mark against her on any list that prevented me from longing to hold her—to be near her. That was love, you idiot, my mind screamed at me.

"That list. I didn't mean any of the things on it," I said into her hair. "I desperately wanted to, because I was scared. But I didn't." I couldn't tell whether she or I was trembling harder.

She gripped my shoulders, and the feel of her nails digging in gave me hope. "I don't believe you," she said, still regaining herself.

I let my chin rest on her head. "Then we are going to work on that."

CHAPTER 51
SYBILLA

I'd thought Sahlmsara was hot, but the land between the Sahlm-saran cities was unbearable. A balmy heat encased me like the sun had joined forces with the winds to carry oppressive humidity from the volcanic shores. We'd descended into a flat valley when Sahlmkar came into view.

The city was made up of primarily flat-roofed buildings and open-air markets. Businesses and row housing were stacked on top of one another. The streets were dust-coated and narrow. All the structures were coated in brown or beige stucco and there was little greenery.

Despite the lifeless hues, the city bustled with activity. The people here had harder edges and gave us skeptical glances as we passed through. Most seemed keen on finishing their day's work; no one paid their King any mind or honors.

In the mud-caked clothes from my unfortunate encounter with the river, I longed to be off my horse and clean. My thighs chafed against the leather saddle. Luckily, the horse was unharmed from his stumble—luckily, I was too.

"Are we safe here?" I whispered to Krait.

"Mostly," he answered. Comforting.

"We are heading to my flat. The building is heavily guarded. You'll be safe there."

The way Krait had clung to me on that riverbank had shaken some of my resolve to be cold toward him.

Stop giving him reasons to infuriate you. My friend's words were easier said than done.

"Please tell me there's somewhere to bathe there," I said.

"Afraid not."

I chanced an annoyed glance at him, and he stared back with a glint in his iron gaze.

He added, "But I've made other arrangements." His eyes crinkled with surprising softness.

I scoffed, "Well, good—I smell like a swamp. And stop looking at me that way."

He grunted, "What way?"

"Like you *like* me."

"I do like you," he answered. "Which is a lucky thing. Liking your future wife is something to strive for, is it not?"

My cheeks heated. I only hoped the coat of mud would protect me from him noticing. "Enjoying bedding me is *not* the same thing as liking me."

"That's an added benefit," he retorted.

I returned my attention to the narrow road as the men before us started pulling their horses aside toward a stable.

The buildings around us were all three-to-four-story flats, with stucco-rimmed balconies. Clothing hung from lines overhead.

"We'll drop the horses here. Keep your weapons with you," he instructed as he dismounted, and I followed. A groom came to retrieve our mounts, and Krait led me down the brown cobblestone road. A soldier on horseback, accompanied by a few guards on foot, followed with our packs.

The sun was, thankfully, setting, and an orange and red glow illuminated the town. The sunset added vibrance to the otherwise monochromatic surroundings.

Krait stopped at a cart and bought a loaf of bread and a few wax-sealed cheeses. A few yards later, I waited while he stopped at another cart to pick up a bottle of wine.

No one here seemed to treat him any differently than a common patron. Though the intense gaze of some made the hair on my arms stand. I let my mind slip into the cracks of a man's mind as we passed.

"If our King is here, maybe the rumor is true...Maybe our true Origin has returned..."

My throat constricted. They didn't just worship Caym here; they truly thought him the better choice to lead them. Krait's words on our journey rang true. I shivered despite the heat.

We'd been traveling all day, and I was still too hot to feel hungry, but the wine sounded nice. Krait made one last stop for fresh pitted fruit—apples and pears that were bruised but not rotted.

The guards kept their distance, but still flanked us. We dodged carriages through the narrow streets until Krait stopped.

"Here, this is the flat." He motioned to a building much like all the others—beige stucco, three stories, and flat-roofed.

When we approached the door, Krait asked, "Hold these?"

I smirked and said, "Fine, but you are not getting the wine back." I took his bounty of cheese, fruit and wine off his hands.

Krait hefted our packs onto his shoulders and thanked the guards who had trailed us. "Stay near," he told them, and they nodded their agreement.

"I can get mine." I tried to argue about him carrying my pack.

"You know the way in. Get the door for me."

Reaching the entry, I whispered, "In the Shadows we trust." The lock clicked, and the door opened for us.

Krait dropped the heavy bags in the entryway. Before us lay an empty stone-floored hall with little decor outside of a wooden candelabra that hung above with flickering tealight candles.

I ventured beyond the entryway and into a sitting room with two deep leather sofas and a frayed red rug. The walls were all covered in white stucco, and there were brown wooden beams running across the expanse of the ceiling. To the right was a staircase up to the second level. To the left was a small kitchen with a hearth. I placed the food down on a butcher block.

A vase of striking freshly cut larkspur was set on a small kitchen table in the corner, giving the air a clean, subtle scent. It was as though someone had prepared for us to be here.

"I like these," I noted and trailed my fingers over the delicate blue petals.

Krait kicked off his wet boots and peeled off his still-damp red tunic. I watched with interest.

How could the man be caked in mud and still somehow appeal to me?

He glanced at the flowers. "I had Ryn bring them. I know you like them."

"So *Ryn* brought me flowers?"

His expression seemed downright playful when he said, "At *my* request."

Trying to focus on his face without melting into a puddle at his feet, I asked, "Do you visit here frequently?"

"Not anymore—Elsedora or Ryn typically handle matters here when needed."

He was taking off his pants now.

My hand found my throat, which had gone dry.

"Have you no shame?" I gasped out, shielding my eyes.

Huffing a dark laugh, he said, "It isn't anything you haven't seen before—don't you want out of that filth too?"

I desperately wanted to remove the scratchy, damp material. *Modesty be damned.*

Unclasping the charmed quiver and bow from my back and discarding my sword onto the sofa, I sighed, having not realized how they'd weighed on me. My hands found the seam of my tunic. The feeling of the fabric peeling away from my skin was glorious.

Luckily, I'd worn conservative undergarments, but they did little to hide anything with the fabric clinging. "What are these *other* bathing arrangements?"

"You'll see," he said.

"Are you playing coy with me?"

He smirked. "I have no idea what you're talking about."

At the river, he'd insisted he didn't mean the things on that list. Yet he'd written them.

Though who was I to judge someone for writing things they didn't mean when I so often fired them off verbally? I hadn't meant most of the fire I'd spewed his way. It scared me to admit it, but my reasons to keep him at arm's length were dwindling.

As I peeled off my breeches, Krait walked over to a closet and retrieved what looked like two bedrolls, two pillows and a leather satchel, where he stowed the food and drink from the kitchen.

"We're ready to go," he declared.

"Wait. Like this?" I glanced down at myself and the thin white fabric barely covering me, and then to him, where his thin under-breeches left little to the imagination.

"Just like this," he said and held his free hand to me. "There won't be anyone else where we're going."

Reluctantly, I clasped his hand. An eager flutter settled in my stomach.

CHAPTER 52

KRAIT

Sahlmkar was not my favorite city by any stretch of the imagination. But in a remote corner of the northern Sahlms was my most treasured place in the realm. I'd never shared it with anyone before.

Sybilla reluctantly took my hand, and I Shadowed us into the cavern behind the falls. We weren't far from Sahlmkar, but the spot was impossible to reach on foot.

A natural spring had formed here amidst the dry lands to create a curtain of water flowing down into a crystal pool. It later split off into smaller streams that headed toward the volcanic shores.

Water cascaded off the rich red rock above us. I released Sybilla's hand before setting down the bedrolls and unraveling them there in the cavern, where we'd sleep cooled by the mist and breeze.

Not many ever wandered toward the volcanic shores. I'd discovered this place by chance centuries ago. Since having found it, when in Sahlmkar, I rarely slept in the flat. Instead, I found solace in the head-clearing sounds of rushing water.

Sybilla's lips parted. As she dipped her hand into the waterfall, her eyes glistened. "We're staying here?" An edge of excitement leaked into her voice.

Even with the mud coating her cheeks, she was a beautiful sight, standing there, appreciating one of the places I treasured.

"Is this acceptable accommodation for a Queen?" It only then occurred to me—what if she hated this gesture?

She glanced over her shoulder and shrugged. "I'm not sure I know what's acceptable anymore."

I couldn't tell if there was insinuation in her voice.

"You seemed to have two bedrolls ready quite quickly."

I smirked. "I may have prepared ahead."

She stared at me with skepticism.

A nervous flutter formed in my chest. Maybe I'd miscalculated how angry she was. I added, "It's my favorite place in the realm. Usually, I sleep on the ground, but I figured you might want a bedroll and pillow. A bit more comfortable."

Her posture softened as she scanned my face. "Are you trying to court me, Darvanda?"

No. Yes.

I scoffed back, "I have no idea what you mean." I fought the way my lips wanted to pull up at the sides. Rubbing my chin, I observed her closely.

Her hands were on her hips, now with only a thin white layer of fabric hugging them. It took all my restraint not to cross the cavern, replace her fingers with mine and dig into the supple skin that she was drawing my attention to.

I felt like a fumbling boy without any idea of what to do with my hands, so I ran them through my hair. She kept staring at me unnervingly.

All I knew for sure was that no matter what we faced next, I did not want to move forward with her continuing to hate me. Not when I'd grown so sure that I'd never be able to give her up.

From the satchel, I retrieved a lantern and a bar of lilac soap—her preferred fragrance. My preferred scent.

Her arms fell to her sides, and her expression softened. "You are, aren't you?"

"Sources, does it really matter?" I took a deep breath. "If you'd like to not smell like a swamp, come this way. And be careful on the rocks—they can be slick." I led her out of the cavern, avoiding her attempts at eye contact.

The moonlight guided us out onto the rocky banks of the spring, and its glow reflected off the water. A small canyon of red rock surrounded the area—a perfect, private oasis. As we stepped around the natural pool, I whispered a Brennac charm to light the lantern and then set it down.

"You can go first. I'll give you some privacy." I reached out to hand her the soap.

She stared at my outstretched hand. The rise and fall of her chest grew more erratic. Then, instead of taking the soap, she took my wrist and pulled me toward the spring.

"What are you doing?"

"Making sure that you bathe too," she answered. She had me guessing whether I was hearing things.

"Why?" I asked as the thrill of being tugged into the water behind her sent a cool shiver down my spine.

"Because you smell like a swamp, too." She looked at me over her shoulder and added, "And I haven't decided whether I want to fuck you or filet you tonight. I'm leaning a certain direction—despite my better judgment."

Thanking whatever miracle had her contemplating the idea, I stifled a laugh as she dragged me deeper into the spring. It was a shallow pool, so I did not worry about my newfound discovery of her lack of swimming skills.

As though hearing me, she answered, "And also what if I'm to drown without you to save me again?"

I shook my head. "It is shallow."

"I know—you're thinking loudly and doing little to ward me."

When she hit breast-high water, she dropped my wrist and dipped her head back to submerge her hair. She spent some time wiping the mud from her face.

When she went beneath the surface, I pushed away the image of her being pulled into the river's current earlier. My arms itched to reach out and lift her.

She popped her head back up a few steps closer to me.

To distract myself, I used the soap to clean the lingering mud and grime of travel from my arms.

"This might be my new favorite place, too," she said as she looked up at the waterfall. The way the water slid over her lips, the way her hair stuck to her neck, left me breathless.

"May I?" I asked, holding out the soap again. This time, she raised a brow.

She returned my question with some of her own. "You're going to bathe me? Isn't that a little intimate for someone who considers me so unbearable?"

"Yes—if you'll let me. And if anyone is the unbearable one, it is not you."

Sybilla pouted. "Well, it isn't any fun to rib you if you're going to be self-deprecating about it."

I expected her to move away or decline my offer, but instead, she swayed closer in the water and faced away from me so I could begin with her hair. I lathered the soap between my hands. As my fingers worked against her scalp, she hummed and leaned into me, her back pressed to my front. I swallowed hard and let my hand trail along her neck before running the soap down her shoulder, pushing down the sleeve of her undergarments.

She lowered to rinse her hair, and her body slipped down mine, causing me to stifle a groan. When she emerged, she lifted her arms and slipped her top undergarment over her head.

She said, "You can't properly bathe while clothed." My breath caught as she shimmied out of the bottoms and let them float toward the banks.

When she turned toward me, the sight of her tightened nipples at the water's surface drew my attention.

"I suppose you're right," I mustered. "I might need assistance." I didn't. But the words sparked interest in her eyes.

"Courting me. Asking for my help. Who is this new man?" Her fingers trailed down my torso to find the waist of my underbreeches. She pushed down, and my already hardened length was freed, brushing her hip.

"Tell me again everything you hate about me," she whispered as I kicked the remaining layer of clothing off between us, not caring if it was lost to the spring.

I shook my head. "There is nothing that I hate about you. It's the most infuriating thing."

When she looked up at me, I did not let my memories squash my hope.

CHAPTER 53
SYBILLA

The words on that parchment had been cutting. But his actions were adding up to something different, something *more*—something that neither of us seemed prepared for, but neither of us could prevent either.

With nothing between us but clear water and the light of the moon, I'd made my mind up.

I still wanted all of him.

No halfway point, no moderation.

I knew he was capable of more.

"There are plenty of things a prospective husband should loathe about me. For one, I can't promise to be polite, cordial or patient when I don't want to be. I won't be mild-mannered or obedient. I can't help but curse when I'm angry—"

"Sybilla," he said, trying to cut me off.

"Let me finish, you insufferable bastard," I snapped, and his brows lifted with entirely too much interest. Sadistic prick.

A prick that I'd happily climb and let take me right here in the spring. I wanted him too much to deny it any longer. I'd rather be angry with him, than angry without him.

I continued, "I am not without faults—I will fight you, every day, tooth and nail, on everything. My corridor may come before your needs. My duty to my realm may make our discussions heated. And if you even think about touching another, then I'll be blind and murderous with jealousy."

The lamplight flickered across his satisfied expression, which made me want to lay my feelings bare.

"But I will also fight *for* you and your realm just as hard. I will not falter in the face of anything, because I've fallen for you. Somehow, no matter how intolerable you act, you're who I see in my future. I see you leading beside me. Maybe not always together on every matter, but I see you there no less."

He was quiet, all amusement washing from his face.

A lump formed in my throat. Being naked had nothing to do with how vulnerable I felt.

My confidence faltered.

I'd misread him.

"If you do not feel the same, say so now. We can forget this."

"I wouldn't be able to," he said.

My shoulders deflated. He'd said so few words in response to so many.

"I couldn't forget you," he clarified. "Nor would I have been able to let you walk away easily, knowing that you might have wanted something more. I tried so hard to convince myself that I could never be what you want—what you need."

He stepped closer, intensity flaring in his eyes as he put a finger beneath my chin and tipped my head up. Water from his hair dripped onto me.

"It's you that I see for my future too. And it has nothing to do with an old book or a prophecy within it. I want *you*. However you come, however many obstacles you set in my way. I will never be the perfect husband, but I can work on being perfect for you."

There was no current in the water, yet I felt pulled closer to him. My breasts brushed against his chest. "I have some conditions," I added.

"Why does that not surprise me?" His hands skated up my arms and left goosebumps in their wake. "Name them."

"You were right about that list. While I want a child, I want to be ready to be a mother...and I am not. I need you to understand that. However long it takes, I will work to set Caym back until I am sure."

His hands halted on my shoulders. He looked pissed off.

Will he turn away now?

"You think that still weighs on my decision to want you?" Signature annoyance had leaked into his voice, but also something akin to worry.

I tried to reason with him. "I know the prophecy requires urgency but—"

"Fuck the prophecy. We'll change it," he cut me off. He brushed his lips against my ear. "I said I will take you as you come. If you look in that satchel in the cavern, I even brought tonics to prevent conception in case you might consider being with me again. I don't have conditions, Sybilla. So keep naming yours."

His lips moved down my neck, dancing across my pulse point. So distracting. My core tightened with anticipation. I wanted so badly to feel him inside of me again. His words were even more distracting—the absolution in them. I would have his heir, but he was giving me control of the timeline and that lifted a weight of stress off my shoulders.

His willingness to offer so much more of himself than I'd ever imagined left me dizzy. A future, a partner, someone to laugh with, fight with, grow old with.

I almost forgot my next condition as he nipped at my shoulder and then kissed away the sting.

"Good then," I choked out as one of his hands squeezed my waist and I pressed into him. "The next condition is that you will remove that statue from the bell tower."

This time, he faltered and straightened. His expression dropped to something torn between anger and melancholy. It mirrored the look he'd had on his face when he'd started piecing together Ryn's betrayal.

I regretted the way I'd phrased that sentence.

"Shit, no," I continued. "Freya has been in that dark room alone for too long. Don't you think? She deserves to see the light, to be seen and celebrated. I shouldn't meddle...but I've already told you that isn't something I can help. It seems she might like the main hall more...or maybe to be in Luz, where she'll be closer to her homeland?"

He stood stone-still and silent for a beat. Then his posture softened, and his arms abruptly wrapped around me.

Thank the Sources.

My fingers dug into his back, and the weightlessness of being in the water made it easy to hitch my leg up on his hip. One of his arms slipped below my thigh to balance me. His free hand caught in my wet hair before his mouth took mine and I let out a breathy gasp.

There was something decadent about the way he tasted on my tongue—something tender about the way he felt. The last time we'd come together had been so frantic, so rushed. This kiss and his gentle touch were something new to savor.

Our bodies, slick against one another, tangled together. With my breasts pressed to his chest, his length rubbed against where I craved him most, and I groaned into his mouth.

We broke apart only to catch our breath. "Any other conditions?"

"We'll settle the rest later," I answered. "We have other things to settle tonight."

His fingers dug into my hips as he whispered into my mouth, "Bedroll?"

I quickly nodded and squeaked in surprise when he lifted me out of the water. My legs wrapped around his waist as he carried me to the cavern. He placed me in front of one of the bedrolls. Feeling the press of his hard length against my stomach made my breath hitch when my feet met the rock ground.

Placing a hand on his chest, I pushed him back toward the rolled cushion. Lowering himself, he brushed his thumb along his bottom lip as he looked up at me gluttonously.

My inner thighs were already slick with need, and his unfiltered hunger as his stare dragged down me undid me further. My core clenched when he leaned back on his elbows, waiting for me. I straddled his hips and lowered myself onto my knees. Just one thrust up and he could fill me.

With merciless slowness, he grabbed my hips and pulled me down onto him, stretching me. I nearly broke then—my mouth hung open as a guttural sound left it.

"Do you even understand how beautiful you are when you're too full of me to speak?"

He lay back, and his hands roamed from my hips up to my breasts. He took my nipples between his thumbs and forefingers.

I strung curses together beneath my breath, which ended up sounding more like nonsense than language, further proving his point. I had no more words. Only sensations that overwhelmed my senses as he drove up into me.

My hips rolled against him, seeking more.

"Use those filthy words now, Sybilla. Tell me how this feels."

"Fucking incredible," I gasped out. "You are incredible."

He reached up and hooked one finger into my mouth to pull me by my lower lip to his. When he kissed me, it was a brand that would never leave me—a day without him in it wouldn't go by without me noticing his absence.

"More," I demanded between kisses. I tried to rock against him faster—hurried and reckless.

The moment had required no planning yet was heavy with so many commitments to each other. The only future I cared about was one where we tried to make it out of this mess alive so we could have more moments like this one, again and again.

"Slow down," he said and grabbed my hips to hold me still as he thrust into me with labored breath. "I don't want this to end so soon."

Those words tore at a part of me that I'd long guarded. He loosened his grip, and we continued with a slowness that was more tender than hurried, more...just *more*.

"This is never going to end. You told me that before." I leaned down and kissed him.

The faint groan he let out into my mouth was indulgent to all my senses. The stubble that rubbed my chin, his sounds, the smell of spice and smoke—it all enveloped me, and I couldn't get enough. He thrust up, and I had to grip his hair to hold off my release.

"No, it isn't," he answered. Another thrust. Another groan.

His mind's wards dropped. I felt every sensation he did, and he felt all of mine, too. Humming with each other's pleasure, we toed the edge of release.

"We can't keep fighting it," I said. He answered by flipping me with one arm onto my back and driving into me deeper.

I gasped out, "Fuck..."

"We can't," he agreed and sucked in my lower lip, swallowing my string of curse words. He had no complaints about my vulgar language now.

My legs circled his waist, and there was nothing more I could say as he pushed into me once more and my walls around him clenched. Crying out, my resolve to hold out cracking, I tumbled over into a wave of pleasure. He buried his head between my neck and shoulder, riding out the end of my release.

He lifted to look me in the eyes as a satiated groan escaped his lips and he spilled into me. He wasn't a man of many words, but as he pulsed inside me and his eyes searched mine, all his unspoken sentiments dawned upon me.

He'd never wanted to filet me.

He did not hate me.

He feared losing me.

He might even love me.

Krait used his Shadows to uncork the wine, and I unwrapped the cheeses with ravenous enthusiasm. He handed me a small vial of yellow-colored liquid that tasted awful but gave me the peace of mind that our romp wouldn't have the consequence of a child. Not yet.

It would be on my terms.

We laid out the other bedroll and set up a small picnic there. Once half the loaf was gone and we'd eaten away at the skinned fruit, Krait watched as I took a drag of the wine bottle and settled down next to him.

There, naked, lying on his side and propped on an elbow, he looked like a painting. My very own debaucherous work of art—one that I could run my hands over. I'd sunk my fingers into the hair on his chest without thinking, and he smirked.

"You aren't scared of this? It could go poorly." I bit my lower lip.

He shrugged. "We have worse things to fear. Whatever comes next, there isn't a soul alive that I'd rather face it with," he said before taking the wine bottle. He stared at me with some indescribable intensity.

"Why are you looking at me like that?" This time, there was no sharpness to my tone; there was only curiosity.

"Marry me," he answered.

I raised my brows. "That has already been settled."

Our betrothal felt different now. It felt real. I'd skirted marriage for so long, yet I had no doubts this time.

"Tomorrow," he clarified as he handed me the bottle.

I sat up on my elbow. "Tomorrow?" I balked, staring down at him as he relaxed into the bedroll.

"Yes."

"Here?" I asked.

"Does it matter where?"

"No," I answered. "No, it doesn't matter. Tomorrow. Tonight even."

His expression softened before he reached over and drew me to him. The bottle was discarded, spilling onto the rocks beside the bedroll. We fell asleep to the sound of the waterfall and each other's hammering heartbeats.

CHAPTER 54

KRAIT

On our way through the streets of Sahlmkar, Sybilla nervously babbled about a wedding she'd attended for a couple of nobles in the South Corridor—something about it being a dockside ceremony and losing rings to the ocean.

My excitement had risen too much to actively listen to her story. But, seeing her by my side, chattering amicably, flushed and energized felt right. We burst into the Temple of Shadows midday.

A Divine was lighting the candles around a charcoal-colored statue of my great-great-great-grandfather Desidero. Sybilla wandered about the temple while I explained to the man of worship, who only spoke Brennac, that we would like to be wed. The conversation went by in a blur of anticipation and adrenaline.

Waiting even a moment longer to make our union official seemed foolish when there would be no carrying on without her. We'd already wasted too much damned time fighting.

I'd eloped once and it had cost me my heart—even that didn't deter me. Instead that rusty organ in my chest swelled, thinking about the second chance that lay before me.

The Divine raised his brow. He looked over at Sybilla. "She is the one?" he asked.

I watched Sybilla as she stared up at the gray tapestries adorning the walls with her hands clasped behind her back. The space was windowless and built from dark lava stone. Torches lit only the wall hangings and the monument to the Shadow Origin at the center of the room. Darkness danced around us.

Sybilla wore the dark breeches and cream tunic that I'd had Ryn pack in the satchel for her. She'd tried to tame her curls into a loose braid over her shoulder, which had become frayed and now poked out in places. I wore something similarly plain and unpressed. It didn't look like any royal wedding I'd ever attended, but it would be *ours*.

She glanced back at me and smiled.

"She's the one," I answered.

I'd rushed one marriage. I'd let my Source Match bear the consequences of marrying the wrong man. My chest tightened, and Sybilla frowned as she approached me.

"Is something wrong?" She placed a hand on my chest. "Are you going to leave me at the altar, Darvanda?" she asked with a playful tilt of her head.

"That would be more of your move," I joked and her frown deepened. My hand slipped over hers as she met my eyes. "I've never been more sure that I am in the right place with the right person."

Her expression brightened again. "Well, good. You'd be a fool not to recognize what a catch I am."

At that, I dropped my forehead to hers and let a chuckle rumble in my chest.

I would be a fool.

There were no witnesses, no carriage processions, no crowds or applause or pomp.

We stood before the Divine. Our vows were short and in Brennac, which meant she didn't understand them. I opened my mind so that she could hear me translate as we recited them together.

"May the Origins honor our union.

When the sun breaks, this hand thou shall take.

Through both shadow and light, we shall together face future plights.

Let our roots grow deep in the soil for when winds raise ocean shores,

The fire within me is forever yours.

And when the moon and stars rise, our love shall be written in dark skies.

Until death do us part, our love shall conquer all.

My heart is now thy heart."

Her Brennac was sloppy and barely accurate, which made me smirk as we finished repeating our promises.

By the end of our vows, I felt her hands shaking in mine and realized I was trembling too. It was not with fear. It was from an end to fear—holding her there, knowing that I'd wake beside her for as many tomorrows as we were graced with.

Her eyes glistened like emerald pools as she looked up at me and squeezed my fingers. Her encouraging smile melted me; it would be all I saw in my dreams, replacing so many nightmares.

The Divine finally said, "You may seal your union with a kiss."

She seemed to understand his words just fine because she pulled me down. When she kissed me, every muscle in my body relaxed and I lifted my hands to cup her face.

When we parted, the Divine held up two wooden rings, which were typically provided by the temple to those who could not afford metals. That tiny piece of smoothed wood would be my most priceless treasure.

As soon as she slid the ring onto my finger, my heart skipped a few beats as though readjusting. Now it matched the rhythm of hers.

"Let's go prepare beasts to fight for our future," she whispered into my ear.

Forever stubborn, forever efficient. Forever mine.

CHAPTER 55
SYBILLA

Krait hadn't given me trouble about immediately wanting to meet the beasts of Sahlmkar after we were wed. If anything, he regarded me with adoration for it.

We did not have the luxury of time. The scorching dust-coated air burned my lungs as we met the afternoon sun outside the Temple of Shadows. Not even the harsh climate and oppressive heat could shake the lightness in my step; not even the pain in my joints would ruin my wedding day.

I ignored the steady throb of pain in my ankles. I'd take my tonic when we got back to the flat before it got any worse.

I would be fine.

As though sensing my worry, Krait reached into the satchel to retrieve a green vial and handed it to me.

Sighing in relief, I said, "How did you know?"

"Your brow pinches a bit, and your gait grows stiffer. You're sure you want to do this today?" he asked.

I downed most of the vial and teased, "I deal with you daily—how much more monstrous could these beasts be?"

Huffing a laugh, Krait said, "Sources save us. We've been married not ten minutes."

We stepped carefully around textile tents and avoided collision with carriages on the narrow dirt-coated cobblestone street.

"Where are they kept?"

"They lie in the tombs below the city."

"And now...you want *me* to wake them up? Just like that?" I asked uneasily.

He took my hand. When he spun the wooden ring on my finger, warmth flooded me. For once, when I had approached that altar, there had been no hesitation—no inclination to run.

"Just like that." He quirked a brow. "Frightened?"

"Of course not," I scoffed the lie.

We passed a barren block of row houses with boarded windows and cracked foundations. Sahlmsaran guards stood watch at each end of the streets, and a few trailed us wherever we went, keeping their distance at Krait's request.

Krait led me into an alley just behind the row houses; the narrow path was devoid of any foot traffic. Barely any light reached the cobblestones here, and the shade was a reprieve from the sun.

At the end of the alley, an iron door stretched at least twenty feet tall.

When we reached the entry, Krait placed his free hand just above the doorknob. He whispered a charm in Brennac. I reminded myself to tell him later that I'd like to learn his ancestors' language.

After he spoke the charm, gears turned within the door, making an awful grating noise. We backed away, and the door swung open.

It was pitch black inside—a void reminiscent of Krait's Shadows. He stepped forward and took a torch off the wall. With another whispered charm, it sputtered alive with flame.

"Can Source-wielders control any Source?" I asked.

He shook his head. "Small charms here and there are possible, like that one. It's much harder, nearly impossible, to hold and wield other Sources than one's own; it takes too much energy. Power isn't a bottomless well. At some point you do reach an end, a moment when you can't go on. Even for you—that is a universal rule."

With the flame he held, he lit more sconces on our way down a stone stairway.

"Asterie was able to light all the sconces at once in the Luz crypts," I challenged him.

He smirked. "I don't deal in light. I'm weakest at charms that require fire or sun. She also had a piece of Fen's magic too."

We continued to step into the belly of the tombs below Sahlmkar. The stone walls around us were dark gray, and the air grew sticky and too warm. It smelled of soil, mold and dust. When we reached the bottom, the tunnel forked in four possible directions.

"Oh, joy. A maze," I mused.

He brushed back cobwebs. "Purposefully so."

I tried to remember which direction we went—left, left, right, straight, left, right. The winding path had so many turns that I grew dizzy, and my anxiety mounted. Finally, we reached another door. This one was as large as the entry but a sooty color and carved with a pattern reminiscent of the Shadows often ebbing from Krait.

"Was Desidero an ally to Isolde?" I asked, finding it oddly comforting to think our ancestors may have aligned once.

"Desidero was thought to have been in love with her daughter Isleen." His words were darkly alluring. I rose to my tiptoes to brush a kiss across his bottom lip.

"Of course he was," I mused as Krait's hand dug into my hair to steady me.

"As thrilling as it would be to take you here, we need to focus, my Queen."

I returned to flat feet. "Fine," I huffed.

Krait leaned down to kiss me once more, before he whispered another Brennac charm to unlock the door. It opened to a large cave.

The dark lava stone domed high above us. When Krait began to light torches around the perimeter, I finally saw *them*. They towered above us, their vicious intentions set in stone.

They had obsidian scales that covered their long lengths and legless, snake-like bodies. Their curved faces resembled the angular shape common in the rattling serpents of this realm. Feathered wings stretched high above their serpent heads. They were utterly terrifying to behold.

Any prior confidence drained from me.

"Giant flying snakes? You've got to be kidding," I whispered mostly to myself.

Krait looked over his shoulder at me as he lit another torch. "Don't tell me you're getting cold feet about this," he said.

I shot him a pointed glare. "No, I am just unsure how *I'm* meant to control something so...horrifying."

Krait stepped behind me. "There is only one way to find out. We start with this one," he said as he turned me by the shoulders toward the largest. "This is Lymrasi—their leader. We'll speak with her first. It's believed that if she accepts you, the others will too."

Before I could think twice, Krait stepped behind me and urged me forward with his front against my back. He placed my hand on a giant scale of the beast's nose. He kissed the top of my head as an amber glow shone bright, which made me stumble into his chest.

I squinted against the glare. Life seemed to return to Lymrasi's dusty stone scales, and they glimmered black against the lamplight. Krait pulled me back a few paces as the serpent wound and stretched.

He kept me between him and the beast. Motherfucker.

"Now? We're waking her *now?*" I gasped as the serpent licked the air, still coming out of its stone sleep.

"If not now, when?" he whispered in my ear. I would kill him if we made it out of this cave alive.

A low hiss escaped the beast's mouth before it stretched its neck toward the ceiling and shook it side to side with a lethal grace. When the serpent's double lids lifted, a slitted pupil of gold stared right at me.

Luckily, I'd relieved my bladder back at the falls; otherwise, I'd have surely pissed myself for the second time in front of Krait.

She hissed out, "Who holdsss the power to wake me?" Lymrasi's tongue tasted the air in front of my nose.

I held my breath, cold sweat building on the back of my neck despite the cave's sticky heat.

"I-I—" I stammered. Krait squeezed my shoulders tight. "I am Sybilla Wymark, Queen of the Central Corridor and the Last Daughter of Isleen."

Lymrasi tilted her neck as her wings flapped twice, blowing back the curls from my face. "Ahhhh, yesss. And with an heir of Desssidero. How prophetic. But are you worthy?"

Her gaze beat down on me as her mouth opened just enough to reveal venom dripping from her fangs.

She smelled of mourning and death—not putrid or rotten but like the very essence of loss. The feeling tugged at my mind, wanting me to think of all I'd personally lost. It was like a mental attack on my very soul.

It took a great deal of energy to push Lymrasi out of my thoughts, and I strained to ward both my mind and Krait's. "Ahhh and she lovesss him too. It is a shame that Caym cursssed me to kill his brother's kin," she hissed, and coiled back as though about to strike us.

"No!" I ordered with a raised hand, and Lymrasi's neck halted mid-swing. "You answer to me, not Caym. I seek your help against him."

Krait said nothing but held onto my unraised arm and let me press into him, steadying me. We stood our ground against the beast of nightmares, and she sized us up as though we were mice to be swallowed.

But she did not strike.

I'd stopped her.

"Ssso you can control me. What reasonsss do you have for needing my help?" Lymrasi asked.

"We require reinforcements against Caym's rise. I've come to offer you freedom in exchange for your help," I said. The beast coiled its long tail around itself.

"I do not bargain," she answered. "That is Death's way."

Setting these beasts free seemed unwise anyway.

"Then what will it take to gain your favor in the impending war against him?"

"I only require one thing. Then me and my children will help you," Lymrasi said as she licked the air.

"Name it," I challenged. Dealing with conditions had always been my strong suit.

She hissed, "That when the time comesss, you will not hesitate to defeat him. No matter the cossst."

I looked over my shoulder. Krait's brow furrowed, but he nodded.

"Deal. How do we wake the others?"

"Only I can do that. Come to me when Isssolde's power hasss been restored to Caym."

A lump formed in my throat. They would not help until our doom was imminent.

"Fine...We will be back," I said. "Do not leave here. Am I understood?"

Lymrasi whispered as she slunk deeper into the cavern, "Yesss, young Isssleen. We are now indebted to one another. But you are on borrowed time."

Her words made me shiver.

I'd make riskier deals with beasts of nightmares if it meant Caym never got the chance to destroy our realms.

I hoped we were not too late to fight him, to return him to a state of sleep until the next black moon.

On our walk back to the flat, Krait grabbed my hand and pulled me aside. He pressed me against the wall of a shop just a few blocks from our destination.

"Can we consummate our marriage right here?" he asked. "Something about watching you command a giant snake has gotten me all sorts of eager."

I smirked and swatted half-heartedly at him. "Someone will see. There are guards right over there."

"Let them."

He leaned down, and when his mouth took mine with feverish indulgence, my knees went weak. Kissing my husband here, open to prying eyes, open to whatever judgment was dealt us, felt too good not to be wicked.

There may have been a man slinging leathers into a cart yards away. The sound of a chime might have meant someone opened the shop door feet away from us.

None of it mattered, because I was drunk on a man I never should have fallen for, but had anyway. I moaned into his mouth as he reached down and pulled my thigh up around him, seeming intent on exactly what he'd asked for.

"My King." The sound of clanking armor grew louder. Not now. I was too consumed in his kiss to be stopped.

He parted from me, staring into my eyes with swollen lips and mussed hair. "When we get back to the flat, we're finishing this," he promised.

"My King," the soldier repeated, and Krait righted me on the ground. We turned to face the disorderly group of soldiers that stood at the corner. They were winded and huffing.

"Officer Ryn requires your help at the prison. He requested that you come alone."

A young soldier approached with a note, and though I couldn't make out the words, I recognized Ryn's handwriting. I looked between the soldier and my husband. "I stay by your side."

Krait scanned Ryn's note. "I promise when I determine it's safe, I will come get you," he reasoned. "If Ryn thinks it unwise, trust him. Please."

The lust of our prior moment of wild desperation had passed and had been replaced with the stone facades of two rulers negotiating.

"I'll determine whether it is unwise. Hand it over."

He passed me the note.

Something is very wrong with the prisoners here. They've grown rapidly ill. Come quickly. For the love of all things good, keep Sybilla away in case it's contagious.

"I'm coming with you," I demanded again.

He took both of my hands and brought them to his lips to kiss the palm of each. "Please stay in the flat until I understand what's happening. The last thing I can handle is losing you to some mortal illness that could have been avoided, Sybilla."

If I pressed him, he would break. But logic won out. "You come right back."

Krait's head dipped so he could whisper into my ear. "Of course. I'm very motivated to pick up where we left off." Then he planted a kiss just below my ear that made my knees weaken again. Heat spread across my cheeks as the guards looked away.

"Okay," I agreed, still hating the idea of parting from him.

He passed me the satchel and then he turned his attention to the guards and said, "See her safely back to the flat."

CHAPTER 56
SYBILLA

I paced the space, memorizing every crack in the stucco. Krait had only been gone minutes when a knock came at the flat's door. Warily, I tried to look through the keyhole but then heard a familiar voice.

"Queen Sybilla? I was sent from Luz. I'm here with your tonics." Thank the Sources.

I flung open the door. The man who had seen me through the worst of my health and had been a constant in my life for so long was on the flat's doorstep.

I breathed a sigh of relief to see him, then I exclaimed, "Healer Mortag!"

My healer offered a smile and an outstretched arm. Two guards stepped between us. One said, "He has been searched for weapons, my Queen. We escorted him here, but shall remove him if necessary."

My heart sank, as I realized that he'd likely been questioned and interrogated to get to me.

"All is well," I assured them and then turned to Mortag. "Come in, come in."

The guards stepped aside.

"How did you get here?"

Mortag kissed the top of my hand and followed me inside.

He looked just as he always had—a neat cream-colored robe with bronze buttons down the front, dusty brown hair cut short, and a sharp nose. Healer Mortag was an immortal without Source magic. He'd been my mother's healer and her mother's before her. He'd mentioned once that he'd been alive to see the Great Wars.

"Sit, sit." I motioned toward one of the sofas. "It is good to see a familiar face. What happened to you during the battle of Luz?"

"Ah. I was just fine. I got summoned to deal with some family matters in Eros," he said and reached into his robe pocket. "But I stopped in Luz on my way here and brought your favorite." Mortag pulled out a small wooden box full of tea bags, which were stained bright blue. My heart warmed, and I took the tea box from him with a giddy smile as he sat.

Eager to drink the earthy, floral nectar, I said, "I'll go fetch some water. Make yourself at home."

I left the flat with a kettle to gather water from the spigot outside. The sun had set. Glancing around, I found the street completely empty—no market carts, no guards. Where had the two who had brought Mortag gone?

My brow furrowed. It worried me that something more dire might be happening at the prison and I was relegated here.

A lump formed in my throat. My visitor, at least, made for a pleasant distraction from the absence of my husband.

When I stepped back into the flat, Healer Mortag had risen and now faced a window. He looked out at the street below.

"Tea?" I asked him.

Mortag waved a hand. "No, I brought that especially for you. I know how it clears your mind."

I pursed my lips as the kettle hissed. After searching no fewer than six cupboard doors, I finally found a cup to pour water into. As the tea steeped, the water twisted in blue cloudy wisps, and I drew in a deep waft of the sweet, earthy scent. Perfection.

"You are a long way from home, my Queen. And to be married, I've heard?" Mortag asked. His tone was laced with surprise and what one might construe as judgment.

"Guilty," I admitted. "I am married already. It is what's right for Luz—this alliance, this marriage. I think you'd like him. It is a good match."

"Your mother thought her marriage a politically gainful one, too. And Death found her quite easily."

I wasn't sure when Healer Mortag had developed the nerve to speak to me in such a way, and my awareness heightened. My teeth ground together. "Yes, well...she was foolish to trust my father."

My healer hummed and said, "Drink your tea. It will ease your nerves."

As I drew nearer to him, I instinctually lifted the cup to take a sip. Upon noticing something familiar on the sleeve button of Mortag's cream robe, the tea sloshed in my mouth.

The deathmark.

He still faced away from me. All the hairs on my arms stood as I lifted the cup to my lips, backwashed the tea into it, and set my cup down on the windowsill beside his arm, trying not to let my hands shake.

"You..." Healer Mortag's voice turned darker as he said, "You have skirted Death your entire life, haven't you, Isleen? Don't you find that odd?"

I faltered, taking one step away from him. "That is not my name," I reasoned. "Healer Mortag, you know that I am Sybilla. You've cared for me since I was a girl."

Healer Mortag laughed—a horrid sound that filled my ears with smoky terror, like his essence was seeping into my mind. When he looked at me, his eyes were a terrible shade of murky green—Caym's envoy.

Fuck. Think, Sybilla, think.

I glanced down at the cup of blue liquid on the sill and felt nauseous. A family recipe. My mother had loved it, her mother.. .daughters of Isleen.

What the fuck had he been doing with the tea?

Then it hit me—how easily my power had started to come to me while in the Sahlms, how scrambled my mind had felt for the first few weeks here. It felt like a punch to my stomach.

He had been suppressing my power for my entire life.

I caught sight of the moon through the window behind him. It was a deep shade of gray, nearly devoid of color with only a silver lining.

We were supposed to have years. This could not be happening so soon.

Mortag hunched, and I watched as the brown in his eyes returned. His mouth agape, he stared at me with dread written across his features. "I'm sorry, my Queen. Please, run..."

My heart pounded. "We can fight him, Mortag. I will help you..."

"It is a shame that you fell in love with my nephew." A dark, grating voice came from the door of the flat.

I hadn't heard anyone enter over the blood throbbing in my ears. A man in a heavy gray robe stepped into the room, the top half of his face obscured by the shadows of a hood. Barden followed behind him.

Emmerick, Barden, Mortag...The three envoys. But this was a fourth threat.

My eyes widened at the sight of my cousin—his hair ruffled, cheeks red and eyes bloodshot.

The gray-clad man continued, "We could do *marvelous* things together. But time and time again, you always choose *him*." The way the man's lips had shaped the word "marvelous" would haunt me until the end. With blackened fingertips, he drew back his cloak hood.

That same sense of inevitable doom I'd felt the night Asterie and I had used the moonstone together struck me.

Caym.

His eyes were a piercing shade of green that seemed to smoke with amber from within. He combed back golden locks with one hand. If it didn't feel like I was about to be rotted from the inside out, then his sharp features might be considered handsome.

"Ah. I cannot kill you...I won't kill you. Not when you hold such beautiful power. We will be unstoppable, Isleen."

Barden and Mortag now stared at me with hungry expressions, like wolves set on prey. He was influencing both of them. Isolde's powers had been restored.

You are on borrowed time, Lymrasi had said. I'd been so damned foolish.

"Cousin, Mortag, you need to push him out. This isn't you." Panic sank in, and I drew a hand to my throat.

"Oh—it has *always* been me. Watching you, waiting for when our paths would cross under this black moon," Caym said. "I once wished to see you dead for your ancestors' betrayals. But now...I see what we may accomplish together. Come with me willingly, and I will not harm them..."

He waved a hand at Barden and Mortag and my heart pounded. His voice was like venom in my veins, alluring in a horrific way. I almost faltered, almost approached him.

He'd done this to Firose.

I'd seen it in her memories—his lure, his ability to sink into people. He had his sights on me next.

"So now you wish to see me leashed to you instead?" I spat back, my sense of self-preservation giving way to anger. He'd hurt so many—killed so many. "I'd rather be dead."

Barden and Mortag stood still, but their arms went limp at their sides. Caym looked murderous, nostrils flaring. "I warned you. When the Origins released this body from that tomb below Helos, these pawns were a means for me to regain strength through. They are useless to me. They'll make better use as Death. So we start here until you bend to me..."

Caym let a sinister smile cross his face as he cracked his neck and outstretched a hand toward my cousin. The putrid smell of dark magic roiled as a ghastly amber smoke swept around Barden. It robbed him of breath, then of color, then of skin. His pocket watch fell from his hand—it landed face up, revealing the deathmark carved into its gold body.

I gasped out in horror as my cousin's muscles decayed until there was nothing but dust on the tile. I threw a hand over my mouth, stifling a scream.

There were no guards to hear me.

Caym's eyes closed with a satiated shudder as though he'd just taken the first sip of a fine port. His lids opened slightly, showing me the whites as his eyes rolled back. He extended a hand toward Mortag next.

"You can stop this, Isleen." Caym held out his other hand to me. "Just come to me."

"Mortag—no!" I tried to run to my healer only to realize my legs were trapped in place.

I had no control.

All that training, all that false hope that my mind would be any match for him. He would kill everyone I loved until I accepted his terms—until I surrendered to him.

I reached deep into the depths of my mind, and I screamed to the one who I knew might hear me, not knowing if from a distance his mind would let me in.

"He's here. Caym is here. Run!" I helplessly slammed against the shield of his mind as if it were a pane of glass.

The smoke descended over Healer Mortag.

No, no, no. The dust of what had once been my healer fell into a pile next to my cousin's. My heart cracked in two.

I tried to scream out, but a hand wrapped around my neck and squeezed. Caym had killed them both so quickly, and the shock of the moment washed over me as I gagged for air.

"I may not be able to kill you, but what an impressive partner you will make once you give in," Caym said. "Pity, really. My nephew had been so happy with his first wife—didn't even notice when I made her an envoy. What was her name? Fiona? Farah?"

Freya. He'd taken Krait's first love. My stomach churned.

"She was only strong enough to change the moon cycles by a few years before her untimely demise. Will you be more useful than she was?"

"Never," I choked out.

"We'll see." He frowned. "Pity this black moon had to sour your honeymoon. I suppose there will be no heir. That was what you were going to try, wasn't it?"

He made a *tisk-tsk* sound before he slammed my back against the stucco wall so hard that debris from the ceiling rained on us. I cried out as he released my throat, but his face was so close that I shuddered. He closed his eyes as though he might kiss me and then breathed out that awful amber smoke. I gagged as it slipped into my mouth, caressing my tongue. He would devour me, take me under his command and never release me.

I could be worse than Firose, worse than any other under his command.

That future flashed before me.

Fallen cities.

Nothing but ruins.

Smoke, ash and annihilation.

"No!" Slamming against every mental barrier I could find in Caym's mind, I pushed against them, looking for a movable wall. I held my breath and fought against his attempt to let that awful smoke consume me. He tore through every dark thought and tried to ignite my despair.

With one final mental strike, I let all my rage lash toward him.

The intoxicating feeling of control overtook me.

Caym reeled back into the butcher-block table, falling as though I'd physically struck him.

As I took hold of his mind, our thoughts tumbled to-gether—memories mixing, intentions warping, emotions cutting through the night like glass against delicate skin.

Blue tea being poured.

Amber smoke filling a battlefield.

Finding journals written in my mother's hand.

Freya atop a moonlit roof with Caym at her back.

My sixteenth birthday.

Poisoned eggs.

Screams of women in a pleasure hall as amber smoke engulfed them.

A ruby-encrusted sword.

Barden letting soldiers through an Egress to assassinate me in Luz.

The fall of a guillotine.

My mother's face was the last memory I saw.

Caym writhed against the tile floor as I held him down with just my fury. My screams cut through the night. It took so much strength to hold him there that my body hunched and slackened. Moving backward toward the door, I wondered how far I could get before he would be released.

Then I ran.

Out on the streets of Sahlmkar, I sprinted without aim. Realizing I had no idea where the prison was, I felt helpless to find Krait. The bustle and life that I'd seen upon arriving had ceased. I didn't see a single soul.

Empty shop windows blurred past before I turned down the alley toward the one power in this land who might be able to help me.

KRAIT

There was an eerie sense of dread in the air as I made my way to the prison. The sun had set, and the wind kicked up dust—shops had closed and tents were left unattended. It was as though not a soul walked the streets except those we'd brought from Sahlmsara. Maybe it was the hour of worship. The Temple of Death still stood in Sahlmkar; it was upkept by the citizens here.

Ryn stood with a somber expression just inside the gates of the prison, in the courtyard. He had mostly healed from when I'd lashed out at him. Sahlmsaran guards were swarming the iron prison door, with weapons raised.

"*What* is going on? Is this how we treat the ill now?"

"It's a bloodbath, Krait. The prisoners revolted. They looked like rabid animals—eyes blackened, faces gray. They began to grow ill this afternoon. It's chaos in there. We need to secure the perimeter and keep them contained."

A sense of dread continued to churn in my stomach. Ryn's instincts to keep Sybilla away from here had been right. The prison's dark stone walls stretched up five stories, and thousands of people were kept there.

Slam, slam, slam.

There was a pounding sound on the prison door, like a bull trying to break free from a pen.

"Where did everyone in the city *go*?" I asked Ryn. My heart sank…None of this was right.

He seemed to finally notice how silent the streets outside the walls of the courtyard had become and scratched his head.

Ryn started to say, "It's as if everyone here…" Then his face paled as he stared up at the sky. I followed his gaze. A gray-rimmed darkness began to cover the moon.

The black moon.

Death's rise.

Those who worship him will give their lives to become his vessels of destruction.

"It's as if they are dead," I finished for him. Cursing beneath my breath, I pulled a dagger from my boot.

Slam, slam, slam.

The giant iron doors of the prison burst open. Bloodcurdling, lifeless screams filled the air as prisoners piled out of the building. They looked ghastly…touched by death. Their eyes gleamed amber, their cheeks were sunken, and nothing separating their grayed skin from bone.

"Ryn…they're Moirai. He's here. He's raised them."

"We don't have any chance of winning here," Ryn yelled to me. The Moirai were deathwalking—traveling in a way much like my ability to travel through Shadows. They couldn't sustain it far, but it meant they were upon us quickly. With the dagger, I began to cut through those who approached. Ryn covered my back, sword raised, doing the same.

"Retreat to Sahlmsara!" I yelled over the commotion to my men. Ryn was right—there weren't enough of us to fight off this attack. "Now, go!"

Sybilla. I needed to get to her.

As though I'd summoned her, a familiar feeling seeped into the edges of my mind before I felt her slam in with desperation. I gasped as Sybilla took hold of my mind. Everything grew cloudy and cold. She gripped me only for a moment and images flashed.

White stucco walls, leather sofas, blue flowers. Piles of dust.

"He's here. Caym is here. Run!" she screamed into the void between us.

When she recoiled and no essence of her was left, it felt like my world shattered.

"He has her! Caym—he has Sybilla."

"What? How?" Ryn shouted as we struck through the prisoners and ran through the gates and into the city.

"I left her at the flat." Panic seized me.

Shadowing myself away, I prayed to Desidero that my worst nightmares were not being realized.

It all came back to me in waves.

A wooden box—delivered to the palace gates of Brennax. A note atop it.

"Since your marriage could not be annulled, it needed to be ended."

Signed by King Toth, Freya's father. When I'd pulled the nails from that box, the tufts of silver hair had been the first things I saw. Hair, and then so much blood.

Nausea mounted as darkness whirled past.

It was said that once your heart realized you'd lost your Source Match, it never recovered—a wound that could not heal. And yet one woman had begun to make me feel capable of some healing, some warmth, and now she was facing our greatest enemy. Alone.

I burst into the Shadows of the flat. There were two piles of dust on the tile by the sofas. I choked on my fear, spinning around but finding no one else.

"Sybilla!" I called.

On the windowsill sat a full cup of blue tea. I lifted it and smelled—the earthy, sweet scent of garrot root. *Fuck.* I prayed to any Source Origin listening that she had not drank that tea. Her sword, bow, and quiver lay discarded on the floor. She would be defenseless.

My muscles seized up against my will.

"Hello, nephew. I knew you would come for her."

A cloaked figure stepped from the shadows of the kitchen with a painful slowness. As Caym's boots stopped in front of me and I met the eyes of Death, all air left my lungs.

"Stygian," I hissed.

My ex-Commander stood before me. The man who had betrayed me centuries ago by leading the massacre in Phynx.

"I don't go by that name any longer."

"Krait?" Ryn burst through the door of the flat, looking winded. Damn loyal bastard.

"Run!" I shouted to my dearest friend. He needed to get out of here, but instead, he'd drawn his sword, ready to fight for me.

Ryn launched himself at Stygian, the mastermind behind so much destruction. My friend froze next to me mid-charge, sword up, and a wicked smile crept across Caym's face.

Fuck.

With all of Isolde's power returned, we were doomed. How does one battle the inevitability of Death? I feared for Sybilla, feared for us all.

"Prince Toth, your sister's death gave me much power—so very sweet. Yes, she was such a willing servant, albeit only for a short while. I wonder if your Death will taste like hers." Caym licked his upper teeth.

My jaw clenched. He had no right to mention Freya.

I scanned the flat once more, looking for signs of Sybilla. I would not let him draw me in with lies about my dead wife. I would not let him push me back into that abyss of anger. That was exactly what he wanted.

"Where is she?" I ground out.

Caym lifted a hand toward Ryn. "Don't be concerned with the young Isleen—she will live on by my side as she was meant to. But my brother's line ends with you."

Ryn turned on me, face blank. My boots felt stuck to the floor as he approached me, drawing up his sword. I tried to scream, tried to reach out to him, but not a muscle moved. The whites of Ryn's eyes went wide as he realized what Caym would compel him to do.

A droplet of sweat ran down my forehead as Ryn approached. Silenced and still, I stood helpless against Death.

Ryn pulled back his sword, ready to cut through the air and slice through my neck. My eyes welled.

Internally, I screamed out to her.

"Sybilla. You are my eternity. You always were."

CHAPTER 58

EMMERICK

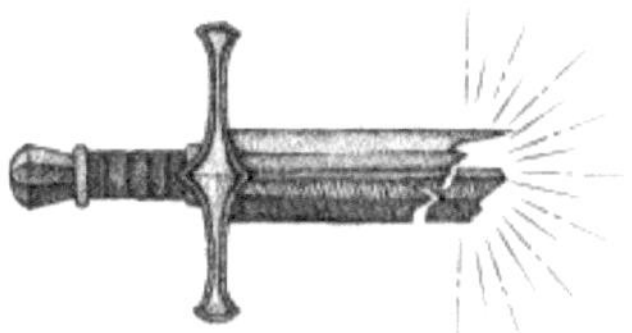

F irose approached my cot silently, but her eyes begged for distraction from our shit predicament. I sat, propped against a stone wall and patted the space next to me.

Instead of sitting, she curled up beside me and placed her head in my lap, facing away from me. I gently rubbed her shoulder, half trying to comfort her and half trying to calm my own anxiety. For Sybilla to have shown mercy, whatever she had seen in Firose's memories must have been horrific.

Soon I may be cursed to sleep for who knows how long, but Firose...what would they do to her? My heart clenched at the thought. She'd stayed quiet since we'd arrived here, and I'd been too afraid to ask her what was running through her head. This was the first moment of tenderness we'd shared since she had been Ryssa to me.

Since Sybilla had left with Darvanda to the northern region of the Sahlms, it felt like a weight had lifted off me.

I wasn't too big of a fool not to have realized her feelings for the Sahlmsaran King. My boyish ideals of her had been squashed, but she was still my dearest friend. For that, I would work on removing the view of her I'd crafted in my head as someone to be won.

A sound rang out, loud enough to vibrate the metal bars of the dungeon. The bell tower above began ringing with each second. I squeezed Firose's shoulder.

That was a warning call in Henosis.

Light footsteps padded down the stairs a few minutes later, and Elsedora appeared. "Get up. We need to go."

"Go?" I dumbly asked as Firose straightened to sit beside me. Elsedora's glare narrowed on the enchantress, and she pursed her lips.

"Yes, a threat has been detected from the watchtowers north of the city."

Firose stiffened beside me. "What sort of threat?"

"The sort where thousands of gruesome-looking foot soldiers, traveling at a speed which I can not understand, are approaching our city gates from the direction of Sahlmkar. Firose, you are intimately familiar with the region, are you not?"

The ice in Elsedora's tone, as she noted the place where Firose had drawn her army from, made me grip the cot's edges. She wouldn't again—she couldn't have. I'd been with her this whole time.

The ceiling above us rumbled, raining down stone debris, as though people were running through the estate above. The bell tower kept its constant rhythm, and my heart pounded.

"Do they seem to be moving through Shadows the way Krait can?" Firose asked, ignoring Elsedora's biting question.

Elsedora's posture softened slightly. "Yes, in small distances. I've been told it looks as though they disappear and reappear closer by the minute."

Firose was on her feet instantly. "Then they're Moirai," she said. "They can deathwalk. They're of Caym's creation—what does the moon look like tonight?"

Elsedora's body went rigid, and she shook her head. "I noticed a gray ring and figured it was a crescent moon. It can't be…We were supposed to have years."

The blood drained from Firose's scarred cheeks, and her eyes went as wide as saucers. "He is back, *fully* back." I'd never seen her so panic-stricken.

"If they are what you say, how do we fight them?"

"Head and heart. They'll survive fire, water and most mortal wounds otherwise," Firose answered.

Their exchange was so rapid that I reeled to keep up.

"Where is Sybilla?" I demanded, standing up and crossing the room to the redheaded thief who had kept watch over me in Helos.

"I don't know. She and Krait haven't returned." When Elsedora met my gaze, I saw the same horror reflected back at me. The people she cared about were out there too. "And, when I last checked that map, it no longer showed me an envoy's location. Up, let's go."

Blood coursed hot through me. My friend was out there, where the approaching threat had come from, where Caym was.

The last time I saw her was not supposed to be the last time I spoke to her. Those weren't meant to be our final words to one another. She had to survive.

Elsedora motioned up the stairs, and I began to climb with shaking knees; Firose trailed me. My cuffed hands shielded against the assault of lamplight at the open door. The estate was in an uproar of activity—guards using it as a staging area for weaponry and maids grabbing their belongings.

We approached the estate's entry, and Elsedora said, "Go to Luz. Warn Asterie. The Egress is in the courtyard, to the left—you'll need to push through the crowds."

The courtyard thundered with the mayhem of hundreds of running feet and hooves mixing with the sound of carriages being loaded and the blare of horns.

A guard yelled, "All civilians to the Plateau! Move on! Move on!"

Elsedora shouted to a guard on our left, "Prepare every Warhorse, and send them north of the city! When the Moirai reach us, aim for their heads or hearts." The guard nodded and then sprinted away.

The bell tower ringing above us heightened my anxiety with every stroke. There was a haphazard mob of people around the Egress.

Elsedora glanced between me and Firose. "Don't make me regret not leaving you as food for the wolves. Send reinforcements. As many as you can, but you both stay away from here." She gave me one hard look and then thrust her hand out—in it was a key. She placed it in my palm and then ran toward where the guard had headed.

Wasting no time, I grabbed Firose's hand, and we helped uncuff each other's wrists, freeing our use of Source power. We ran toward the mob of people crowding around the small Egress.

Tall enough to see over most of the crowd, I noticed people were leaving three at a time. A child sobbed in her mother's arms beside us. My throat constricted, but I pulled Firose onward.

We elbowed our way through the panic. By the time we reached the Egress, my tunic was torn and I'd likely whitened Firose's fingertips with the strength of my grip.

A man shouted, "Wait your damned turn!"

Ignoring him and sinking into the shade of the carved space, I shouldered away anyone else from entering. Then I commanded, "To the South Tower."

There was no way I would bring Firose to Fen and Asterie's doorstep. I trusted Amara to listen to me.

I trusted she of all people would understand how wholly Caym could overtake someone.

CHAPTER 59
SYBILLA

I mpossible language.

There were so many fucking vowels, and the inflection held so much nuance. I struggled over the Brennac words that Krait had used to open the alley doorway into the cavern. Ready to give up, I heaved out a breath, with my forehead pressed to the door.

With Caym inevitably on my heels, doom crashed around me.

Krait had told me that I would never face dangers alone again, and I longed for that to have been true. I wanted him here.

"Repeat," a feminine voice whispered to me. She sounded familiar but her voice was so vapory at the edges that I knew no physical form accompanied it. I shivered to think that it resembled my mother's cadence.

The voice whispered Brennac to me, and I repeated it, hoping this wasn't just an illusion of my own creation. As I spoke the words, I somehow understood their meaning. "Welcome me. For I seek not darkness but cannot find the light. In the Shadows we trust."

The lock gears turned, and the door beneath my forehead gave in. I whimpered in relief. Running into the tunnels, I tried to remember the way.

"Left, left, right, straight, left, right." The whisper in the wind continued to guide me. Every muscle in my body burned, every joint aflame, but still, I ran. Adrenaline and fear fueled my hurried pace.

When I burst into the cavern, Lymrasi hissed. She coiled and lifted her serpent snout in my direction. "I knew you would be back sssooner than you expected."

I gasped for air, but approached her without fear. "How do we wake them?" I motioned toward the other stone serpents. "I'm calling on you for help *now*."

"Ssso many have sought us for Death. What is it that you wish to ruin, child?"

"Nothing!" I huffed out, "We don't have time for riddles. I don't plan to *ruin* anything. But Caym will if we do not stop him. You told me not to fail—to come back to you when Isolde's power has been returned. I beg you. Help me, Lymrasi."

"Lymrasssi means 'center' in the Brennac language. It was not my given name."

I groaned, clenching my fists. "Then what is your given name?"

"Isssleen."

My back straightened.

My cousin and healer had been envoys, and my ancestor was a winged snake. No possibility seemed off the table. I felt as though I knew nothing.

She hissed, "When we laid him to rest, he changed me and all but one of my children—made usss monstersss. We want to be free of him, so *she* must sssspeak with you now."

I looked around; no one else stood in the cavern, yet the distinctive feeling of being watched overwhelmed me. The same voice that guided me here said, "Sybilla, forgive me."

I spun to face the woman who had both broken and shaped me. "Mother?"

She stood there in iridescence, like a shimmering cloud atop a mountain. My mouth hung open as I took in her face and curls—so similar to mine. I'd never had a chance to face her as the woman I'd become.

"We do not have much time," she said. "He will still rise once more, but you can stop him today, Sybilla. You have always had access to one of the ways to stop him—he fears the weapons Isolde created, for he cannot wield them, but they can destroy him."

"How..." I glanced at Lymrasi, or *Isleen*, and then back at the ebbing form of my mother. "How do you know? How are you *here?*"

A pang of guilt settled in my gut. My father had driven a wedge between us long before the day she'd been executed.

"Because I am a daughter of Isleen, my child, as are you. I am the reason your father had visions, the reason he thought himself an Oracle. Your father's prophecies were never his. I made him hide the boy and train him."

Her words shattered everything I'd thought I knew about my childhood.

"But Caym found me all the same. So long as he thought me naive about my power, I was safe. *You* were safe. But Mortag discovered what I had been doing and..."

"They killed you..."

My mother nodded. "The tea Mortag served us stifles our power—muddles it to a dim portion of what we are capable of. But the garrot root helped you stay well."

That's what he'd been doing with the tea.

"He was our healer for years—why didn't he just kill us?" I asked.

My mother's cold hand found my cheek. "At first, he did not know what we were—who we were. And then...he could not." She looked at Lymrasi.

The serpent spoke. "My mother's bargain with Caym had one caveat. He losesss her power if he killsss a child of Isleen. It's why, instead, he coveted me, why he turned us to ssstone instead of killing us. He can tear the world down around you, but he cannot kill you or your child himself—try as he might."

"I only hoped that you would remain unaware until you were ready," my mother whispered. "I ran out of time to prepare you."

"I'm still not ready," I snapped back, feeling like the petulant teenager I'd been when she left me. "I don't understand what I should be ready *for*."

My mother rubbed my cheek once more. "You are. *It* would not come to you now if you were not. You are ready to face him, ready to prevail today so that your daughter can one day end his reign."

My daughter.

She spoke in such absolutes.

Something gleamed at my feet, and when I looked down, a sword rested there. "What is this?" I asked.

My mother answered, "It is the sword Isolde crafted to defeat Caym. It is one of three relics your child must wield against him. It can stop him tonight."

Isleen's serpent head nodded as she tasted the air.

I reached down and picked up the sword, assessing its weight. It was oddly familiar—mostly steel, but the handle was cut with gold. Rubies encrusted the guard. My hackles rose to see a deathmark on the very bottom of the pommel. This was not just any sword...It was Emmerick's broadsword.

The one he denied naming after me.

"I made him hide the boy and train him." I'd always found it odd that my father had been so willing to train the baker's son. He hadn't been charitable with his time when it came to me.

"It was you," I gasped. "You protected Em. You made Father protect him. Father gave him this sword..." My eyes welled, tears threatening to spill over.

"Yes. Your father never knew what weapon he'd gifted young Mattock. And neither did Caym. Even after he put his awful mark on it, it still longs to destroy Death—and because Caym built that bond to the sword, it can now find him. All you must do is ask it to."

I stepped toward my mother and reached out with my free hand, longing to take hers. The luster of her felt like cold air as my hand went through her. "This can kill Caym?"

"Ssstop. Not kill," Isleen corrected. "He will rise once more. But do as you can to delay him until your child has all the relics."

"Then how do I *kill* him?"

"You will not," Isleen hissed back. "Only a child of my lineage and the fifth heir of Shadows will know the way."

My head tilted. "And if no child comes?"

But something warmed within me. I envisioned Krait as a father; he held our swaddled daughter to his chest and looked down at her with a smile that I'd never seen him wear before. It flashed like a memory I had not yet made.

My mother's voice seemed to grow farther away as she cut in, "There are many ways to fulfill a single prophecy. The path you carve is uniquely yours."

The iridescent shimmer started to fade until my mother's face dissipated into nothing but fog, which drifted to the ceiling of the cave. "Don't go!" I shouted and reached out for her. "Please."

My mother whispered, "I will be with you through it all. Always."

She was gone. It had been so abrupt. I slumped, and the sword's blade touched the ground.

I turned to Isleen, wanting to scream, *"Bring her back!"*

Instead, I asked, "Why does he seek destruction? Why does he want *me?*"

"In early timesss, I'd married a mortal man with whom I had ten children. But when my mother made her bargain with Caym, that changed me. I did not age, while my husband grew old and passed. Desidero was there for me when I mourned. He cared for me and that care blossomed into love. But Caym grew jealousss. He wished for my hand. I chose Desidero but met my end before we could marry. He wasss my second love."

I wiped away the tears from my cheeks, looking up at the beast before me. Not a beast. Isleen—a woman who had loved, lost, and lived. My resolve built in my chest.

"What am I to do?" I asked her.

"What does your heart tell you to do?"

Before I could answer, panic seized me. Not my own.

"Sybilla. You are my eternity. You always were."

No—no, no. Krait. I needed to reach him.

"I told you, child," Isleen hissed. "You cannot fail, no matter the cossst."

The sensation of falling overtook me as I plunged into a depth of my mind that I'd never visited before. It felt like peeling away viscous mercury.

Krait stood before me, helpless and veiled in a thin layer of gray translucent fabric. I reached out through the darkness, fumbling toward him. Then I grabbed the veil and yanked it away from his face.

I cupped his cheek and said, "Then fight for me. And don't you dare fucking die."

Krait's eyes widened for a moment before he ducked and then disappeared.

Unable to hold onto that place, unable to stay with him, I crumbled to my knees in front of my ancestral power. When I came to, I stared up at Isleen's fangs.

"I wish to end Death's reign. I will do whatever it takes. *Please*," I begged.

"Very well." She slithered around me, her feathered wings tucked tightly to her sides. "Climb up, and we shall go."

The stone of the other nine beasts began to crack—ten beasts of nightmares. *My kin.* I carefully climbed up Isleen's scaled back, less than gracefully. Once seated, I looked down at the sword in my hand and said, "Lead us to Caym."

The creatures hissed and stretched, awakening around me. "Caym created usss, but we answer to only you now," they sang together.

We left the cavern, and pounding wings took to the wind of the night sky.

CHAPTER 60
KRAIT

"*Then fight for me. And don't you dare fucking die.*" Her voice reached me, just before Ryn swung his sword. She was alive.

And she had ripped Death's grip on me away. No longer frozen, I ducked and felt the *swoosh* of the blade against the hairs atop my head. Caym roared and pointed a hand at Ryn. Amber smoke leaked out toward my friend, and his eyes widened.

With only a moment to spare, I Shadowed to Ryn. Grabbing him by the tunic, I pulled him back. Caym's magic hit the vase of flowers behind us in an amber flash. The glass shattered, and the flowers wilted.

I held Ryn's arm. Caym grabbed my shoulder just before I Shadowed us away.

We tumbled and fought through the Shadows. I tried to kick Caym off me. Death's hold prevailed, and he dragged us off course. I'd been too slow to decide where we should escape to.

So instead of traveling a few blocks, we crashed through the darkness—a lusterless heap of flailing bodies. I cried out and tried to regain control, but I could no longer guide us. Everything turned to amber smoke as we plummeted and hit sand with a horrid thud.

Ryn clung to my forearm as we rose together.

We stood at the center of the amphitheater in Sahlmsara.

No, please not here.

I'd led him right into my city. I felt too weak to Shadow back to Sahlmkar now. My only thought of hope was that Sybilla had escaped—she'd spoken to me. I hoped she had found a way to Lymrasi without me.

The bells of Umber House rang, and horns blared. They were evacuating.

Caym was no longer at our side. Instead, he stood on the flat marble stage above one of the entry archways. The iron gates had been drawn shut and, judging from the faint amber glimmer across their surface, also warded. The Death Origin held out his arms on both sides, looking like a horrid gray-cloaked statue.

I gasped, trying to regain my strength.

"And now we wait for the *show*." Caym's voice boomed down on us. "I tried to serve you a quick, humane death, nephew. Let us wait for your Isleen to come so she can watch her loved ones fall. She will learn how futile her fight against me will be."

He was luring her here.

I tried to step toward him—tried to push Shadows out. My legs refused to move for the second time, and I roared in protest. The most horrific pain I'd ever felt encased my whole body, and I crumbled.

The agony had me blind to any reason to live.

Ryn kept running toward the podium, making it a few paces before he, too, dropped and writhed. Our pained shrieks mirrored one another.

My hands grasped at the sand, taking fistfuls of it and squeezing.

A cold feeling crept up the back of my neck, and everything grew dark. A gray veil had clouded my vision.

No matter how hard I fought, control no longer belonged to me.

474

CHAPTER 61
EMMERICK

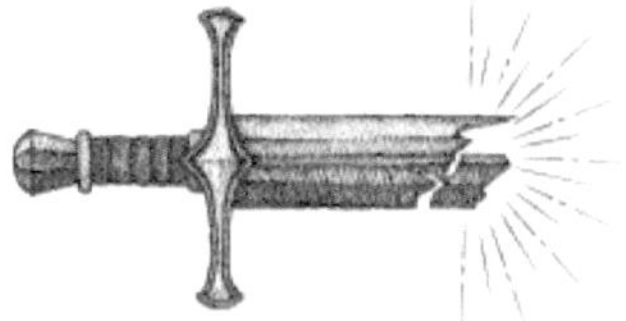

The Egress dropped us into the halls of the South Tower. I ran toward the drawing room. I'd only been here once, for that dreadful meeting when I'd enraged Sybilla by allying with her cousins.

"Amara! It's me, Emmerick. I'm not here to harm you." Entering the room, I raised my hands.

Amara stood with one hand pressed against a pine desk, a black triangular stone next to her fingertips. She wore a simple beige dress with gold seams and brown boots. Her eyes were bloodshot, and she seemed forlorn until she set her sight on me and brightened. "Emmerick? Thank the Sources—you are safe."

Safe? Debatable. I wouldn't worry her about that now.

As Amara gazed beyond me, her whole body stiffened.

"She is not here to harm you either," I said, keeping my tone as calm as possible.

Amara stammered, "You—you are dead. How are you here?" A bright light formed in Amara's palm, and she began to aim it. Her eyes burned with golden fury. "What have you done to him?"

I stepped into the path between Amara's ball of sunlight and Firose.

"Please, please listen first," I begged.

She glanced between me and Firose. With her glowing hand shaking, and her lip trembling, she said, "You never told me what Corric was. He never told me you were helping him." Her voice cracked. "For centuries I thought you kept him from me, that you were hurting him. How? How are *you* here and he is not? Tell me that this memorandum is not a cruel trick."

She motioned to the black stone on the desk before approaching.

"It *had* to be that way. You would not have given up on him if you knew Corric still loved you. His love for you was a liability. He wanted you safe. There is no room for love in Caym's grasp."

I looked Amara in the eyes. "Now he has me too. He's risen to his full power; he is in the Sahlms. We can stop him...but I need your help."

Amara's posture straightened, and the light in her palms blinked out. Running her gaze over me, as though auditing for any sign of harm, she whispered, "I cannot lose you too."

Firose stepped up beside me. She carefully said, "Then hear us out."

"You lied to me for centuries," Amara answered. She pressed her lips into a hard line.

Firose nodded once. "Yes. I have spent so many years hiding things. But you were *always* my friend, Amara...even when it did not feel that way to you."

Firose's words lingered between us like stale air, burning with truths she'd never say.

She'd spent decades helping Corric hide me from Caym and centuries before that training Asterie to be strong enough against him too. My birth father's fall to the Death Origin had never been her fault. "I tried my hardest to save him for you," she whispered.

"You have one minute to explain, Firose, before I decide to turn you over to Luz and let Asterie and Fen decide your fate," Amara said, her head held high.

We explained as quickly as we could about what had occurred in Sahlmsara and what had transpired in Helos. About our whereabouts, about Caym's hold on me. She listened but began pacing in front of us—I, too, could never seem to sit still.

With newfound vigor, Amara said, "I will Egress to Luz and gather the others. We don't have time for any more reunions," she said and eyed Firose with reluctant acceptance. "Stay here, away from where Caym might reach you."

As she stepped toward the hall, she gave my shoulder a tight squeeze.

I glanced over at Firose, whose brow pinched. We heard the gentle whoosh of Amara Egressing out of the tower—only then did I let a sigh of relief escape me. Firose mirrored my slackened posture.

I started for the hall.

"Where are you going?"

"To Sahlmsara," I said.

Sybilla might still be in the fray, might still be in Sahlmkar, and there was no way I'd hide across the realms while innocent people fell at the hands of a monster.

"Wait!" she called out and trailed me.

My brow furrowed. "You're sure?"

Her eyes glistened with sapphire fire. "I will not hide from him any longer."

She took my hand in the Egress, and our touch pulsed with our combined magic—palms heating. It felt like her flames grew between our fingers.

When we exited the Egress in Sahlmsara, a ghoulish gray face greeted us with a curdling shriek. I reached for the phantom sword at my side. My fingers didn't make purchase on anything.

A rag was shoved to my nose, and arms wrapped around my neck. Firose squeaked, but was quickly pulled out of my grasp.

"Emmerick!" she screamed before a cloth was shoved over her mouth too.

Hands grasped me from all sides. Horrendous creatures surrounded us. I grew rapidly light-headed, limp and weak—whatever was on that cloth made my attempts to wield my Source power useless. We had no defense against the Moirai.

Why not just kill us now?

Everything blurred around me as they dragged us by our legs down the cobblestone streets of Sahlmsara toward a behemoth domed, open-air structure made of rough, pale marble.

CHAPTER 62
SYBILLA

I t seemed impossible how fast Isleen's wings carried us over the Vallic mountains. "What is that?" I asked, seeing spots of moving objects below us.

She answered, "They are Moirai. Makings of Caym from those who worshiped him."

Thousands of them approached the canyon, the city of Sahlmsara. I shuddered. The front lines had already reached the gates, and Warhorses tried to cut them down. Flashes of amber smoke created a dusky fog where the Moirai traveled.

Tears stung my eyes to think of the empty streets of Sahlmkar and how many had turned themselves over to the Death Origin's cruel intentions.

Source magic was used defensively in bursts of white orbs, golden beams, and red flames, yet Moirai had already breached the city gates.

"Can your children help?"

"Yesss," Isleen said, seeming to get satisfaction from the word. "You command them."

I focused. "Three of you, guard the gates. Avoid harming the soldiers on flaming horses. Attack only the Moirai."

Three winged serpents fell out of formation and swooped down. We continued on, flying low over the city. I looked back, watching as Isleen's children roared and spewed amber flames at the marching Moirai.

Sahlmsara was in chaos. People in the distance fled from the canyon, toward the Plateau. Market tents were upturned, and the canals ran an awful shade of murky amber. Death already tainted this place, and my heart was in my throat as I clung to Isleen's black scales, less than graceful in my ability to hang on. We dipped down toward the amphitheater that I'd spent so many hot mornings training in.

"He is here?" I questioned.

"Yesss." Her voice grated below me, as though it pained her. "I am following the sword's direction."

Flames were being flung at the amphitheater's gates, and I recognized a tussle of auburn waves. Fenris. And Amara. Where was Asterie?

"There," I said to Isleen. She broke away from the others and descended so quickly that my stomach dropped. We landed at the gates. Amara, dressed in casual attire like she'd been unprepared, flung sunlight from her palms at the approaching Moirai, protecting Fenris' back.

"Fen!" I called out. "What are you doing?"

"It's warded! Amara came to Luz to gather us. When we reached Sahlmsara, the Moirai had already arrived. We were separated. Asterie, Wyeth and Hurley were taken inside," Fen rambled. "They have her. They have my love." His voice cracked as he stepped away from Isleen's fangs.

Fenris, looking exhausted, let flames erupt from his palms again toward the gate.

"Help him," I commanded.

Isleen let out a roar, breathing amber smoke that mingled with Fen's flames until the gate rotted through, crumbling.

Fenris turned around, his flames sputtering out. Fear coated my tongue—bitter and sharp—as he took in the creature below me.

With Isolde's sword in my hand, I sat up straight on the serpent's back despite my fatigue and desire to slump over. Isleen swung her tail, knocking away any Moirai that approached us.

"Go! Find them!" I motioned Amara and Fen inside, and they ran toward the gates, their steps slowed down by the deep sand.

I could hear the screams of Moirai as they breached more of the city. The Warhorses at the front lines were not enough to hold them all back even with our aid. Lifeless bodies swarmed and climbed the marble walls, making their way into the amphitheater where my friends were being held.

I knew why he'd brought all of my loved ones here. He wanted me to go inside; he wanted me to try to save them. I could not fail.

"Does that flame you used on the gate kill the Moirai?" I whispered to Isleen.

"Yesss," she answered again. This time, she *definitely* sounded satisfied.

I focused on the circling serpents above and commanded, "Burn any of the Moirai that dare stand between me and Caym. Protect the citizens of Sahlmsara and the Source-wielders in the pit."

Three of the circling serpents descended on the amphitheater, and the others flew deeper into the city to help the Warhorses. Isleen beat her wings, and we flew over the open-air dome.

The winged children of Isleen were beautiful, obsidian feathers tucked back and mouths open as they whirled down, ready to breathe amber flames upon their enemies...upon *my* enemies. I kept trying to justify to myself that they were no longer citizens of Sahlmkar, but instead weapons of Death. My heart sank anyway.

While it was a heady feeling to hold this much power at my fingertips, that power could be so easily molded into something ugly—something dangerous—in the wrong hands.

"That is why you must not let him take you, child." Isleen's voice broke through the wind, answering my worries.

"I'll die before I let that happen."

CHAPTER 63

KRAIT

Everything around me happened in a blurred gray fog. None of my actions were my own.

So much rage roiled through my veins, yet they ran ice cold.

I longed to release that wrath.

The Moirai dragged in Firose and Emmerick first. Asterie, Hurley and Wyeth next. Then Elsedora.

My heart cracked.

Thousands of Moirai began climbing over the amphitheater walls and filling the stands. They stared with hunger into the pit, like piranha awaiting a bucket of chum.

"Nephew, you will end these new Origins before they rise. The Sources know that their younglings are no match for me. They bargained recklessly."

New Origins.

On Death's command, I turned and faced the group of Source-wielders. Their expressions were blank, eyes glassy—the effects of garrot root had taken hold of them. It wasn't even a fair fight.

All the natural Sources were here, in one closed space.

Sun, Moon, Stars, Flame, Soil, Water...the Wind Source was unaccounted for. I wondered if the Commander, Cassidee, had evaded capture. Had they grabbed Elsie by mistake?

I tried to fight out of Caym's grasp, tugging and pulling at the thread of my consciousness that allowed me free will. The more I fought, the more numb I grew.

Beside me stood my silver-haired...friend? Did I know him?

Things began to break at the seams—my ties to the world thinned. Everything seemed unimportant. The Moon-wielder looked clear-eyed, the only one who hadn't been root-gassed yet.

He screamed, "Krait! Fight him."

An internal growl from Caym told me that it infuriated him to be unable to control more of our Source magic at once. His energy waned from controlling so many Moirai.

"How could their prayer not have been enough? The people of Sahlmkar have not worshiped me properly," he snarled into my mind.

So much Death, yet he craved more.

The Moon-wielder approached me and Caym made my Shadows wrap around his neck.

Death's wrath mixed with my own as he wielded my Shadows against the other Origins. Dark vines snared Asterie, her young ward and Wyeth, cutting the air around them. I desperately tried to release them.

Why did it matter?

Their cheeks turned blue.

That woke me up some. I felt caged in a thick glass box; no matter how hard I pounded on the panes, all I could do was watch. My Shadows caught Firose, Elsedora and Mattock. Tendrils of darkness spanned everywhere, like black and amber roots climbing the amphitheater walls.

"Come out, little Isleen. You can stop this!" Caym screamed over the roar of his Moirai, who'd begun to descend from the stands.

Asterie struggled against my Shadows and let the wolf-demon out from the ink on her arm. The beast was immediately wrapped in gritty vines and pulled to the ground with a whimper.

The tether of Caym's power forced me to squeeze the vines tighter.

I'd kill them all.

Everything felt numb. Cold.

Darkness shrouded the arena. Something was overhead. A giant serpent flew into the arena with a rider atop it—honey-toned curls blown back in the wind.

Sybilla...

Her presence returned some of my warmth.

"You are strong, so strong." I tried to push the words to her and heard Caym's internal growl again.

Then Caym faltered at the sight of the flying beasts. An opening.

I peeled back enough of my Shadows to release Ryn and then Elsedora. Ryn's feet became unstuck, and he and Elsie began running toward the stage where Caym stood.

No sound left my lips as I tried to scream at them to stay away from Caym, to run from danger, not toward it.

Hope seemed lost.

They'd die by his hand or mine in this Sources-forsaken pit.

CHAPTER 64
SYBILLA

The Origin of Death stood with his arms outstretched, atop a podium high above the pit—an orchestrator of chaos, the bringer of doom.

"Come out, little Isleen. You can stop this!" he boomed. All of this pain, all of this suffering, and for what? For unrequited love, for envy, for greed?

He'd lured me here.

I'd bite.

Isleen's wings beat back the putrid amber smoke that clouded the arena floor. Through the dust, I could make out dark vines in the pit below—barbed and violent.

"Krait!" I called out. When the dust cleared some, I saw him; his arms were stiffly outstretched, matching Caym's position. Dark tendrils were wrapped around Asterie, Hurley and Wyeth. They'd snared Emmerick's and Firose's ankles too. "Stop, Krait!"

"You can stop him...You know how," Caym yelled. "Let's make a bargain..."

Between the swarming Moirai and Krait's Shadows, my friends were doomed. A lump grew in my throat.

I contemplated his words. I could give him what he wanted. *Me.*

"We do not bargain with Death," Isleen hissed below me.

Sunlight and fire flashed below as Fenris and Amara fought into the arena, cutting down the Moirai, trying to get to their loved ones.

It all needed to stop before any of them were harmed.

The shriek of a Griffith pierced the air, and an East Corridor fleet joined Isleen's children in fighting for the city beyond the walls of the amphitheater. I could hear Cassidee, shouting orders.

The way to end this today stood up on that podium.

"You told me not to fail," I shouted to Isleen. "You know where to go."

The beating of her feathered wings thundered. Caym stood, staring with an intent gaze down at the arena, a cowardly fucking puppeteer. Rage spurred me to grip Isolde's sword tighter at my side.

As we descended, Ryn floated, levitating up through the amber smoke toward Caym's podium. His form glowed brilliant white against the night sky.

"*Ryn, stand down!*" I tried to scream into his mind.

He either did not hear me or wished not to. Elsedora had almost scaled the wall. Her boots were about to hit the podium behind Caym. The two of them would get themselves...

A bright white crescent-shaped light collected in Ryn's palms. All light pulled to him, eclipsing us in complete darkness.

My mouth hung open.

He looked beautiful—illuminated.

"Hurry!" I yelled.

Isleen's wings beat faster as we approached the podium, but even she seemed to be struggling to see through the glare emitted by my Moon-wielding friend.

Ryn aimed and released his power—the crescent moon left his palm in a spinning white beam toward the Death Origin.

But amber smoke formed a helix around Caym; he strained with a scowl. The light refracted off the shield. Elsedora ducked, and the beam slammed into the amphitheater's walls, missing her by a hair. Marble crumbled, cascading down into the pit.

"Stand down, Ryn!" Tears streaked my cheeks. Isleen lowered, opening her mouth as though she would spit fire. "No!" I commanded her. Not with my friends in the way.

"At all costs," Isleen hummed the horrid reminder.

My Moon-wielding friend readied another orb of light. El stood on the marble slab of the podium with a throwing dagger aimed and ready to leave her fingertips.

Ryn glanced over Caym's shoulder at Elsedora.

In the moment of distraction, Caym raised his arms again.

Ryn needed to move, to run.

Amber smoke snaked rapidly from Caym's fingertips.

"Ryn! No!" I screamed, clinging to Isleen's scales, the sword hanging in my tired hand as I watched in horror.

The tendrils grasped Ryn's arms first, his flesh rotting as the smoke snaked up his torso.

I choked on a sob. In a single breath, Ryn was dust. His ashes were blown away and carried over the amphitheater walls into the streets of Sahlmsara.

Elsedora's scream erupted in an unnatural gust of wind.

She did hold Source power…

Isleen's wings were caught in the gale, blowing her backward. I sobbed and held on tightly to her scales.

The wind had knocked Caym forward. His eyes widened as he tumbled down into the pit with a sharp bellow.

Elsedora's outcry had blown away all the smoke from the arena below. My heart seized when I saw Krait's arms were still outstretched—his Shadows wrapped around the others.

Everything had gone to shit so quickly.

My friends were dying. One was dead.

Caym was one step closer to overtaking the realms.

He would not stop until he saw both realms fall. He would not stop until he saw all of my friends turn to dust before me.

Then he'd take me anyway.

Caym had hit the sand below, and now lay there, splayed on his back.

"Stop!" I yelled to Isleen. She flapped hard once, halting us in midair. I wished for my bow and arrow—there was a clean shot to the bastard's heart from this angle. Drawing near would give him time to rebuff any attack or compel me.

Holding Isolde's sword tight, I chose the next best option to an arrow.

I glanced at Krait, sending a silent goodbye.

"We don't fail. For Freya, for Ryn, for my mother..."

I slipped from Isleen's back, plummeting down, sword first, without giving myself time to think about the height.

It felt like miles as I took aim.

The wind pulled at my cheeks.

Caym stared up and raised his hands—too late, fucker. You can't compel a person to stop falling.

The sword pierced his chest.

Caym erupted in a flash of amber.

The force of his energy threw me back. I tumbled sideways through the air before hitting a solid marble wall. My vision faded as the putrid smell of Death filled the air and a smooth, deep voice shouted, "Sybilla!"

CHAPTER 65

KRAIT

Caym's hold on me cracked.

I lifted the dark, airless prison of vines that held the others in the pit. Their gasps of relief sounded around me as I turned toward the podium. The Origin of Death had plummeted to ground level. Moirai swarmed us.

I needed to get to Caym, to let my Shadows tear him apart before he was able to get hold of me again. The ground shook. The amphitheater's marble walls swayed.

Cassidee's Griffith landed with a thud behind her partner. "Wyeth, get on!" she shouted with an outstretched hand. Amara stood at Mattock's back, fighting off Moirai, and my officers were nowhere to be seen.

Fenris reached Asterie and Hurley, protecting them in a ring of flames from the onslaught of undead.

Then something glimmered above and caught my attention. Something was falling toward Caym.

Someone.

Sources, no.

"Sybilla!"

My hand slammed out; there was no time to craft Shadows to break her fall. It was too late.

She sank the sword deep into the Death Origin's chest. Caym's magic erupted out of him, and his skin crumbled like the burning pages of a book—his mouth hung wide before he turned to dust.

An amber blow of smoke knocked Sybilla backward and everyone in the pit off our feet.

It rattled the amphitheater's already compromised walls.

She'd done it.

I rolled and ended up on my side. With a cough, I looked out into the arena. Every Moirai in the stands and pit began to collapse, disintegrating into heaps of putrid-smelling dust. Half of my realm was gone—sacrificed to Death's path of destruction.

Groaning, I stood and fought through the settling amber fog, yelling, "Sybilla!"

Falling from that height would be lethal.

I didn't let myself linger on that thought as debris rained down from the walls. The theater was going to cave in...I needed to find her.

Elsedora ran to me with tear-soaked cheeks.

I waved her away. "Get yourself and everyone out! The walls are coming down."

We had only minutes before we would be beneath rubble. El ran from me, obeying. I heard her bark orders to the others.

"Sybilla!" The dust kicked up more as marble struck the ground in chunks around me. Fuck.

In the heart-pounding, ear-thudding moments that I couldn't find my spitfire wife, I prayed to any Source who would listen. "Please," I cried out.

The woman who I'd just today committed to making my eternity could not be gone so quickly. I longed for her to jab some insult about my incompetence my way or tell me I was insufferable. I'd kill to hear her voice cut through the air.

"Sybilla!"

Finally, I found her.

She'd been thrown against a wall of the pit and lay flat on her stomach in the sand with a gash on her head and her arm twisted back in an unnatural position.

I bolted to her and drew her carefully into my lap. Darkness whisked us out of the amphitheater and onto the streets of Sahlm-sara a few blocks away.

So much of my power had been drained, and I slumped over her too-still body. *Please breathe.*

I trembled and checked her pulse. "Please, Sybilla. Throw some fire at me, stubborn woman..." I could not lose her.

Her blood pumped to her pulse point; it was the most exquisite sensation. Kneeling with her rested across my knees, I rocked forward and back.

"Thank fuck," I rasped. "You need to wake up...I need you to yell at me for leaving you at the flat."

Her arm was still cocked at that awful angle, her skin pale as a ghost, her hair lusterless and strewn with marble dust and sand except in the awful places where it was stained with blood.

Tears ran down my dust-stained cheeks as I lifted her up, cradled in my arms, careful not to jostle her broken arm, and stood.

Footsteps shifted the gravel behind me—Elsedora approached with a small party. We were a few blocks from Umber House, and I needed to get Sybilla to a healer. Glancing back, I assessed who she was with Asterie, Fenris, Amara, Hurley followed her.

"Krait!" El sobbed.

"Where's Wyeth?"

"She flew toward Umber House," El answered. She gasped and put a hand over her mouth as her gaze found Sybilla. "Is she?"

"No...she's breathing but we need a healer." I carefully cradled Sybilla's head to my chest. "Where is Ryn?"

The way Elsedora's face fell destroyed me. She sobbed again, before grabbing my arm.

He hadn't made it.

"No," I denied.

But Elsedora's nod confirmed my fears.

"No, El...where is he?"

"He's gone," she choked out.

Horrified numbness crept over every inch of me. That couldn't be. "That can't be," I repeated the thought that kept repeating in my head.

My friend could not be gone; we'd just seen each other—minutes, hours ago? My brow pinched, and my tears fell into Sybilla's hair.

Elsedora winced. "I saw...She saw." She nudged her chin down at Sybilla as her lower lip trembled.

Fenris hugged Asterie's shoulders, and her wolf-demon's head hung low.

"We need to find Wyeth. Asterie, Fen, can you run ahead? I don't want to jostle her by moving too fast."

Asterie nodded. "Yes, my King." She grabbed Fenris' arm and ushered Hurley away. They ran south toward my home to find the healer. The city around me looked like Luz the day after the attack—upturned and charred.

As marble crumbled from the highest parts of the amphitheater, heavy footfall rounded the corner. Mattock approached us. I shielded Sybilla away from him, fighting back a growl. His mouth fell open upon seeing her in my arms. He was uncuffed, but his eyes shone a warm brown.

"Please, Darvanda." The young King's voice wavered. "I just want to see her. Is she alright? Please."

My knees shook. Nothing would ever be the same for any of us. "You'll see her when she's well," I barked.

The ground rumbled again. We were still too close to the likely fall of the building. City blocks would be destroyed.

Emmerick braced, his fists clenching, and El stopped him with a hand to his chest. "We don't have time for this. Down, puppy—we need to get her back to the house quickly. Follow us." She began to guide him by the shoulders, pushing him toward the street parallel to the main canal.

I followed El and Emmerick. The faint feeling of Sybilla's breath on my tunic sparked a sense of hope. "You don't get to die on me," I whispered to her.

We traversed streets of turned-over tents, discarded carts and busted windows. So damned depleted of energy, I grunted, straining to not stumble or lose my footing.

"There was enough time to evacuate—just barely," Elsedora called out. "We sent everyone to the Plateau."

The destruction was thankfully isolated to the northern portions of the city, far away from where my people had fled to the south. Relief and guilt were at war within me.

We reached the courtyard. Should the amphitheater fall, we would be out of harm's way.

Moments later, the crash of the dome crumbling shook the city. A cloud of white dust blasted through the streets, coating every surface.

We rushed into Umber House and closed the door behind us.

CHAPTER 66
EMMERICK

*C*rumbling marble. Firose stared at me from within the amphitheater.

"Come on!" I yelled.

But instead of following me out the gates, she stood still with her brow furrowed.

"What are you doing?"

She closed the metal gate in front of me and worked a charm to lock it. "Go," she commanded.

I shook my head. "You'll be crushed—won't that kill you?"

"Maybe," she answered with a weak smile.

My throat closed. She stepped away from the gate and met my gaze. "Go, Emmerick."

Tears welled, but I understood.

There would be no living with the sort of guilt she held. The darkness that had leaked into my mind the past months left me feeling like I, too, would truly never be the same. She had lived with that weight for four centuries.

The walls began to cave, marble falling into the pit. "You don't have to do this—we can leave here now, go somewhere quiet, live a peaceful life."

Firose smiled wider. "It is nice to imagine that someone will live on to think well of me," she said. Then she stepped back into the dust.

Clutching the metal gate, I swallowed hard before feeling the vibration of the impending fall of the walls.

I turned away from her and ran.

The magic coursing through my veins shuddered as though part of me died in the collapse behind me.

"Tea?" Elsedora interrupted the memory that had repeated itself since I'd left Firose in the falling theater.

Her eyes were bleary and red, and her posture held none of its usual swagger and confidence as she walked across the sitting room of Umber House.

Death had not taken me yesterday. Yet I felt so damned empty.

"No, thank you," I answered.

Darvanda had brought Sybilla to their bedchamber, where Wyeth was treating her wounds. I'd gritted my teeth when I'd realized they'd already begun sharing quarters. It felt like I was encroaching on a delicate new life she'd woven, with new friends to rely on. New hands to mend her. New lips to kiss her.

Intense anger still gripped me even with Caym gone, but the sadness in realizing how much I'd destroyed weighed down my will to act on any emotion lest it taint my morals further.

Elsedora watched me, taking inventory of my eyes. We still didn't know if ridding Caym of his true form meant *I* was rid of him too.

Surprisingly cozy, the sitting room was fitted with a few dark leather sofas and a reading nook that overlooked the now grayed courtyard. The terrazzo glinted in the rising sun, and the walls were wainscotted in dark wood.

Elsedora had not seemed to have heard me because she poured me a cup with a shaky hand.

"The Moon warlock—he was your friend?"

Her mouth drew into a line, and she nodded. "Something like that. Firose?"

"Something like that," I answered.

I sipped the tepid, earthy tea.

"I'm sorry," she said.

I nodded. "Me too."

Fen entered the sitting room, and Van trailed behind, which told me Asterie must be nearby. She entered behind Fenris with a stack of clean clothes.

"Em." Her shoulders sank upon seeing me, and she set the clothing down on a sofa. "You're alright?"

I sighed. "Right as rain."

Asterie's lips pursed. "Liar."

At that, I offered her a weak smile and said, "It's good to be back." *Was I back?*

Fenris sat down beside me and slapped my shoulder too hard. I grimaced.

"Quite a mess you've made," he said in jest, but I stiffened.

"Fen," Elsedora warned. "He's not done anything."

"It's fine, really," I said.

It wasn't. Nothing seemed fine.

I bottled that rage. It could be neatly packed beneath heartbreak, confusion and regret.

A creeping chill climbed up my neck; it was a horrifying, familiar sensation. I gasped and met Elsedora's stare. She'd never stopped assessing my eyes.

"I know that look," she whispered with a haunted expression. She turned to Asterie and Fen. "Fetch binding cuffs! Now!"

Then, everything around me blinked out into a void of nothingness.

CHAPTER 67
SYBILLA

I woke to the smell of spiced cologne and smoke, feeling more sore than I'd ever experienced. *Could I move?*

I tried to run my hand over my face, but found my arm constricted in a sling. I winced. *At least the grime of the arena was gone.*

Someone had dressed me in a nightgown and tucked me into familiar divinely soft silk sheets.

I felt his presence.

Turning my head was painful. I did it anyway to watch Krait sleep in a chair beside our bed in Umber House.

He had cleaned himself up, too. There was a furrowed line in his brow as though he'd not left the battle in the pit behind him. My heart sank as I realized there *was* someone we had left behind in the amphitheater.

Visions of my silver-haired friend glowing, levitating, hit me. That was before…The next memory nearly made me choke.

"Krait," I croaked out and pushed up onto my good elbow. I needed to hold him—needed to know he was really there.

His smoky, iron eyes snapped open, and the lines in his forehead softened. "You're awake."

"How long have I been out?" I asked. He rose and leaned over to place a glass of water to my lips, making me drink before he'd answer.

"A couple of days," he finally said. He sounded as though those were the first words he'd spoken in just as many days. Knowing him, they might have been.

Tears ran before I could say anything more, and when I reached out and grabbed his shirt, he softened and slipped beneath the sheets to hold me. I clung to him with my good arm, not wanting to face the day, not wanting to understand the gravity of what had occurred, not wanting to hear what, or who, else we may have lost.

As though sensing my concern, he smoothed the curls away from my temple. "Everyone else made it out."

"Everyone else is safe?"

He nodded, but his expression seemed guarded.

I shoved my face into the space between his neck and shoulder, breathing him in. We lived, so many did not. "He killed them *all.. .*All the civilians of Sahlmkar."

He hummed sadly. "They will be memorialized. The people of Sahlmkar long ago promised themselves to Death's bidding...As I told you, they were not bad people. They placed their faith in a cruel Origin."

I sobbed into his shoulder and said through the tears, "I tried to get to Ryn. I should have gotten there quicker. I could have stopped him." The image of my friend's body turning to dust made my stomach twist and nausea build. During our last interaction, we'd been short with each other. I'd taken that time for granted.

He squeezed me tighter and kissed me on the top of my head. "Don't do that. There is only one person to blame."

Meeting his gaze, I whispered, "Is Caym gone?"

Krait offered me a sad smile. "Yes. For now. It seems you aren't so shit with a sword anymore."

Choking back a weak laugh, I shook my head and said, "I got lucky."

Isleen's words haunted me. *Stop. Not kill.* How would the Death Origin come to rise again? It couldn't be predicted by any prophecy. We'd reached the end of those pages unless another scribe stepped forward.

I winced against the pain in my ribs.

His jaw tightened as he ran a hand through my hair and gently brushed my temple with his lips. His eyes stayed closed, and he rested his forehead against mine. "You *did* get lucky. What were you thinking?"

"I was thinking failure wasn't an option. I saw a way to stop Caym from taking this city, and others, and that seemed worth dying for. Lymrasi said at all costs."

He shook his head against my forehead. I raised my good arm to take a fistful of his hair and brought his lips to mine in feverish gluttony. Having him here with me was the only thing tethering me to this reality—the one where Death had risen, where I'd stopped him, where we'd lost a friend and had nearly lost another city.

He deepened the kiss, sliding his tongue across my lower lip, as though he too was drinking in the moment. Humming with relief, I grasped the back of his neck, feeling him, anchoring to him.

When he broke for air, my cheeks tingled from the rub of his stubble. He commanded, "Never do that again."

"Kiss you?" I retorted.

He let a half-hearted growl build in his throat. "No, risk your life. I won't have it."

I spun the wooden ring on my left hand, and answered, "That is not a promise I can make. You fight, I fight."

He grunted in response, and I claimed his mouth once more.

He broke to say, "You'll never let me win one, will you?" For once, he didn't seem annoyed about it.

My heart swelled. I'd happily fight *with* and *for* him until death parted us. I couldn't imagine living what remained of my life any other way.

"I may forever be unwilling to give you the higher ground, but I'd be happy to face a hundred more battles so long as at the end you are by my side."

His lips turned up. "I love you. More than I ever thought myself capable of loving again."

Letting my hand rise to meet his cheek, I offered him a weak smirk. "I know."

Krait tried to tell me I was too injured to go down to the dining hall.

He knew better. I glared at him in a way that made him let out a deflated sigh.

Wyeth had done great work stitching my head and then had used Source power to heal as many of my injuries as she could. To avoid scarring, she'd recommended not healing everything all the way and letting my wounds scab over.

She'd cast a charm to speed the healing of my broken arm. Sources, the bone rapidly growing back together hurt.

I dressed in my new favorite cream-colored linen dress and woven-leather mules. Krait wore an equally light tunic and breeches. Though he was *heavily* armed with his broadsword strapped across his back, two daggers poking out from each of his boots and another dagger holstered on his belt.

He still seemed tense despite there not being an immediate threat. Krait sported dark circles below his eyes, and the wrinkle had returned to his brow line.

Asterie was the first person we came across in the halls—Vangard trailed at her heel, panting. Her eyes lit up when they landed on us. She smiled. "You're awake, Sybilla."

"I am—if you can call this *awake.*" I reached out and scratched Van between his curved horns. He kicked up one back leg. "Where is everyone?"

"Most are gathering for tea."

"Who is most?"

"Well, all but Elsie. She sent a note down that she would not be joining us for breakfast. And Emmerick told us that Firose was not found after the fall of the amphitheater. She is presumed dead. I cannot pretend that I am not glad we do not need to face her."

There was a pang of sadness in Asterie's voice as she spoke of her former mentor. I could feel that she longed for closure, but she knew a reunion between Firose and Fenris outside of the chaos of that arena would have been catastrophic.

My thoughts exactly—hence why we hadn't originally told them she had lived.

"Never presume," I warned. "We've done that once before with her. The woman is like a roach—she just never seems to die." Callous as it sounded, I still couldn't separate the good and bad in the Fire-wielding enchantress. The damage she'd inflicted had scarred the realms too deeply.

"You spoke with Em? He's well?" I asked her and noticed Krait's grasp on my hand tightened.

Asterie's face fell, and she looked uncomfortable.

"He hasn't told her." Asterie was still shit at warding her thoughts.

My head snapped toward Krait. I spat out, "What haven't you told me?"

"We have *temporarily* placed him back in the holding cell for monitoring," Krait answered. I pulled my hand out of his, ready to huff a response but he spoke again. "Sybilla, he was one of Caym's envoys. Destroying the Death Origin's true form may not have cut those ties. Caym has acted without a body before."

"I'll be the judge of that," I snapped. "It is me he's after..."

Krait's jaw stiffened. He wanted to argue—I could tell by the hard lines on his face. Why did he have to look so damned attractive when he grew angry with me?

Caym's other envoys were dead, and he had been within his true form when I killed him...he couldn't still have Emmerick.

He will rise once more. But do as you can to delay him until your child has all the relics.

Remembering Isleen's words, I asked, "Where have Lymrasi and her children gone?"

I'd tell him later of meeting my ancestors—of my mother's help. There was too much to unravel now.

"They were creatures of Caym's creation—they, too, were free as soon as you struck his heart."

My pulse quickened, and I shook my head. I needed to understand so much more from Isleen. I still couldn't wrap my mind around what had happened in that cavern.

"I want to speak with Emmerick."

"I go in alone," I demanded. Krait glared—it was a definite *filet me* expression. "Stay right outside."

He growled, "If he makes one wrong move against you—"

"Then I can handle myself. Keep your Shadows to yourself, husband dearest. Marriages can be easily annulled if not consummated." I laid a hand on his chest and rose to my tiptoes to press a kiss to his lips.

Krait softened against me and pushed a stray curl behind my ear. "That would be a hard technicality to hold up."

He reluctantly stepped back, allowing me to open the door to the stairway. It surprised me that he hadn't fought harder to come with me.

Guards led me down the dank-smelling stairs to the cell. Emmerick sat against the wall, staring down at the floor. He wore a fresh tunic; his stubble had grown out but his face was clean, wounds tended to.

"Leave us," I instructed the guards after they let me into the cell.

Em wasn't wearing binding cuffs. I found that a promising sign that Krait was only holding him as a precaution. Untouched, a tray of food and water was on his cot.

"Em."

He looked up. I crossed the cell and crouched beside him.

I swallowed hard, fighting back tears, at a loss for what to say. His expression looked haunted—jaw clenched and stare dull.

He looked at me with shaking hands pressed to the stone floor. The jovial boy I'd once loved had hardened into someone I didn't recognize.

I reached out and grabbed one of his hands. "It won't ever be the same, will it?" I asked with visions dancing in the back of my mind of tree forts and the hunt for squirrels in the woods, our first kiss when he was a stable boy and all the firsts after that.

"No, it won't," he said, his voice full of unspoken sorrow. "But my hope is that maybe, someday, it will all make sense why."

I'd given all of my heart to Krait, but I was certain that a piece of it had been carved out and gifted to Emmerick long before. That piece would always care whether he was well, safe and happy.

"I'll get you out of here. I am going to skewer him for putting you down here again," I ground out.

Emmerick met my gaze with a sad smile. "Syb, I need you to listen to him. I know you—you aren't going to like what he tells you. You aren't going to like your hand being forced."

I bristled.

His stare pleaded with me. Then my dearest friend stiffened. His grip on my hand grew tight, and I gasped with a wince.

"He's coming..." Em choked out. "Sybilla...You need to get out of here."

Blood pumped in my ears. When I met his gaze again, his face was contorted into a cruel scowl that was not Em's. His eyes gleamed that awful shade of green.

I tried to pull away, but he held onto my hand with crushing strength. Emmerick stood abruptly. He pulled me up with him and spun me to press my front against the wall.

"Did you truly think killing one part of me would stop me, Isleen? You'll need to kill this one too, or I'll simply rise again from the ashes."

Straining against his grip, I shouted, "Guards!"

"You can't, can you? I knew you wouldn't be able to see this one fall."

"Guards!" I screamed.

His hands slipped around my throat. I heard the clatter of armor, but before they arrived, Shadows pried the fingers from my throat. Krait had Shadowed in, and he pulled Emmerick's possessed body away from me.

"Cuff him now," he told the guards, who had finally reached the cell. *Now?* Why not before? When Krait's eyes met mine, the same sadness lingered there that I'd seen at the top of the stairs, which made me pause.

He'd known.

"You needed me to see it," I said through clenched teeth, and Krait nodded, a flash of shame crossing his features.

"I'd planned to be quicker to Shadow in—I'm sorry."

I could kill him.

That seemed to be how my life would be with the King of the Sahlms—in a constant flux between wanting to kiss or kill him. Or both.

"We need to use the Sethe curse," Krait said as the guards bound Emmerick's wrists. Em slumped down against the wall, subdued again. Panting, he stared at the ground before he drew in a deep breath, warm brown gaze returning.

"No. The cuffs can keep Caym at bay," I argued. But even I knew that was a risky plan. Cuffs could be removed.

Emmerick avoided making eye contact with me and said through a heavy breath, "He's right, Sybilla. I am not safe for this world. Keeping me alive at all poses a risk. Darvanda offers the mercy to let me live. The curse will give you more time—and if, in the end, it is the only means to end Death's reign, then you kill me."

Our backs were against the wall, and all the Sethe curse gave us was delayed inevitability.

"How long?" I asked them, hating that it seemed like they were teaming up against me. The two men who cared about me most had discussed this—they'd gone behind my back while I was incapacitated.

"We agreed on twenty-five years," Krait said, and Emmerick swallowed hard with a nod.

"Syb, this is the right decision—you know it. I've left a letter with all my requests for while I'm asleep. A letter for my parents too. I don't want them to have to say goodbyes."

I slumped in defeat. Twenty-five years of sleep.

Hopefully it was enough time to search for a way to wake Emmerick from the curse, to raise a child, and to find the relics needed to end Caym for good.

We had so much damned work to do.

Death would not take me. He would not keep Emmerick either.

"Fine," I agreed. "But I have conditions."

CHAPTER 68

KRAIT

12 YEARS LATER

Our trunks were packed and piled by the Egress, ready for our journey back to the Sahlms, where we would spend the winter. Asterie and Fenris would have a good handle on affairs here in the Central Corridor in our absence.

Walking into the Luz Palace's main hall, I found Sybilla loitering, looking up at two bronze statues displayed between the grand staircase. She leaned down to light a candle at their feet. Hundreds were scattered around them in varying colors. We held open hours for those who wished to come and celebrate the fallen rulers of Phynx.

Sybilla had convinced me that Ryn and Freya's memorial belonged in Luz, just miles from the ruins of their ancestral city. Some days, it still pained me to look at their faces. But most days, there in the hall, with sunlight spreading rays across them, the memories I had of my late wife and her brother shifted to brighter moments—their smiles, their laughter. They were not ghosts here.

It had taken time to settle the unease in the realms. Now that the crops were bountiful everywhere, all seemed at peace.

The corridors were adapting to the presence of Source magic in Henosis. Bringham remained a thorn in our side, as he still outlawed its use in the West Corridor. Luckily, he only had a small landholding, which didn't impact most trade. Amara spent her time in the South Corridor, helping to prepare Sheffield's young nephew for the throne and keeping the isles in order.

The way Sybilla looked wistfully up at Ryn and Freya made my heart swell. She wore a rust-colored satin dress with the Sahlmsaran crest embroidered on each shoulder. Her curls were pulled back in a Luz-blue ribbon. Some silver threads of hair poked out in unruly protest—she blamed me for them.

Sybilla liked to point out every wrinkle and slight change that occurred in my face as though my aging was some grand experiment to her. She'd touched the corners of my cheeks last night and whispered, "Are these smile lines? You better be careful—someone might think you are friendly."

My mouth curved up at the thought. We faced an inevitable fight against Caym, but even if the next thirteen years didn't yield the results we wanted, I looked forward to each moment spent with her, no matter the task. We hadn't yet found the remaining two relics. Sybilla had returned to taking garrot root; it seemed to be the only remedy that kept her inflammation at bay, but with it her power was also stifled.

"Papa! Which texts do I need to bring?" Lark called over the balcony railing, and my attention snapped away from her mother.

Larkspur had turned ten a few months ago and was growing awkwardly lanky. She had Sybilla's eyes—bright green and expressive—and had been graced with her mother's curls, though they were dusty brown. She'd inherited my darker complexion, but I was glad that was the only quality I'd gifted her; she was her mother's daughter through and through.

"*All* of them, Larkspur," I grated out. *I'd told her that four times already.*

Our daughter's head lived in the clouds. She didn't fully grasp how to keep others' thoughts and emotions out. We'd had to teach all those closest to us how to ward against her Reverist abilities. There were some things a young girl didn't need to reckon with just yet—despite the weight of the realms she would one day hold on her shoulders.

"Right!" Lark said and clattered back to her bedchamber.

When I looked at my wife, she caught my gaze. She smirked before she approached me. "Have patience with her," she warned.

"I *am* patient," I ground out. Sybilla let out a knowing huff of laughter which made me smirk too. We both knew I was far from a patient parent. Neither of us was.

But we were trying.

On our worst days, there was the beauty of Lark's five aunts to help us—she was surrounded by enchantresses willing to teach her, guide her, love her.

We were having a bad month. Nightmares had visited Lark for weeks, and though she was far too old to be crawling into bed with her parents, it was hard to deny her when we knew the real nightmares she would face. That soft spot in my resolve meant Sybilla and I were *never* alone, even when our work for the day had concluded.

Neither of us had been ready when Lark graced us. We'd been carefully taking tonics, waiting until we were both sure. But, like her mother, Lark had had her own plans.

I wrapped a hand around Sybilla's hip and pulled her to me, stealing a kiss. Sybilla sank into me, hungrily capturing my bottom lip between her teeth, with a desperate groan.

It had been over a month since I'd felt all of her, been inside of her, heard her gasp out my name.

"My King and Queen, care to get a room? Some of us have work to do."

Elsedora approached from the entry. Yet again, we'd been interrupted. El wiped a bead of sweat and dust from her brow. She wore fitted breeches, and a tunic cropped at the stomach, and she was heavily armed with throwing daggers strapped at her waist. Her boots were muddied. Judging by the bags beneath her eyes, she hadn't slept in days. She looked like shit.

"Before you harp at me—Hurley is *fine* alone in Sahlmsara for a few nights. He can't do that much damage in a short time," El argued.

She frequently visited the Sahlms, helping Hurley learn his role as my newest officer of Sahlmsara. With the help of the young Water-wielder, the Sahlms no longer struggled with droughts.

Sybilla had negotiated to seat us as interim rulers of the North Corridor while Mattock remained in his cursed slumber. Only when he awoke would we revisit the arrangement. It had brought me great satisfaction to have been able to see the ensuing tantrum from Bringham.

"I didn't say anything. He's doing well. *You're* doing well with his training. Did you find anything?"

Her sour expression and piss-poor mood told me all I needed to know. "The tomb was dripping with traps from the moment I entered. I got through them all for nothing except this gaudy thing..." She dropped a necklace with many dangling iridescent beads into my palm. It glistened in a curious way.

"It could be something," I said. "Why don't you bring Fen or Hurley next time? It worries me that you keep at this alone."

"Pfft...They always just end up slowing me down."

Since discovering her Source power, Elsedora spent much of her time following the wind to ancient ruins and tombs. There, she hoped to find relics to help us defeat Caym. So far, to her dismay, all she'd been able to find in the last twelve years was an ancient mirror that seemingly had no purpose.

Larkspur tiresomely begged to go with her aunt *every* time El left.

In her off time, Elsedora visited us here or stayed at her estate in the North Corridor. El was Lark's favorite person in the realms. Aside from us—for now. We'd see what her formative teen years handed us.

I was a moment away from letting my daughter go with El next time, just for a minute alone with my wife. In truth, I was at least six years away from letting her go tomb raiding.

Ryn's death had impacted us all. It had made El's drive for vengeance against Caym ravenous. It was as though she never stopped moving. I'd asked her once if Ryn had been her Source Match—she'd thrown one of her daggers at my head.

Sybilla took the necklace from my fingers and held it up before she handed it back to El. "It looks like these are moonstone beads. Give it to Asterie to inspect when she returns from the cabin this afternoon."

"Aunty Lora!" Our daughter's voice burst from over the balcony. Lark had created the nickname when she'd been too young to pronounce Elsedora and had jumbled her name together into something new.

Lark sprang down the stairs and into El's outstretched arms. In a blink, Elsedora went from looking exhausted and pissed off to melting like putty in the girl's grip, as she usually did. She lifted Lark and spun her around twice. "Hello, little troublemaker. Gah! You're getting *way* too big for this. Can you stop growing?"

"No! I need to grow so I can come with you to the catacombs! I asked for throwing knives for my next birthday so I'll be ready."

Elsedora laughed. "Why don't we go for a walk in the gardens while your parents finish...packing?" Elsedora gave Sybilla a not-so-subtle wink before setting Lark on her feet.

Lark squealed, "Let's go!" and then dragged El by the arm, sprinting toward the back doors that led to the garden.

"Alright, alright," El said as she was dragged away by our spitfire, our whole heart.

I'd been pretending not to notice that Elsedora had been allowing our daughter to visit Emmerick's chamber with her. Sybilla wouldn't approve, but I thought it wise that Lark saw the realities of the world as it had been. She needed to see the consequences of things she would later face.

Still, it was difficult to be so harsh on Lark about her studies and training. El offered her childish games, silly faces and the fun a child needed, and I couldn't be more grateful to her for that.

Sybilla's voice interrupted that thought. "I think Elsedora might be my favorite person today." She touched my abs and pushed me back toward the steps. She glanced at the maids, who were dusting the main hall. "Asha, Lex—leave us. Please."

I smirked as Sybilla grabbed me by the collar and claimed my mouth. The staff knew very well from the early days of our marriage what "leave us" meant. Get out of the room or prepare to get a show.

The Luz maids scurried out of the room.

I knew well, too, and my length already pressed against the seam of my breeches as her fingers found the buttons. She pushed me further toward the staircase. She had my waistband pushed down and my length freed before my ankles even hit the first stair.

We were not going to make it to the bedchamber.

I hissed when my bare ass landed on one of the marble steps, and I ran my hands under her dress, delighted to realize she was wearing nothing beneath the skirts. When she straddled me, and I pushed deep into her welcoming warmth, I groaned between our lips.

This was what eternity felt like.

None of it had been perfect. We'd loved and lost and still stood to lose so much more.

Yet every time a muscle ached or a joint cracked in a way it never had before, I realized that growing old with her might be the best form of forever I could have imagined.

EPILOGUE

LARK

We strolled through the garden, and Aunty Lora swung my hand happily, pointing out everything that was in bloom. Fall flowers were my favorite.

"Did you remember *all* of your texts this time?" she teased.

"Yes," I sighed, unhappy that Papa seemed to have gotten to her too.

I could never tell if he was truly angry with me, and Mama often called him many things that I wasn't allowed to repeat. She said he was far less grumpy than he used to be, but that was hard to imagine.

Schucks.

There *was* one book I'd forgotten. I'd left it in the boathouse by the pond. It was a spell book that Aunty Asterie had gifted me. I had wanted to see if I could turn a toad into a prince like in the storybooks. Turned out, there *wasn't* a spell for that, and all I'd ended up with was seven unhappy toads.

There had only been *boring* enchantments in the book. Like how to light a candle or move an object from one side of a table to the other.

"I forgot one—I'll go get it!"

Auty Lora released my hand. "Hurry back. We'll be leaving soon."

I ran down the winding path to the pond. "Hello!" I shouted to two guards, both of whom saluted me.

"Hello, Princess." Their words whistled away as I ran, feeling faster than the wind Aunty could control. Soon I'd have all of Papa's Shadows—they kept telling me that as though it should mean something important to me. I hadn't yet learned how to travel through them like he could.

Out of breath, I opened the rickety door of the boathouse. A rowboat bobbed in the water, and the book was exactly where I'd left it on the dock. I snatched it up and was about to run back up the path when something caught my eye in the tree line beyond the pond.

Someone was watching me—a boy. He ducked back behind a tree, hiding. No one else was allowed in the gardens. I stomped over to the tree.

"*You* are trespassing. Who are you?"

The boy's tawny cheeks reddened—he looked a couple of years older than me. He didn't answer and stepped away like he might flee.

His hair was a mop of black curls, and his eyes were the prettiest shade of blue—like a watercolor painting of the sky. "I *said*, who are you?"

"Please, don't tell anyone I was here. It can be our secret."

Before I could yell for the guards, he opened his palm. Light and fire bloomed there—I gasped.

"For you, Princess," he said.

In his palm, from a spark of light and fire, a single red rose formed and glistened as though lit by flame from between the petals. It reminded me of the roses that often appeared outside the sleeping man's door. The same man Mama was so adamant about me never meeting.

Aunty Lora always seemed so distraught when we found the roses, and the maids would not admit to leaving them.

I took the rose from the peculiar boy with a smile.

"Our secret," I agreed.

ACKNOWLEDGEMENTS

To my readers—I wouldn't be here if you hadn't fallen in love with this world. Thanks for joining me on this journey and motivating me to keep putting the words down. Your support has made me feel all warm and fuzzy inside. I hope you enjoyed this adventure, and I can't wait to bring you more!

I am sure it isn't easy being married to someone who is plotting books in their head ninety-nine percent of the time. So thank you, Dan, for constantly repeating yourself and understanding why you have to. Your love and support are felt everyday. And if I go first, I expect you to have a bronze statue made in my honor and for you to worship it for four hundred years. I feel like this book should count as legal documentation of this very reasonable request.

So many thanks go to my editor, Britney Waldrop. You've become half of my brain when it comes to the realms of Henosis and the Sahlms. I feel like you could write a textbook on them. Your guidance took this story to levels that I'm so proud of.

Mom, thank you for reading my magic smut. You played a huge part in making this story resonate for others with chronic pain and autoimmune diseases. Sybilla was easy to write—I grew up watching you be a badass.

To my lovely alpha and beta readers—thank you for reading this when it was still a heaping pile of disjointed ideas.

I'm forever grateful to have such an amazing support system of people who care about me, the person behind the author title.

ABOUT THE AUTHOR

Mariet Kay is a fantasy romance author who lives in Phoenix, Arizona, with her husband and a pack of rescue animals. Her debut novel, *Born of Starlight*, is the inaugural installment of the Legends of Henosis series. Mariet has a decade-long career in digital marketing and has always possessed a passion for digital media and content creation. For more information visit marietkay.com